The Red Word

The Red Word

Sarah Henstra

TRAMPPRESS

This edition published 2019 by Tramp Press
www.tramppress.com

First published 2018 by Grove Atlantic

1 3 5 7 9 10 8 6 4 2

Tramp Press gratefully acknowledges the
financial assistance of the Arts Council.

ISBN 978-1-9997008-7-4

Thank you for supporting independent publishing.

Set in 11 pt on 15.5 pt Electra by Marsha Swan.
Printed by Clays, London.

Book I

STROPHE

(circling)

I. INVOCATIO

(calling on the muse)

Sing, O Goddess, of the fury of Dyann Brooks-Morriss, teller of unbearable truths. O sing of the rage that kindled one young woman's heart and the next until it drove us together from our homes, battlethirsty, into the secret places of the enemy. Sing how the young men scattered and fled as before the thunderbolt that lashes the sky. The storm is not appeased until the green leaves are torn from the trees, until even the great pines are uprooted from the mountainsides and lie down for the shipwright's axe. It does not stop until bodies are rent and scattered as easymeat for curs and crows.

*

I receive two bits of news less than thirty minutes apart:

It is eleven thirty in the morning, September 20, 2010. Here on the eighteenth storey the sun trampolines off Lake Ontario and strikes both the floor and ceiling. I've just made my breakfast, squinting against the glare on the kettle, and I am back at my desk in the bedroom with the blackout drapes pulled tight. I am pretending to work, but the image I've got open in Photoshop on my monitor screens is not for work. It's an arrangement of hydrangea and coneflower in a tarnished silver vase. They are two images, in fact, shot at two slightly different exposures. I am toggling back and forth, fiddling with saturation levels, when the first news arrives. It's an email message from Annabeth Lise with the subject line *Karen I am so so sorry.* Her nanny's mother has died in the Philippines.

I scroll through three quarters of Annabeth's frantic, rambling message before I grasp her point. Her point is the International Conference on Lifestyle Photography, three days away: she is so, so sorry but there is just no way she can swing it; I will have to give our 'Domestic Dreams' presentation on my own; she could send me what she's written so far but it's so rough at this stage; I'm so good on my feet that she knows it'll go great; the photos are the best part of these things anyway, right? Annabeth really is so sorry.

She owes me big-time, she says.

I delete the message and stumble out of the bedroom. Sun-blinded, heart racing, I pace a few lengths of the kitchen and living/dining room. I have never been to a conference before. I'm fairly sure I made that clear to Annabeth when she asked me to go with her. I am no writer, certainly not a public speaker. All I was supposed to do was cue the slideshow.

If all this blood is your blood you'll be dead soon. If not not. This is what runs through my mind when Jen Swinburn calls me – twenty-four minutes later – to give me the second piece of news: that Stephanie McNamara has passed away. As I sit there on the phone at my desk in my office in my apartment in Toronto, with my feet in slippers and with the taste of cheddar-on-toast on my tongue, I do not think of poor Steph at all but of myself. *If all this blood* – it's a memory.

I look up and, on the heels of the memory, I spot the detail I've been searching for in the twin images on my screens. An overripe melon lies next to the tarnished vase, its seeds sliding onto the tabletop. The tabletop itself is scarred like a butcher's block, and there is a divot at the spot where the seeds are oozing against the wood. The light meets the slime and slows down, bends, pools. A tiny wrinkle in the visual plane.

On the phone Jen says she had access to my phone number because she's on the Alumni Relations Board. We small-talk a bit: I say I enjoyed that piece she wrote a few years ago for the alumni magazine about journalism after 9/11. She says she saw my byline in *Covet My Home* while on a cruise with her in-laws and couldn't help googling, and 'who would have thought a militant anarcha-feminist like yourself would end up employed in the Martha Stewart sector, ha ha'.

And then she tells me about Steph. She received the notice at the alumni office. 'I remembered you two were close, but I didn't know if you'd still be in touch,' she says. 'It's just not the kind of thing you'd want to read in the back of an alumni bulletin.'

'Are you calling anyone else?' I ask. It isn't quite the right question. It sounds like I think Jen has been nosy or presumptuous. I try to fix it: 'I mean, in case you need updated contact info for anyone.' Not that I would have updated contact information for anyone. I was one of the first to leave – back home to Canada even before my student visa expired – and fifteen years later everyone else is more or less scattered across the United States.

'Just a small list,' she says. 'It's not normally our role.'

'Thank you for calling, Jen. I appreciate it.'

A quick search reveals there is to be a campus memorial service for Dr Stephanie McNamara this coming Friday. It's the day after the panel presentation, in the very same US city as the photography conference. I know that Steph teaches – that Steph taught – in the Women's Studies Department in that city, but I haven't thought of her during my travel preparations. I haven't thought of Stephanie McNamara, period, in years. The coincidence seems important in a spooky, literary way, like tragic destiny. Her college isn't far at all from the Ivy League school where, in 1995–96, my sophomore year, Steph and I and three other girls were housemates.

If all this blood is your blood you'll be dead soon. If not not. Everyone knows the trouble with myth. The trouble with myth is the way it shirks blame. It makes violent death as unavoidable as weather. All that tragic destiny lets everyone off the hook. Some bored god comes kicking up gravel and, just like that, a noble house explodes into carnage.

But then, I photograph interiors for a living. Myth is what I do. I mythologise.

O soulwithered Stephanie, keeper of all our sorrows. You tried again to open your eyes to the dark and this time it must have worked.

2. EXORDIUM

(urging forward, introduction)

I squinted up at a shadow blocking out the sun. A man was standing over me. He wore faded jeans and a huge oval belt buckle etched with a triple X. I lifted my elbow to my brow and the man became a woman, a girl my age. If I'd learned anything last year at college, I'd learned that just because someone was wearing a military crew cut and a white T-shirt tight across a flat chest and had a pack of cigarettes folded into the sleeve of the T-shirt like James Dean, it didn't mean you went and assumed she was male. Some of my education seemed to have worn off over the summer.

'Are you okay?' the girl asked.

I turned my cheek to the grass in an effort to mute the stereophonic whine of cicadas and grasshoppers. I was lying in somebody's backyard. Gray fencing teetered overhead, but the only shade on me fell from the massive, hairy leaves of some kind of vine I was curled beside. Slug trails dazzled the undersides. 'What is this plant?' I asked.

'Um, pumpkin,' the girl said. 'Last year, after Samhain, we couldn't fit all our jack-o'-lanterns into the composter, so we dug a big hole back here and buried them.'

'Samhain?' My voice cactused my throat.

'Halloween. Look, are you okay? What happened to you?' she asked.

'I had sex with somebody,' I said. The uprush of memory, and the shock that I'd spoken it aloud, made me retch a little. I rolled over and sat up in the grass.

'You had sex with somebody,' she echoed. 'On purpose?'

I waggled my head side to side, testing my headache. The yard kept swinging when I stopped moving. 'There was a frat party,' I explained.

It came back to me now with another lurch why I'd walked all the way from the fraternity house to this particular spot, early this morning before I'd passed out. 'Oh,' I said. 'Oh, damn. Is this 61 Fulton Ave?'

'Yes. Well, at the moment we're standing in 63,' she said. 'Our backyards are connected.'

I looked around. There was a line where the neat lawn became a jungle, and this was the jungle side. 'I came about your ad for a roommate,' I said.

The girl crouched beside me, barefoot in the grass. She held a mug of coffee and a lit cigarette. She offered them both, reaching out one hand at a time and pulling it back to indicate she'd make either substance disappear if it proved offensive to my hangover.

'Thanks.' I took a sip of the coffee, heavily sugared, and then a drag from her cigarette. I brushed at the ants crawling over my bare legs.

The girl was a few years older than me, I guessed, maybe twenty-three or twenty-four. 'You're a little early for the room thing,' she said. 'Some of us have class this morning. Didn't whoever you spoke to tell you that on the phone?'

I held out my hands to show the girl my dirt-ringed fingernails. 'Well, I wanted to make a good first impression, you know?' I laughed, but misery poked its black fingers all through the laughter. I was making it worse. I was making her feel sorry for me. 'Look, let's just pretend I was never here.' I heaved myself to my feet – if I didn't notice then maybe she wouldn't either, how my knees and shins were smeared with green, how I must have been crawling on all fours that morning by the time I reached the back fence.

This would have been a good place to live, too. The roommate-wanted ad had stood out from the others at the Student Housing Office, where I'd been browsing yesterday for an alternative to my on-campus housing placement. The ad was much wordier, for one thing. *Committed feminists only,* it read. *Vegetarian/vegan/macrobiotic meal-sharing,* and *Queer-friendliness a must*. That last phrase had stuck in my head because I wasn't sure exactly what it was supposed to mean. 'Queer' was a slur *against* gays, I'd always thought. An insult, not something friendly. It was something the rednecks in northern Ontario were fond of shouting at tree planters on our days off, when we dressed up in thrift-store tuxes and dresses to go dancing at the Valhalla Hotel bar. Buncha queers.

The contact name on the ad had stood out for me too: Dyann Brooks-Morriss. Dyann had been one of the only sophomores in my freshman Great Writers class last year. I was impressed by her vocabulary and the boldness with which she would interrupt the professor with questions about things like 'patriarchal assumptions' and 'ideological blind spots'. I came home once after hearing Dyann speak up in class and looked up 'hegemony' in my dictionary. Dyann sat in the front, and I was in the back, so I'd never really had a look at her up close.

I wobbled across the lawn behind the girl. 'Hey. Give my apologies to your next-door neighbours too, okay?' I said.

Her smoke huffed out in a laugh. 'If they noticed, which I'm sure they did not, I don't think they'd mind. Look, why don't you come in for a coffee.'

'That's okay.'

'Please, come on in for a minute. I'm Steph, by the way.' She steered me to the deck on the tidier side of the yard, where the patio doors stood open. 'This is Marie-Jeanne' – she pointed at a blonde girl peeling an egg at the table, and the girl gave me a quizzical wave – 'and over there is Dyann.'

The living room was shadowy after the bright backyard. Dyann was a silhouette on the couch. 'I'm Karen,' I said. 'Would you mind if I just used your washroom a sec?'

Steph pulled the string on a bulb over the basement stairs. 'It's down to the left,' she said. 'Charla's room and mine are down there. The other three bedrooms are up on the second floor.'

I had been looking forward to meeting Dyann Brooks-Morriss face to face. And I'd been planning to dress a bit like this girl Steph – in jeans and maybe my army-surplus boots. I'd definitely have worn my plaid shirt, the men's worsted-wool Pendleton I'd found at a logging camp during the spring planting contract, the shirt I'd fallen in love with because it reminded me of the one Sal goes back for, in Kerouac's *On the Road*. I had a feeling Dyann would approve of that shirt. I'd planned to impress her with exaggerated tales of environmental destruction and workplace discrimination in the Canadian tree-planting industry.

Instead I was wearing a pair of men's boxer shorts, one turquoise jelly sandal, a pink T-shirt with a sparkly palm tree on the front, and no bra. My hair in the bathroom mirror was dew-frizzed and studded with bits of dead grass. An inchworm made its way across my breast, down a frond of the sparkly palm tree. I stank of booze and, probably, sex.

When I came back upstairs Steph said, 'Do you take milk and sugar?'

'I should go,' I said. 'You've been really nice.'

'We figured we may as well not make you come back again this afternoon,' she said. 'Why don't we all just talk for a minute now instead.' She hovered the milk carton over the mug until I nodded, then she poured and stirred. Steph's face was kind: a full-lipped smile, freckles, light brown eyes with dark lashes. It wasn't a soldier's haircut after all – more like a little boy's, with soft brown bangs cut straight across but ruffled out of place.

3. DIASKEUE

(graphic description)

We sat down in the living room, Steph next to where Dyann sat cross-legged on the couch, Marie-Jeanne in the chair opposite mine. There was an orange tie-dyed bedsheet stapled to the ceiling in billows like psychedelic clouds. The sofa was covered with a Persian rug in ruby and sapphire hues that were repeated in the votive candles gathered on the sill of the big bay window. The coffee table was a water-stained steamer trunk with massive brass clasps. In the corner stood a female mannequin, naked except for a man's necktie and a Viking helmet with horns.

Two posters hung on the wall behind the sofa. One was a grainy black-and-white image of a female singer screaming into a microphone. Janis Joplin, I guessed, though I wasn't sure. The other poster was solid black, with lots of colourful text and American Indian motifs. Most of the text was too small to make out from where I was sitting, but I could read the heading: *WOMEN WHO RUN WITH WOLVES.*

It was probably rude, the way I was staring at everything. The only interior decorating I knew how to do was taping up pages torn from magazines. Last year the one thing on my side of the dorm room was a *Rolling Stone* picture of Prince playing at a club in Amsterdam called the Horse. I'd tried a bunch of images, but the masking tape kept letting go of the concrete wall. Everyone in the dorm had assumed I must be a devoted Prince fan, if that was my only décor. But it was just the only thing that stuck.

'Did you say someone named Charla lives here? As in Charla Klein?' I asked.

'She moved in before the summer, yes,' Steph said. 'You know her?'

'She was on my floor in Pittman Hall last year.'

I waited for one of them to respond to this – wasn't Charla great, or weren't dorms such a drag, or how had I found it, living with four hundred other women? But they didn't even glance at one another. This really was going to be an interview, I thought.

'Would you like one of us to drive you to a hospital?' Marie-Jeanne asked. She had a heavy French accent. Not just French: French-Canadian. Quebecois. There was no 'h' in her 'hospital'.

'Why?' I glanced over myself. I'd washed most of the dirt off, and I'd checked the boxer shorts for stains but they were fine.

'Karen, what we're asking is if you were raped,' Dyann said.

'No,' I said.

'You should have a kit done right away. Even if you can't remember the details,' Steph said.

'*Especially* if you can't remember the details,' Dyann corrected her. 'They might have drugged you. Or, if you were drunk enough to pass out in our backyard, then you were too drunk to give informed consent, and that means it was rape.'

'No,' I repeated. 'Rape' was a sharp word, a greedy word. It was a double-sided axe brandished in a circle over the head. It drew all kinds of attention to itself.

Dyann swung her legs to the floor and leaned forward, elbows on her knees. 'It's called a rape kit. It's a series of swabs they do at the hospital. They can analyse the DNA, so they have proof, later, in court. But you have to do it right away.'

'I know what a rape kit is, all right?' I said. 'I do remember the details, and it wasn't rape. Haven't any of you been to a frat party before?'

Dyann stared at me. I could feel the others waiting for her to decide what came next. Dyann Brooks-Morriss had very bright, dark eyes and a narrow, high-bridged nose. I thought of raptors, of a falcon. The impression was heightened by the earrings she wore: a single bird feather, striped rust-brown, dangled from each earlobe all the way to her shoulders. Her hair was a wild tangle of dreadlocks piled atop her head. I forced myself not to ogle her, to study the pattern on the Persian rug beside her shoulder instead.

'Which fraternity?' she said, finally.

'GBC,' I said. 'Gamma something?'

'Gang Bang Central. Perfect,' Dyann said. She flung herself back against the sofa, tipped up her head, and stared at the ceiling with her mouth hanging open. Her hands flopped to either side and hit the cushions, palms up, fingers slack. Her whole body said, *Too much; this is just too much.*

'It *is* perfect,' Steph said. 'Isn't that Bruce Comfort's fraternity?'

For a moment my torso was warm and full of gold coins. Bruce Comfort. It was marvelous, I thought, how even his name, even just his *name*, was enough. Then I saw them all noticing my reddening face.

'Oh, *mon dieu*, he is not your seducer from last night, is he?' Marie-Jeanne said.

The front door of the house banged open. A shirtless boy braced his arms on either side of the archway from the hall and leaned into the room. He was mouthing a long frond of dry grass so that the seed tassel jumped and trembled in the air before him. The sandy fluff of his armpits exactly matched the hair on his head.

'Do you live here?' Steph said.

The boy half-fell into the room and stuck out his hand. 'I'm Stick. Simon Pinkney, but everyone calls me Stick. Next-door neighbour. And you are …?'

'Look, we're kind of busy here,' Steph said.

'Karen Huls,' I told him.

Stick pumped my hand and then turned it over to look at the calluses. 'Wow. What are you, a cowpoke? Roughneck? What?'

'Um, tree planter,' I said.

'Is he already high?' Dyann asked. The question seemed to be directed at Marie-Jeanne.

Stick let go of my hand and disappeared into the kitchen, where he let out a trumpeting fart.

I joined in the looks exchanged around our circle, sharing in the girls' wide-eyed disgust, pleased with Stick, whoever he was, for the sudden camaraderie he had created amongst us with his intrusion.

He reappeared with a carton of milk, and Dyann shot up and crossed the room to intercept him. 'Not again. No.'

He held the carton out of her reach. 'Dude, ease up. I'll get you back.'

She blocked his way, shuffling side to side as he tried clumsily to pass. 'We are not your wet nurses!' she said.

'Oh, for fuck's sake,' said Marie-Jeanne – 'fooks', it sounded like, with her accent – 'I borrowed eggs from them only this morning.'

'Five dollars in the grocery jar the next time you set foot over our threshold,' Dyann insisted.

Stick gave a little bow. '*Heil* Hitler. Hey, did you guys introduce Karen to Ms Dentata?'

'You know,' said Marie-Jeanne, when the door had slammed behind him, 'we didn't pay them for the pot last week.'

'They said that was a sample.' Dyann huffed back to her spot on the couch. 'He just pushes the boundaries on purpose, to make a point.'

'Or else he thought the new girl was hot,' Steph said, 'and wanted to make an impression.'

'Who's Ms Dentata?' I said.

'Our mascot,' Steph said, pointing at the nude mannequin in the corner. I looked closer: someone had inked a circular symbol at the V between its legs. It was like a sun with the rays pointing inward.

'Oh, *Vagina Dentata*, I get it,' I said. 'Nice.'

The three girls exchanged glances, and I realised I'd just passed some kind of test. A little flare went up inside me. All this time – during all that rape talk, before – my brain had been lagging behind the conversation, flailing wrong-footed through its swamp of embarrassment. Oh, but I wanted to live here, in this house, with these women! It was like an alternate universe, this room, with its riotous colours and textures and its in-your-face femaleness. But it also felt like I'd entered the real world, the world beyond the campus. I could almost feel myself maturing, becoming sharper and more ironic and self-possessed, just having been inside this house for the last twenty minutes. I wanted this house to be my home.

I got out of my interview chair. I strode to the archway and leaned against the wall next to it. I cleared my throat. I said, 'I got back to campus forty-eight hours ago from a tree-planting camp in northern Ontario.' I held up my hands to display the blackened calluses across my palms. 'I'm crashing with my dorm roommate from last year and her friends. Rachel Smythe – you know her? Self-declared shopaholic? Bedspread matches her wastebasket, which matches her desk organiser? She used to dry all her chenille sweaters on that rack in the common room?' I flicked my hair off one shoulder and then the other, imitating Rachel's empty-headed preening. 'Anyway, Rachel and her friends spent all of last night drinking and deciding what to wear to this fraternity mixer, and then at the last second they dragged me off the couch to drive them over there.'

I could paint a good picture when I wanted to, even this hungover. My bloodshot eyes probably added to the effect. I began to pace the carpet. 'My God, that frat house!' I exclaimed. 'It's like the Panopticon in there. A Foucauldian wet dream. Everyone surveilling everyone else, dying of self-consciousness. Everyone looking for the authentic heart of the party, like, "Where is it *really* happening?" Everyone wandering from room to room: "Are we missing it? Are we missing it?"'

I flopped back into my chair. 'I think I sort of snapped.'

'So you decided to have sex with a frat boy.' Dyann's hawk eyes were half-lidded, as if my story had bored her. But she sat perfectly still against the cushions, and I somehow knew that the lack of interest was feigned.

'Well, it was something to do,' I said. Brazening it out.

'And? How was it?' Steph said.

I laughed. 'Fucking awful,' I said.

They laughed too. Even Dyann gave a little snort.

'It wasn't Bruce, though,' I said. 'He's not exactly my type. The eternal brawn-versus-brain dilemma, you know?' If the frat house was the Panopticon – and really, the analogy didn't work in the first place; the reference to Foucault had been a shameless bid to sound smart – then Bruce Comfort was the closest thing to its control tower, its true centre. He wasn't self-conscious so much as simply aware of his own magnetism. Every time I saw Bruce Comfort in action I thought of Kerouac's line about the moony night – *a night to hug your girl and talk and spit and be heavengoing.* Even though Bruce was a sophomore like me and had only joined the fraternity in the spring, he was already at the heart of it. He had his own gravity, drawing the others into orbit, pulsing with his own heat like a star.

Brawn versus brain. What if they actually liked Bruce, though? What if one of them was related to him or something? 'How do you know Bruce Comfort, anyway?'

Steph sighed. 'Oh, he got a woman pregnant at a party back in May,' she told me. 'Too good for a condom, some typical bullshit like that. She came into the Women's Centre yesterday looking for help. Apparently he told her, to her face, that it wasn't his problem.'

'At least he didn't participate in the charade,' Dyann said. 'He could have gone down the whole "Well-it's-your-decision-I'll-support-you" road, and she'd still think he was her Romeo.' As she talked, Dyann clawed through her hair with both hands, freed a sharpened pencil from her dreadlocks, and shook them loose across her shoulders. 'It's like Sylvia says. Our first mistake, as women, is to ask for a fiction and then to accept it as a truth.'

'Well, Sylvia would say that Bruce is just as inscribed in the mythologies as Susannah,' Steph said.

'Who's Sylvia?' I asked.

Dyann didn't seem to have heard me. With the pencil's tip she was scratching little white lines onto her bare knee. 'Yeah, but the myths *serve* the Bruces and *penalise* the Susannahs,' she said. 'There's no point studying the myths unless you understand who profits from them.'

'Dr Sylvia Esterhazy is a professor,' Marie-Jeanne told me. 'Dyann took her class last year, and Steph is her teaching assistant.'

'The course is called "Women and Myth",' Steph said. 'Enrollment's already at cap, but I could see if I could still get you in, Karen. It's one of those really great fundamental explorations in feminist thought: where do our ideas about masculinity and femininity come from, originally? Sylvia takes us right back to the Greek epic for answers. Heroism. Victimhood. Sacrifice. Stuff like that. We go right back to the source.'

Dyann jabbed the pencil in her direction. 'But it's what you *do* with that knowledge.'

Marie-Jeanne sighed. 'So, Karen, you have a taste of our discussions now. Some poor girl is pregnant from a fraternity boy, and our arguments go on for days and days.'

'That's exactly what I'm saying, MJ,' Dyann said. 'Talk is cheap.'

*

O hindsight. Look how the whole thing unwinds from a single mistake. The tragic hero is late to learn, and myth can be so smug! That road bandit you killed was your father. That queen you married was your mother. Your own cleverness your hubris, your downfall.

Pregnancy hadn't even occurred to me. I tried to remember if the rubber I'd found glued to the mattress that morning had been whole. There'd been a neat knot tied in it. It had felt bulbous and powdery inside my fist before I wrapped it in toilet paper and put it in the trash. No, all of Mike Morton's semen must have been safely trapped inside.

4. EUSTATHIA

(promising constancy in purpose and affection)

Cloudshadow. The airplane lifts off from Toronto, and the landscape below my window congeals into camo print. The lakes glitter and blacken in the sun. The Canada-US border is right there, right underneath me already, but of course the two countries are indistinguishable from this height. Higher up I am confronted with the unlikeliness of clouds: the oil-painting indigos and vermilions, all that billowing top-lit rapture. It's like a cartoon, like a video game, and I fall into a sort of free-floating excitement.

I never get to travel for work. Freelancing means that if I pitch a faraway location, I have to haul all my photography equipment there at my own expense. My steadiest commercial clients are all in Toronto: real estate corporations, a major grocery chain, the Liquor Control Board's quarterly glossy. Much as I prefer the creative leeway in the editorial shoots I do for magazines and interior designers, those jobs don't pay enough to warrant chasing them very far outside of the city. And shooting for *Urban Idyll*, Annabeth Lise's blog, doesn't pay me anything but lunch and an occasional free throw pillow.

Ironic, then, that it's her blog paying for this trip to the convention. Annabeth was invited to participate in this 'Domestic Dreams' panel, and she invited me along, offered to pay my plane ticket since they were paying hers. Her empty seat next to me reminds me that I still have no idea what I'm going to say for our presentation. I'm grateful it's a short flight and there've been no delays.

In the cab to the hotel, Greg calls from Geneva to wish me luck. 'Did you pay the hydro before you left?' he says.

'We still have to talk,' I remind him. My lower back aches from sitting, from standing in lines.

He sighs. 'I know.'

But I don't want to talk any more than he does, not now, not on the phone. Greg still has to move out of our apartment. We've already agreed that he will move out. It's just a matter of when he'll be back in Toronto long enough to pack, and to transfer the lease and the joint bank accounts into my name.

I can hear Kristina's voice in the background, speaking German.

'Oh, Greg,' I say, 'come on.'

He says something with his hand over the mouthpiece. Then: 'Sorry about that. So you're good to go? Your conference thing is all ready?'

'Yeah, I'm good,' I say. I haven't told him the news about Annabeth ditching me, or the news about Steph. Anyway, Greg has stopped listening. I can hear the burrs in his silence, can hear him already thinking about something else. I look at my watch: it's eight in the evening in Geneva. Kristina is probably dressed and waiting by the door to go to dinner. I have found only one photo of her online: a group shot, a bunch of women in white coats. *German Women in Policy Innovation*, the online translator informed me.

'I have to go, Greg,' I say.

'Listen, I'm sorry I can't be there. With you. At the convention.'

'Why?' I ask.

'Okay, bye,' he replies. 'Bye, Karen. Love you.'

I hang up, wincing, thinking that Greg will have to answer to Kristina for that one. She'll have caught the 'Love you'; her command of English must be excellent if she works at the World Health Organization with Greg like he claims. The words are just a reflex, of course, just a habit from two years of long-distance phone calls. I shouldn't hold it against him, and neither should Kristina.

I notice a missed call from my mother and feel a ping of dread. I've been putting off telling my parents about Greg and me. My mother in particular liked Greg, though she hardly got to know him in the five years he and I were together. My mother likes smart men – 'men with something going on upstairs' is how she puts it. 'You can do better,' she would say whenever, as a teenager, I showed any interest in a boy whose looks she thought were too 'obvious'.

I look out the taxi window as we pass an ivy-covered building with a soccer pitch in front and schoolboys in uniform and look, here is Bruce. Striding up from my memory fresh as yesterday, here is godsfavoured Bruce Comfort, nineteen years of age. He's all aflush from the rugby pitch, all aquiver with his own heartsurfing pulse. A decade and a half later, he still comes up on me like this whenever he likes.

Look how the room is thicketed with dancing girls, five for every boy. The room is the dining room at the Gamma Beta Chi fraternity chapter house. For this first mixer of the fall term it is forested with girls like poplars in a rising storm, their limbs tossed and shaking to the thunderous bass beat. I spy you by degrees, Bruce, framed by the gilt-plaster mantel of the fireplace.

Bruce, I glimpse you through the flashing limbs and the trembling foliage of hair. You mark out territory simply with your stillness. A girl is balanced on your lap – Mona, her name is; I remember her from the dorm, spiral curls tossing, drunken giggles – and your mouth is pressed tight to her nipple through her blouse. Monumental Bruce Comfort, your muscles all packed in casually under your tanned skin. Your head is close-shorn, sleek, the better to show your great golden brow and your curled-back ears. Your bicep wraps round Mona's ribs and your powerful jaw works against her breast. I cannot look away from the glare of your golden power and her nipple comes away from your kiss puckered in a dark wet circle that fills my groin with a prickling heat and I do look away, I must, thrilled and terrified and despairing.

O heavengoing Bruce. You learned it too, didn't you: nothing mythical can touch the lives of mortals without catastrophe.

5. HAMARTIA

(error in judgment)

I painted a good picture, but what I told Steph and Dyann and Marie-Jeanne was the truth. I'd chauffeured my ex-roommate Rachel and her friends to the fraternity party and had ended up inside. For seventy-five minutes I had stood there among strangers drinking and chatting and smoking and watching Bruce with the dancing girls. Then I had veered away, sweating and dizzy, my skull vibrating with the noise and marijuana, through the kitchen where the floor was sticky with spilt beer and out the back door of the frat house.

There was nobody in the backyard and nowhere to sit, either – just a pile of empty boxes and a few bicycles lying in the grass. A weird red glow crawled across the patio stones from a room in the basement. I hoisted myself onto a rain barrel and rested my head against the fence, listening like a caught feral thing for the faraway nightquiet.

And then Mike was out there with me. Cute Mike Morton from my freshman philosophy class last year, Mike with the startled brown eyes in the narrow white face. He and I had been assigned to the same group for a presentation on Machiavelli, and at the end of term he'd told me that I was the most intelligent girl he'd ever met. I was flattered, since someone had told me Mike Morton scored the class's only A+ on the midterm. We hung out at a couple of dorm keggers, me and Mike and his dorm roommate, Bruce Comfort. I remembered them saying something about rushing a fraternity. About Bruce being offered a bid by several frats right away, and Mike thinking maybe he could get in on Bruce's coattails.

Mike led me back inside the house and danced with me and fetched me a beer and paraphrased Sophocles: 'Let us take pleasure where we can; the morrow comes ever blind,' he said, and his eyebrows rose in an anxious little question.

I lifted my cup and felt how my whole face smiled at him. 'Aren't you supposed to be a Golf Pro?' I asked. The mixer theme was Golf Pros & Tennis Hos. Rachel and her friends were members of the guest sorority and had dressed in sequined bustiers and white miniskirts.

Mike, though, was wearing a seersucker blazer. 'New pledges are on lube duty,' he explained. 'I was going for country-club bartender.'

'Nice,' I said. I held out the hem of my palm-tree T-shirt and curtsied. 'I was going for not-a-sorority-sister, didn't-plan-on-going-out-tonight.'

'Nice,' he said.

I kept drinking until I couldn't feel my own skin, until I was wearing my own face strapped around my head. Time became a tongue darting in and out of a gap-toothed mouth. We danced. Bruce wasn't in the dining room anymore. Some girl was being passed around the dance floor from frat brother to frat brother. She was too wasted to stand up on her own, so they passed her back and forth, moving her boneless limbs like a puppet to demonstrate comical dance moves for one another.

Mike and I got more drinks and stood on one of the balconies, and Mike searched through his pockets for some paper and asked me to write down my phone number.

'Why, do you have more duties to attend to?'

'No. I'm duty-free. I just thought, it's late, and I don't want to lose you if you take off soon.'

I didn't have a phone number to write down. Mike had given me his checkbook to write on, and when I handed it back to him he laughed. 'You just wrote me a check for seven thousand dollars.'

'I don't have seven thousand dollars,' I told him.

'It's not your checkbook, either. You're really drunk, aren't you,' Mike said.

I was trying to remember something I'd been curious about earlier. 'Is it true there's a dungeon in the basement?' I asked him.

'Sort of. Not an actual dungeon. It's called the Black Bag.'

'Can I see it?'

'It's not all that exciting. Unless you're planning on taking the GBC Express.'

Rachel and her friends had been talking about the Express in the car. 'Do girls do that? Have sex with all the frat brothers at once?'

'I think it's more like one at a time. That's why it's called a train, not a ... whatever you'd call the other thing.'

'An unrailment?' That was not a word, though; that was a drunkword. I struggled to stay on topic. 'One at a time, wow. That's gentlemanly.'

Mike shrugged. 'I was just kidding. They don't actually do it.'

'Where do the stories come from, then?'

'We have a reputation to maintain. It's mythology. You know.'

'Compensating.'

'Very funny.' Mike's eyes were joyous, though. In my experience most boys backed away from a sharp tongue, a clever rejoinder, a challenge. One of the crew bosses had said it to me only a few weeks ago, during the summer tree-planting contract: 'That's a real turnoff, you know, when you get all catty like that.'

Not Mike, though. He was hungry for it. There must not have been enough intelligent repartee around the fraternity for his taste. Mike was too smart for Greek life, I thought.

'I just want to see the room,' I said.

Mike led me down the back steps to a basement rec room with couch cushions on the floor and an elaborate video game system. At the other end of the room was a closed door. Mike opened it a crack to peek inside, then stepped back and waved me in. This was where the eerie red light in the backyard originated: there was a tinted bulb screwed into the ceiling fixture. It was a weight room, or had been, once: mirrors on the walls, frames for free weights, an elaborate tension rack with pulleys. A sagging vinyl sofa sat against the mirrors.

On the wall was a porn-mag centrefold of a girl on her knees, wearing a ball gag and studded leather restraints. She smirked over her shoulder, her labia hanging wrinkled and slimy past the G-string.

I went over and slapped her greased round buttock. 'Classy,' I said.

'Sorry. That's disgusting.' Mike put his arms around me, turned me, and tipped my face to his.

We kissed, swaying, for several moments. Then he said, 'You know, I do have an actual bedroom.' Oh look at those wet, hopeful brown eyes!

Mike's bedroom had two twin beds and a bookshelf and nothing else. A suitcase spilled clothes onto the floor.

We kissed, and the kissing progressed to the removal of clothing; I wasn't wearing that much to begin with. I lay on the bed, and Mike sprawled on top of me. The room rotated around us, steadied, rotated again.

I thought of sacrifice. Not because I didn't want to have sex with Mike, although I wasn't particularly turned on by him. Not because I was having sex at a fraternity house, either, although the party at the frat house certainly had something to do with what was happening. It was a sacrifice of Mike and me both. It was a rite bigger than ourselves that had to be carried out a specific way dictated by all the people who had performed the rite before us. We were two strangers assigned to the task, drunk, uncoordinated, unfamiliar with each other's bodies and therefore ungraceful in our efforts.

And it was effortful. He was working hard, Mike Morton: his cock prodding between my legs, his back flexing with the effort, his chest shining with alcoholic sweat. We slid hip over hip. Mike worked faithfully and hard, and I did my best to facilitate his efforts with movements that might parallel and complement his own.

'Member' is a word for the phallus. There's 'remember'. And then there is 'dismember'. They teach you this in college. You know it before they teach it but they teach it anyway. They tell you of the golden calf, of altars, of the Dionysian bull-god. They tell you that whenever it enters the lives of mortals the mythical tears a hole. It jabbed and prodded and bruised me, and after a few more clumsy, gasping thrusts Mike sighed and said, 'Oh, oh, God,' and dug his hot forehead into my shoulder, and I gripped him tight with my thighs.

*

In the earliest morning between stumbling, still drunk, from Mike's bed and walking the twelve blocks to 61 Fulton Ave, where I passed out in the backyard, I barged in on Bruce Comfort peeing in the bathroom.

'It's okay, it's no problem. Come in,' he said.

'Come in?'

'Sure.' He flipped up the waistband of his sweatpants and flushed the toilet.

So I went in. I reached past Bruce for a length of toilet paper, wrapped up Mike's used rubber, and dropped it into the wastebasket. Then I pulled down my boxer shorts and sat on the toilet to urinate.

'Or do you want privacy?' he said. He was shirtless. His pectoral muscles were gentle, sleepy swells under his skin.

I shook my head. The shower curtain hung from only two of its rings. Behind it, in the tub, slept a girl in lacy panties and a football jersey. 'Who's that?' I said.

'No clue,' Bruce said. 'Mine are still in my bed.'

'Yours "are"? Plural?' I asked. Then I winced: it stung when I peed.

'This is kind of a weird thing we're doing,' he said.

We both laughed. We washed our hands side by side at the sink. He stood behind me, and we looked at ourselves in the mirror.

'So, Karen Huls,' he said.

'So, Bruce Comfort,' I said. My back shivered, sensing bare skin nearby. He'd remembered my last name. My whole name.

'Do you have any idea how sexy you are?' he said. His thumbs nudged little circles at my hips and then stopped.

I looked at my reflection: flushed cheeks, raw lips, eyes still hectic with booze. Bruce's bare skin was like the sun at my back. I knew what I looked like. I looked like that line from *Gatsby*, the one that went *At his lips' touch she blossomed for him like a flower and the incarnation was complete.*

He pressed his nose into my hair. 'You smell like Mike.'

The sun! It was hard to breathe. 'I'm sorry.'

'It's okay,' Bruce said. 'I'm happy for him.'

6. KHOROS

(group that comments on the action)

Dyann and Steph and Marie-Jeanne decided I would make a good room-mate after all. The interview had more or less ended with Stick's intrusion. Marie-Jeanne had asked me what the fraternity boys had thought of my hairy legs. 'Airy,' she called them, and it had taken me an extra beat to make sense of what she'd said. I blurted, 'This is the weirdest interview ever,' and they laughed and agreed with me.

'I think she is okay,' Marie-Jeanne said, and she stood up and started stacking books from the dining table into her bag. 'I have to go to class. Yes?'

Dyann frowned. 'That's not exactly ... We at least need to check in with Charla.'

'We need to choose someone, and the phone has not exactly been ringing. Karen is okay, I think. A fellow Canadian! *C'est assez pour moi.*' Marie-Jeanne smiled at me with her even white teeth, her red lips, her blue eyes.

And Steph had called me that same afternoon at Rachel's to report that Charla, too, thought I'd be a great fit. 'She said you spent all last year in the dorm hiding in a corner reading poetry, when you weren't taking pictures. Which is enough for Charla apparently.' I assumed the hint of disapproval in her voice was for Charla, not for poetry or photographs. Steph had liked me from the start, I thought.

'What do you think of the name "Femhaven"?' she said.

It sounded like a menstrual pad company. 'For what?'

'For the house. Charla wants "Moonmere", but MJ thinks that makes us sound flaky.'

'What does Dyann think?'

'She thinks naming the house is dumb. She keeps coming up with "Raghurst", sarcastic stuff like that.'

I laughed. I could picture it perfectly: all of them sitting around that gypsy-caravan of a living room debating the politics of various names for the house. The socio-discursive implications. And now they were letting me into the debates too. They'd picked me! 'I like "Raghurst", actually,' I told Steph.

✳

A few days after I moved in Dyann sent me next door to retrieve her thermos from someone named Jake – roommate of Stick – who'd borrowed it without her permission. 'I would only say something I'll regret,' Dyann said. 'We may need to stay on the good side of those guys, but that doesn't mean I have to put up with their shit.'

'Why do we need to stay on their good side?' I asked.

Dyann shrugged. 'Marie-Jeanne and Stick go way back, from some engineering summer camp or something. That's how we found this house. Through him.'

Stick and his housemates had built a skateboarding half-pipe in their living/dining room. I tried their bell, but the racket of wheels on plywood drowned it out, so I went in and waved and watched from the hall as they ollied and three-sixtied and crashed into each other. Their house had exactly the same layout as ours but no furniture, just piles of their belongings – clothing, books, stereo equipment, rock-climbing accessories – all over the floor. The ceiling above both ends of the half-pipe was dented and cracked and smudged.

A boy named Wheeler rinsed the thermos out for me. He had to keep pushing his glasses back up on his sweaty nose. 'So you're an Esterhazian?' he asked.

'What's that?' I said.

'You're telling me that you passed muster for roommate and you don't even know who Sylvia Esterhazy is?'

'Oh, the professor?' I said. 'Steph might try to get me into one of her courses.'

Wheeler wiped the thermos dry on his T-shirt and handed it to me.

'Um, are you an Esterhazian?' I asked.

He laughed. 'My point exactly, man! I'm in computer science. Like, why would I even know that name, Sylvia Esterhazy? But you can't even be their neighbour without drinking the Kool-Aid.

'I love those women, don't get me wrong,' he said, toeing aside a pair of barbells in the hallway so I wouldn't trip, 'but they are intense.'

I smiled at the way he'd made 'intense' into two words. I wanted intense. 'Intense' was exactly what I wanted people like Wheeler to be saying about me.

I didn't have class till the afternoon, so Dyann invited me to come hang out at the Women's Centre. We cycled to campus together. Her bike had a metal rack for a water bottle attached to the crossbar, and the thermos, filled with coffee, rattled back and forth as she pedaled. Her pants were rolled up over her knees. I spent the six-minute ride from Raghurst to the main campus watching the muscles of her calves bunch and stretch, bunch and stretch.

The Women's Centre shared a second-floor room in the Student Life Building with the Centre for Students of Colour and the Environmental Alliance. The Women's Centre only got Mondays and every second Thursday, Dyann told me, but many of the members also belonged to one or both of the other groups, too, so it worked out fine.

A powerfully familiar odour hit me when Dyann pushed open the door. In the dorms last year most of us had had a kettle to supplement our meal plans with ramen noodles and Cup-a-Soup. The scent of MSG-enhanced broth had had a way of lingering even in the washrooms where we rinsed out our mugs and spoons. I had been happy to leave it behind for tree-planting, where our camp food was of the from-scratch variety, and to have settled at Raghurst, where we seemed to share a common will, at least, toward healthier eating. But now here was the Women's Centre, where someone had obviously stayed late or skipped breakfast and had defaulted to dormitory habits, and to me the place smelled like the good old days. It was like coming home.

There was powdery linoleum tile and some chairs draped in batik fabrics. Placards and banners and xeroxed pamphlets covered every surface of the room. A handful of girls were gathered around a folding table under the windows. 'Hey, Dyann,' one of them called, 'come and look at these illustrations and tell us whether you think they're serious enough.'

'That's not the point, Melanie.' A girl with a messy French braid spoke with a tone of exhausted forbearance. 'It's our content that's serious; we want the illustrations to counterpoint that, remember?'

Dyann and I peered over the girls' shoulders. There were spidery cartoon figures with grimacing faces and waving legs. 'We'll reduce them when we photocopy, of course,' Melanie said. 'Nestle them in there right among the blocks of text.'

'Is this the STD section?' Dyann said. 'Are these supposed to be, like, "Hello, Mr Gonorrhea? Hi, Ms Genital Warts, want to go get a drink sometime?"'

'Is this for a zine?' I said. Dyann hadn't introduced me, but I knew one of the girls. 'Hey, Jen,' I said, and I nodded round the circle at the others. 'Karen Huls.'

Jen Swinburn was the editor of the student newspaper, the *Campus Eye*. I'd taken a few pictures for her last year, including a front-page shot of a doe and fawn grazing in front of the campus war memorial. My parents had framed the clipping I'd sent them and displayed it on the bookshelf in the den.

'Janine. Hi,' said the girl with the braid. 'This is Melanie. It's sort of a zine, but we're aiming for a glossy cover because we got funding from Health Services.'

'Cool. What's it called?' I said.

'*DIY Gynaecology*.'

'But we've been tossing around *HOT PANTZ*,' Jen Swinburn said. 'All caps, with a "Z" on "pants". You know, to signal the levity aspect right up front.'

Jen was a member of Kappa Sigma, the largest women's sorority on campus. Last spring she'd badgered me to rush. She'd gone on and on about how great sorority membership looked on a resume. I wondered if the Women's Centre staff knew a sorority sister was helping publish their zine. Based on my recent experience, Greek life seemed sort of incompatible with feminism. Or maybe I had it backward. Maybe the Centre wanted buy-in from the sororities for better distribution, and they'd sought Jen out specifically for that reason.

'Sure. Whatever else we do, let's just make sure nobody takes us seriously,' said Dyann.

Janine put her fists on her hips. 'Come on, Dyann. You said you were ready to leave that discussion behind.'

Dyann rolled her eyes and plunked herself into one of the chairs to unscrew the lid from her thermos.

I took the chair next to her. 'What's the matter?'

'They won't include my herbal abortion recipe. The farthest they'll go is "A Gentle Natural Way to Bring on a Late Period". They're worried it would get the zine banned on campus.'

'Would it?'

'Probably. Which would actually get it some readers.' She'd raised her voice on this last comment, but none of the girls at the table responded. Dyann shook her head. Her feather earring dipped into the cup of her thermos as she drank.

She held the cup out to me, and I sipped the strong, bitter brew. 'Does it work?' I said.

'Censorship? Sure. Look at 2 Live Crew.'

'No, the herbal abortion.'

She nodded. 'If you're not too far gone.'

'Why don't you give the recipe to that pregnant girl who came in here?' I suggested.

'Susannah? Steph did. She was horrified.'

'Oh,' I said.

'Women are our own worst enemies, Karen. If you learn anything at all from Dr Esterhazy, you'll learn that. We play nice, and we play along, and so men just go ahead and write us into their fantasies exactly as they see fit.' Dyann jumped to her feet, stalked over to a wall-sized bulletin board, and began tearing off outdated posters and notices. 'Give me a hand here, will you?'

Together we cleared the board, leaving only a row of information cards along the bottom displaying contact numbers for the campus meditation centre, the Acquaintance Rape Task Force crisis line, and the local women's shelter. There was a 'No Means No' postcard too, the iconic black background with the purple script listing all the excuses girls give for not having sex: *'I'm tired' means NO*, and *'Let's just go to sleep' means NO*.

In the dorm we'd played a drinking game called No Means No. Someone would give an excuse and the girls would decide whether it warranted a NO. 'I'm on the rag means ___,' a girl would say, and the rest of us would yell 'YES!' and she would have to drink. 'I've got herpes' meant NO, the girls had generally agreed, as did 'I'm an ugly dog' and 'I'm your sister, you perv.' Most everything else meant YES.

I pulled down a clipping from the newspaper – not the *Eye*, the city paper – from last winter with a picture of Steph wearing a camera around her neck. Her brush cut and the saggy cords she wore made her look like a street urchin from Dickens. *Turning the Lens Around*, read the headline. *Women's Studies Students Stage 'Operation Sex Shop'*. The article explained how she and Dyann waited outside the adult video store and snapped photos of the men emerging.

'"It's about accountability," claims sophomore Dyann Brooks-Morriss, aged 19. "Most of these men are here to purchase or rent pornographic images of women. They're here to look, to get pleasure from looking. So we're making the point that women can look too. We're not only objects of the male gaze."'

'This is awesome. I read about this,' I said. 'So this was you and Steph?'

I read on: 'Stephanie McNamara, 23, a PhD student in the Women's Studies program, goes further: "Porn is the theory; rape is the practice," she says, quoting Women's Studies professor Sylvia Esterhazy. "We want these perpetrators to know we have them on record, that we know who they are, even if it's only an image of their faces."'

'We talked about this in my Ethics class last year,' I told Dyann.

Dyann snorted. 'Ethics? What, it's unethical to return the gaze?'

'Well, the right to privacy, I guess.'

'And what was the classroom verdict?' She was taunting me, I knew. But she also wanted to hear my answer. After a few days of being Dyann Brooks-Morriss's roommate I was starting to grasp how she worked in conversation. Silence, or mild politeness, meant she was bored. Sarcasm meant you'd piqued her interest, maybe irritated her. Head-on attack meant you'd hit close to the mark. The easiest way to disappoint Dyann was to back down, to tell her she was right and you were wrong.

'Well, it's not illegal to photograph people unless you're publishing the photos,' I said. 'And the sidewalk *is* public property. I love the idea of using a camera as a weapon.' My Nikon F90 was one of the first things I'd unpacked in my new room at Raghurst. I wished I'd had it on me when I retrieved Dyann's water bottle that morning from the boys next door – I couldn't wait to shoot their living-room skate park.

'That article's full of inaccuracies anyhow. That's a Catherine MacKinnon quote Steph gave them, not something Sylvia said. And Sylvia was pretty pissed we'd mentioned her at all; she hates anything to do with activism.'

'I thought you guys all loved Dr Esterhazy,' I said.

Dyann was writing in a notebook with a black Sharpie. She tore out the page and pinned it at the top of the bulletin board. *SHAME*, it read. 'Steph loves her. Don't get me wrong, Sylvia's a brilliant thinker. She's great for learning the basics, where our fucked-up ideas about women actually come from.'

'But for you it's about action,' I guessed.

'For me it's about action.' Below the word *SHAME* Dyann pinned a picture of Bruce Comfort. She stood back to appraise the effect, grunted, and started writing again.

I stared at the grainy image. The sleek golden head haloed by sunlight. The naked brown shoulders. Bruce was barefoot against the deep green of the main quad, cradling a football in his arms like a newborn baby. I'd seen the picture before – last spring in the *Eye*, some kind of campus life year-in-review spread. Dyann had made a colour enlargement of it.

'What are you doing?' said Melanie, behind us. She had a wide, round face with fleshy cheeks that looked even puffier because she wore her fine hair tucked tight behind her ears with barrettes. 'Where did you get that picture?'

'Just a sec,' said Dyann. She gnawed on the end of the marker and wrote some more.

Janine looked up from the craft table and gave a little groan. 'Um, Dyann? I don't think we want to …' She trailed off, pushed back her chair, and walked over to us. 'Is that another fraternity thing? Why don't you just put it in the frat file, then?'

'Our frat file is a *file*. Nobody ever sees it,' Dyann said. She pinned the second sheet of paper next to Bruce's picture. *Refused to use condom*, it stated. *GBC booze cruise, May 1995. Told Susannah her pregnancy wasn't his problem.*

A small, shared exhalation went around the circle of girls gathered at the bulletin board. We locked eyes with each other, one by one.

'Holy shit,' Jen Swinburn said.

There was surf-sound inside my ears, sudden sweat-sting in my armpits. Gossip was one thing. Gossip was a bunch of us feeling unhappy about the way we were treated and feeling temporarily better when we complained about it to one another, and then feeling worse, probably, afterward. But this was the opposite of gossip. It was declaration, accusation. It was visible and solid. It wasn't about feeling better or worse; it leapt out ahead of our individual feelings into collective action. Right here on this ordinary weekday morning in this ordinary, homely room, Dyann was giving us permission for something we'd never even considered an option.

'Do any of you women want me to take this picture down?' said Dyann.

Janine cleared her throat. 'I have a picture I want to stick up there, actually,' she said.

'Me too,' Melanie said, and she giggled.

Dyann's feathers curtsied. Her hair lassoed itself. 'Okay, then,' she said. 'Bring them in. Add them to our Wall of Shame.'

The women of Raghurst hold forth amongst themselves on the subject of myth's purpose:

Steph: The Greek myths – all myths, really – strive to answer the question, 'What was it all for?' The myths ask, 'Where are the gods amid all this carnage?' And the myths answer, 'Here they are, down from Olympus, taking sides.'

Karen: Whose side are they on?

Dyann: The men's side, of course. Greek mythology is one long excuse for the rape and murder of women. Just like all history.

Steph: Homer laments the bloodlust, though. 'What greater monster is there than man?'

Dyann: 'Man,' you see? It's always men. The myths don't have a clue what to do with women. They have nothing to say about us whatsoever. We need to build our own fucking mythology.

7. OPTATIO

(ardent wish)

O sing of the American college campus, great crucible of human excellence. Here we are gathered in from the far corners of the continent, plucked from the skyscraper alleys and the benighted suburbs and the picket-fenced hinterlands. *Success doesn't come to you. You go to it.* Here we are planted deep in the fertile soil of culture, history, tradition, legacy. *Your generation will learn from the last and serve the next.* Here we are nourished by the nation's finest minds amid settings of unparalleled natural beauty. *Take wisdom from your books but also from the trees that made them.* Here we discover kindred souls whose thirst for knowledge inspires our own. *The friendships you make here will last a lifetime.*

I had saved my stack of recruitment brochures for months, even after I was accepted at several schools and had made my choice. I wasn't an athlete but I looked and looked at the shining-eyed girls in ponytails and knee pads arrayed behind the trophy, the sweat-slicked boys on the football field clutching one another in openmouthed euphoria. I'd studied the photographs so carefully that I'd memorised them, and in some strange way the images shaped my reality, infiltrated it, so that I arrived on campus already seeing things in a certain light. I wasn't a scientist but I looked and looked at the grad student holding a test tube of pink liquid over a Bunsen burner while her lab partner watched with a serene half-smile. I wasn't an actor but I looked and looked at the backlit, costumed figures with arms outstretched on the theatre-program stage.

There was the image of students sprawled on their bellies in the grass amidst scattered books. The one of the robed professor laughing with his acolytes in front of a stained-glass window. The one of the boy skateboarding with his backpack past the bell tower. The one of the raised arms flinging the mortarboards high against the blue sky. What had I imagined campus life would be like before I was living it? I'd imagined it would be like the brochures, of course – and the strange thing was that it actually *was* like the brochures. To look back over the images with my mind's eye was not at all an exercise in disillusionment. Were the images an accurate reflection of the experience I was having, then? Or was my experience a faithful imitation of the images I studied so ardently?

The terms of my foreign-student visa stipulated that I wasn't permitted to work off campus, so I took a job waitressing at the Faculty Club. The dining room was accessed through a red-carpeted foyer with a marble sculpture of Pygmalion and Galatea and restrooms whose doors were disguised with dark wood paneling. There was even an old-fashioned coat-check counter, with brass number tags arrayed on a board for retrieving your garments after dinner. Inside, soaring windows framed a patio above a bowl-shaped lawn called Faculty Hollow and, beyond it, a ravine. During my first shift I stood breathless at the window as a massive hawk climbed the wind and glided overhead, so close I could see its hooked beak and a small, limp body clamped in one of its talons.

The kitchen, though, was no fancier than any other I'd worked in: dishes stacked above the stainless-steel prep counter, steam billowing from the dishwashers, a greasy resin coating the floors. I was trained by Hamish, a dour exchange student who informed me he would be dropping out and heading home to Scotland the moment I was competent enough to take over.

Arriving for my third shift I saw Steph and Dyann sitting with an older woman at a booth along the far wall. They had salads and teapots. Their notebooks were spread out beside their plates, and their heads were bent together in earnest conversation. I didn't particularly mind my new roommates finding out that I waitressed, but in fact I hadn't yet told them about this job. Most of my fellow students didn't need to work for tuition – many had never in their lives held a part-time job – and I'd grown weary, last year, of how novel and exotic my various jobs on campus were to my dorm-mates. Rachel Smythe had adored informing her friends that if they called the meal-card office to make an official complaint, they had better be *nice* because it could be her *roommate* on the phone, and didn't that just go to show that you never really knew *who* you might be dealing with, even in the service industry?

Steph and Dyann took me right in stride, though. They introduced the woman as Dr Sylvia Esterhazy. Dr Esterhazy was old in that but-who-knows-how-old? way all professors had: snowy curls, delicate features, and a web of tiny lines and freckles all over her face. She wore a black linen tunic and a chunky necklace with an arrangement of silver disks. She propped her elbows on either side of her plate and folded her small hands together. Her middle finger had a silver ring with a large moonstone twisted around to one side.

'Sylvia is a Cavendish scholar, originally,' Steph had informed me. 'She was trained in early modern women's autobiography. It's all Greek and Roman mythology now, but her monograph on protofeminist social societies is still cited by everyone in the field.'

'And what do you do?' Dr Esterhazy asked me, as if we were colleagues at a cocktail party.

'English Lit,' I told her – I had just declared my major – 'and waitressing. My bursary doesn't quite cover the foreign-student fees.'

'Canada – how foreign,' Steph said, and they all three laughed and nodded and rolled their eyes sympathetically.

I kept an eye on them as I did the rounds with my tables. Their conversation seemed to absorb them utterly. Dr Esterhazy's hands traced shapes in the air as she spoke, and Steph's head bobbed in metronomic agreement. Dyann leaned in to interject. Her index finger stabbed the tabletop in front of her. Dr Esterhazy shook her head and laughed, and Steph joined the laughter. Dyann sat back, arms crossed, smiling too. Then Dr Esterhazy reached out both of her hands – one across the table and one beside her – and Steph and Dyann each took one of them. Dr Esterhazy tipped her chin, and my roommates leaned in close to listen to the professor's secret words.

Envy erupted inside me. My feet marched me over to their table. I stood before them with a face that must have been volcanic with yearning. I caught Steph's eye and touched my chest and crooked my fingertip in Dr Esterhazy's direction.

Steph nodded and winked. 'Would you consider one more student in Women and Myth?' she asked the professor. 'Karen would really enjoy it, I think, and she'd be a real asset to the class.'

A crease appeared between Dr Esterhazy's fine dark brows. 'Oh, but we're so oversubscribed already.'

'But maybe by next week? You said you expect the numbers to drop, right?'

'I would love the challenge,' I said, my cheeks lava-hot. There was something about the intimacy among these three, Steph and Dyann and their prof. Or maybe it was how perfect Sylvia Esterhazy looked here in the Faculty Club with her wide, pale eyes and her angelic hair, like an aging Rossetti muse. She cast an aura, and my roommates bathed in it, but I, I stood alone at the verge in my stained white shirt and my polyester skirt and my odour of kitchen grease and ignorance.

'Have you any background in Greek myth?' Dr Esterhazy asked me.

'She's only a sophomore,' Steph said, 'but I could help her along.'

'But you're not paid to offer extra help. I told you, Stephanie, it's deplorable how little funding they gave me. I won't have you exploited by working in excess of your grading hours.'

'I live with her too,' Dyann said. 'I'll help too.'

'I wrote a paper on Persephone for Dr Mandel last year,' I said. 'I could give you a copy if you'd like.' In fact my paper had compared the character of Hades to the Biblical depiction of Satan. I had only mentioned Persephone in relation to Eve in the garden.

It seemed to do the trick, though. Dr Esterhazy sighed. 'Oh, all right. The more, the merrier, I suppose. And I'll have you, my faithful *dexiteros*, to share the yoke,' she added, touching Steph's hand again and sending a pleased flush into her cheeks.

Dyann rolled her eyes at this. She slid out of the booth and took my hand and pumped it in sarcastic congratulations.

'Thank you, Dr Esterhazy,' I said. Her name folded sweetly in my mouth, and I swallowed it like a secret vow. I would learn what this wise woman knew! I would learn what they all knew, and I would know it as well as they.

Dyann must have read the ardour on my face, because she rolled her eyes once more. 'Welcome to Esterhazy Island,' she said. 'Did we mention it's a one-way ticket? There are no return flights.'

*

That day I had planned to meet Marie-Jeanne at the cafeteria before her field hockey practice. I would have liked to sneak her into the Faculty Club – I'd heard that the manager would turn a blind eye and let the waitstaff dine with friends after our shifts sometimes, but I couldn't afford the food even with my employee discount. At the caf I went on autopilot, collecting what last year had been my standard, most-nutrition-for-cost meal: a small milk and an egg salad pita loaded with all the free fixings it would hold – green peppers, extra cheese, hummus, olives, pickles. Then I had to wait with my tray while Marie-Jeanne picked her way painstakingly through the salad bar. 'You can't combine ferments with carbohydrate,' she complained, wrinkling her nose at the coleslaw and bypassing the croutons. Her finished plate contained small piles of chickpeas, shredded carrot, tuna, and cottage cheese.

'Are they pretty strict with your diet on the hockey team?' I asked her when we'd found a seat by the windows. 'At home, too, I've noticed that it's never you eating the Doritos or digging into the ice cream.'

'I'm the strict one with myself,' Marie-Jeanne said. '*Je suis anorexique.* I have to be very careful, all the time.'

Marie-Jeanne didn't look like an anorexic. She was round-cheeked and thick-waisted, with solid, muscular arms and legs.

She must have seen the skepticism on my face. 'Anorexia doesn't go away. It's like *l'alcoolisme:* you can only manage it, not cure it.' She pulled her wallet from her backpack, dug out a snapshot, and slid it across the table to me. It was a little girl in a baby-blue leotard and pointe shoes. The girl held one foot over her head, her rib cage thrust forward and her back arched at an impossible angle. Blonde braids were wrapped around her head.

'I was a ballerina back at home in Trois-Rivières,' Marie-Jeanne explained.

'This is you?' I brought the photo closer but I couldn't see Marie-Jeanne anywhere in the little girl's face or body.

'That's me, yes – at seventeen years old. Yes, only three years ago, 1992. In fact I still had not got my period, my breasts, nothing. That is what happens when you are near starvation.'

'Holy shit,' I said. 'Sorry.' I looked up from the photo, but she just nodded and shrugged.

'*C'est grotesque, oui?* I keep it nearby me so that I can measure myself.'

'You mean like weigh-ins, stuff like that?'

'*Non*, no. I mean if I look at this picture and I don't see it – if that girl's body looks okay to me, or normal, or nice and strong – then I know I'm in trouble. I know I need to get myself back on track.'

'It's your touchstone.'

Marie-Jeanne smiled and tucked the photo back into her wallet. 'My touchstone. *Oui, c'est ça.*'

After lunch I walked my bike beside Marie-Jeanne, and we wandered toward home through the campus dormitory block. Students had spread out blankets and backpacks and were snoozing on every available green surface in perfect mimicry of my recruitment-brochure photos, albeit featuring fewer schoolbooks and more cumuli of pot smoke.

At the first major intersection past the main gates we came upon a charity car wash with a banner that said GREEKS GET WET. A blonde girl in green flip-flops and a green-and-white-striped bikini bounced up to us carrying a green-and-white-striped box with a slot in the top. The letters 'KS' were embroidered across her left breast and printed in matching script on the box. 'Alzheimer's research?' she chirped, and shook the box so it jangled.

Before we could take off our backpacks to dig for change, the girl veered toward a car pulling up to the light. The driver, male, unrolled his window, and the girl leaned her elbows on his sill to speak to him.

All the girls wore the same bathing suit. The boys manned the hoses in the convenience store parking lot where the cars were being washed. They all wore baggy green board shorts. I spied Mike Morton sponging off the hood of a car and then Jen Swinburn standing on a newspaper box. Jen waved at Marie-Jeanne and me and lifted her megaphone to her mouth: 'Kappa Sigma Sisters!'

The bikinied girls – ten or twelve of them – dropped what they were doing, stood at attention, and raised their right hands toward Jen.

'Rush Crush! Two o'clock!'

The girls jogged over to us and dropped to one knee on the sidewalk. They clasped their hands together over their hearts, ponytails all drooping to the right as they cocked their heads and made exaggeratedly pleading faces.

Marie-Jeanne and I exchanged baffled looks. A couple of passing cars honked at the spectacle.

'All right, back to work, you dirty whores! Let's go,' Jen ordered, and the girls scrambled to their feet and scattered to their duties.

Jen strolled over. She wore a green tank top over her bikini. *Kappa Sigma* was written out in full across her breasts. 'Hi, Karen.'

'Hi, Jen. I didn't realise you were actually the boss of your sorority.'

'I'm pledgemaster for this week is all,' she said.

I introduced her to Marie-Jeanne, who asked her if the bikinis were mandatory.

'We have one-pieces too,' Jen said, 'but let's face it, the bikinis bring in way more cash.'

'I can't believe they make you do this,' I said.

'It's the whole point of being Greek, Karen. I keep telling you. Having fun and giving back.'

Behind her I saw the GBC brothers lashing each other with wet towels. Mike was pointing at me and saying something to the boy next to him when he got hit full in the face with a sponge. He staggered around to hoots of derision, yelling about soap in his eyes, and the brother holding the hose blasted his head and shoulders.

I told Marie-Jeanne to go on ahead and take my bike. When Jen and I approached the boys, Mike shook himself like a puppy. He'd lost one of his flip-flops. 'You said you'd call,' he said.

'Yeah, ho, you don't leave a brother hanging,' drawled a nearby brother, twirling his towel into a whip.

'No, no, no. Wait a second now.' A boy with shaggy, bleach-blond hair strolled over and put an arm around my shoulders. 'This girl is a KS Rush Crush; did you not hear? That means it's Chet being the emotional slut in this particular case, begging her to call. She doesn't owe his sorry ass a thing.'

'Who is Chet? And what is a Rush Crush?' I said.

'Chet is our boy Mike here. And a Rush Crush means you're a highly desirable PNM – Potential New Member,' he added when I shook my head. 'And for Kappa Sigma, that means you're at least a seven, seven and a half –'

'That is *not* our criteria, you zoo animal,' Jen interrupted him. She grabbed his hand by the index finger and flung it off my shoulder like it was something rotten.

The blond boy placed the hand to his chest. 'All right, all right. It means you're highly intelligent, you've got your head on straight, tons of ambition, blah blah blah. And you still know how to have a good time. All right, your High Holiness?'

'Better,' Jen said. She introduced the boy to me as Duncan Larson, GBC house president.

Mike had turned back to the car window he was polishing. Across the lot I saw Bruce Comfort with a girl on his shoulders. She'd hooked a toe into the band of his shorts and was trying to push them down with her foot. A crescent of white skin flashed at his hip and across his buttocks as he whirled and dipped to make her shriek.

I stepped over to Mike, dropped to my knees on the wet pavement, and pressed my palms together as the KS pledges had done. 'What can I possibly do to atone?' I said.

Mike went pink at the chorus of praise that met my subservience. He patted the crown of my head in kingly beneficence, then dabbed his towel at the droplets his hair had dribbled onto my cheek. 'Walk with me,' he said.

We drifted to the shade of the storefront. Mike's collarbones were sunburnt. He said he thought I should come over and hang out with the brothers at the house. 'When there's no party on, sometime. You know, so they can get to know you better?'

'I don't think hanging out at a fraternity is really my thing,' I said.

'What is your thing, then?' Mike frowned. 'The drunken party fuck?'

It felt like a slap. 'You were there too, if I recall.'

'Yes, but I would like to turn it into something more than that. Or at least see if it could be something more. Don't you think that would be better? I mean, I don't know about you, but I didn't feel fantastic about it the next morning.'

He had a point there. It hadn't felt fantastic.

'I'm not saying we have to start going out to dinner and the movies together. But we could try to just *be* together, and see what happens.'

I'd had bad sex at a party with a relative stranger, but maybe there was a way to make good on it after the fact. Mike Morton was a smart guy, a great talker. He'd told me that GBC had nearly rejected his pledge because his grades were too high; they were worried he'd spend all his time studying. He was pretty sure his freshman grades had won him the physics prize and thought maybe the calculus, too, although the prizes wouldn't be announced until October. Even in the philosophy class we'd shared last year – his only arts elective – Mike had made all As on his papers, just like me. He'd lent me his copy of Herodotus, and it had been all marked up in the margins with his handwriting, even though it wasn't even on the syllabus.

He offered to pick me up at Raghurst, but I laughed and told him not to push his luck. I'd come by the frat house some afternoon, I said, when I had time, and see if he happened to be in.

*

Hindsight. Look how all the mythic motifs are right here waiting: the host, the guest, the gift, the stranger knocking at the door. All those trusty old hospitality rites. And look how late the tragic hero is to learn! He is marching along the straight tracks in the snow and some cavorting god runs over him with a snowmobile.

8. PRAEPOSITIO

(statement of theme)

In Dr Esterhazy's class a single Greek word appeared on the screen: αἴτιον. She told us that it meant 'originary myth'. She said it was different from the more common Greek word 'mythos', meaning 'tale' or 'story'. It had to do with deeper beliefs, with causes and beginnings, with our most basic understandings about the world. I copied the word in pencil onto the cover of my notebook, drew an outline around the strange letters with my black pen, and then inked them in with red.

'We won't be working with much actual Greek or Latin text this year,' Dr Esterhazy reassured us. 'We're English scholars, Women's Studies students, not classicists. But every now and then we'll take a look at a word or phrase and poke around at its etymology. We'll explore the options it presents for translators, and sometimes the problems it creates. The debates it generates.'

There were no male students in Women and Myth. We were twenty young women – eighteen white, one East Asian, one Indian or Pakistani – gathered around a conference table in the School of Graduate Studies Building. I'd understood that my fourth roommate, Charla Klein, was also enrolled in the class, but she hadn't shown up today. The room had stone walls, a dark wood floor, and tall windows made up of tiny, diamond-shaped panes.

The first module of the course focused on sexual difference as the basis for early myth systems. On Dr Esterhazy's screen was a terracotta fertility goddess from the early Mycenaean period. She had been collecting these images for years now, she told us – painted pottery fragments, cave drawings, charms, and talismans. They all depicted the female body in a way that emphasised its femaleness. Many of the figures were nothing more than a pair of big breasts, a swollen belly, and a slit beneath.

'Woman's body is irreparably bound to the earth and its rhythms,' Dr Esterhazy said. 'Our menstrual cycle, the cycles of gestation and birth – these things connect us to the natural world, don't they? And the natural world, for ancient peoples, was a terrifying thing. Flood and famine. Earthquakes, plagues. Art is the antidote to human terror. We can view all cultural production, right from its earliest manifestations in these fertility figures, as an attempt to escape from nature. To control it somehow. To transcend it.'

Dr Esterhazy's voice was soft, low, and as musical as brook-song. She'd brought a big stack of reference books to class, and I sat close to her end of the table so I could copy down the titles. *The Lives and Loves of Sappho*; *Women in the Ancient World: A Sourcebook in Translation*; *Fragmentary Lives*. Except for the *Iliad* all our required texts were collected in a course reader Dr Esterhazy had compiled. I was in the habit of using the library a lot, though, for all my courses. I brought dozens of books home and read them at night in bed. Usually I didn't read so much as skim, or get halfway through the scholarly introduction and doze off, but I liked to know where the ideas were coming from. It made me feel like part of an inner circle, even in bigger classes where my professors knew me only by my student number.

Dr Esterhazy flipped forward in the slide deck to a relief carved in stone: a little creature with a gaping mouth and, right below it, a gaping vagina. 'You wouldn't know it, but we've just jumped two thousand years forward, to a twelfth-century church in England.' She smiled around the table at our murmurs of surprise. 'Yes, this is on a church: you can go visit Herefordshire and take your own photos, if you like.

'Ravenous, isn't she? Here you can see how the female body has come to represent the devouring forces of nature. All cultural production – organised religion as well as art, and science, too – is patriarchy's flight from woman's devouring body, from the arbitrary and cruel ways that nature hurls him into the muck.'

'As if it's our fault.'

We all swiveled. A girl down the table stared straight across us at Dr Esterhazy, her face scarlet, her eyes round with unshed tears. She wore a silky pink blouse with shoulder pads, and her streaked hair was curled in a little fringe around her face but hung straight in the back. 'I'm sorry to interrupt, but I was with a boy this summer, okay? A frat boy. Like I didn't know better.' She rolled her eyes, and then swept a manicured fingernail along each lower lid to catch her tears before they melted her mascara.

'Anyhow, he gets me knocked up. So when I tell him I'm pregnant he says he's *moved on*, okay? And I just – I'm sorry, I know this is really off-topic, but I just don't see why he gets to *move on*, and just, like, walk away from his responsibilities.'

I stared. This had to be the girl Steph and Dyann had told me about, the one who'd come looking for advice at the Women's Centre. Bruce Comfort's girl.

At the start of class Dr Esterhazy had asked us each to write our name on a folding card and prop it on the table in front of us. Now the professor folded her hands and leaned forward, squinting to read the girl's card. 'Susannah,' she said, 'may I ask – and it's okay if you don't want to share – have you been to a doctor? Are you getting the support you need?'

Susannah emitted a kind of sob-laugh. 'My parents are making me quit school. They're making me move back home with them.'

'Are you keeping the baby?' someone asked.

Dr Esterhazy's frown deepened. 'That's not really an appropriate –'

'Of course I'm keeping it,' Susannah cried.

Congratulations burbled all across the seminar room. Hands reached toward Susannah; one girl shoved back her chair and lunged over to embrace the mom-to-be.

I found myself smiling automatically so as not to be the only unsupportive classmate. Then I stopped, remembering Dyann's comment about women being our own worst enemies. Was it right to congratulate someone on a pregnancy that would ruin all her ambitions in life? I was surprised someone like Susannah was even registered for a class like Women and Myth. Did this expose my own sexist victim-blaming – that I'd assumed the knocked-up girl couldn't be interested in a topic like this? Or that she couldn't be smart enough to understand it?

I turned to check for Dr Esterhazy's reaction, curious whether she'd be upset over Susannah's fate or upset about her class being interrupted, or both. But the professor was simply waiting with her silver-ringed fingers folded together on the table. The slide projector's glare caught her profile and lit the tiny hairs on her cheek and jawline. Her white hair erased itself against the screen. My eyes became so fixed on Dr Esterhazy that I couldn't look away even though I might be staring. And the others' eyes must have followed mine and been fixed, too, because in a moment the murmuring died away like a wave broken across the professor's bow.

She let the silence settle until it was disturbed only by sniffling, stifled now, from Susannah. Then she said, 'Would someone like to accompany her to the restroom?'

For a few moments no one even volunteered.

9. IN MEDIAS RES

(in the midst of the action)

Charla Klein. I have been saving her for last. I didn't actually see Charla Klein at Raghurst until nearly two weeks after I moved in. Apparently she had gone to a conference in New York City on natural medicine, a subject she was interested in pursuing after she finished college.

Then one afternoon I walked into the kitchen, and there was Charla straddling Dyann's lap with a pot rattling and fizzing behind her on the stove and Dyann's hands up her skirt. Charla's back was turned to me, her face pressed hard into Dyann's neck.

Dyann grinned widely at me and mouthed, 'Charla.'

I walked over and turned off the stove, telling myself yes, that's right, just turn off the stove for them so they don't have to deal with scorched cookware in the midst of passion. It would have been nice, though, if my feet were less heavy, my bones lighter inside my body. Transparent would have been good.

Charla made a sound that was neither male nor female but animal. Three breaths came harsh as sobs, and then she was quiet. Dyann wrapped her arms tight around the quivering shoulders.

'Someone's here, right?' Charla's voice was muffled.

'Indeed,' Dyann said.

I darted for the doorway, but Charla had already lifted her head. 'Karen Huls,' she said. Lipstick smeared her chin and smeared Dyann's collar. The skin of Charla's cheeks, jaw, neck, and chest was suffused with a different, more intimate crimson.

'Hi, Charla.'

Dyann licked her thumb and rubbed at Charla's chin. 'I swear I'll make a convert of this woman yet.'

Charla rolled her eyes. 'Uh-huh. Because lesbianism is a religion.'

Dyann was still grinning. 'And that there was communion. Let the sisters say amen.'

'So, how do you like living here so far, Karen?' Charla said.

'It's a little tame for me.' I shrugged, and they both laughed loudly.

'You're coming out with us tonight, right? Come!' Charla said.

And that was that. That was Charla greeting me at Raghurst after the four-month summer break and, before that, only the most superficial and casual of dormitory acquaintanceships.

*

The Thirsty Camel Bar & Grill cast a sickly glow over the street. The south-west and north-east corners of the intersection had tiny workers' cottages with blighted lawns and chain-link fences, empty driveways with weeds sprouting through the asphalt. North-west was a laundromat/video store whose proprietors liked to throw empty liquor bottles into the street from their apartment above. The glow emanated from an oasis-green Heineken sign and a cheery Corona sun, and it belied the darkness and the fetid smell just beyond the Thirsty Camel's front door. No daylight was permitted to penetrate the plate glass for fear of fading the dartboards. There were rumours of dogfights, and Charla once swore she'd heard snarling through the heavy back door, but when we asked the bartender, Stan, he only laughed.

On this my first visit to the T-Cam I made the mistake of wearing sandals. I was tired when I got home from class, and I'd contemplated bowing out altogether, but Steph said they needed another sober cyclist to double Dyann who, along with Charla, was somehow already drunk. Marie-Jeanne would be meeting us there after practice, Steph said.

Our feet crunched and shushed through a thick layer of peanut shells on the floor. Under that was a more worrying sponginess: years and years of beer and vomit, blood maybe, soaked in and ground up and roach-chewed into chocolate-coloured loam.

The room was mostly empty. We ordered two pitchers of beer and carried them to a booth with a heavily scarred table.

'When it's full we get Charla and Dyann to sit at the bar and make out,' Steph told me. 'Then the men steer clear of us the rest of the evening.'

'I would've thought that would *attract* attention,' I said.

'Well, yes, but the attention's on us anyhow. When they realise we're queer they get all protective. It's really quite tender.'

Dyann sloshed beer over the rim of her glass as she poured. 'Well, "tender" is generous,' she said. 'They want to lynch us, is what. So then, when they get drunk enough, they suddenly start feeling all fatherly, thinking about all the *other* men out there who must want to lynch us too. They assume we'll never make it home alive.'

'They want to call us a cab,' Charla said with a laugh.

The waitress in me took over, and I relieved Dyann of the pitcher, filled the rest of our glasses. Meanwhile she hooked her fingers through her belt loops, puffed out her belly, and swayed. 'You girls are so young. You don't know how dangerous it is out there.'

'You'll get married someday,' Charla said, 'and you'll see.'

'My daughter was a lezzie in college,' Dyann said.

'They don't say that,' I said.

'They do!' they chorused.

'You better watch it, Karen.' Dyann pointed at my new bracelet. 'They're going to think you're one of us.' It was a braided leather cuff I'd bought at a craft fair on campus the day before. It wasn't nearly as butch as Steph's – she wore a wide black leather one snapped over each wrist – but Dyann was right: I'd been influenced by their fashion sense. Sharp-eyed Dyann. No detail got past her.

The T-Cam's grease-stained menu card listed seemingly infinite combinations of cheese and previously frozen, deep-fried starches. We ordered onion rings and waffle fries. Steph fed quarters to the jukebox and pumped her fists to the opening chords of 'Livin' on a Prayer'.

The conversation came around to Susannah's pregnancy, as it had so many times over the previous weeks at Raghurst. 'You should have seen everyone in Dr Esterhazy's class when she told us,' I said. '"Oh my gosh, congratulations! Is it a boy or a girl? Do you have a name?" It was like we were in some kind of pageant from the Middle Ages. We should go back to hanging the sheets out the window of the bridal chamber.'

'I hate her,' Dyann said.

'Esterhazy?' I said.

'Susannah. She gives us all a bad name. Being so weak and sappy – it's like lying down and asking to be trampled by patriarchy.'

'Well, we have a name for that hatred,' Steph said. 'It's called internalised misogyny.'

Dyann frowned. 'It's not misogynistic to say that a woman is stupid. It's not misogynistic to recognise that women are their own worst enemies.'

'But women are imbricated in a misogynistic system,' Steph reminded her. 'The whole system operates by ascribing agency to the very objects over which it exercises power – the very objects whose agency is robbed by its operation.'

Charla gave a gigantic sigh and lifted her empty glass. 'Me, I can't wait to have babies,' she said.

When I pushed the second pitcher toward her, though, Steph said that they had had enough; they should wait.

Dyann gave a theatrical shudder. 'It's like a horror movie. Something foreign *takes over* your body, dictates how you feel every second. Totally dominates you through your hormones. It even tells you what to eat.'

'Growing something, though,' Charla insisted. 'Your body knowing how to do that, without any work or learning or expertise on your part.'

'And then it tears you apart on the way out.' Steph made claws with her fingers and splayed them in front of her nose like a mole digging underground.

'I want a water birth. With a midwife,' Charla said.

'What's a water birth?' I said. How did my roommates know so much about life after college? Our conversations always seemed to go like this. We'd be talking about something from class, something happening on campus or some theory one of us had read in a textbook, and then they'd suddenly veer off into a discussion of an experience I knew nothing about. Something I'd never even heard of.

'You can rent this tub, like a hot tub but not as hot. They set it up right in your living room.'

'Why, though?' I said.

Dyann rolled her eyes. 'It's supposed to relax you.' She put on a high, breathy voice: 'Don't think of it as labour; think of it as a trip to the spa.'

'No, it's true,' said Charla. 'Instead of fighting gravity by pushing and everything, your muscles relax and the birth canal can really open up. The baby just floats out. They can even let it swim around underwater for a while, before it has to take its first breath. It's a gentler transition into the world, less traumatic.'

'That's idiotic. What if it died? What if *you* died?' Dyann was slurring her words, and Steph must have heard it, too, because she put her hand over Dyann's glass to stop her refilling it.

'It's completely safe,' said Charla. 'Safer, if you count all the infections people get from the germs in hospitals.'

'You have big plans for your life. Very ambitious.' Dyann shoved her chair back, and it overturned when she stood up. 'Whoa,' she said, and laughed. 'Charla, just promise me you're not pregnant right at this moment? Because the kid would have three heads or something.'

Charla had swigged from my glass; she laughed, and choked, and beer dribbled out of her nose. She and Dyann moved to the pool table and racked up the balls. 'We should at least get a kitten,' I heard her say. 'Or birds! Let's get a pair of budgies, and they can lay eggs.'

*

O sing of Charla, iron–velvet paradox! When she grew up, Charla said, she wanted to be a barkeep in a diner where truckers stopped to refuel. She used that actual word: 'barkeep'.

'Pain is a door,' Charla would say, or, 'We are all merely creatures in creatures' bodies,' or, 'When your clothes are on fire you take them off.' She said crazy things, deafening things.

Little Charla Klein, petite enough to make the people around her giants, prone to craning her neck and standing on tiptoes. We could have passed for sisters, Charla and me – from a distance, anyhow, or in photographs. We had the same shoulder-length dark hair, the same dark eyes, similar facial features. Charla was a smaller, curvier, more exaggerated version of me. Wrists like wishbones, a long white stem of a neck, a dizzying cello flare from waist to hip.

I have only one photograph of Charla. In it she holds a lighter to the bowl of her little hewn-quartz pipe. The flame illuminates the red leather cuff of her jacket, her chipped black nail polish, a curl of hair falling into her eye. It's a strangely discomforting image. The visual plane is crowded, opaque, as though there wasn't enough room for the camera's lens – or there isn't enough room for the viewer, maybe. There is no invitation to look. Charla's eyes are half-closed, focused inward on the smoke she's inhaling, on her plea- sure or her anticipation of pleasure. She is sealed off from us like an egg.

Charla was soft focus, gin fizz, Etta James on cassette, flavoured rubbers, smoke rings, Rozencreme, catnap, fountain pen, dressing gown, hundred- dollar bill, chocolate pudding, Kathy Acker, *No, just one sip of yours*, dog-eared, incense, silkscreen, *Is it already afternoon?*, smoked trout, dirty laundry, Earl Gray, cedar water, the Rolling Stones, *How now, ladies?*, parasol, *Every Woman's Herbal*, fishnet stockings, Egyptian kohl, cowboy boots, kiss on each cheek.

I will never finish my list of Charla. Nor will any list capture just how revelatory she was for me. Charla put 'freedom' and 'terror' into the same sentence. Without ever aiming to, she said things and did things that made my brain stop in its tracks, overheat, and seize. She ground my mind to a halt.

I'm glad I met Charla last, but also that I knew Charla first and separately from the others. I'm glad that she was separate from the rest of us even more than I was separate from the rest of them. I'm glad to have a separate memory- tunnel to travel through, back to Charla Klein, so I can visit there from time to time without having to brave the whole blacksmoking labyrinth.

Joan Jett came on the jukebox singing 'Crimson and Clover'. Steph sighed and leaned forward with her freckled forearms propped under her chin. 'You know what I am?' she said. 'The husband. I feel like the husband.'

'Do they always get this drunk together?' I said.

She laughed. 'That's not what I meant. And no, they don't; it's an exper- iment. I meant the fact that I'm Dyann's ex, and now she's with Charla, and here we all are. Lesbians never actually leave each other, you know. It's just' – Steph shrugged – 'LBD.'

'Little Black Dress?'

'Lesbian Bed Death. It's so cute that you don't even know the term.'

'It sounds awful.'

Another shrug. 'The sex just dried up, and we sort of drifted over from that into regular friendship. Of course, my depression doesn't help my libido much, either.'

They were all lesbians, my roommates – except Charla, who called herself a 'staunch bisexual'. I'd assumed it about Steph and Dyann, that first morning in the living room, figured they must be the 'queer' in 'queer-friendly' from the housing ad. But Marie-Jeanne had been a surprise.

'MJ? Are you kidding?' Dyann had responded, five or six days after I moved in, when I'd finally found a tactful way to ask. 'She's the biggest dyke of us all. She's such a dyke she can dress like a Banana Republic ad and still outdyke the rest of us.' Marie-Jeanne did dress like a Banana Republic ad. Immaculate khakis, pastel polo shirts, little nautical-print scarves tucked around her neck. Her blonde hair shone like a schoolgirl's in its chin-length bob, the bangs cut straight across. 'My stylist does trims for free,' she'd told me. The comment stayed with me because it was the first time I'd ever heard someone my age use the word 'stylist'.

A whoop drew our attention to the pool table. Charla had tried to twirl her cue like a baton and clanged its tip against the brass light shade.

'Keep it down, cowboys,' Stan yelled from behind the bar, and Charla and Dyann collapsed with laughter.

Steph lit my cigarette for me. She caught my hand and held it up. 'Your callus is peeling off,' she noted.

'From manual labour to the life of the mind,' I said.

We were quiet a moment, watching the girls whirl and stagger. Marie-Jeanne arrived. She took the pool cue from Charla, who wrapped her arms around Marie-Jeanne's shoulders and kissed her on the lips. 'A Jell-O shooter for my fine friend here!' Charla hollered at Stan. 'A blue one!'

'Blue is for boys,' Dyann corrected, prompting Charla to perform elaborate gagging gestures. 'The blue was disgusting,' she informed Marie-Jeanne. 'What the hell kind of flavour is *blue raspberry* anyhow?'

'Is that why they're so hammered? They were doing Jell-O shots?' I said. It didn't seem like a Raghurst sort of activity.

'The boys next door brought them over,' Steph told me, and the two of us exchanged a look of amused toleration. The parents, I thought, not the husband. Steph and I were the parents. I drained the pitcher into my glass.

10. EFFICTIO

(blazon, word-portrait)

I thought long and hard about the image I wanted to present to the fraternity. I'd let the hair on my legs grow out since spring, since the start of the tree-planting season, and it was getting more noticeable as my summer tan faded. Instead of shaving I biked to the drugstore for a package of extra-strength cream bleach and spread it over my shins. It made the hair a soft, almost translucent blonde. I borrowed a white eyelet-lace blouse from Charla and wore it with frayed cutoffs and a leather choker. I tweezed my brows and put on red lipstick but left my hair uncombed. Altogether the look was miles away from sorority girl but still feminine enough to please at least some of the frat boys, I thought. None of my roommates asked where I was headed.

The Gamma Beta Chi chapter house was about the same distance as Raghurst from the campus but on its north side, where the student ghetto gave way to the bigger, older, and more expensive homes of professors. My bike ride was still only ten minutes.

The front lawn of the frat house was littered with furniture and sprawling male bodies. It looked like all the boys had moved permanently outdoors. The brick building loomed up behind them into the maples. Even in the full sunshine it was as shadowy and misshapen as a Victorian asylum, its upper stories encrusted with dormer windows and rickety balconies. The tableau was a cross between a beer commercial and a Brueghel painting, and I was immediately sorry I'd left my camera at Raghurst.

Mike popped up from one of the couches on the lawn and came down to meet me on the sidewalk. 'Hi, honey,' he said. He held my jaw on both sides and kissed me in front of everybody.

I squirmed out of his grasp. 'You've got lipstick now,' I said, swiping his lip with my thumb.

'Gentlemen, this is Karen Huls,' Mike announced. He hoisted my bicycle to his shoulder and carried it up the steps to the porch.

'Hi, Karen Huls,' they all droned, like pre-schoolers greeting their teacher.

'Hi, Karen Huls,' said Bruce. I hadn't seen him there on the grass but I saw him now, feetfirst flat on his back shorts no shirt hands behind his head elbows out. A golddark valley between his thighs and goldbright tufts under his arms – the secrets of Bruce's body laid out carelessly for the whole world.

I'd begun reading the *Iliad* for Dr Esterhazy's class, and I kept picturing the hero Achilles as Bruce Comfort. *Blessed by the gods*, the book said. *Beloved of Athene*. I pictured how Bruce's broad chest would look plated in bronze, how his blond hair would become shaggy and sweat-stiffened under his iron helm.

Even if I had brought my camera with me, I couldn't very well take a photo of Bruce Comfort – not in front of all these frat boys, not in front of Mike. But if I could, oh, if I could! I wouldn't bother with the beer-commercial tableau at all. Here was the essence of the scene, right here: it would be a single close-up of Bruce's ribs curving under his skin, sweeping down into the grass like the hull of a wargoing ship.

Achilles was described in the *Iliad* as 'godsfavoured'. I liked how the translator would mash two English words together when no single one could accurately capture the Greek.

'Offer the lady a drink, Frodo.' A thin brother with dark hair curling out of his shirt shoved the boy next to him off the couch.

'I'm Frodo,' the boy told me, blushing. He had watery, pale blue eyes and blond eyebrows. 'Would you like a rum cooler? White wine?'

'Beer's good, if you have it,' I told him. There was a chorus of shouts at this – approval, it sounded like – and a number of requests for refills.

I followed Frodo through the dark, oak-paneled foyer into the kitchen, and Mike followed me, saying, 'Frodo's helping out because you're our guest and I'm your ... host. Otherwise I'd be doing the bartending. Libations are my expertise.'

A blond brother met us in the kitchen doorway and introduced himself as Chris. 'So you're Code Blue, I take it,' he said.

'What are the other options?' I asked.

'Karen, Charlie. Charlie, Karen.' Mike nodded at a fullback type with coppery hair sitting at the table, wolfing scrambled eggs with a spoon clenched in his big fist. The room smelled of sulfur, stale sweat, and alcohol.

Chris pointed to sheets of coloured circles arrayed on the table. Stickers. 'White, pink, red, and black,' he said.

'And green, for pukers,' Charlie supplied. 'I don't think you're supposed to tell girls, though.'

'Tell us what?' I said.

'You don't want to be black. That's all you need to know.' Chris swigged the last of his beer, added it to the dense collage of empties on the counter, and cracked a fresh one.

'Or gold,' Mike added. 'Where're the gold stickers?'

'It's a golden ticket, not a sticker,' Chris corrected him. 'It's a whole different thing.'

A bare-chested brother in boxer shorts wedged past Mike into the kitchen, pausing to squeeze him against the doorframe, hump his hip several times, and belch against his cheek. 'Oh, yeah, baby, Chet, you are *sooo* fine,' he said. He crossed to the fridge and grabbed a beer. He waved the game controller he was carrying at Frodo and me, then used it to scratch his hairy stomach. 'Baby brothers, just you wait till the Tribal Warfare party tonight,' he slurred. 'Those State skanks are unbe-fucking-*liev*able. We'll be peeling them off the tracks tomorrow, if you know what I'm saying.'

The *Campus Eye* that week had printed a letter of complaint from the Women's Centre about the invitation poster for the intercampus party to which the boy was referring. Jen Swinburn had let me take the newspaper's camera out to find a good photo of the poster, and I'd snapped a long row of them pasted outside the men's washroom in the Earth Sciences Building. It was a great photo, I thought: the men's symbol on the washroom door lined up perfectly with the last poster and generated what Jen would call a 'visual argument'. The poster itself featured a crude caricature of an Indian squaw being dragged by her hair by a tomahawk-wielding brave.

'Do you mind? There are ladies present,' Charlie said. He folded his toast and shoved it into his mouth.

'I take it that State girls are Code Black,' I said.

The bare-chested boy looked startled. 'Red, anyhow. Who's telling her about our system?'

'What do you do, put the stickers on their foreheads when they come through the door?' I asked.

Chris punched Mike in the bicep. 'Watch this one, Chet. She's sharp.'

The bare-chested boy looked me up and down. 'She's kind of West Coast, don't you think?'

'She's Canadian,' Mike explained.

*

Frodo, Chris, Charlie, Blackie, Duncan, Tim, Bruce. I recited the names in my head. Mike and I were back outside after all the introductions in the kitchen, sitting side by side on the front steps of the frat house. 'How many people live here?' I asked him.

'Twenty-six, right now. Thirty-two, once the football team is back from fall training.'

Two boys were decorating the porch rail with a dandelion chain. Mike introduced them as Pits and Jeeves. Their work was being supervised by Alec, the thin, hairy brother who had pushed Frodo off the couch when I arrived. Apparently all the pledges, Mike included, were given nicknames and kept busy with various meaningless and degrading tasks for a three-week period after initiation at the start of each term. Mike told me it was no different at any of the other thirty-plus frats on campus. 'Twenty percent of the undergraduate population is scrubbing toilets with toothbrushes as we speak,' he said.

Mike bragged about me to Pits and Jeeves. 'Karen is the best photographer I've ever met,' he said. 'She's going to be an artist. Remember the name "Karen Huls", because in a few years you'll see it everywhere.'

I rolled my eyes and let the blush take over my face because I thought it would look gracious and humble. I was flattered that Mike remembered I took pictures. Last year he'd riffled through some photos on my desk in the dorm and commented on how 'arty' I was. They were black-and-white shots I'd developed in the darkroom in high school – some of the items that kept falling off my dorm room walls. I wondered if Mike knew I'd snapped a few pictures for the *Campus Eye* last year too.

'Eighty-two!' someone called out from a BarcaLounger beside the lilac hedge.

The others took up the chorus. 'Sixty-seven! Forty-five, seventy-eight, seventy-three point five!'

A passing group of girls stopped on the sidewalk. 'Point five? What's the point five for?' one of them asked.

'You get three and a half points for the Green Day T-shirt,' the brother called back.

I looked around at the brothers on the porch. 'What's my score?' I asked.

'You don't get one,' Mike said, hastily. 'They don't grade girlfriends.'

'Why not?' I couldn't decide what was worse: being graded, or not being graded because I'd somehow graduated to 'girlfriend' even though Mike and I had spent only one night together so far.

'It's a different category,' Jeeves said. 'It wouldn't be respectful.'

'Who teaches you guys all this stuff?'

Mike grinned. 'You pick it up pretty quick.'

He took me back inside for a proper tour of the house. 'They don't really let girls in most areas, especially during the day,' he explained. 'It's kind of an inner-sanctum thing.'

Upstairs, Frodo and another brother were wrestling Mike's mattress down the hall. 'Tell us whether you like the bookshelves where they are before we set up the stereo on them,' the second boy said.

'They're moving me because of you,' Mike said. 'I'm switching with Blackie and Pits. Their room is bigger and more private.'

'And you don't even have to have a roommate?' I said. 'That's nice of them, to switch. And nice of these guys to help move all your stuff.'

We consulted about the brick-and-board bookshelves they'd reassembled under the window of the new room and decided they looked good there.

'GBC is such a small fraternity that pledging is pretty strenuous, compared to other houses,' Mike said. 'And the initiation is completely insane. I'm still having nightmares about it.'

'What did you have to do?' I said.

'I can't talk about it,' Mike said.

'Was it, like, drinking urine and being buried alive?' I'd heard the stories. A few years ago a freshman at a nearby college had been hospitalised by a Greek initiation. It was one of the 'trust tests' pledges had to take – in this case, diving blindfolded down the stairs into the arms of his brothers – only he'd somehow jumped on an angle and brained himself on a baluster.

Mike smiled tolerantly. 'Something like that.'

'Oh, come on,' I said. 'I'm curious now.'

'I told you. I can't talk about it.'

'Yeah, but you can tell *me*,' I said. I lowered my voice. 'I promise not to tell anyone.'

'No, I can't,' he said. 'I'm sorry, Karen, I really am sworn to secrecy. It was part of my oath.'

'You're kidding,' I said. But I could see now that he wasn't kidding at all.

Frodo came in and dumped a pile of bedding onto the mattress. 'There you go, Chet. You're officially off the Stage. You're welcome, Karen.' And he gave a little bow.

We went back downstairs and gathered as many beers as we could carry to replenish the cooler outside. Mike distributed cans to the boys on the lawn. Bruce had moved from the grass to a lawn chair, I noticed. He hadn't come inside to talk to me.

A fresh-faced girl in a sundress sat on the porch, hand in hand with Alec. 'I'm Grace,' she told me. 'Kappa Sigma.'

'Karen,' I said.

'Karen is with Chet,' Alec told her. 'Karen, you know Jen Swinburn, right? Is it true they've got some kind of fraternity blacklist set up over at the Women's Centre?'

'I don't know,' I said.

'Jen says Bruce Comfort is on the list,' Grace said. 'She saw his picture and everything.'

'Can you get us in there to see it?' Alec said.

'The Women's Centre? It's not locked or anything,' I said. Actually I was pretty sure they did keep it locked. I remembered seeing a reminder note about the importance of returning the key to the desk downstairs if the room was used after hours.

'But isn't it supposed to be some kind of "sacred space"?' His voice had a sneer in it.

'I don't know,' I said. 'I'm not really involved – maybe you should ask Jen.' I didn't want these guys to think of me that way. I liked feeling like a sort of double agent – being admitted to the club, learning the secret passwords and codes. What had Mike called it? The *inner sanctum*. To be a double agent I had to fit in, not be singled out.

Grace said, 'Anyway, Karen, you're off the Stage now.'

'What *is* the Stage?' I asked. When they didn't answer right away I turned and called down the stairs to the boys on the lawn, 'Why is Chet off the Stage now that he's in another bedroom?'

'It's just about privacy,' Mike said. He was beckoning me to come and sit next to him and Charlie on one of the sofas, but I hung back. I wanted an answer.

'You may as well tell her, Chet; she'll hear all about it eventually,' Jeeves called.

'Start off your relationship on a footing of honesty,' Charlie said. He hooked a finger in Mike's waistband and shoved his other hand down Mike's pants. 'There's not as much down here as you might have thought, Karen.'

Mike shoved Charlie off the couch and hurled himself on top of him. The two of them rolled a ways down the grassy incline.

'It was dark. He used a dildo, Karen!' Charlie bellowed. He grabbed Mike in a loose headlock.

His words were addressed to me but meant for Mike. Roll with me, they meant. Tussle with me. Bruce and another nearby brother flung themselves from their chairs onto the lawn to join in. The one named Pits strolled over, sprinkled some beer from his bottle onto the tangle of bodies, and was tackled and absorbed into the fray.

'Come on. What's the Stage?' I asked Grace.

'Oh, it's just that you can see into some of the bedrooms from the third-storey terrace,' she said. 'People can watch you having sex in there, if you leave the light on.'

'On purpose?'

I must have sounded shrill, because Alec reached past Grace to pat my leg. 'Not girlfriends,' he said.

'Yeah, only a true asshole would Stage his own girlfriend,' Grace said.

'Babe, that was an *accident*,' Alec said.

'Frat boys like to share,' Grace told me. 'You have to watch your back.'

'Karen, you're Canadian, right?' Pits called. The play-fighting had paused, and the brothers sprawled, grass-stained and sweaty, in each other's arms.

'Yeah, I'm from Toronto,' I said.

'Is it true that Canadian girls give great head?'

Pits yelped as Mike's forehead drove into his side. 'It's true! I read it somewhere, I swear. It's a proven statistic.'

Bruce watched. He was propped on his elbow like a golden idol. Separate, talismanic, benevolent – he blessed the brothers with his presence in their midst.

'No, no, you're right, it is true,' I told Pits. 'It's actually part of our school curriculum. In sex ed, you know? We practice on icicles.'

Howls of delight came from all corners of the yard.

'Is she serious?' someone said. There was another, louder round of laughter and jeering.

Mike practically glowed. He crawled on all fours toward my feet. 'Please, please sleep over tonight,' he whined, playing it up.

I wasn't going to have my readings done for Dr Esterhazy's class tomorrow. This was important too, though, I reasoned, getting off on the right foot at GBC. It would affect my overall quality of life this year a lot more than a few chapters of the *Iliad*. Also, Grace was whispering something in Alec's ear. I didn't like the attitude those two projected at me – me the naïve new girlfriend and them the experts on fraternity love. And then, too, there was Bruce lying down there sending gold through my veins, gilding every nerve.

'I'll pencil it in,' I said, pretending to write it on my hand. 'Demo amazing Canadian blow job skills for Mike Morton. What do you think, 10:30 pm? Eleven?'

'Put me in at nine,' Pits joked, and got another head-butt in the belly from Mike.

They made me think of hunting dogs, all these boys together. The way they nosed each other and nipped at each other's hindquarters. The loose-jointed, sprawling repose and then, at the slightest provocation, the frenzied baying. The separate human minds furred and fused with pack love.

II. KAIROS

(occasion, context)

My International Conference on Lifestyle Photography program states that the Welcoming Reception begins at 7:30 pm in Ballroom A. I've already changed into a floral skirt and heels, but instead of heading down to the party I sprawl on the bed, swoony with hunger and travel fatigue, and thumb through the conference program. Annabeth was supposed to be sharing this hotel room with me. 'A girls' getaway!' she'd said, though ours has never become more than the most shallow of friendships. If she were here she'd probably at least have ordered a bottle of wine up to the room. We'd have already clinked glasses a few times, gossiped about some art director or editor who cannot keep his hands to himself, touched up our lipstick. Annabeth is the kind of person who likes to do things right, do things well.

I flip to the presenter bios. Annabeth's is cribbed from the 'About' page of her blog: 'Annabeth Lise is mama to three little ones: Harper, Magnus, and Georgia. Three years ago they moved into a sprawling, neglected house on a ravine lot in Toronto. There's lots of play, many traipses through the woods to the pond and, in the best of moments, harmony and creativity in their family of five. The rest of the time is filled with chaos and craziness, but they love that too! Annabeth started the blog *Urban Idyll* in 2006 to document the transformation of her homestead into an urban farm. Since then the blog has grown and changed along with her family. Her first book, *Urban Idyll: How to Nurture Your Family and Connect with the Nature in the City*, was released in 2009.'

Annabeth wrote and submitted a bio for me too. Here it is, under 'H': 'Karen Huls photographs interiors and homescapes for a variety of print and online magazines. She specialises in 'chasing down the light,' ie finding the beauty and enchantment in even the shabbiest spaces. Her photographs are featured throughout both the blog and the book *Urban Idyll* by Annabeth Lise (Riverstone Press, 2009).'

Reading this, I am aware of the extent to which it subsumes my work in Annabeth's, and also of the extent to which Annabeth's habit of putting others' names in the service of her own has been a contributing factor in her success. It makes me suddenly nervous about tomorrow afternoon's 'Domestic Dreams' presentation. She can't be comfortable having left things to me like this. She'll have a spy or two in the room to report back to her, at the least.

I decide to skip the reception and work on my presentation. I carry my laptop down to the hotel restaurant, tuck into a darkened booth, and order a pint of beer and a plate of fries. For a while I concentrate on ordering images from the blog, adding notes to each slide to recount the basic story of Annabeth's house reno, the twins' birth, the planting of the vegetable garden, the arrival of the baby chicks. Then my mind drifts, and I open a photograph of bearded irises in a clay jar. I'd brought them home from a shoot once, and forty-eight hours later discovered that my whole apartment reeked of rotting garbage. Blue pigment from the wilting petals leaked in rivulets down the jar. A single, flaccid leaf obscured what would have been the highlight on the jar's glaze.

I'd shot it in natural afternoon light on the lowest stop I could manage. Postproduction, I'd darkened the image further, lowered the exposure, and burnt it in until the white wall behind the jar was a smoky gray. I'd taken out 78 percent of the colour. Most crucially, I'd layered four different exposures to boost the dynamic range well past what the human eye could discern in the dark.

The result is hyperreal, and even here on my laptop at relatively low resolution it sends a visceral thrill through my body. My half-finished beer sings in my skull. I feel my face heat, and I glance self-consciously around the restaurant as if my screen revealed pornography.

The stench of dying iris floods my nostrils, my sinuses, my brain. The stench is somehow in the picture itself, in the flaunting of its lurid, impossible detail. The salacious ghosts of flowers.

*

We didn't manage to double each other home on our bicycles after all, that first night at the T-Cam. Dyann perched on my crossbar and I pushed off the curb, but we veered and wobbled and fell onto someone's lawn in a laughing heap. We stayed where we'd landed – Dyann smoked one of my cigarettes, I remember – until Stick showed up in a taxi, locked my bike to a fence, scooped up Charla from the lawn chair in front of the Heineken sign where she'd passed out, and brought the three of us home. Steph and Marie-Jeanne must still have been sober enough for the bike ride.

The next morning, pausing on the stairs, I heard Dyann arguing with Marie-Jeanne. She didn't want the neighbour boys involved, she said.

'They *are* involved,' Marie-Jeanne said. '*C'est trop tard* – too late. Stick is part of it, no matter what you like. And I am not comfortable if we are hiding things from him.' 'Eye-ding tings,' she'd said.

'*I* am not comfortable with him acting as our babysitter. Or our pimp,' Dyann retorted.

'You don't even make sense now. You're probably still high.' 'Eye,' she'd said.

12. QUAESTIONES

(debatable points)

My week was divided between Raghurst and GBC. There were parties or mixers at the frat house every Friday and Sunday night. Saturday night was supposed to be for clubbing, but most of the brothers would end up staying in, watching sports or MTV or playing video games. At first Mike and I would go out to dinner, see a band or a movie before coming home to the parties, but after a few weeks we started staying in, too, hanging out at the frat house with everyone else. Once things got going it was hard to get motivated to leave. We'd drink too much or get too high to make decisions, and the evening would slip by.

One Friday night – typically a GBC night for me – the Faculty Club was slammed with doctors and medical students from a pediatrics conference, and they called me in to help. The doctors ordered ribs, duck, kidney pie, pork belly – all the least nutritionally sound dishes on the menu – and drank round after round of whiskey sours. The female med students all sat together around two small tables by the windows, talking soberly about their residency prospects and which profs they had a better chance with if they wore lower-cut tops. Not everyone was like the Raghurst women, I was reminded. Not everyone was interested in the power imbalances informing our experiences on campus.

Most didn't care about any of the things we cared about. Some just wanted to get through college and get a decent job afterward.

My emergency shift was supposed to end at nine, but I didn't get off until after eleven, and I decided I wanted to sleep in my own bed.

A set of bells hung over Raghurst's front door: three round, brass bells, like sleigh bells, clamorous when I pulled open the door. Another three bells hung from the other end of the ribbon on the inside.

'What are you doing here?' Dyann asked as I walked in. She sat at the dining table tying twigs into a five-pointed star with red yarn.

'I live here,' I said. In addition to the sticks there was a little bundle of dried leaves that, when I picked it up to inspect it, smelled like soup. 'What's going on? What's with the bells?'

She took the bundle from my fingers and stuffed it into her backpack. 'Nothing. It's just to mark the comings and goings.'

'For Christmas?'

'No, not for Christmas, Karen; Christmas is two months away.'

Marie-Jeanne and Steph appeared from the basement. 'Oh, hi, Karen,' said Steph. 'Are you coming with us?'

'Nope,' Dyann said.

'Five is perfect for a coven, though,' Steph said.

'A coven? As in witches?' I asked.

Dyann glowered and disappeared into the bathroom.

I tried again: 'What's going on?'

'It's called Meditrinalia,' Steph told me. 'Some obscure Roman festival. We're using it as an excuse to do a circle down in the ravine.'

I didn't know what this meant. 'Why doesn't Dyann want me?' I asked.

Steph shrugged. 'It's easily misunderstood, I guess.'

I turned to Marie-Jeanne. 'Have you done it before? A circle?'

'The solstice, in June. It's *très romantique*.'

Steph said, 'See, I don't think she'd want it called *romantic*. It's not supposed to be a feel-good thing.'

'Each witch brings her own meaning to the ritual,' Marie-Jeanne retorted, primly.

'Yeah, but it's not what we *get* out of it. It's the acknowledgment of some-thing older than ourselves, something female-centred, something violently erased under patriarchy.' Steph had raised her voice partway through this speech, so that Dyann could hear from the bathroom. They were at it again: what would Dyann say? Does Dyann approve? We don't know how to think about this without Dyann in the room.

'An it harm none, do what thou wilt,' Charla said. I hadn't seen her there on the couch. Easeful, sprawling Charla, breathtaking in tight jeans and a red leather jacket.

'I would really like to come along.' I moved to the bathroom door. 'Dyann. Can I come? I'll be respectful, I promise.'

'It's not lack of respect,' she said. 'It's that you can't hide behind your camera. You can't just observe a circle from a safe distance.'

'She can *sweep* the circle,' Charla called.

'Couldn't we at least have gotten a good wine?' said Marie-Jeanne, stuffing the bottle into her backpack.

Dyann emerged from the bathroom and looked me up and down. Then she looked around at the others. 'Maybe we should just talk to her right now,' she said.

Marie-Jeanne and Charla took seats at the dining table, and Dyann motioned me into a chair. Steph placed a thick green file folder on the table in front of me.

'What's this?' I leafed through the contents: newspaper clippings, photocopied journal articles, transcripts of court proceedings.

'It's the fraternity file from the Women's Centre,' Steph said. 'We thought you should have a good look.'

'Every one of those is a documented case of sexual assault,' Dyann told me. 'All across the country, every fraternity house at every college.'

'Well, not *every* frat house,' Marie-Jeanne said.

'Of course not,' Steph said. 'But this file only goes back twelve years. Four fraternities on our campus were investigated, years back. Yes, Gamma Beta Chi was one of them' – she'd seen the question on my face – 'but it's not the only one.'

Dyann said, 'And more than half of these cases are multiple assaults. It's almost never just one guy. They pour drinks down a girl's throat –'

'Or drug her,' Charla said.

Dyann nodded. 'Or they drug her, and then they set her up somewhere in one of the bedrooms and take turns with her.'

I'd never heard about any criminal investigation into Gamma Beta Chi. *Years back*, Steph had said. I wondered if Mike – if the current generation of GBC brothers – even knew about this. Mike would be offended at the very suggestion. 'Was anyone ever charged?' I asked. 'Expelled?'

Steph shuffled through the file and pointed at a *Campus Eye* story dated from 1987. 'See here? Almost a decade ago. One of the other fraternities had its official status suspended for a year, but no individuals were disciplined.'

'The brothers all defend each other,' Marie-Jeanne said. 'They lie for each other.'

Charla nodded. 'They blame the victim: they say she wasn't incapacitated, say she told them she *wanted* to screw the whole frat. They'll say anything at all.'

'And the sickening part', Dyann said, 'is that people believe them. They believe deep down that it's the woman's fault for going to the frat party in the first place, or for wearing a short skirt or too much makeup, or for not making sure she had a sober friend to drive her home.'

'For getting wasted,' Marie-Jeanne said.

'Right. It's her own fault, for getting wasted,' Dyann said.

'It's exactly like in the *Hippolytus*,' said Steph. 'Any overt display of female agency automatically calls down violence. Phaedra, as the female, needs to be chastened and humiliated or else she poses a threat to the male.'

'All male–male relationships are triangulated around the female,' Dyann said. 'She is the currency through which the transaction is effected, right? Sylvia calls femininity a kind of fund through which patriarchal society –'

'Anyway,' Marie-Jeanne interrupted. 'Karen, you get the point, I think.'

'You guys, I don't need the lecture,' I said. 'I can take care of myself.'

'There used to be a room in the basement at GBC called the Black Bag,' Charla said.

I rolled my eyes. 'It's disgusting. It looks like a torture chamber.'

Steph put a hand to her sternum. 'They're still doing it? The Express?'

I looked around at their wide eyes. 'Not for real. It's just talk.'

'What kind of talk?' Steph asked.

'Like, macho frat talk.' I shrugged. 'They call it "pulling train". They're always joking about it: making train whistles, or "Dude, lemme hitch my car to that" when one of them is getting somewhere with a girl – that kind of thing. But it's just talk.'

'You need to get us in there,' Dyann said.

'What?'

'We would like to come to a frat party sometime,' Charla said.

'We want some firsthand data on the culture, instead of just combing media reports and official statements,' Steph said.

I laughed.

'What's funny?' she said.

'You make it sound like some sort of safari park. I can just see you in there with your binoculars and field notebooks.'

Charla smiled. 'Good point. But what do you suggest, then?'

'How about just coming to a party? There's no guest list; you just show up.'

Steph waved a game-show presenter's hand at her haircut and biker T-shirt and then at Dyann's dreadlocks.

I laughed again. 'Okay, maybe you two would stand out a little. Charla and MJ, you could pass, if you dressed up a bit.'

'When?' Dyann said.

'Any Friday night, really. But I'll ask Mike what would be good.'

They looked at each other. 'Don't tell Mike about this,' Steph said.

'Honestly, Mike would think this whole conversation is hilarious,' I said.

'Still,' Dyann said.

I sighed. 'Listen, are you sure this is about fraternities in general? This isn't a personal grudge against GBC? Because of Bruce Comfort, and that whole thing with Susannah?'

'Oh, we don't care about Susannah,' Dyann said.

'Well, we care about her as a fellow female citizen of the world,' Charla said.

'Susannah is an idiot,' Dyann insisted.

'No, no. This is precisely *because of* women like Susannah,' Steph said. 'We're willing to step up for women who may be unwilling but who have less self-awareness, less agency.'

'Charla is willing, you mean,' Dyann said.

Charla put a hand on Dyann's shoulder. 'Are *you* willing, Karen?' she asked. 'Your being involved with GBC gives us way more access.'

I picked at a dried splotch of Thousand Island dressing on my skirt. It felt good to have something my roommates wanted. To know things they wanted to know. They'd collected all these studies and statistics, but they didn't understand frat boys at all. They didn't understand how nothing was taken seriously over there, how everything – every conversation, every activity – served the singular purpose of having a good time. When I thought about it, life at GBC was the precise antithesis of life at Raghurst.

I said, 'Just come really late one night, when everyone's already good and hammered. Then nobody will care what you look like. Nobody will even notice you.'

Marie-Jeanne stood up. 'Good. Okay. Do you have rubber boots, Karen?'

'Don't forget, though,' Dyann added, 'the personal is political. And vice versa.'

13. ENIGMA

(riddle)

I changed out of my uniform and then squeezed into the backseat of Steph's rusty Corolla between Marie-Jeanne and Charla. We parked at the western edge of the campus and picked our way down a dark path through the brush, Steph leading the way with our only flashlight. A bright moon silvered the leaves on both sides of the trail and lit a series of laminated information cards staked into the muck. *Turtle Nesting. Tundra Swan Migration. Invasive Species: Asian Carp. Drowned River Mouth.* Charla wondered if it might be a full moon – it was swollen, glowing coolly in its web of cloud – but Dyann told her it wouldn't be full until tomorrow night.

The path cut through a grassy plain and then opened onto a boardwalk through the bulrushes. I'd always wondered exactly where this place was. Last year I'd heard some of the girls in the dorm talking about going for a run on the boardwalk, and I remembered reading about some chemistry prof getting fired for poaching fish from the pond. But I'd never had occasion to go exploring.

Marsh air pressed against my face and lungs, rank-smelling despite the strong breeze ruffling the surface of the open water beyond the rushes. There was some disagreement about where the ground would be dry enough to duck under the railing, but we found a path that led through cedar and poplar to a sloped clearing. Here we dropped the bags we carried and stood a moment without speaking: the silky grass and velvet moss tussocks underfoot, a black wreath of maple leaves overhead, and O, that white glowpearl of a moon!

I thought Charla had been joking about sweeping the circle, but Dyann scuffed out a shape seven feet across, pulled a wooden-handled brush from her backpack, and handed it to me. 'It's mostly symbolic. You don't actually move anything with it,' she said.

I wondered if she meant symbolic of my servitude: was I being initiated? Everyone was busy and hushed, though, unpacking, laying things out, setting things up. Charla poured water from a thermos into a bowl and filled a large seashell with table salt. Steph consulted her compass. I swept and thought about the drowned river mouth, imagining moving water buried below us, struggling and then lying still. There was that dark smell.

Steph lit a stick of incense and a candle at the North point. Dyann lifted a pair of tiny brass cymbals on a leather cord and chimed them together three times.

'Just do what we do,' Marie-Jeanne told me. 'It's very repetitive.'

We crouched, and each of us dipped a finger in the bowl of water. 'Water is life; here is life,' we said. Then we took a pinch of the salt: 'Earth is life; here is life.' We repeated the words with 'fire' and 'air'. Dyann took the salt and water, Charla lit another candle, and Marie-Jeanne held the lighter to the bundle of leaves I'd seen at home – sage, from the smell of the thick smoke. We filed around the circle, following Dyann as she poured salt in a thin line all around, and then around again, stopping to chant, 'We bless the North with salt to purify and protect our circle,' and so on at the four compass-point 'watchtowers'. North got salt, South got fire – Charla pushed the candle into the soil – West the dish of water, and East the herbal smoke curling into the air.

The four watchtowers seemed to offer different fortifying qualities. Everyone except me had brought an incantation, blessing, or meditation, either memorised or written out on scrap paper. I felt left out but too self-conscious to improvise. Marie-Jeanne prayed for physical balance and strength. Steph got down on all fours and said, 'Keep me loyal to this earth and to my life upon it. Keep me grounded in gratitude to the past and hope for the future.'

My favourite part was what Dyann called 'drawing down the moon'. She poured wine into a cup and we gathered in to hold it, collectively, up to the sky. 'We call upon the Goddess in all her crone forms of old, under this past-harvest Moon. As summer meets winter, as day meets night, aid our efforts here.' Dyann said it first, and we all repeated it.

Charla took off her necklace – a coiled snake on a silver chain – and dangled it over the cup. She said, 'I purify and bless this charm, that it may remind us of the power invoked in this circle and protect us with good fortune.' She dipped the snake into the wine, sucked it dry, and replaced it around her neck.

There was some burning and burying of bad things – a makeup ad (Dyann), a rejection letter from an Ivy League grad school (Steph), a postcard from home (Marie-Jeanne), a man's watch (Charla). There was a prosperity charm made up of a dish of coins with a tied red thread laid on top and the words, 'Goddess and Horned God, bless us with abundance to keep us well and warm.'

I didn't believe in God, not really, not unless I was worried about an exam or I missed my parents. Nor was I prepared to throw in my lot with this Goddess and Horned God, whoever they were. But I said all the words anyway, and somehow, without any of the others telling me, I knew that it was the saying and not the belief that mattered here. The words were the whole point.

During the purging exercise, when Charla was about to bury the wrist-watch, Dyann asked me whether I had anything I wanted to put to the earth.

'No,' I said. 'I don't know,' I said. Sadness sprang on me. The smell was hellish: fungal, rotten. It glued my throat together.

'What needs less? What needs more? That's what this ritual is all about,' Dyann said.

A few nights earlier I'd gotten drunk again at the frat house. In Mike's bedroom there had been music, brandy in real snifters, a barefoot slow dance, a naked one. There had been the dark, deep expanse of the bed and Mike's hot breath in my throat. 'How do you want me? What do you want?' he had said.

'I want to be your fantasy,' I'd slurred – a line from the Prince song I'd heard downstairs earlier in the evening.

I looked at the little hole Charla had dug in the drowned river mouth. 'I want the real thing,' I said.

Dyann snorted. 'What, like true love?'

'No. Dyann,' I said, 'will you get off my case for five fucking seconds, please?'

Her eyes widened a little at the look I must have shot her. The others were quiet.

I crouched to get Dyann Brooks-Morriss out of my field of vision. Mike had brushed the hair back from my face and held his palms there, his fingers interlaced like a wreath around my head. 'Draw your knee up,' he'd whispered. 'Guide me into you.'

When I did that it hurt, and the condom snapped and tore. 'You're too dry,' Mike said. I'd fished in the shoebox under his bed for another rubber, but by the time I tore open the foil he'd fallen asleep. My last thought, bobbing seasick drunk in the crook of Mike's arm before I passed out, was how this would never happen to Bruce.

'Do you guys think I hate women?' I said.

'What?' Steph said.

'Do you think me dating Mike, me partying at GBC – do you think it's because of my internalised misogyny?'

Charla squatted beside me so she could look into my face. 'It's just survival instinct, Karen.' She looked up at the others. 'I mean, let's face it. Women don't have a lot of options for how to behave with men. You can choose the Susannah route – cry about it to everyone who'll listen, and then go martyr yourself to early motherhood. Or the Dyann route, and have nothing more to do with men forevermore.'

'Or the Charla route, and follow pleasure,' I said.

'Is that what you think I do?' She was startled.

'That's what you *said* you do. Playing pool, that night at the T-Cam.' She'd sprawled flat on her back across the pool table with her hands stretched up toward the top corner pockets. 'The pleasures of the flesh,' she'd sighed. 'Those church people are right to make up all those rules, all those sins. Otherwise nobody would ever do anything but this.'

Now Charla laughed. 'I swear I lost thirty hours of my life that weekend. I can't remember a single thing.'

I looked into the wet black hole in the earth. 'I want the real thing,' I said again – again, not really knowing what I meant by it – and I cleared my throat against the tears pinching there and spat them into the hole. My hands had gone numb against the damp grass. 'Goddamn it,' I said.

'Look there,' Charla whispered, and I looked up to see a screech owl sitting on a nearby buckthorn. A small, feathered sphere just level with our heads, round yellow eyes returning our gaze with humanoid directness. A solid ten seconds passed before it flew off.

Someone sighed, and I felt my own sigh go down through my lungs into my spine. A sinking into the spongy greenblack air, a giving over into unlikelihood and wonder.

Minutes later, after we'd shared the wine and thanked the watchtowers and told them each to take for their use any powers that had not been used, Dyann reached her arms out to the sides, spreading her fingers and pointing her thumbs to the sky like a preacher. 'Hey, Karen. This is real, right?'

'What – Wicca?'

'No, *us*. This. Five women in the woods.' She grinned at me, and I saw, suddenly, something generous in her face. I'd met her impatience with impatience of my own. Anger with anger. Was that what she'd wanted all along?

'This is real,' she said again. 'Okay?'

'Okay, it's real,' I said. 'Yes.'

14. KATHARSIS

(cleansing)

I ran into Bruce in the second-floor bathroom. After we washed our hands he wrapped an arm across my waist, pressed his cheek to my temple, and swayed us back and forth in the mirror. No talking this time, just a half-smile, a low-lidded parody of romance.

'Hello, Patrick Swayze,' I said, after a long while.

'Nobody puts Baby in a corner,' he murmured.

Something inside me tipped off its shelf and fell to the floor. That a person like Bruce Comfort should know a line from a movie no boy would ever admit to having enjoyed. That he should quote it unselfconsciously, without even bothering to open his eyes.

I said, 'Did you know that in Greek mythology gods and goddesses cannot gaze upon themselves?'

Then he did open his eyes, and he looked at me in the mirror and grimaced and touched my arm. 'I wonder if any of these bruises are mine,' he said.

'I think you were a few layers up,' I reassured him.

He meant the party from the night before. Nine Inch Nails' song 'Closer' had come on, and all the brothers had crowded into the lounge together and started jumping around, jostling and hoisting each other overhead, mosh-pit style. I liked the song. Our tree-planting crew had developed the habit of playing it right at dawn, riding the old school bus along the bone-rattling logging roads into the cutover – like the helicopters playing 'Ride of the Valkyries' in *Apocalypse Now*, I always thought. The lyrics were outrageously crude, and Trent Reznor's electronically altered voice delivered them with a snarl that gave me the temporary ability to feel my heart beating between my legs.

I'd wedged my way into the room with the boys and thrown myself into the hot crush of bodies just as they started to move in a more orderly fashion, started to stream clockwise around the room with a small open space at the centre. At the song's chorus the brothers all pumped their fists in the air and began to chant, 'Rut! Rut! Rut!' The chanting got louder and louder, and they turned a faster and faster ring around the room, until the song was only background and the noise and movement was all there was.

'Karen! Get out of there,' Mike yelled, trying to be heard over the din. He reached an arm out for me but I was already caught up in the tangle of limbs, lifted clear off my feet and swirled around like water down a drain. I got one foot up onto the sofa but was pulled back under, yanked by the arms and turned onto my back.

And then I was down on the rug with stomping feet all around. Someone landed hard on top of me. Charlie said, 'Oh shit!' when he saw it was me, and he made a protective cage of his arms over my face and torso. Then body after body fell on top of us, a grinding, crushing pile of boys. Charlie grunted once, twice. My nose was squashed into his larynx and I turned my head for air, noting the private scent of his sweat.

The music stopped. 'Get off! Get up – Karen's under there!' Mike screamed. 'Get up!'

I must have blacked out for a few seconds. The next thing I noticed was I could breathe again, and Duncan, the house president, was leaning over me and saying my name.

Charlie squatted beside me, grimacing and flexing his elbow. Beside him I saw a brother lying with his eyes closed and Pits with one ear to his chest, checking for signs of life. Everywhere around me were boys struggling to disentangle themselves, crawling around to retrieve lost shoes and pocket change, panting and groaning and exclaiming over their injuries.

Then laughter burbled up through the crowd as though from a spring. I could barely breathe, but I felt the laughquake moving in my guts too.

The jokes came fast and jubilant: 'You dry-humped me, you asshole!'

'I brought you closer to God.'

'You rapist. That was rape.'

'That was your wedding night, bitch.'

'Blackie, fuck, man. You're bleeding in my hair!' someone complained.

I turned my cheek to the rug and watched Blackie remove his T-shirt, wad it up, and press it to his face in an effort to stanch his nosebleed.

'That was righteous,' Frodo said, and at his words a sigh tore through each of us in the room.

Alec looked over at me. 'Weren't you on the very bottom? How are you not pulverised?'

'Charlie kind of boxed me in,' I said. I turned to thank Charlie, but he had crawled off somewhere.

'I saw her in there, right at the start. But, I don't know, I didn't even think of her as a girl,' Pits said.

'Fuck you very much,' I shot back.

'You know what I mean,' he said. 'You can take care of yourself.'

Fresh cups of beer were passed from hand to shaky hand. Lacking strength to stand, we all stayed sprawled on the rug in front of, or half-underneath, the furniture.

I raised myself up to my elbow to drink. 'Can someone please explain to me what just happened?'

'Hey, Chet, I've been meaning to ask,' Alec said, as Mike wedged in beside me with his beer. 'Has Karen had a ride on the gold car yet?'

'Ha ha,' Mike said. He had a nasty scratch on his cheek.

'If you're too busy we could help you out,' Alec said. 'We wouldn't want her to miss out on the experience, right?'

'What's the gold car?' I asked.

'How about I go ask Grace what she knows about the gold car first,' Mike said, 'and then we can talk about Karen.'

A long 'Ohhh!' went around the room to signify that it was *on*, that Mike had thrown down some kind of gauntlet.

Mike ignored it and put his arm around me. 'Officially that was called a rut,' he informed me.

'Officially? Like, it's in the rules?'

'In the fraternity charter, yeah,' he said, when I must have looked incredulous. 'It's an actual thing. Spontaneous, but pretty predictable when certain songs are played at a certain point in a party.'

'And the gold car? What's that?'

'That has nothing to do with this,' he said. 'Alec can be kind of an asshole.'

And then these bruises, early this morning, dotting my arms and legs like ripe plums.

'Do they call him Chet because of the Hardy Boys books?' I asked Bruce's reflection in the mirror.

'What?'

'Chet Morton. The sidekick.' Already I wished I hadn't said it, I wanted to bite my tongue, because I knew it was true. On Mike's desk was a family portrait with a mom, a dad, and two zit-riddled teenagers, a boy and a girl. The girl had braces and hairsprayed bangs; the boy had his arm wrapped around her shoulders. It had been a shock to recognise the pudgy boy as Mike. He was maybe sixteen in the photo and maybe twenty-five, thirty pounds heavier than he was now. I had stared at the portrait a long while, thinking, You don't know a person. You can't know.

'Can we please not talk about Chet right now?' Bruce said.

*

Saturday mornings I went to my second job, as a life model for an adult-ed art school that leased space on campus. The pay was four times what I made waitressing, and all I had to do was take my clothes off and stand very still. There was a faithful core of old ladies who'd attended the class for years – it was more like a club than a class for them – a few artists struggling not to let their day jobs win, and one new mother who apologised for her presence on the first day. 'I'm no artist,' she said, 'but this is my only *me* time.'

The instructor's name was Modesto Ricci, known in class as Desso. Rumor had it his paintings were represented by a Manhattan gallery, but I never learned which one. He worked as a floor manager at a major department store. He used to be a life model himself. It could be very erotic, modeling nude, Desso told me, and I shouldn't worry about becoming aroused.

'The male models get erections all the time,' he said. 'It's something about being watched. The students are used to it. It makes better art, in my opinion.' He would tell me these things through the door of the art cupboard where I got dressed again after class, balling my bathrobe into the back of a shelf full of paint canisters. No one from the adult-ed school was allowed to store any of their stuff in the studio, but so far no one had taken issue with my bathrobe.

Desso was the first obviously gay man I'd ever spoken to. He wore pink dress shirts and silver rings, covered the gray in his hair with Grecian Formula, and referred to his partner Larry as his husband. The old ladies loved to hear stories about Desso and Larry. Desso and Larry going grocery shopping was enough to keep them blushing and twittering the whole class.

I wasn't exactly aroused by posing naked. I got cold and sleepy, day-dreaming so deeply that whenever Desso asked me to change position he had to repeat himself, even if the class was only doing three-minute sketch exercises. He had to set strong lights on me to keep me from shivering, to stop gooseflesh from pimpling up all over my arms and legs. He reminded me to let my stomach pouch forward, not to hold anything in. 'You have this little swayback, pardon my touch,' he said, poking me with his thumbs. 'These little divots are focal points for anyone painting you.'

The old ladies liked to fuss with their supplies. One wore latex gloves and used antiseptic wipes on her stool, the handles of her brushes, her plastic palette and knives, the ledge of her easel. Sometimes it took her half an hour of class to set up.

Today the new mom kept weeping as she sketched. The old ladies clucked over her, giving her Kleenex, patting her shoulders. 'No, no,' she said, 'it's good. It's so cathartic! Art-making after all this round-the-clock caregiving. It's so good for me.'

After two hours in the hushed, spotlit studio the campus was like a green hammer raining blows on me. The clouds bounced along the blue sky. Fluttering banners announced that today was our annual Inspire! Day, when the college hosted high-profile alumni to get us excited about our futures. I remembered that a famous Indian writer was supposed to be speaking. I wanted to hear his address, so I went to see if the *Campus Eye* might have an extra ticket to the event. Jen Swinburn was doing layout for Monday and she told me no, the paper didn't have any tickets.

'Could you go shoot the funeral, though?' she said.

'What funeral?'

'The protest, from the Women's Centre. I thought you'd be involved in it, but it's good you're not. I've sent Gita to write it up, so look for her.'

'Where?' I said.

'Down in the east quad. You won't be able to miss them, I don't think. They have a megaphone.'

I slung the camera around my neck and went back outside. The quad was peppered with dads in khakis and moms in floral dresses. Lower-profile alumni were invited to Inspire! Day too, as well as the parents of current students. They were being inspired to donate generously to the Strategic Campaign. Groups of happy folk gathered in various configurations on the lawn for photographs, the ladies tottering as their high heels poked through the grass. It was strange to see older people on campus mingling with the students. All these families murmuring and hugging, cradled together on their soft lawnshadows.

Homesickness jumped me. My mother had cried on the phone earlier that week. Something hormonal, she'd said, and something about my brother Keith not having a kind word to spare her. Her tears had sent tiny hooks through the receiver into my eardrum. I wanted to hang up but I was guilt-pinned. How could anyone cry in front of another person, even long-distance? How could anyone cry, period?

I wandered past the tents with reps from life insurance firms and car dealerships handing out free key chains and mugs. The bookstore had a cute wood-sided booth selling varsity rings and those jackets with the white leather sleeves.

The Women's Centre had set up its protest to the north of the main auditorium, so that anyone being dropped off for the famous writer's visit would have to walk its gauntlet. The protesters were all dressed in black for mourning and stood out dramatically from the crowd.

Dyann stood next to an enormous painted-cardboard headstone. She wore a black hat and veil, and she held up the megaphone. 'She won't be among us as an alumnus,' she said. 'She'll never get to experience the sense of achievement, the bright future you are all celebrating today.'

I took some photos of the blown-up, slightly pixelated portrait beside a painted-wood coffin displayed on a table draped with a bedsheet. White blouse, blonde hair, shimmery pink lipstick. Then I looked at the name on the headstone. *Susannah Christine XXX*, it said. It gave the year of her death as this year, 1995.

The megaphone screeched and steadied back into Dyann's voice: 'We're gathered here today in memory of a fellow student, a young woman forced to leave this campus because of the criminal irresponsibility of all-male environments. We call for an immediate ban on fraternities on this campus!'

Many of the protesters were nervous as street pigeons. They shuffled and clumped together and didn't meet anyone's eyes. A few carried photocopied flyers and thrust them into people's hands.

Steph, by contrast, was moving easily from one family to another and engaging them in light-hearted conversation. She wore a crisp white shirt with black armbands, black trousers, shiny black brogues, and a bowler hat. She tapped her silver-tipped walking stick against the sole of her shoe and said something that sent laughter drifting across the quad. She was right on message, though, because when I came closer I heard her saying, '... Victorian morality holding sway despite our talk of equality'. I snapped her picture.

'Hi,' I said when Dyann saw me. 'Jen Swinburn asked me to cover the protest for the paper.'

'Jen Swinburn is such a chickenshit,' Dyann said.

'Why?'

'She wants to put "Women's Centre" on her resume, but she doesn't want to jeopardise her run for Student Union president by actually doing anything in public. Here comes Security again; I guess the guy found his supervisor.' She raised the megaphone. 'Showtime, people!'

Some of the girls struck up a shrill, wordless song.

'It's keening,' Dyann told me. 'You know, like women do at funerals in Ireland and Greece? Steph played them a recording, but they're not imitating it very well.' She frowned and stalked toward the singing group. I recognised that hawk-like gleam in Dyann's eye, that raptor focus. This was going to go the way she'd planned, or there'd be hell to pay.

The security guards sat in their car at the curb. Their presence seemed to embolden some of the onlookers. 'Bunch of dykes,' I heard a male student say.

'I'll bet they don't want to ban sororities,' a woman said.

More dads than moms were lingering to read the placards, I noticed. I could tell they saw their own daughters in Susannah's face. There but for the grace of God goeth my Courtney, my little Amber. Many of these fathers had probably been frat brothers, back in the day. They'd probably participated firsthand in the kind of debauchery for which Susannah was suffering.

'Of course she has options,' one mourner was saying. 'Our point is that *he* had options too, and he made a mistake too, and the responsibility shouldn't fall solely on her.'

I'd heard from someone in Dr Esterhazy's class that Susannah's family wanted nothing to do with Bruce, not even to sue him for child support. That her family had ten times the money the Comforts had anyway.

The mourner continued: 'But the whole problem, the whole structure of fraternities, diffuses responsibility from the individual in a way that makes victimisation easier.'

I took a picture of Marie-Jeanne in a veiled hat like Dyann's. I'd identified her by her accent. 'Yes, okay, as you say, your fraternity taught you how to be a man,' she said to a grandfatherly figure in a pale green blazer. 'It taught you to be a leader. The best men, the best leaders. So that you can go and lead businesses, lead companies.'

'Exactly right,' he said.

'But there are two problems with this,' Marie-Jeanne told him. 'First, it means that companies end up looking a lot like fraternities. No women, no minorities – only frat boys, grown up to men.'

The man nodded. 'Well, sure. Most of the partners in my firm met thirty years ago, right here on this campus. Half of us rushed Alpha Tau in the same three-year period.' He smiled, and I snapped a shot of the lines spreading from the corner of his eye, although I knew the newspaper wouldn't use a decontextualised close-up like that. 'It's like a family.'

'Second,' Marie-Jeanne continued, 'everything you do in a fraternity teaches you not to have your own thoughts. You are only supposed to go along with the crowd. So how can you be a leader that way? How can you make a decision about right and wrong?'

'We just hired a black girl,' the man said. 'Real nice girl. She talks a little like you, in fact. Raised in Germany. Are you German?'

Steph appeared at our side and pointed at the cop car. 'Look at that. They must have been told not to shut us down.'

'That's good, right?' I said.

'No. It just means we're not being disruptive enough.'

I edged her away from Marie-Jeanne and the old man. I was feeling uneasy. My roommates talked like this all the time at Raghurst, of course, but that was in the privacy of our own home. Out here in the quad felt different. 'Steph,' I said, 'isn't this whole issue kind of private for a protest?'

'That's the whole problem. People see this as the actions of one man, behind closed doors, when he's part of an entire system that supports this sort of behaviour.'

'I mean private for Susannah.'

'We exed out her surname on the gravestone,' Steph said. 'It's not an issue.'

They weren't extending Bruce the same courtesy, though. I'd heard several of the protesters cite his surname. 'Bruce Comfort is the poster boy for fraternities on this campus,' I'd heard someone declaim.

Spotting the camera around my neck, Gita came over to show me what she'd written so far: *Not everyone is celebrating at Inspire! Day today. Some female students are remembering a classmate whose future is darkened and whose choices, they feel, have been unfairly limited.*

Steph was reading over my shoulder. 'Frats are the whole problem,' she said to Gita. 'That's the whole point of this. Make sure you get that down: fraternities are the problem.'

The women of Raghurst hold forth amongst themselves on the subject of the erotics of learning:

Charla: All this gender theory is so *hot*. There stands Esterhazy droning on about the patriarchal circumscription of female desire, and here I sit creaming in my skirt. It's like she has no idea. Or it's like everything about her guards against the idea that what we're talking about, when we talk about male and female – male *versus* female, especially – is sex.

Steph: It undermines the impact of feminist criticism to say that it's hot.

Charla: Talking about sex is a sex act.

Steph: Not when you're trying to disinvest those discourses from their patriarchal underpinnings.

Charla: The word 'disinvest' is hot. The word 'underpinnings' is hot.

15. IN UTRUMQUE PARTES

(arguing both sides of the case)

'Was that good?' Mike would say. 'Did you climax?'

'Why does it matter so much?' I would say.

'My pleasure isn't complete unless yours is too,' he said.

'I'm not sure that's how it works,' I said.

'What do you mean?'

'Your pleasure seemed pretty complete to me.'

He frowned. 'I don't even want to come if you're not. If it's not happening for you.'

'It is.' I sighed. 'I do.'

'When? Every time?'

'It's not something to put under the microscope, Dr Morton,' I would tell him. 'It'll crumble under pressure.'

Drunken sex was our most common kind of sex. It was clumsy and fast. Stoned sex was weirder, more intellectually interesting. I pictured my body as a gigantic amniotic sac, my limbs liquid, my tongue floating free in my mouth. When Mike rolled atop me I thought I would burst and splatter the walls, but then I realised my hide was thick as a whale's. I was buoyant and supportive. He could sprawl and roll and I would suspend his solid weight, disperse it all across my entire surface.

Because of sleeping beside Mike I had been practising making no discernible movement or noise when I masturbated. I would lie there lustcrisp up to a whole hour waiting for him to fall asleep. Charla had told me some women could reach orgasm just by sitting with crossed legs and flexing their muscles. I still needed to lick my index finger and slip it down between my legs, but I was getting more and more efficient. I pictured that laughing mouth pressed to that nipple – that strong jaw, that honeygold skin, that dark puckered circle – and I could make myself come with just a few nudges. Sometimes I could do it counting down from ten.

One night there was a picture of Susannah – the same one the Centre had copied for its funeral protest – taped to one of the refrigerators with the words HORE OF BABALON inked across her tits.

They taunted Bruce about Susannah, of course, about the fuss she was making on campus. They called him Big Daddy. They served him beer in a baby bottle. They crossed their index fingers and chanted 'Shame' at him when he entered the room, in reference to Bruce's place of honour at the top of the Wall of Shame in the Women's Centre. But then, everybody taunted everybody at the frat house, all the time. It was one of the things I liked about the place. There was a refreshing lack of curiosity at GBC. No one cared what the others were really like, what they felt or believed or wanted do after college. No one talked about anything with any seriousness, not even sports. It was just jokes, sarcastic comments, put-downs, and comebacks.

In high school I had never managed it, the insulting banter between boys and girls. I'd sit dumbly while my girlfriends giggled, or I'd say something too cutting, and later I'd hear that the boy had thought I was a bitch. Even tree-planting – I'd never fully joined in the rapacious partying or the casual tent-hopping that happened on weekends. I'd been too keen to do the job well, to make good money. At the frat, though, I was good at it. I just did what the boys did. A couple of beers and I'd join right in, taking it and dishing it out, just like one of them. 'Karen, when are you going to clean up all these dirty dishes?' one of them would ask, and I'd shoot right back, without missing a beat: 'Just as soon as you suck my dick.'

93

'Karen, when are you going to earn your golden ticket?' Alec teased one night when we were all watching boxing on TV.

'As soon as Grace does,' I said. 'Call her. Get her over here.'

*

'Was that you?' I asked Bruce in the bathroom, early one morning. 'That picture of Susannah.' I hadn't asked him, ever, about her. I wanted not to care whether he was the father of Susannah's baby or not. I wanted him to be above it, somehow, exempt from both the juvenile ribbing of the frat boys and the tiresome moralising of the Susannah-supporters. Or I wanted *me* to be above it. I wanted to be exempt myself.

He lifted my hair in his fist. 'Even I know how to spell "whore",' he said.

We never went farther than this, Bruce and me. These half-dressed, drunken exchanges in front of the mirror.

'W, H, O,' he spelled. Between letters he touched the tip of his tongue to the nape of my neck. 'R.'

I waited, and then pulled away. 'Um, that's not how you sp –'

'E. Gotcha.' He scraped my jawbone with his stubbled chin.

There was no past and no future in the frat house except the recent and local past and future: that time Blackie puked on that girl, that party with the State cheerleaders coming up in January. There was no abstract thought. There were no consequences to anything.

'WHORE,' Bruce said, lazylaughing, blowing hotsweet breath on my skin through the 'wh' sound, and he took my earlobe between his teeth.

A touch or two, some hurried words. And once I brought my camera into the bathroom and took a few pictures of him. That was the extent of it between Bruce and me.

The trouble, though. Everyone knows myth would like to be more than a touch, a picture, a word. Myth would like to be flesh.

*

'Helen of Troy is different from any other Greco-Roman female figure,' Dr Esterhazy told us in class. 'Like other female characters, she is the object of male desire and the male poetic imagination, of course. But Helen is constantly on the move. As an object she constantly dissembles, constantly eludes, constantly slips beyond our grasp, just as her body is shunted back and forth between Sparta and Troy. I'm curious, students: what struck you about Helen, on reading about her for today's class, knowing what you know from our cultural repertoire? Knowing "the face that launched a thousand ships" and so forth?'

'Homer calls Helen "daughter of Zeus" a lot,' said Melanie, whom I'd met at the Women's Centre when Dyann was setting up the Wall of Shame. Her round cheeks went very pink with all of us looking at her. 'It's kind of ironic, since didn't Zeus, like, disguise himself as a swan and rape her mother, Leda, and then Helen was born from an egg?'

'Why is that ironic?' Dr Esterhazy asked her. I'd noticed that our professor was very exacting about word use. It was probably because her PhD was in English.

'They're all scared of Helen,' Charla said from the chair beside me, before Melanie had a chance to respond. She wiggled her fingers for my *Iliad* and fanned through the pages until she found what she wanted. 'The old men in Troy say she is "terribly like a goddess" in appearance. As in scary. As in terrible to look at.'

Dr Esterhazy nodded. 'Charlotte, right? Yes, great observation. Like the beautiful and terrifying Medusa, Helen's beauty shocks onlookers. She's nearly always veiled, and we're never given any specifics about her physical appearance in the texts.'

Charla didn't correct the professor about her name. Dr Esterhazy had insisted we use our name cards for the first few classes so she could get to know us, but Charla hadn't returned to campus until after that.

'If you will look at the footnote on page one hundred and twelve,' Dr Esterhazy said, 'you'll see it's not clear whether Helen is feeling lust for Paris, or anger, or what. Her desires remain as veiled as her body. Is she abducted, or does she go willingly? The question of Helen's agency remains crucially, essentially undecidable.'

Charla was tucked into her chair like a pretzel, knees up and ankles crossed so that leaning forward to write was a yoga pose. She wore a black camisole and a gray sweatshirt with the neck clipped out like Jennifer Beals in *Flashdance*. It was an unfashionable outfit for the nineties but my roommate, as always, made it sexy. As Dr Esterhazy talked, Charla twisted her hair into a knot and wove a pencil through to fasten it. A handbreadth of smooth white skin showed above her waistband.

The professor said, 'The drive to know Helen, to see Helen, becomes the driving force of the action in the myth, the thrust of the plot itself. She is *casus belli*, the cause of war, precisely because she cannot be taken or possessed.'

Casus belli, I wrote in my notes. I wondered if it even really mattered what Helen of Troy was all about in the myth. She was nothing, just collateral damage, a better prize than most but still a trophy. She was the spoils of war.

16. VITA ACTIVA

(a life active in the political arena)

On the last Friday of October I accompanied Mike to his Faculty of Science awards banquet. He'd won not only the physics and calculus awards but also the prize for overall academic excellence. It was my idea to go to the dinner – I'd seen the poster at school and told him we should take the time to celebrate his achievement. I was trying to amend for not inviting him to a movie the week before. The repertory cinema downtown was running a series of John Hughes brat-pack films on the second Tuesday of every month. I'd gone to *Sixteen Candles* alone, last minute, and I'd run into Bruce Comfort and his date at the theater, and Bruce had then mentioned to Mike that he'd seen me there.

'It's that you didn't even think of me,' Mike said.

'I did think of you. You guys went to that basketball game, remember?'

'I might have said no, but it would have been nice to be asked. Or maybe I would have fit it in. Bruce said, "Oh, I saw Karen at the movies," and I was like, "What?" I didn't even know you were going. It was humiliating.'

'I'm sorry,' I said. There were lots of things I did without Mike, though. I wondered what sort of reporting structure he had in mind.

'I don't think we can share this bathroom,' Bruce had said when I'd seen him in the lobby partway through the film. He slid down the wall beside the ladies' room door and patted the faded red carpet beside him.

We sat hip to hip. 'Ask me a question,' he said.

'Like what?' It was my first time being near Bruce Comfort without being at least somewhat drunk. He seemed bigger, more rigid. It was like sitting next to a bronzed version of Bruce.

'Anything,' he said. 'We never get a chance at home.'

Home. Like we were siblings. Like I was the girlfriend of his brother. 'Um, okay. What do you want to be when you grow up?'

'Teacher,' he said.

'Of what?'

'History. High school, maybe.'

'Didn't you fail history last year?' I'd heard it from Mike – that Bruce had managed to fail one of the easiest freshman courses.

He reached forward and began to fiddle with my sneakers. I couldn't see his face, only the broad wings of his shoulder blades, a ripple of ribs, and a ladder of spine. 'Well, I'm not going to be a teacher anyway,' he said. 'I'm going to be Comfort Insurance Services, Inc.'

I'd heard the name. Comfort Insurance was huge. I had never realised that the 'Comfort' part was a surname – was Bruce's surname. 'Is that your dad? Comfort Insurance Services?'

'Dad. Grandfather. Brothers, aunts, cousins.'

My hand cupped the ribs under one of the wings. The blood beat strongly there. 'It's your destiny,' I said.

A shrug lifted the ribs, and a sigh snuck under them.

'So, screw history,' I said.

He laughed and sat back, and I took the hand away. 'Screw history,' he said. 'Screw school, period. You gotta live, right?'

When we got up he said, 'Careful,' and caught me in his arms. He'd tied my shoelaces together.

'Nice,' I said.

He knelt to untie them, and I rested my hand on the crown of his head. 'You gotta live,' he said again. The rim of his ear was red. I slid my fingertips against it and warmed them while he worked.

So I'd told Mike I wanted to go with him to his banquet. I wore a long tuxedo shirt of Steph's with black tights, and I wrapped a silk scarf around my waist like an obi.

Mike looked good in his suit too. His brown hair flopped into his eyes, and his GBC tie contrasted pleasingly with the school colours repeated everywhere, from the banners above the stage to our cloth napkins. During dinner, though, he was restless and unhappy. He kept jumping out of his seat to talk to people or to go to the washroom. His hands stayed shaky even after he went up for his awards. He didn't touch his food.

'I wish we'd stayed home,' he kept saying.

'Why can't you just enjoy it?' I said. 'This tenderloin is actually really good.'

'These people don't get it. They think that this is what matters to me, that these *grades*' – he said the word like *plague* – 'make any difference to me. You know I don't care about this stuff.'

'My roommate is listed in here.' I showed him Marie-Jeanne Ouellette's name beside the sophomore mathematics award. 'I'm besieged by nerds,' I joked.

'The notions of value are totally fucked up,' Mike said.

I thought of Marie-Jeanne's ballet photo, her girlish body whittled down to a cage of bone. Yet she was now so solid and strong and smart! Carrying that picture around, carrying that past – I was sure it must feel like being haunted.

I said, 'Okay, you're too cool for school. I get it.' I earned good grades, too, but I *earned* them: I studied like mad, agonised over every essay I wrote. Mike never cracked a book in my presence. He hated it when I stayed late at the library or said I had to get to bed early – he even complained when I left the frat house in the morning to go to class. 'What are you going to remember about college?' he'd say. 'Not what you did in class. It's the people. That's what will last.'

Now he picked up his merit certificate from beside his plate, slipped off its silver ribbon, and unrolled it. 'They expect me to pin these things to my walls. Like this is the final goal or something.' He folded the paper in half, quarters, and eighths, creasing it with his thumb, and slipped it into his jacket pocket.

'The money's good, though, right?' I said.

Mike looked at me. He took all three prize checks out of his wallet, signed the backs of them, and dropped them into my lap. They totaled forty-five hundred American dollars.

'Cut it out.'

'You deserve it, Karen,' he said. 'That's a kind of value, at least: economic value. The fact that you have these part-time jobs? You work to earn your attendance here. At least that has integrity.'

'Stop it,' I said. Mike had pushed aside his place setting in order to sign the cheques, and the woman beside me had watched the whole thing.

'It's how we came together, remember? You wrote me a check, that first night.'

I leaned into Mike and spoke as softly as I could, close to his ear: 'I know you're too smart for all this institutional stuff. The decorations, the awards. It's the main thing I like about you, your *cerebrum thermonous*. It's a pretty rare thing to find in a person. But, Mike, you have to suffer the lesser. You need to be gracious. Otherwise your life will be unbearable.'

'"*Cerebrum*" is brain,' he said, 'but what's "*thermonous*"?'

'It's something like "brain on fire". It was a huge problem for Greek oracles and prophets.'

Mike kissed me, smiled, and sat back in his chair. 'God, I love that. You have the exact word for everything.'

I put the checks back into his wallet. I untied his discarded certificate ribbon and wound it around my wrist. 'Can you tie a little bow?' I asked him.

'That's why the fraternity is such a relief, you know? They don't care about all this, this external stuff. You can just be. Just … be!'

'The drugs help, too, with the not caring,' I pointed out. 'The booze helps.'

'I want to take classes with you next semester,' Mike said. He fumbled the ribbon and tried again. 'I want to sign up for Shakespeare with you.'

'Shakespeare is a full-year course,' I told him. 'Twenty-four plays in twenty-four weeks – says so right in the course description – and you've missed eight already.'

'That feminism one, then. Myths.'

'Same thing. Our only half-year courses are the core English ones, and to get into those you have to be an English major.'

'We should do an elective together,' he persisted. 'How about astronomy? We could go to a field and lie down on a blanket and make our own star map.'

'It'll be a bit chilly.'

'At the end of term. In the spring.'

The knot had slipped and pulled too tight. My fingers ached, and the veins on the back of my hand bulged like worms. I bit at the ribbon, but it was buried in skin.

'We're two halves of a whole,' Mike said. 'Remember from our class last year, what Plato said in *The Symposium*? People are souls split in half. They find each other.'

'Yeah, but Plato hated women. He banned women from his Republic, remember? Said they had to stay home and shut up.'

'That was his politics. I'm talking about his philosophy. The truths he discovered.'

I slid my bread knife under the ribbon and tried to saw it off. It pulled tighter still. 'Maybe you should switch majors,' I said. 'You really liked philosophy.'

'Maybe I'll switch to English,' Mike said. He frowned. 'Although to tell you the truth I don't really see the point in it, any more than science. I would quit school in a second if I could still live at GBC.'

The ribbon frayed and finally came loose with a pop. My hand throbbed.

'What did you do?' Mike said. 'I thought you were going to wear it. It looked pretty.'

17. PERIPETEIA

(reversal of fortune)

When we got back to the frat house a costume party was under way. It was a sadomasochism theme, loosely connected to Halloween a few days away, and every room was packed with girls in skimpy leather shorts and spiked dog collars and stilettos. None of the brothers was wearing a costume. It was the same with all their mixers, I'd noticed. CEOs & Office Sluts, Prom Night Cherrypop, Priests & Whores – only the girls played their part. They had to wear the costumes to get in the door. The new sorority pledges were scored, and the rankings were passed back to their big sisters, so they outdid themselves in the outrageous sluttiness of their outfits.

Before the banquet we'd finished only half the bottle of wine I'd brought, so Mike and I went straight up to his room to continue our date.

Mike presented me with what he called an early Christmas gift: a floor-length kimono with a print of butterflies and water lilies. 'Feel how it flows against your skin,' he said when I stripped and tried it on for him. 'It's pure Japanese silk.'

It wasn't silk. There was a metallic thread running through the fabric that scratched and caught at my fingertips. I didn't say anything, but I couldn't understand how he hadn't read the label. It was printed right there in the collar: *100% NYLON. MADE IN CHINA.*

Mike moved me to his bed and eased me onto my back. 'I fantasised about this. Untying this, just like this,' he said.

Mike and I made love. He'd asked me not to call it 'fucking' or 'having sex'. I practised it in my mind. *Lovemaking.*

After we made love, Mike fell asleep right away. The party was loud, and I lay there a long time listening to it. When I did sleep it was only a few hours before I woke up again, my back sweaty where I lay on the kimono.

I got dressed – a T-shirt and boxers from Mike's dresser – and crept down the hall to the lounge. Two girls crawled around on the carpet, looking under the furniture.

'Did you lose something?' I said.

'The sapphire fell out of my ring,' one of the girls said.

On the sofa, face-down, was a frat brother whose name I thought was Zane. 'What's the matter with him?' I asked.

'He wasn't feeling well,' the girl said.

'Brave guy, sleeping out here,' I said. If a brother couldn't hold his liquor at a party or keep up with the others, he'd usually be subjected to all manner of indignities: being stripped, shaved, decorated with permanent marker, or worse. Frat boys were like marines in their derision of weakness, their dogged pleasure in disgracing the fallen. I was surprised to find Zane unmolested.

The second girl gave up combing the carpet and flopped into a chair. Her leather halter-top had a heavy steel loop at the neck for attaching her to things. 'This party sucks,' she said.

'It's, what, 4 am?' I said. 'This party's over.'

'Not down in the Bag it isn't,' said the girl in the halter.

'What's going on in the Bag?'

'Shut up, Julie,' said the first girl.

'What's going on in the Bag?' I repeated.

The first girl sat back against the couch, crossed her ankles, and lit a cigarette. 'It's disgusting, if you ask me,' she said. 'Those guys are pigs.'

'Some State skank volunteered for training,' Julie explained. She rolled her eyes.

'I heard they hired someone,' said the first girl.

'Training. Like, they're pulling train?' I said.

'There's no way a hooker would let them do that,' Julie said. 'Unless they paid her a *lot*. She's tied up and everything.'

'They tied her up?' I said.

'Well, it is an S&M party,' Julie said, and giggled.

Another brother slept at the kitchen table in a pool of spilled beer, the overturned bottle trapped under his hand. Two more were sprawled open-mouthed in the recliners downstairs with game controllers in their laps. One appeared to have vomited on the arm of his chair. The third guy – Charlie, the redhead – still stared at the screen, which was frozen on Pause. I thought of Sleeping Beauty's pricked finger, her curse spread over the whole castle.

I crossed the room, heading for the door of the weight room, and Charlie lurched to his feet and dropped his controller on the floor. Then he swayed and fell back into his chair. 'Only brothers in the Bag,' he slurred.

'And sisters, right?' I said.

'You're wearing too many clothes for a little sister, sister.' His gaze swung back to the screen. He hadn't even recognised me.

'You should go to bed,' I said. 'Really, Charlie. You don't look too good.'

'I'm good, I'm good,' he said. But he struggled back out of the chair and shuffled off toward the stairs.

I watched him pull himself up, hand over hand, along the wall. I'd never seen any of the brothers this wasted. Maybe it was always like this, and I was usually asleep or too far gone myself to notice.

The door to the weight room wasn't locked. I slid inside the room and closed the door behind me. I kept both hands wrapped around the doorknob at the small of my back.

I was inside the Black Bag.

The red lightbulb squinted back at itself in the fogged-up mirrors. Sticky gymnasium air licked my skin. The stench was wrong for a gym, though – saline, mushroomy.

Bodies. Skin. Naked orange legs and feet. Hair sweeping over shoulders. A boy's bare orange ass.

A naked girl hung by her wrists from the weight-bench frame, knees against the bench, moaning ...

Charla. I knew it was Charla despite the fog and glow, despite the blind-fold she wore and the way she kept her head tucked down, away from me. Chris held her around the waist with one arm. Fly open, rubber on, he held his cock in his hand and tried to angle it between her legs.

'Charla,' I said.

Dyann was in front of me. Her hands came up hard over my mouth. 'Quiet, Karen,' she hissed.

I couldn't let go of the doorknob. I jerked my head and stood on tiptoes to see past Dyann. She moved with me, swayed, dodged. The weight of her whole body pressed her hand against my mouth so that my head went back hard against the door. I felt my tooth cut into my lip.

The door opened, and we fell out into the rec room. Dyann lunged for the knob and closed the door of the Black Bag behind us.

'What. What.' My teeth chattered, and I lost the rest of the question.

Dyann said, 'I thought you weren't going to be here tonight. Is MJ with you? Steph?'

'Steph?' I wiped blood from my mouth.

She looked at me. 'Go back upstairs, Karen. Just go back to your party, all right?'

'The party is over. It's four in the morning. It's over,' I yammered.

'If you see Steph up there, tell her I've been tapping at that goddamn window for twenty minutes. We're done here; we need to make a move.'

'But Charla's ... Charla is –'

'Go, Karen, please. Fuck, I'm begging you!'

I obeyed her. My legs shook so I could hardly climb the stairs. I stumbled around the main floor, searching for Steph, but Steph was nowhere. The very idea of Steph at a frat party was too absurd for my brain to hold on to. I felt very tired, chilled and weak, and I wanted more than anything to crawl into Mike's bed. But when I finally made it up to the second floor I found his bedroom door locked. I'd forgotten to spring the knob when I came out.

I wept. My nose ran. I sat on the stairs wiping my face over and over with Mike's T-shirt until it was streaked with snot and with blood from my cut lip. It's not fair, I thought, it's not fair. I knew the thought made no sense. I was so tired!

Eventually I found an empty bedroom, dragged a dresser in front of the door, and crawled under the covers.

Mike found me in there early the next morning. He got the door open a crack and then shouted until I moved the dresser and let him in. I explained about his locked bedroom door, and he was angry with me for leaving without waking him up. 'You shouldn't do that, Karen, not during a party! How many times do I have to tell you?'

I snapped at him for being patronising, for treating me like a child. Somewhere in the middle of the argument I remembered about the Black Bag, and I rushed past Mike to the bathroom to vomit.

'I think I have a virus,' I told Mike. I told him I had to work a special event at the Faculty Club. I told him there was no way I could get out of my shift, not even if I was sick. I told him I was already late and had to leave right away. I told him no, I didn't want to wait a sec and see if he could find someone to give me a ride.

Mike argued with me, but when he followed me downstairs and saw the brothers still passed out everywhere, he got distracted and let me go.

When I was sure he wasn't watching anymore, I circled around to the backyard and crouched by the basement window. The red light was off. I couldn't see anything.

There was a noise behind me, and I scrambled to my feet. Bruce Comfort was slumped in a lawn chair. Slack-jawed, shirtless. The belt and button of his jeans hung open, and a half-full bottle of beer was wedged between his thighs. His nipples inside their blond whorls of hair were tight points against the chill. I slid two fingers around Bruce's wrist and felt a small jumping pulse. I wiped away a spider's web of drool. Even like this, nearly comatose, Bruce appeared perfectly poised. Posed. A movie cowboy propped against his saddle after a bad night in the tavern.

Book II

ANTISTROPHE

(counter-circling)

18. DICAEOLOGIA

(making excuses)

I wander to the photography conference's Happy Hour Meet & Greet in the hotel atrium. Hibiscus and other tropical plants are arranged in a two-storey pyramid in the centre of the room. Just inside the door a woman I know from Toronto named Nicola Zwitter leaps upon my arm and steers me directly to the bar.

'Margarita, right?' she says.

'Wow. Good memory,' I say.

'You didn't come to the CMA awards,' she says. 'We Canadians should be sticking together, don't you think?'

'I'm not a member of the ...' I've already forgotten the acronym she used.

She frowns. 'The Canadian Magazine Association. Seriously? Karen, you should be. There's way too many writers at those things, not nearly enough art people.'

Nicola has recently been hired as art director for a new publishing imprint that specialises in home design and cookbooks. 'Chalet', they're calling it. I offer my congratulations and ask her what titles she's working on.

'Something called *Slow Home*,' she says. 'You know slow food? Well, it's a whole home movement now.'

'Sounds right on trend.'

Nicola wrinkles her nose, and I wonder if I've offended her. I miss Greg. He's way better than I am at small talk. He remembers details about people, like the names of their dogs and how many kids they have. When Greg came to these parties with me he always knew exactly what to say to someone like Nicola Zwitter to make her believe I was the nicest, most authentic person in the entire world of photography.

I feel as if his absence suddenly shows on me somehow, as if a wound has started to bleed. And sure enough, Nicola says, 'Is Greg in town with you?'

'Greg's in Geneva,' I say.

'Right, he took that job. How's the long-distance thing going?'

'Well, he's there for good, I'm afraid.'

Nicola's face composes itself for sympathy. A throaty hum revs up as she thinks of what to say.

Now why did I go and share that information with this woman? I've alarmed myself. To compensate for it I close my eyes in a slow blink and say, 'It's for the best, for both of us.'

The bartender hands us our drinks, and Nicola raises hers and shrugs. 'My marriage went down the crapper ages ago. The divorce just came through in July. Here's to starting over, right?'

She leads me to a bistro table surrounded by a jowly woman with dark-rimmed glasses, a tall, handsome man in jeans and a white shirt, and an older man with a red bandanna handkerchief spilling from the pocket of his tweed blazer. 'Joan, David, Douglas. This is Karen Huls,' Nicola says. She touches the older man's sleeve. 'Karen, this is Douglas Reeve. He's the king of our little Chalet fiefdom.'

'Hi,' I say. Douglas Reeve is CEO at Nicola's new publishing house. I remember reading something about how he's sworn never to retire, and how this bullheadedness has resulted in a plutocracy, or has made the glass ceiling worse for the women in the senior ranks, or something like that. We shake hands, Joan, David, Douglas, and me.

'Karen is a crackerjack photographer,' Nicola tells them. 'Her macros are phenomenal. Do you remember that piece in *Food and Drink* with the prosciutto? That was Karen.'

The others clearly don't remember the *Food and Drink* piece, but Nicola is undaunted. She's got her hand on David's sleeve now. 'Karen, tell them the lemon story.' She laughs, then starts talking again before I can say anything: 'So we're shooting a two-page spread, the whole table, right? The intern takes a bag of lemons and dumps it upside down in this bowl without looking twice.'

I set my drink down and, wiping the condensation off my fingers, I am distracted by the note in my blazer pocket. Through all of the conference sessions today I've been distracted by this note. It's from Dyann Brooks-Morriss. It was delivered to my hotel room. A handwritten note: *Dear Karen, I'm in town for Steph. Will I see you at the memorial? Love, DBM. PS: Good Luck tomorrow.*

I've been rereading the note all day. Could it really be her? I can't imagine her stooping to such conventionalities: *Dear Karen,* and *Love.* There is a softness, a tentative tone, in the question *Will I see you?* There is a generosity in *Good Luck.* But then there is the arrogance of signing only initials after fifteen years without contact. Can I still call it arrogance, though, if I knew at once whose initials they were?

Of everyone at Raghurst I missed Dyann the most, and for longest. After everything fell apart – when I returned to campus the following fall, and Dyann was gone – I went mad with grief for her, mad with missing her. I would have walked off the earth to find her that year. I would throw my heart at her feet all over again.

I wrench my attention back to Nicola when I hear her say my name: 'Karen's all the way across the room setting up the shot, but suddenly she's dragged the whole tripod right up next to this bowl, and she's snapping like crazy. Yelling at the assistants to find her other lens.'

'I didn't *yell*,' I say.

'Everyone is standing around wondering what in the hell is going on with the photographer.'

'Nobody was standing around. The table hadn't even been styled yet.'

'So what were you doing?' David asks me.

Nicola leans into him playfully. 'What she was doing was, she's shooting a moldy lemon. There's one lemon in the bowl that's totally covered in mold. The rest of us are all like, *Eww, throw that out,* and meanwhile Karen for whatever reason is going apeshit over it with her camera.'

'And did you end up using it?' Douglas's voice is too soft for the chattery space of the party. I have to lean in and ask him to repeat himself. When he touches his hearing aid before saying it again, I realise he's compensating for deafness by trying not to talk like a person who is hard of hearing. 'Did you use the shot in the story?'

I smile at him. 'Can you imagine? Charcuterie and moldy citrus.'

David puts an inch of space between his arm and Nicola's. He raises his glass. 'To artistic compromise!'

'I'm not a diva on set, I swear,' I tell them. 'It was just for a side project of mine.' It was one of my 'darks', that photograph of the lemons. That bright dimpled peel doing exactly what is expected of it. Then that shock of gray-green fur.

'You're right, I am not selling you very well,' Nicola says. 'Karen is fantastic. We will definitely want to work with her.'

I lift my glass to theirs and take a sip of my margarita. I suddenly feel sorry for Nicola. It's easy for me to live without someone. I'm used to it. Even with Greg I spent most of my time behind my camera or alone at my desk. But Nicola. Her divorce explains the extremely aerobicised condition of her ass and thighs in that tight dress she's wearing. The ultra-blonde hair, the layers of makeup she never used to wear. Poor Nicola Zwitter is, as they say, on the prowl.

'I can't wait to see your portfolio, my dear.' Douglas smiles, gives a little sigh, and looks off across the atrium. He probably isn't all that anxious to see my portfolio. He's probably seen it all so often that he can barely stand it anymore. A hundred thousand country loaves on maple bread boards. A hundred thousand matelassé bedspreads with piled-up pillows. All the tired old fantasies entering through the eye and benumbing the veins.

I touch the note in my pocket again and – O Bruce. How his hair used to stick up over his right ear. How that ear would be flushed a deep red and hot to the touch, so that when I met him in the bathroom I would know he'd slept on that side.

One night Mike's pills kept up an itchy, humming pressure under my scalp. When Bruce slipped up behind me I was drumming my forehead with all ten of my fingertips to counteract the feeling. 'My brain is twitching,' I complained. 'Picture it in there. It's kicking like a wild stallion.'

He rested his chin atop my head and waggled his eyebrows at me in the mirror. 'What colour?'

I closed my eyes. 'Gray. With white spots and a tangled yellow mane. He's huge. Massive. The ground shudders when he gallops.'

'Does he go after the girl horses? The mares?' Bruce humped the small of my back in illustration.

'No. Light. He chases down light,' I said.

'A lighthorse.' He nodded, bouncing his chin on my skull as though it made perfect sense. 'Hey, did you bring your camera? You should get a picture of us in the mirror like this.'

*

Pictures, though. Look at my pictures, perhaps especially the ones no one sees, those stylised still lifes with all their obsessive fussy detail that I call my 'darks'. Sing of Dyann Brooks-Morriss, keeneyed warlover, a searchlight for the truth! Dyann wanted the cleansing tide of blood. She wanted to rouse the world from its torpor. She thundered right down to the wellsprings of life, past them, down even further to stare unblinking into the murk of Tartarus. Meanwhile I tiptoe along the surface, taking pictures, looking at pictures. Looking at pictures and looking at pictures. Looking at all these pictures to avoid looking at that one.

19. KATEGORIA

(accusation)

'I'm driving you back there,' Steph said. The keys were already in her hand moments after I jangled through the front door of Raghurst.

They'd been sitting in the living room, Marie-Jeanne with a breakfast smoothie, Steph with papers spread all over the coffee table. If Steph hadn't leapt to her feet when I walked in, I'd have wondered if I was completely insane, if I'd imagined the entire scene in the Black Bag the night before. 'No way,' I said. 'Not until somebody tells me what the hell is going on.'

'You saw for yourself, apparently,' Marie-Jeanne said.

'What I saw …' I couldn't say what I'd seen. My mind dodged around it like repelling magnets. 'Where is Dyann? Where's Charla?'

'They're fine; they're sleeping. You need to go back there and make sure everyone is okay.' Steph took off her sweatshirt and handed it to me. 'Here, you can wear this; it'll look like you just popped home to change. Come on, let's go.'

I planted my feet. 'Who? Whom? Make sure whom is okay?'

Marie-Jeanne said, 'A lot of those guys were mixing all kinds of drugs, alcohol. Do you know – are you sure they were all up and accounted for this morning?'

'No one in the hospital?' Steph added.

'No one was even awake yet,' I said. 'I can call Mike and see, if you want.'

'Let's go,' Steph said. 'You can't say a word to Mike. I mean it, Karen.' She steered me out the door. 'This is really, really important, and we don't have time to explain it all right now.'

*

Normally the pledges, at least, would be up by mid-morning after a party. They'd be collecting empties, opening windows, righting chairs, and wiping up spills in anticipation of the cleaning service. Someone would have gone out for groceries and cooked a big, hangover-busting breakfast of bacon and eggs, pancakes, real maple syrup – 'real maple syrup' was actually listed somewhere in the house rules, apparently – and the smell of that, along with the prospect of Chet's Tequila Sunrises, would draw the brothers into the kitchen in stumbling, half-soused groups of two and three.

I'd come to enjoy these feasts almost more than the parties themselves. All that prowling and stalking and strutting the night before, and here they would gather in the morning, droopy and deflated. The puffed eyelids and rumpled hair – even the stale smells – reminded me of my younger brother. The boys scratched and mumbled, and they groaned when you touched their bare shoulders.

But today when Steph dropped me off it was quiet. The lone pledge I encountered in the hallway, little red-eyed Frodo, looked harried and ill. 'Fucked if I know,' he snapped at me when I asked where everybody was. He hadn't been able to rouse anyone to help him clean up, he complained, and nearly everybody had gotten sick at some point. I checked the backyard, but Bruce wasn't there anymore.

Mike had gone back to bed, too, so I crawled in next to him.

'I'm sick,' I reminded him when he reached for me. 'I wasn't on the schedule after all, thank God.'

We slept until noon. When we came downstairs again, two women in baby-blue aprons were steam-vacuuming the furniture. Batches of Hunch

Punch had gone wrong before, Mike told me, and there were routine procedures for global vomiting. Ana's Housekeeping Services was number six on GBC's speed-dial.

Eventually everyone was awake again, showering in twos and threes so the hot water wouldn't give out, mixing beer with tomato juice. Mike set up a station in the kitchen for his Sunrises and everyone filed through for his shot, and soon enough the chatter was loud and there was talk of golfing, of fishing, of heading up to Duncan's father's cabin for one last lake cruise before the freeze.

I pretended to have lost my bike key. 'Not last night. Sometime in the last few visits,' I said. 'Someone took it, remember? It was this big drunken joke about stealing my ride? I can't even remember who it was now, but I'll know him when I see him.' Lame as the lie was, Mike bought it, and we paraded all around the house, scanning all the common areas and poking our heads into every bedroom. I checked everyone, made sure they were breathing.

'It wouldn't be in there,' Mike said. He grabbed my hand before I could turn the doorknob of a third-floor bedroom.

'How do you know?'

'You've never been in there before, have you?'

'How do you know?' I repeated. I reached for the knob, and he stopped me again, frowning now. 'What?' I said. I didn't have time for this.

'You haven't been in there before, right?' he said.

'No, but I want to check anyways. Maybe the key fell out of somebody's pants, all right?'

Mike held me back as he opened the door. 'Oh, gross,' he said.

I pushed past him. There were bunk beds and a desk with an overturned lamp. Bedding and clothing were strewn everywhere. A vintage gymnastics vault stood in the centre of the rug. The whole thing – the segmented wooden sides, the padded leather top – was spray-painted gold. And sprawled over the vault on her stomach, with one leg hanging down each side, was a naked girl.

'Is she breathing?' I said.

Mike put his hand on the girl's back.

'Don't touch her!' I swatted his hand away. 'I mean, let's get her dressed before she wakes up.' I caught my breath, held it, trying to slow my frantic heartbeat. My whole body shook with the effort.

'She looks pretty comfy to me.' Mike shrugged. 'I doubt it's her first time on the gold car.'

'The gold car.' I looked at him, then at the girl on the vault. '*This* is the gold car? This is what Alec was talking about that time, with that stuff about me earning a golden ticket?'

'That's why I was sort of hoping you hadn't been in here before.'

I found the girl's jeans, blouse, and brassiere behind the horse, and her panties in the bottom bunk. She was so groggy that Mike had to hold her up while I guided her limbs into the clothes. Then we helped her downstairs, sat her in a kitchen chair, and gave her a glass of orange juice. Between the shaking of her hands and her swollen mouth, she could hardly drink. She said her name was Sheri Asselin. She asked if we could call her a taxi.

Pits brought her a handful of ice in a paper towel. 'Sheri, tell me, how did you enjoy your evening?' he said.

Mike glared at him and made a slashing gesture across his throat. They both looked at me.

'Just call her a cab, you asshole,' I said to Pits.

'Ouch! That's what we get for doing good deeds?' he said.

I stalked across the kitchen, grabbed the phone off the wall, dialed the taxi number, and gave the dispatcher the address. Sheri watched me with eyes that weren't seeing anything.

Next I called Raghurst. 'Pick me up. Right now,' I said to Steph.

'What is your problem?' Mike said. He sat next to me on the porch as I lit a cigarette, waiting for my ride. 'That girl is not your problem, all right? She can take care of herself.'

'Yeah, she looks really well taken care of. And by more than one frat boy, I bet.'

'So she's a slut, so what? It's not for us to judge.'

I looked at him. 'Do you do it?'

'Do what?'

'Ride the gold car, or whatever you call it.'

'I was with you last night, remember?'

'Other times. Do you join in the Express?'

'No, Karen. I told you, I'm not into sharing.'

I was pretty sure he'd never actually said that to me before, not explicitly. 'Why not?' I said.

'Oh, come on.'

'No, I'm serious. You share everything with your brothers, right?'

'Not that. Not you. I'd never share you.'

'Remember that whole discussion you guys were having a while back, about "rapeability"?' I said. 'Remember how you were all saying some girls are just more "rapeable" than others?' Some girls wore it like a sign around their neck, they'd joked: 'Insert dick here.'

Mike leaned way back, away from my smoke, to remind me he disapproved of the habit. 'That was totally a joke, Karen, and you know it.'

'Well, it wasn't funny, Mike.'

'You're taking it way too personally. They didn't mean you. And they didn't mean, like, *rape* rape; they were talking about that kind of thing' – he flapped a hand over his shoulder to indicate Sheri. 'Drunken debauchery kind of stuff, the gold car. That would never be you.'

'Why not?'

Mike rolled his eyes. 'You wouldn't put yourself out there like that.'

'You're always telling me not to leave your room at night.'

'Not because of *rape*.'

I didn't answer. Of course, I was thinking about the Black Bag, not the gold car. I was thinking about Charla, not Sheri. But I'd promised my roommates I wouldn't say anything about that to Mike.

'You saw in the rut that time,' he reasoned. 'They didn't hit you with their full weight. They wouldn't hurt you.'

'You were panicked about the rut,' I said.

'Not because of *rape*,' he said again.

Was I taking it too personally? It wasn't about me, really; as Mike had pointed out, I wouldn't 'put myself out there' like Sheri must have done. Yet Mike worried every time I wandered the frat house alone. If it wasn't rape, what was it? The word cut its way back and forth, double-sided, in my mind.

20. OICTOS

(show of pity or compassion)

Dyann and Marie-Jeanne were at the dining table when Steph and I got back to Raghurst. 'Well?' Dyann said. 'All the noble party warriors accounted for?'

Steph looked at me. When I didn't say anything, she said, 'Karen said they were hungover worse than usual this morning, but otherwise okay.'

Dyann nodded. She and Marie-Jeanne exchanged a look, and Marie-Jeanne nodded too, then gathered the lunch dishes from the table and took them to the kitchen.

I didn't even know where to start. I followed Marie-Jeanne halfway to the kitchen. 'Why weren't you at your awards banquet last night?' I turned to the others. 'She won the math prize, you know.'

Nobody said anything.

'Really, it was a lovely evening,' I said. 'The food was great. They even had crème brulée. And there weren't nearly enough women up there at the podium. I would've thought you'd make it a priority to show your face.'

'We had – how do you say it? – bigger fish to fry?' Marie-Jeanne said.

'Like pimping out your roommate at a frat party?'

It was momentarily satisfying to watch their faces go rigid with shock. 'We weren't … we didn't pimp Charla out,' Steph said.

'Then what was Charla doing in the Black Bag?'

'You'll need to ask Charla that,' Dyann said – and then she lunged out of her chair to block me from the basement stairs. 'Later, I mean. She's sleeping. She needs to rest.'

'Fine. What were *you* doing in the Black Bag, Dyann?' I asked.

Marie-Jeanne came back to the table, and Steph and Dyann sat down too. They looked at each other around the circle.

I took a chair and folded my hands in front of me. 'Grand Council. Excellent. Meeting is brought to order. On the agenda today is "Tell Karen what the hell is going on already."'

'It makes sense you're angry. But can we set aside the sarcasm?' Steph laid both hands flat, palms up, on the table. 'It just isn't helpful.'

'Look, Karen.' Dyann's hands were on the table too. 'We need to apologise to you, okay? We've talked it over, and we realise that we should have told you we were making our move last night.'

'We didn't think it through, that you'd be going back to the frat house with Mike after the banquet,' Steph said.

'We never meant to put you in that position,' Marie-Jeanne said.

I grabbed Dyann's wrist and dug my nails into it. 'Tell me one thing: how many of the brothers had a go at Charla?'

Steph said, 'Charla was willing, Karen. We did this for all the women who *aren't* willing.'

Dyann was trying to twist away from me, but I held on, held her eyes with mine. 'How many?' I repeated.

'Lots, all right? It was lots,' she said. There was more pain in her face than my grip on her arm could have caused. I let go of her.

The bells clanged. We all jumped, and Steph swore. 'November first, those things come down,' she told Dyann.

Stick and Wheeler appeared in the dining room. Stick clawed my shoulders in a friendly massage. 'Everybody alive over at Gang Bang Central?'

'*They* knew?' I said.

'Get out, you guys,' Dyann said.

Wheeler set a box and a couple of books on the table. MAGIC: THE GATHERING, the box read. 'It's our game day,' he said. 'We have to set up.'

'What's wrong with your house?' Dyann said.

'Come on. Is that any way to thank your pharmacist?' Stick said.

'We told them they could play here today,' Marie-Jeanne said. 'We didn't think of the dates, I guess.'

'I cannot handle this,' Dyann said. She yanked her jacket off the back of Wheeler's chair.

Steph got up too, and sighed. 'Let's go to the bookstore,' she suggested. 'I want to see if they have the new Eve Sedgwick.'

I followed them down the hall. 'And what about Charla?'

Steph looked at Dyann, who glared up from tying her shoes, shook her head, and said, 'I can't talk about this right now.' She blinked hard a few times, as though trying to clear her vision. 'I'm serious. I feel like I could kill someone.'

Steph sighed again. 'Charla will sleep,' she told me. 'I gave her some Xanax.'

Once they were gone and Marie-Jeanne was occupied with the boys, I snuck downstairs to the basement. Charla's bedroom was dominated by a massive antique bed. She'd placed it in the centre of the floor rather than against a wall, and she'd hung heavy brocade and velvet drapery panels from its canopy frame so that it was totally enclosed. Her 'bower', she called it. 'I'll be in my bower if I'm called for,' she liked to say, in a Southern belle accent.

I groped for a slit in the curtains and peeked. It was almost too dark to make her out. The scent of her lemongrass soap. A thick sigh. A white swell of cheek, and Charla's whole face suddenly quite close to mine as she moved the covers.

'How're the Lethean waters?' I asked, thinking of the Xanax, and then, 'Shit. I shouldn't joke. I'm sorry.'

A muffled laugh. 'They're good, Karen. The waters are good. Want to join me?'

I did want to join her, suddenly – very badly. Steph's prescription bottle was on the desk. I shook two tablets into my hand. They were two different sizes, but I ate them anyhow. Then I crawled into the bower next to Charla.

'I heard you crashed our little S&M party last night,' she said.

'I'm sorry,' I said. 'Although if anyone was crashing it was you guys.'

But Charla was asleep again, or had been all along. I stared up at the shadowed curlicues of the drapes until the drug dropped me away too.

21. PARADIASTOLE

(reframing)

I had an appointment to see Dr Esterhazy during the office hours listed on her syllabus. I'd never gone to see a professor one-on-one before, but Steph had told me that a student's grade went up by an average of 10 percent if the prof had spoken to her, in person, on at least one occasion outside of class.

I'd planned to make notes on a possible essay topic, but the extra hours in Mike's bed and then in Charla's bower had sucked up the weekend. I thought about it as I searched for the right room number through the maze of short hallways on the seventh floor of the Arts Building. Helen, maybe, the *casus belli* of the Trojan War? I could write about how men in Homer are active subjects but women are passive objects, obstacles to be overcome or trophies to be fought over. How femininity is related to justice, or vengeance, or something like that.

Dr Esterhazy's office was more like a supply closet. Two walls of bookshelves, with more books stacked on the floor, and a narrow aisle between them. A desk crammed at the back under the small window. No computer. No phone, either – at least not one visible under the piles of papers.

The door stood open but Dr Esterhazy wasn't there. 'It's the cross-appointment,' her voice said, behind me, and I turned to see her coming up the hall with a glass teapot and two mugs. 'They didn't know where to put me, you see: English or Women's Studies.'

She waved me into the office ahead of her. I had to shuffle and lean against the books to give her access to her desk.

She put the teapot down. 'Where shall you sit?' she said.

There was no place. 'I'm okay,' I said. 'I just have a quick question.' I hoped Steph wouldn't find out I'd actually come. Dr Esterhazy obviously never had actual students visiting her during office hours.

'There are chairs around the corner, by the mailroom,' she said. 'Perhaps you wouldn't mind bringing one of those?'

I found the spot she meant, carried a chair back to the office, and held it in midair while she pushed some books around to make enough room.

When we were seated face-to-face, Dr Esterhazy swirled the teapot. 'Look at this.' Greenery circled and bobbed like seaweed. 'It's called "blooming tea",' she said. 'A friend brought it from India. Jasmine flowers. Isn't it wonderful?' She poured the two mugs full and handed one to me.

Dr Esterhazy's hands were pale, coursing with blue veins, three of the fingers ringed in silver. I wished I could see the rings up close. The biggest one was shaped like a shield and had a pattern, maybe letters, pressed into it.

I told her about my essay topic. She seemed to approve, but she warned me not to fall into what she called 'uncritical readings' of Helen: 'She is a cipher for the male playwright's anxieties, remember. A repository for fear of the uncontained feminine.'

'What should I read besides the *Iliad* for research?' I asked.

'Start with Gorgias' *Encomium*. Then Euripides: he questions whether Helen was even a flesh-and-blood woman at Troy or a mere *eidolon* of her, a spectre, watching from the city walls.'

We hadn't read either of those texts in Women and Myth. I had hoped she'd suggest some secondary sources for interpreting the *Iliad*, not more classics.

'Keep in mind that even as a passive object of sexual conquest, Helen plays a key role in the structure of the story. Absentation, reconnaissance' – Dr Esterhazy paused, when she saw how fast I was scrawling in my notebook, to let me catch up – 'delivery or its refusal, counteraction. The basic units of the epic narrative all revolve around her.'

She must have had such a fight, this delicate, womanly woman, as a feminist student in the 1960s. I thought of the photographs lining the walls of the Faculty Club foyer: the smug groups of men on their high-contrast photo paper. The debaters, the rowers, the soldiers barracked in the gymnasium, the lacrosse team with their woolen uniforms and webbed-leather nets on sticks. All of them with the same haircut and the same squared stance.

'Don't overlook the cultural studies material, either,' my professor said. 'Greek women outside of their domestic spaces were perceived as inherently dangerous. Wayward. Loose cannons. When a man meets a Maenad in the mountains he cannot be certain of his life, after all.'

She smiled at me, and I smiled back. It was as if she was talking to a colleague, or maybe to one of her graduate students. I took a sip of the tea and thought of stems, of nectar. I felt its heat bloom behind my sternum.

I wasn't quite following her line of reasoning, though. Instead I was distracted by the sudden memory of Bruce Comfort slumped in the lawn chair in GBC's backyard. 'Sorry,' I said. 'What do the Maenads have to do with Helen of Troy?'

'Well, Helen is out of place, isn't she?' Dr Esterhazy said. 'The entire problem of Helen is that her absence is an affront to her husband and her social station.'

'But she didn't choose to be kidnapped,' I said.

'It doesn't matter whether she was raped or seduced, whether she was abducted or convinced to elope. She's missing. She's out of place. That alone is enough to link her to the outlaw women, the pre-patriarchal order, the ancient Blood Code that men fought to supplant with modern law. Helen is a structural problem that can only be solved by the narrative progression of the epic.'

I was thinking of Bruce in the backyard, but it was Charla who'd been strung up there in the Black Bag to be swarmed as if by sharks. It was Charla who'd been the object of the feeding frenzy. The strange tea left a sour aftertaste, and I set my cup carefully back on the desk.

Steph had told us that Dr Esterhazy was granted tenure a full eight years after her male colleagues. 'Sylvia Esterhazy had to prove, every single day, that her brains outweighed her womb,' Steph said. I wasn't sure exactly what 'tenure' involved – only that it had been unfairly delayed, and that Steph had sounded less angry than frightened when she'd talked about it.

✣

Desso kept a plastic skull and an assortment of plastic fruit in the art supply cupboard for his still-life classes. Today he arranged the props beside me on a stool for something he called a juxtaposition exercise. I was to keep moving, he said, but in extreme slow motion. The students were supposed to capture the dynamism of the human body in relation to the quietude of the inanimate objects.

I started on my haunches and came up to tiptoes with my hands reaching for the ceiling. I bent my spine, sweeping my arms over the fruit like helicopter blades. Moving slow was way more work than moving fast. At my first break I switched off the space heater.

One of the old ladies liked to paint me with a halo. Sometimes the halo was opaque – she brought in gold leaf to make a glowing Renaissance circle behind my head. Sometimes it was translucent, as if my skull gave off a charge into the air. And one time she asked me to spell my name because she wanted to inscribe it in my halo. She lettered in my whole name, Karen Louise Huls, with a fine-tipped gold pen she used especially for this purpose.

Desso asked me to cross my wrists over my head, bend my knees to one side, and sway back and forth. 'Picture her body in relation to the rest of the tableau,' he told the students. 'Picture her as part of the still life – in tension with it, but always part of the composition as a whole.'

I closed my eyes and imagined red light breaking over my body. My skin ached with the weight and ripeness of the flesh inside. My head tucked itself down to my chest. Picture me blindfolded, I thought. Picture handcuffs biting at my wrists.

The halo lady robed me in blue or green, like the Virgin, but it was always more agreeable to imagine myself as Christ. Picture me crucified, I thought. I posed with outstretched arms, and I imagined blood trickling from my pierced palms, tracking down my arms, and pooling in my armpits. Cherubs fluttered along my ribs to siphon off the holy albumen into their golden bowls. I turned a slow, slow circle on the dais. The artists slashed at their easels with charcoal and paint to capture me.

I was daydreaming again. Picture me a slave to the ancient Blood Code, I thought. I'd liked the sound of it when Dr Esterhazy said it – 'Blood Code' – though I wasn't sure what it was all about, really. Something about matriarchy. Picture me a Maenad, I thought, caught in a net, on display. I pictured myself, pose after pose, imagining snapping photographs of myself next to Desso's plastic fruit.

22. IGNORATIO ELENCHI

(irrelevant conclusion)

No one answered at Raghurst when I clanged through the door and called hello. A draft swept through the hall, and I found the patio door standing six inches open, skewed off its track. Charla was reclining on a blanket at the rear of the yard beside the cedar hedge. I lifted the door back into place, shoving my shoulder hard into the frame to get a smooth slide. Steph had been after the landlord for months to replace the door, arguing that its single-pane glass and cheap metal frame must have cost him a fortune in heating bills over the years.

Charla had spread three or four blankets and piled up four pillows. She lay on her belly reading, her arms crossed under her chin, her feet in wool socks, treading the air.

'Hi,' I said.

'Oh, hi, Karen. Did we sleep together last night?' There was a purple shadow along Charla's jaw with a red scratch in the middle of it. A scab crouched at the corner of her mouth.

'More like this morning,' I said. I took my eyes away from Charla's face, from staring at it, and I looked at the objects scattered all around her: more books, a bag of pistachios, the radio, the cordless phone, and a tray with the teapot, honey pot, and mug. The teaspoon was in her hair, holding the topknot she'd twisted. It looked like Charla had moved her entire bower outdoors.

'I couldn't remember if it was real or not,' she said.

'What are you doing out here? It's cold.'

'It's beautiful.' She rolled to her back and patted the spot beside her. 'Check out this sky.'

O, let us not forget these leaping yellow leaves and the white clouds grazing their skypasture! And underneath us, the many-legged creatures chewing, chewing without cease to make the earth soft again. But it was difficult not to see Charla as a part of the whole, as a natural element within all this seasonal mending and healing. This rosymuzzled, sore-used female, penned here and brooding in her fecundity. I wanted to go get my camera and take her portrait, but it seemed wrong to photograph her in her victimhood. I felt I'd be in danger of aestheticising the violence.

'Can you come with me to the dollar store?' I said.

She grimaced. 'I'm still a bit tender for a bicycle seat.'

'We'll take a cab. It's Halloween tomorrow; we need candy, at least.' She lay here in the backyard like some Leda waiting for her swan, and I wanted to get her out.

In the taxi Charla's white body was close to mine. She opened the window and surfed her hand on the wind-current. Her sleeve billowed, and a dark spiral of her hair escaped from the teaspoon-knot to flutter against her clavicle. I watched how the chill raised the downy hairs on her other arm, too, the one closer to me. I stroked my index finger over the fine skin and felt the sharp-boned wrist where there was another angry red line. The gooseflesh conducted itself from her body to mine. I took my hand back and rubbed my arms for warmth.

'Dyann's afraid to touch me. I can feel it,' Charla said. 'I wanted to fuck this afternoon, and she recoiled. *Recoiled*. There's no other word for it.'

'How could you have wanted ...?' The cabbie's eyes kept sweeping at us in his rearview mirror, and anyway I couldn't repeat what she'd said. I whispered, 'I mean, you're hurt.'

'Yes, it's an unacceptable response, I guess. It is not what one feels or does.'

Charla said such outrageous things. Crazy, unimaginable things. I looked hard for her intention to shock or provoke me, for any sign that she was looking for a reaction, but she just shivered and rolled up the window.

'I want to take you to the hospital,' I said.

She looked at me.

'They can still do a kit on you. It hasn't been forty-eight hours yet.'

'Is that why we're in the car?' she said. 'You want to take me to the hospital?'

I nodded. 'Whatever the others might be saying.'

The car pulled up to the Dollarama. The driver turned, eyebrows up.

'Whatever you decide to do later, we should do the kit first,' I said.

'We should get Halloween candy. I thought that was a good idea.'

'Charla, are you sure?'

She got out of the car. The cabbie shook his head and clicked his tongue at me as I paid the fare.

Charla scratched at his window until he looked out at her, and then blew him a kiss. 'Asshole,' she said. Then she turned to me. 'They all wore condoms. I'm fine. I'll be fine. I don't need the hospital, all right?'

The dollar store had Halloween decorations in one window, Christmas in the other. The entire store seemed to be divided between the two holidays: orange and black for aisles one through four, red and green for the rest. I found an orange lightbulb for our porch and a bag of nylon-fluff web with plastic spiders. The mini chocolate bars were expensive, but as a kid I'd never liked the powdery disc candies or the burnt-tasting toffees in the orange-and-black wrappers. I didn't know how many children might come by Raghurst, either, or if any of my roommates would split the cost with me. Charla had let me pay for the taxi.

She came up the aisle, and I lifted two different boxes. 'What do you think?'

Charla's arms were full of rubber snakes, which she tumbled into my basket at the checkout. I spent an extra few moments pretending to search my purse for my wallet. Finally Charla noticed. 'I'll get it.'

She pulled out a credit card and laid it on the counter. 'I'm going to be Medusa, see?' She dangled one of the snakes over her head. 'I have this so-called executive cruise with this broker friend of my brother's. I'm thinking I'll wear these and nothing else.'

It was the cashier staring, this time.

'You have a date tomorrow?' I said.

'It's not a date. But don't tell Dyann. She hates it when I hang out with older men. Men, period.'

'How old is he?'

'*Old*. My brother's thirty-six, but Raymond's at least forty.'

We carried our bags outside. The sun squatted on the rooftops, igniting shingles and snuffing them out again. We walked together down the sidewalk, edging past a hunched man who swayed and sang inside his overcoat.

'Listen, Charla,' I began. 'I get that I wasn't supposed to be there, at that party. I get that you guys didn't mean for me to find out about Operation Black Bag.'

'You don't have to apologise, Karen.' She put down her bag and raised her hand, and a taxi swung into a U-turn to pull alongside us.

'I'm not apologising,' I said when we were in the car. 'I'm asking for an explanation.'

'About what?'

I slapped my palm down on the seat between us. 'Don't pretend everything's normal. Don't pretend this was all part of some plan. Whatever Dyann planned for at that party, she didn't expect *this* to happen to you.'

Charla looked out the window and rubbed at her bruised jaw. Then she nodded. 'You're right, actually. I think she's pretty traumatised.'

'*Dyann* is traumatised? It didn't happen to her!'

'I expected it, though,' she said. 'I knew pretty much exactly how it would go.'

'You know this is straight out of the textbook, right, Charla?'

'What textbook?'

'The shame? The self-blaming? That's a symptom of being assaulted, an effect of it. That's you experiencing trauma.'

She smiled. 'I think it's a brochure, actually, not a textbook. From the Women's Centre, right? Steph wrote the copy for that one.'

I was being a jerk, she meant, for lecturing her. For telling her how she should be responding to this, feeling about it, even. What had she said before? That her response – or her lack of response – was *unacceptable*. Not only was I being a jerk, I was treading ground she and Dyann had already covered.

Charla brushed my hair from my cheek and tucked it behind my ear, an oddly motherly gesture that made me feel simultaneously less ashamed of myself and less certain in my outrage. 'Has it ever been you, down in that room?' she said.

'The Express? God, no, I'm not –' I was about to say 'not the type', and checked myself. 'I don't let myself get that far gone.'

'You mean that drunk?'

'Well, even if I did. They kind of know me over there.'

23. OMINATIO

(prophecy of evil)

I hadn't invited Mike over for Halloween but he showed up anyway, just as I was scooping the last of the candy into the swollen pillowcases of three preteen zombie brides. Mike was dressed as some sort of desert pilgrim – a bedsheet toga, sandals, and a tall walking stick adorned with what Mike confirmed was a hank of human hair. 'It's Spartacus's – you know that guy Steve?' he said, and I remembered a quiet brother with a ponytail. 'They pinned him down. We got all kinds of costumes out of it. Pits made himself a goatee, even.'

'Gross.'

Mike chuckled. 'Yes, it's utterly foul.' He slipped his arms around me. 'Look at that: we go together,' he said.

'How? I'm a fortune-teller.' I'd tied a scarf around my head and borrowed a long floral skirt from Charla. The skirt had little bells sewn along the hem.

'Well, we're both nomads, right? I'm Carlos Castaneda.'

Shrill screams came from next door. An ashen-faced boy vaulted the hedge onto our driveway, and his friends followed, jeering at him.

I told Mike about the horror tableau Jake and Wheeler had rigged up in their tree. Jake sat in a lawn chair wearing a blood-spattered hockey mask and holding an air rifle in his lap. Whenever a kid came up the walk he'd yell, 'Look out behind you!' He'd fire the rifle, and Wheeler would 'fall' from the bottom branch with a plastic axe in his hands and an enormous bloody hole shot through his chest. They'd practised all afternoon with a noose and a climbing harness but hadn't been able to get the lynching realistic-looking enough. Shooting was the next best thing.

Charla and Steph joined us on the porch amid the clamour of our door-bells. 'At least keep the snaps fastened until you're out on the water,' Steph was saying. 'They won't even let you on the boat like that.'

The last of the trick-or-treating boys froze on the steps, his eyes goggling. He stepped back, tripping a little in his haste to escape, and Charla snickered. I turned and saw that she'd donned her Medusa costume. Her hair was teased and curled into a wild thicket throughout which the snakes were artfully intertwined. She wore low-slung black leather pants and knee-high boots, but she was naked from the waist up. She'd painted targets – concentric rings of red, green, and orange – around her nipples. Her breasts were full, round, and white. A stripy bruise across her ribs seemed only to emphasise the virgin purity of her skin.

'What's your vote, Karen,' Charla said, 'vest or no vest?' She turned a circle, hands on hips, revealing another, smaller bruise below her shoulder blade.

'Karen, tell her she can't not wear the vest,' said Steph.

Charla threaded her arms into a leather biker vest with silver snaps. 'It's *more* provocative,' she argued, tilting her cleavage forward to demonstrate. 'Plus it defeats the whole point. The Gorgon is supposed to shock, not entice.'

'Did you show Dyann?' I said.

Charla grinned. 'She's beside herself. "It's not a display of power if you're wearing it with *men* around," blah blah blah. The poor thing. Be nice to her, will you?'

'I'm Mike,' Mike said from behind me.

I jumped. I'd momentarily forgotten him. 'Guys, this is Mike. This is Steph and Charla.'

'Hi, Mike,' they said politely.

Steph lit a cigarette. 'You know what Freud says, right? It's not actually Medusa's *head* at all. It's the sight of her pussy that turns men to stone. It's the shock of castration. Being confronted with that possibility. Her head, the snakes – it's just a symbolic displacement, like an image in a dream.'

I eyed Mike as my roommates debated the subject a few minutes longer. He seemed impressed by Steph's brains, nodding a little at each point she made. He kept his eyes off Charla. He had wrapped his arm around my waist when I introduced him, and he kept it there even when I bent to retrieve the empty candy bowl from the steps.

A self-righteous pressure built under my ribs. It was one thing to shut me out of their plans, to use me to get at the frat; it was quite another to stand out here half-naked dazzling poor Mike Morton with their psychosexual pyrotechnics.

'Did you know these two were at the S&M party the other night?' I heard myself say.

'What?' Mike said.

'Steph and Charla were at the S&M party,' I said, and this time the words found a home in my mouth. 'Dyann and Marie-Jeanne too. Weren't they, you guys?'

Steph, red-faced, pulled deep on her cigarette and looked off over the hedge. Charla looked from me to Mike and back again with wide, dark eyes.

'Too bad we missed you,' Mike said. 'We had an awards thing to go to.' He flicked my shoulder in mock-sternness. 'Did you invite them and then forget?'

'Congrats, by the way,' Charla said, 'on your awards.'

In the end she left for her Halloween cruise party wearing the vest unsnapped, flapping open.

'Do you have a little time for me?' Mike whispered after we jangled in through the door.

'Right now?'

'In that skirt, with you on top. I'm not even wearing boxers – I shall merely lift my robes.' He pushed against me, making me feel his erection.

We climbed the stairs to my room. I'd hung my four best tree-planting photos above my desk, but Mike didn't notice them. He lay back on my bed and rolled on a rubber, and I was lubricated just enough to wriggle down onto it without pain.

'You're only horny because of Medusa,' I accused him.

He shook his head, eyes closed. 'That kind of display doesn't do it for me. It's so crass, like a bush tribe or something. Like something in heat.'

'Heat' came out in a grunt. I laughed. He'd come so fast. It was so easy.

We kissed awhile, and then Mike said that Bruce was picking him up in a minute to go out with the others.

'Where?' He hadn't nagged me at all about coming out with him for Halloween, I realised.

'Some peeler bar. Don't worry, though, I've already found what I was after tonight.' He strummed his fingers at his crotch, making the toga wiggle and leap.

'You've fulfilled your desert quest,' I said.

'I achieved my higher self.'

'You met your spirit animal.'

'I was one with the universe!' He laughed. Mike loved it when we chimed in together in a joke like this. He liked telling me things, too – sharing something he'd seen or read or done, and hearing me respond – but he was happiest at these moments of consensus between us, when each of us augmented and complemented the statement of the other. It was a very specific type of interaction. I wondered if my own conversational preferences were obvious to him, too, and what they might be.

I saw Mike to the door just as the car pulled up to the curb. I couldn't see Bruce in the driver's seat, and he didn't get out of the car. After they were gone I wandered over to where I could hear the boys still fooling around in the tree. Josh's voice had joined Jake's in the upper branches, and their argument about how to untangle the rappelling ropes was muted by the paper-crumple of dry leaves drifting from the shaken limbs.

Wheeler sprawled in the grass, sipping from a test-tube shooter while Stick filled the rest of the rack from a beaker.

'The chem labs must spend half their budget on replacing those things,' I said, thinking of Mike's potions cabinet in the GBC kitchen, similarly stocked.

'Want one? They're actually not bad,' Wheeler said.

'Told you,' Stick said. 'You just have to get past the name and it's quite pleasant.'

I sat beside Stick and tipped back my tube. Cherry brandy. 'Ew, it tastes like high school,' I said.

They laughed and laughed.

'What's so funny?'

'It's Menarche,' Wheeler said. 'I swear, that's the official name: Menarche!

I followed a recipe and everything.'

'Mm, yummy yummy.' I drank another test tube just to impress them.

Stick dug in his pocket. 'Hold out your hand,' he said, and gave me a quarter.

'What's this for?'

'I'm crossing your palm with silver. I want my fortune told.'

I'd spent the better part of that afternoon on my bed with *Uncovering the Secrets of the Tarot* from the library. Stick was the only one who'd asked for a fortune. It made me suddenly, fiercely fond of him. 'For a quarter you only get one card,' I said.

We sat cross-legged on the bristly brown lawn, knees touching, and he shuffled the deck as I instructed him. His lips moved and his eyelids fluttered as he visualised his Central Query.

'Tell the cards your full name.'

'Simon Alistair Pinkney the Second,' he intoned.

I shushed Wheeler's snorting laughter and fanned out the cards. Stick chose the Moon. 'Wow,' I said, 'you've been drinking too much Menarche.'

'Be serious,' he said. His face was serious.

'Okay, well, the Moon card stands for emotions, the stuff below the surface. You're following a dark road without knowing where it leads. The dog and the wolf there are the flip sides of your subconscious: the tame and the wild selves. You are struggling with insecurity and fear. Self-doubt.'

'Ha,' Wheeler said. 'No wonder you're so overconfident at Magic. You're, like, compensating.'

'I'm not overconfident. I'm just plain confident, from kicking your ass all the time.'

'Oops. Wait,' I said. Stick had laid the Moon card on his knee facing me. I'd forgotten that that meant I was supposed to reverse the reading. 'It's not fear, actually. It's the overcoming of fears. You've got access to the treasures of the pool here.' I pointed to the water with the crayfish crawling out. 'And your intuition is deep and trustworthy.'

'Oh come on, you're just flirting with him now. I question your authenticity.' Wheeler tried to tip Stick over and received a punch in return.

'I asked the cards about you, actually,' Stick told me. 'Whether I have a shot.'

Underneath the smarmy pretend-longing on his face there was a layer of real longing. I billowed my skirt to dump the cards in the grass and put on a gypsy accent: 'Never reveal your Central Query. Now you have jinxed your fortune!'

'Nah, I'm unjinxable.' He helped me gather the cards back into the box. 'I have the treasures of the moon pool, remember.'

*

Dyann, Steph, and Marie-Jeanne had set up the VCR at the foot of Charla's bower to watch *Paris Is Burning*.

'Go get yourself a glass and the other bottle of wine from the kitchen,' Steph said.

'And grab the Cheezies!' Dyann called up the stairs.

I squeezed in beside Marie-Jeanne. On the screen a black drag queen was putting on earrings. 'What did I miss?'

'Nothing,' Marie-Jeanne said. 'It's a documentary.'

'I heard your boyfriend finally got to meet your roommates tonight,' Dyann said. 'I heard you told him we were at their party.'

Her tone suggested I should consider apologising for this. 'Listen, you guys told me you wanted to do *research* at the frat house,' I said. 'I thought you just wanted to see what goes on.'

'Well, we did see what goes on,' Steph said.

'It was an experiment, is all,' Marie-Jeanne said. 'Like an anthropology experiment.'

'A Women's Studies experiment,' Steph corrected her.

I said, 'Why would you need an experiment, though? That room, that house. Those guys are completely predictable. They're like bulls in a pasture or something. You don't let a cow into the pasture without expecting some kind of mass mating.'

Dyann half sat up so she could see me over Steph. 'Actually, your analogy doesn't work. If I brought a cow into the barn, the bulls would tear each other apart. That'd happen with males of pretty much any species of animal during a rut.'

I thought of the brothers chanting, 'Rut! Rut! Rut!' to the Nine Inch Nails song, hurling themselves atop each other. That aggressive group hug.

On-screen two drag queens were yelling at each other over loud dance music. The taller one snatched a feather boa from the shorter one's shoulders.

If Dyann had been upset or unsettled yesterday, she'd certainly calmed down today. 'Come on,' she pressed. 'Haven't you ever seen those videos of elk during mating season? They'll attack cars, passing trains, anything that crosses their path on the way to the female. Those frat brothers, though. They sure weren't in any kind of competition for Charla.'

My hands shook. I wanted, suddenly, to put them around Dyann's throat. 'Because you trussed her up for them like a piece of meat.'

Her dreadlocks leapt. She must have seen my rage but she kept her gaze steady on mine. 'No, Karen,' she said. 'They don't compete for women. They don't compete for sex. That's the whole point. They fucking *collude*.'

O Dyann the serene, her tongue like a blade. Speaker of the last word.

✳

In bed that night I thought of Charla in the backyard, not in her portable bower but topless, painted, lying in the grass. I pictured Bruce happening upon her lying there, discovering her. Easing his heavy golden body down onto her small white one.

I was pent up. I came with a shudder more painful than pleasurable and spent a few minutes chasing down additional orgasms to compensate. I fell asleep, finally, with the picture of Bruce and Charla still radiant in my mind.

The women of Raghurst hold forth amongst themselves on the subject of the cinema:

Dyann: There are over twice as many men than women on movie screens, and yet women are involved in sex scenes twice as often as men. Hetero sex, of course. Think about that, Karen. You go see a hundred movies –

Karen: I know what the statistic means, Dyann.

Dyann: Why doesn't it piss you off? Why doesn't it stop you from spending your time on that drivel?

Steph: I have two rules, if I'm going to spend ninety minutes of my life on a movie. One: it has to have at least two women in it. Two: they have to have a conversation about something other than men.

Dyann: You got that from *Dykes to Watch Out For*, didn't you? What's crazy is how few movies pass the test.

Steph: Well, Virginia Woolf said it first, about books. She pointed out the lack of female friendships in novels before Austen. Women were only ever portrayed in their relation to men.

Karen: Okay, but what about watching movies for pleasure? For simple nostalgia? I go to the theater for an escape, mostly. Just to enjoy it.

Dyann: Pleasure is political, Karen. Enjoying something is a political act.

24. THESMOS

(law of kingly authority)

O, let us not forget why we daily traverse these elm-lined walkways and dappled oaken floors! Here are the eternal starveling scholars pressing their ribs to their desks, parsing Proust and Artaud. Here are the timeless bespectacled laboratory technicians bent over their glowing microbial compounds. Here the rats run their wheels and mazes without pause. Here the great machines of knowledge never sleep. In the face of such, what are we but chaff and noise?

I went to my classes. I carried armloads of books from the library to my bedroom and back again. I studied my textbooks. I sat in the computer lab and read and stared and typed until my eyes shriveled in my head. In these endeavours I was surrounded at all times by other students studying hard, working hard. Not everyone was as disengaged from the idea of academic striving as the GBC boys. Not everyone was part of the Bored Horde, floating through this ivy-wreathed playground from party to party until they were handed their diplomas and introduced, the following day, at their fathers' workplaces. Many wanted to excel as much as I did. Many wanted what I wanted: to experience *cerebrum thermonous*, the mind kindled and the intellect forged in the fires of scholarly study and debate.

I was starting to suspect, however, that all my courses had the same themes and all my assignments asked for the same responses. Dr Davis taught us how, in A *Midsummer Night's Dream*, Shakespeare toys with popular ideas of memory. Titania has a better claim on the changeling child than Oberon does because she remembers his mother, her friend. Oberon's spell induces multilevel amnesia, so that Titania forgets about the boy, falls in love with Bottom, and then forgets this love, too, upon waking.

In my research for Dr Esterhazy's essay I read that for the Greeks, the Furies were champions of cultural memory. They intervened in the drama to enforce the Blood Code, the old matriarchal laws based on kinship, vengeance, and debts to the dead. The Furies insisted on the lessons of the past that the forward-thinking heroes of the myths preferred to forget.

Everything I learned was about memory versus the obliteration of memory. Traumatic amnesia, a *Psychology Today* article stated, must not be confused with ordinary forgetting. Not all childhood abuse recalled in adulthood has been actively repressed for self-protection. Some of it just fades away, along with so many other lived events.

*

The next week was another John Hughes Tuesday. The film was *Pretty in Pink*, and I waited for the bus under liver-coloured November clouds threatening rain. I came in late and stood a few minutes in the back corner while my eyes adjusted to the dark. In the screen-light I picked out Bruce's golden head in the sparse audience. He was slouched close to me, near the back, one tawny arm slung in a casual headlock around a girl. I chose a seat on their side but way up the aisle, fifth row from the screen.

I couldn't concentrate on the movie. It bothered me that the actors were supposed to be in high school but were so clearly older, older than me even, except maybe Molly Ringwald. The men especially, even the extras, had the kind of smooth skin and broad, muscled chests that most of the GBC brothers wouldn't fully grow into for another three or four years. James Spader's hair was thinning, even.

A big, sleek body slipped into the theatre seat beside mine. A hand scooped up my hand and threaded its warm fingers through mine.

'Hi,' Bruce whispered. Heavengoing Bruce. Godsfavoured. There was popcorn on his breath.

I glanced back to his empty seat and then regretted it; now I had to acknowledge that I'd noticed the girl with him. 'Am I your other date?' I asked, trying for levity.

'It's temporary,' he said. 'How are you?'

'Good. You?'

'Good. Well, good *now*. That was one motherbitch of a hangover, after that party last week. I missed a midterm.'

Someone said 'Shh,' behind us, and for a minute we watched the screen.

Bruce let go of my hand, slumped way down, and beckoned me to do the same so he could cup a hand to my ear. The fabric scratched my back; I curled onto one hip to get low enough.

'Did we mess around?' he whispered.

'That memorable, was it?' I joked, but when I turned to look at him he wasn't smiling. 'No. God, Bruce. We did not *mess around*.'

Someone said, 'Shh.'

He leaned in again to whisper. 'Did we do our middle-of-the-night thing? Our slow-dance thing in the can?' His breath strolled on soft feet across my skin. 'Slow-dance' bounced down my vertebrae, a secret on springs.

I shook my head no.

'But you would remember?' he said.

'Of course.'

'I don't remember anything, I blacked out so bad. Nobody remembers.'

'Everybody was badly trashed,' I said.

His hand, still half-cupped, rested against my collarbone, and his other hand had landed on my knee. He seemed unaware of this. 'Did I do anything gross?'

'Like what?'

'Like, I don't know. Was I being an asshole?'

'You have to remember the context,' I said. But the context of that party was Charla in the Black Bag. Sheri Asselin on the gold car. They must be telling stories about it all by now at the frat. No wonder Bruce was worried.

'Even by GBC standards,' he insisted. 'Was I being an asshole?'

'Not to me.' I straightened a little in my seat, and his hand slid off my knee.

'Okay,' he said, and turned his eyes to the screen.

Molly Ringwald's arms were crossed tight over her chest. She was crying. Her 1980s shoulder pads and elevated bangs were unflattering. What did you do? I wanted to say. You must know what you did.

Bruce leaned over again. 'You would tell me, right, if I was being an asshole? To you or to anyone else?'

'Sure. I'd tell you,' I said.

'Okay. Cool.' He glanced back to his date. 'So, this was nice. Can I take you out again sometime?'

'My parents want to meet you first,' I said.

He grinned. 'I'll bring a corsage.' He lifted my hand and touched it to his lips before ducking back down the aisle.

*

I walked home from the cinema in the pallor of night's edge. The sidewalks were narrower and less populous than the ones I walked every day on campus. The fences, the lawns, the brick storefronts, the street signage – everything was flatter and duller than on campus, leached of colour. There was no grounds crew out here. No Campus Cleanup Tuesdays. No Walksafe program, no Adopt-a-Tree, no guerrilla art troupes, no Outward Bound Society demonstrating rappelling techniques on the clock tower, no knitting circle or mindfulness circle or drumming circle on the quad. No quad. The real world had less money.

I thought about how wealthy everyone at school was, how easy it would be for them all after graduation. An Ivy League degree was a key to any door, my parents liked to say. But plain old money was a pretty good key too. Everyone was rich – even Dyann, who loudly spurned everything bourgeois. She could go be a full-time activist after graduation for as many years as she wanted and still slip right back into the upper-middle-class world whenever she finally tired of it. Even the boys next door, with their house devoid of furniture, were rich.

I was envious of all of them. Stick, for example. Fine-boned, moon-faced Simon Alastair Pinkney II, future chemical engineer, fully funded by a merit scholarship from a major pharmaceutical company as well as by family money. Secure in his future successes and yet spritely and silly, Stick was also, apparently, in touch with his deeper emotional self. A boy like that didn't need a fraternity for validation.

Every reading is also a reading for the tarot practitioner, the book had said. The Moon card had faced me, so my fortune wasn't reversed. The dark path between the towers. The well of insecurities. The wild dog and the tame dog yapping at my heels.

25. INDIGNATIO

(arousing indignation)

Friday before lunch I stopped in at the *Campus Eye* office to print my Thucydides response paper for Women and Myth.

'Karen, is that you?' The door to the interview room had cracked open, and Jen Swinburn's blonde head peeked out. 'Come in here. You need to see this.'

The interview room was a tiny closet, the entire floor space of which was usually occupied by a small folding table and two plastic chairs. Today it was crammed even tighter with a TV cart and two additional members of the paper's editorial staff.

'Come in, come in, close the door,' Jen said, and I had to squeeze hip to hip with Derek, the layout assistant, in order to close the door behind me.

'We felt we needed privacy,' Derek said.

'Go ahead, Gita,' Jen said, and after the copy editor bent to press Play on the VCR, Jen flicked off the light.

'Shit, it better not be eating the tape,' Derek said. The image on-screen wavered and disappeared under static.

'It only does that after it's been paused,' Gita told him. 'See? It's good now.'

Damage, was my first thought – that Gita was wrong, and the tape must be damaged after all. The TV screen spat red light over the tiny room, flushing the faces beside me and licking flames through Jen's blonde hair. Then the sound kicked in, turned up loud – a hum of distortion, a murmur of voices, a distant bass thump – and I looked into the red light, and the faces beside me and the people and the entire room and my whole body poured away from me like water down a drain.

It was the Black Bag. It was the weight bench and the frame. It was the red bulb overhead. It was a female body naked orange glowing handcuffed blindfolded. Her back was to the camera, but it was Charla.

I put my hand over my mouth.

'Are you okay?' said a voice. Jen's voice.

The frat brothers – there were two of them – moved in and out of the frame like shoppers testing the merchandise. They turned Charla's face, palmed her breasts, nudged her ankles farther apart. They were talking, but their voices were muffled on the tape, indistinct.

One of the boys, naked from the waist down, climbed onto the bench so that his crotch was level with Charla's face. He said something, and she turned her head away, but he grabbed her hair to hold her still.

It was Alec. The video cut him off at the shoulders now – his face had never turned fully to the camera – but I knew him by the thick, dark hair on his arms. His thighs were hairy, too, and between his legs the thatch was so dense that his cock was barely visible.

The other boy undid his jeans, turned off-camera, and reappeared with a rubber in his hand. He tore the package open with his teeth, dropped it, swore loudly, and picked it up again. He staggered and swayed as he fumbled to roll the rubber into place. Finally, belt buckle clacking, he stalked around Charla and cupped her buttocks with both hands. He said something that made Alec laugh, and Charla jerked back her head and made a long, low noise before Alec thrust again into her mouth.

The image froze. 'I can't watch this, not again,' said Gita. 'I feel like I'm going to puke.'

The overhead light scalded off a layer of my skin. I took my hand from my mouth, and both my hands curled into fists. Damage, I thought. Tatters of red light trailed behind my eyes.

'Karen?' Jen's voice sounded very soft.

I blinked at her.

'Is it you?'

'What?' I said.

'On the tape. Is that you?'

'No. God, Jen! No, it's not me.'

'Sorry,' Derek said. He was red. 'It's just, she kind of looks like you. Or like she could be you, if … We just weren't sure.'

'But that *is* Gamma Beta Chi, isn't it?' said Jen. 'That's the room they call the Black Bag, right?'

I nodded. 'W-where did you get the tape?'

'I knew it!' Jen crowed. 'I mean, I've never been down there, obviously, but I've heard about that weight bench and the centrefolds on the walls.'

'Where did you get it?'

'It came in the campus mail this morning,' she said.

Gita had braced one knee against the wall and was writing rapid, shaky lines in her notebook.

'Two minutes thirty-four: that's when the third dude takes over,' Derek was telling her.

'Don't call them "dudes",' said Gita. 'God.'

'How long is the video?' I said.

'Almost six minutes,' Jen told me.

'Can you believe it?' Derek said. 'Four sexual assaults in six minutes. I mean, this is it for those frat brats. They're all expelled for sure.'

'Expelled?' said Gita. 'They're going to jail!'

'Who else was – how many other boys?' I said.

'There's only one other boy, but that hairy one comes back for seconds,' said Derek.

'Don't talk about it like that,' said Gita. 'Don't say stuff like that.'

'Like what?' said Derek.

'Like "back for seconds". Don't use slang, period.' She was close to tears.

'That's not slang.' Derek looked at Gita and lifted his hands. 'Okay. Whatever.'

'No, she's right,' said Jen. 'We're the ones responsible for this now. We're responsible for what it means. We have to do it properly, from the start.'

Charla, I thought. Oh Charla. 'Maybe you should erase it,' I said.

All three looked at me.

'Or give it to the police. Isn't it illegal to film people like that?'

Jen jabbed a finger at the screen. 'Karen, what's illegal is what they're doing to that poor girl! People need to know about this.'

'Who?'

'Everyone!'

'No, I mean, who's doing it to her? You can't see their faces in the video.' Damage, damage, damage. The word came to me again and again – I saw it, more than thought it, like text scrolling across the inside of my skull.

'Well, someone will be able to identify them eventually,' Derek said.

'We have an idea about one of the perpetrators already,' Gita was saying. She moved her pen down her notes, looking for the name.

'It's Bruce Comfort,' Jen supplied.

'We can't say that for sure,' Gita said.

I took a breath. 'I want to see,' I said.

'I mean, nobody could mistake Bruce Comfort, right?' Jen said, looking at me like she expected me to back her up. 'With that body? You don't need to see his face.' She gestured for Gita to resume the tape.

'Not me,' said Gita. 'I've seen all I can take for now.' She squeezed past us and opened the door to the interview room.

'There you guys are! You have to come see this.' It was Janine from the Women's Centre down the hall. Breathless. Trembling.

We looked at each other. 'What is it?' said Gita.

'It's a sex tape. It looks like rape.'

*

The *Campus Eye* staff had missed the note tucked in the envelope with its copy of the videotape, but the Women's Centre girls had found theirs. Everyone gathered by the windows to examine it while Gita ran back down the hall to check the envelope.

The Wall of Shame had grown exponentially since I'd last seen it. I'd heard Dyann brag about its popularity – how random women were coming in with stuff to post, how it was the best outreach the Centre had ever achieved – but now I was seeing it with my own eyes. Thirty or forty photos of boys were pinned to the board now. *Told my friend I gave lousy head,* I read, and *Put his name on my essay, got me a zero for cheating.*

The two notes, Gita confirmed, were identical: a single line on regular inkjet paper read, *Copies of this video have been sent to local media and key college administrative offices.*

'Why didn't they send it to the police?' someone asked.

'It's a leak, obviously,' said Derek. 'They want the media to spread this, and the police would just hold it as evidence.'

'What do you mean, a "leak"?' I said.

'A fraternity filming its own gang bangs? Even those guys aren't stupid enough to let that get around by accident. One of them is obviously having some kind of moral crisis about it, so he decided to leak the tape.'

'Right.' Jen was warming to the theory. 'He's not about to testify against his friends, like, officially. But he can blow the whole thing open in the media.'

'Someone should call Dyann Brooks-Morriss,' Janine said. 'She'll want in on this one for sure.'

Dyann. With the sound of her name came the smell of the Black Bag. Thick and sour, furred with sex. My throat closed as I remembered. I tasted bile.

'Karen?'

I looked up at them. 'What?'

'Dyann and Steph. Are they at home?' Janine must have remembered that I was their roommate.

'I don't know,' I said. I looked at my watch. 'I have to go to work, though – I have the lunch shift.'

Jen followed me into the hall. 'Who is that girl on the tape, Karen, if it's not you? You must know her.'

'I'm not all that tight with GBC, Jen,' I said.

'But you're dating Mike Morton. Grace told me,' she explained, when I must have looked surprised. 'Look, Karen,' – she leaned in, spoke low and fast – 'you think I don't know it's Alec on that tape, even if it doesn't show his face?

Grace and I are friends, all right? She's going to be devastated by this. I'm going to have to break it to her right away, before it gets around. But that's … it's nothing, compared to what the victim must be suffering. Not to mention what she will be suffering, when this goes public.'

'What do you mean?'

She shook her head. 'They'll blame her for everything. They'll call her a slut, say she set them up on purpose, blacken her reputation, turn all her friends against her. I've seen it before. Hell, it's all over that file in the Women's Centre; you can read it for yourself. Frat boys will say anything to protect each other.'

Oh Charla. 'Maybe we shouldn't be asking who she is then,' I said. 'For sure we shouldn't publish her name in the paper.'

She bit her lip. 'It would be a further violation.'

'Exactly. A violation.' I tried to keep the relief out of my voice. 'If anything, we should argue for her right to stay anonymous. Try to get out there with that before the frat brothers start talking.'

'But we could talk to the girl. Get her story, so it comes out right in front. That would counter the victimisation, right? It would give her a voice.'

'I don't know. Maybe,' I said, miserably. 'I have to go, Jen.'

We were halfway down the stairs. I paused, worried she would follow me all the way to the Faculty Club. But she stopped at the carved oak newel post on the landing and laced her fingers over the griffin's head, stroking his feathers with her thumbs. I could see the videotape exerting its pull on her: she glanced back over her shoulder, as if it had called her name. Finally she said, 'We'll talk, okay?' and turned back.

26. CONFUTATIO

(refuting arguments)

Later I stopped back at the *Campus Eye*. The interview room was locked, but we kept a key on a magnet in the filing cabinet. I sat down and made myself watch the tape all the way through. Alec – he was the one Derek said came back for 'seconds', before the video cut to empty-tape snow. Alec's last name was Moretti. All their surnames were listed on the minutes of the house meetings posted on the second-floor bulletin board. The brothers always referred to Alec's car as the Ginomobile, and at first I'd thought it was just because of its tacky sparkle-blue paint and racing-stripe decals. The joke had seemed less funny when I realised Alec was actually Italian.

Eric Vine was the second boy, maybe. And Bruce Comfort. Jen was right, of course: there was no mistaking that chest, those biceps, that broad back. Even with the red-bulb lighting there was no mistaking that honedgolden skin. Like the others, Bruce reeled and stumbled around the mirrored room. He took off his T-shirt, dropping it on the floor. He ran his palms down Charla's ribs, over her hips.

This time through, I noticed how carefully the video was edited to ensure that no one's identity was exposed. Whenever one of the boys turned toward the camera, or Charla's body swung around so that she faced the camera, the footage was cut and skipped forward a moment or two, so that we never saw anyone's face full-on.

'Condom,' Charla said to Bruce when he opened his belt and fly. The sound was distorted, but I could still hear the words. 'Please. Please get a condom.' She sounded weary. Resigned.

Bruce ignored her. He pressed his forehead into the back of Charla's neck and set up a lazy, haphazard humping motion with his hips. He was nowhere near the right spot. He must have been prodding somewhere along her inner thigh, and Charla was quiet and still.

I couldn't watch but I watched and watched. His buttocks were smooth and round but they flexed as he thrust and became extensions of his lean, powerful legs. He was talking the whole time, nothing the microphone could pick up. His muffled voice was the voice of a bear with its snout in a honey jar.

Then he stopped. 'Fuck, I am drunk.' Loud and clear. And he pulled away from Charla, hiked up his jeans, and tucked himself, half-erect, into his boxers. 'Sorry, sorry,' he said, 'I'm way too shitfaced for this.' He gave Charla's shoulder a friendly pat. Belt buckle flapping, he turned for the door but lost his balance – tripped on his own shirt – and had to catch himself against the wall. He felt his way to the knob like a blind man and fumbled with it for several seconds before staggering out the door.

He must have gone out to the backyard, I realised. I'd found him out there in the lawn chair, still unbuckled, the morning after the party.

Here I sat excusing Bruce. Here I sat, even before the video footage dissolved into gray static fuzz, already telling myself Bruce wasn't really interested in sex with Charla. He didn't really know what he was doing. He'd been too drunk to know what he was doing, he hadn't remembered anything afterward, he'd needed to ask *me* if I remembered him doing anything ungentlemanly at the party. O smoothskinned sunsouled Bruce, unsullied by bad intentions! 'Sorry,' he'd said to Charla, after all – but of course I knew the apology had not been for fucking her but for being too drunk to fuck her properly.

*

When I got home my roommates were drinking wine in the living room. I dropped my backpack and stood in the doorway. 'Are we celebrating?'

Marie-Jeanne gave a tense little laugh. They'd been waiting for me.

'You filmed it. You just set up a camera and hung Charla up there like bait on a hook.'

Charla snorted into her glass. 'Thanks a lot.'

I was really only talking to Dyann, though. 'And then you were like, "Come and get it, boys, she's all yours."'

Dyann rolled her eyes and huffed to her feet, but Steph reached up from the couch beside her and pulled her back down.

'You were hiding in there,' I pressed. 'The whole time they were coming in and out. Were you crouching in the closet or something?'

'I told you she would be pissed off,' Marie-Jeanne said. *Peezed*, it sounded like.

I rounded on her. 'And you. You were in on it too. And the boys next door.'

'Do they know yet at the fraternity?' Dyann's voice was casual. She rested her chin on her fist and gazed out the front window as though already bored with whatever response I might make. Dyann the battlefast general, playing it cool. Closing ranks.

I fetched a mug from the kitchen, took my time with opening a new wine bottle, then poured the mug full. Raghurst was brimming with homey aromas: bread, curry, Charla's cinnamon tea. I took three big swallows of wine and topped up my cup.

There was silence in the living room as they waited, and this gratified me, and then the fact that I was gratified by it stoked my anger further. They'd lied to me. Played me, at least. Or just made sure I couldn't stand in their way, couldn't jeopardise their plans. What I didn't know wouldn't hurt me. Loose lips sink ships. Dyann the strategist, the master of the campaign.

I returned to the living room and sank cross-legged to the floor beside Marie-Jeanne.

Dyann glared at Steph, who was nervously plucking the spring on the arm of the reading light. 'Do you mind?'

Steph stopped, her eyes on me. Their eyes were all on me – all except for Charla's. She knelt at the coffee table stripping the leaves off sprigs of dried herb. There was a tidy pile of naked stems on one side and a white porcelain mortar and pestle on the other.

'What are you making?' I asked her.

'Throat remedy,' she said. 'Stocking stuffers.' She held up a miniature mason jar with a screw-ring lid. 'What do you think I should call it?'

'What's that smell?' Up close it was pungent and Mediterranean.

'Oregano, mostly.'

'Oh, for fuck's sake!' Dyann exploded. 'What do you want, Karen? Do you want me to apologise to your frat buddies?' She'd raked her fingers through her hair, and her dreads stood out in furious disarray.

'Most of the fraternity is away on a road trip,' I said. 'It's the GBC Eastern Convention. A fact I could have told you if you'd let me in on your big media rollout plans.'

They were quiet.

'The Women's Centre was frantic to locate you guys,' I said. 'Did they call? Did you go over there?'

'I went,' said Steph.

'What did you tell them?'

Steph glanced at Dyann. 'Nothing. I pretended not to know anything about it. But I argued for taking a strong stand, obviously.'

'A stand on what?' I said. 'What are they supposed to say about it? It's an anonymous sex tape. No source, no witnesses, no confirmation of time or location. It could be a hoax. They could be actors. Charla could be an actress, or a pro-ho they hired.'

'A pro-ho,' Steph repeated.

'That's what they call prostitutes. Call girls. They hire them once in a while, or they get freebies sent to their parties.'

Dyann leaned forward. 'You're telling us that sex workers will offer their services at the fraternity for free?'

I shrugged. 'Or their pimps send them, or their madams or whatever. I don't know. It's a promotional thing. Those guys never pay for anything.'

'Promo pro-hos,' said Charla, drawing a snort from Marie-Jeanne.

It wasn't true, about the free call girls. I'd heard stories about prostitutes at parties, table dancers in the living room, that sort of thing, but I'd improvised the promotional part, aiming to shock my roommates in retaliation for the shock of seeing that video at school.

'We should have written the statement,' Dyann said.

'No,' Steph said, firmly. 'We're not terrorists, Dyann. The tape has to speak for itself. The master's tools, remember?'

'What does that mean, "the master's tools"?' I asked.

'It's Audre Lorde,' Steph said. '*Use the master's tools to dismantle the master's house.* A sex tape is the perfect tool here. It's an appropriate reversal, on every level: ethical, technological, aesthetic.'

'We thought it would raise too many questions if we wrote a statement,' Charla explained to me. 'Like, who's the author? Who's behind the camera?'

'Except now they're not asking any questions at all,' Dyann said. 'Now it's just another frat party.'

'They want to interview Charla,' I said.

'Please tell me you didn't give them Charla's name,' she said. Dyann the armoured warrior standing at attention.

'Not yet. Jen said it would just exacerbate the violation, to publish the victim's name without giving her the chance to go out with her story first. I sort of let her run with that.'

'We need Karen on our side, Dyann,' Charla said.

'But I don't want to be on your side,' I said. 'Whatever reasons you had, Charla – it doesn't change the fact that now they're going to come after you. They're going to blame the whole thing on you. They'll take you apart piece by piece to protect themselves. And Dyann's just going to stand there and let it happen. Dyann just stood there and watched, and let you get ...' I hesitated.

Dyann made a sucking noise like she'd tasted something bad. 'You were going to say "get raped", right? You were going to say I let her *get raped*. Like *get wet*, like I left her out in the rain or something.'

She stood up and pointed her empty glass at me. 'That's what they want us to do, isn't it? They want us to treat rape like a naturally occurring phenomenon, like weather. They want us to sit around passively and wait until the next inevitable incident' – she repeated the word 'incident', grimacing – 'and then *react* to the victimisation with all the usual, useless moral outrage.'

'Who's *they*?' I said, looking around at the others for help. Surely they didn't all endorse this rhetoric.

'Everyone,' Marie-Jeanne said. 'The university administration. The law. The media.'

'Even women's rights groups. So-called feminists,' Dyann said. 'Look at the Women's Centre women, how scared they are to do anything. We're always supposed to be passive, reactive. The one thing we can never do is *act*. We can never strike first.'

It seemed to me they were missing the point. 'So, okay, you struck first – using Charla? You used her as, what, as a weapon?'

Dyann shook her head. She looked down at me in disgust. 'You know, Karen, it's not a question of being on our side or not. It's about beliefs. What you believe a woman's body is *for*.'

I stood up now, too, so we were face-to-face. 'And what was Charla's body for, Dyann?'

'Oh, hello! Charla's body is sitting right here,' Charla sang.

Dyann lifted her wineglass again, and for a second I thought she would throw it at me. Instead, she let out a sharp huff of air and stomped past me into the kitchen.

Charla held out the pestle. 'Come on, Karen, make yourself useful.' When I didn't take it right away she made a pouty geisha mouth, bowed, and offered it up to me in both hands. The reading light's glow bounced off her knuckles; in the brown of her irises glinted a sliver of white porcelain.

I knelt next to her at the coffee table. She slid the mortar over to me, full of leaves and bits of bark, and demonstrated how to roll the pestle from side to side against the stone.

'We don't think anyone's going to recognise Charla on the tape,' said Marie-Jeanne.

'You know the frat brothers will view the tape too, right?' I said.

'Not even then,' Charla said. 'My face is half-covered the whole time by that blindfold, and you saw how out of it they were. Dyann made sure not to say my name aloud.'

How could the brothers have sex with someone without even having heard her name? But I could believe it. 'Too shitfaced for this,' Bruce had said. How he'd slurred. How he'd staggered and fumbled.

I moved the pestle round and round the mortar. I kept going until Charla grabbed my wrist and said, 'Stop. Geez, Karen, the tea will fall right through the strainer.'

*

On the six o'clock news there was a short segment devoted to the video. Marie-Jeanne called us over and held on to the rabbit ears to make the signal clearer. 'Disturbing footage,' the reporter was saying, 'believed to have been recorded on campus at a fraternity party.'

'They don't live on campus,' I said.

'The university owns all that land, though,' Steph said. 'And GBC has an official affiliation with the school. That's one of the things we'd like to see changed, so the fraternities aren't protected by the system –'

Dyann shushed us, but there wasn't much more to hear: the college administration was looking into the matter, the report said. It wasn't yet clear whether criminal charges would be filed, and members of the fraternity weren't available for comment.

'They didn't even say it was Gamma Beta Chi,' Marie-Jeanne complained.

Dyann collapsed onto the couch. 'They didn't show any of the video. Why wouldn't they show the tape?'

'Too graphic for prime time, maybe,' Steph said. 'We'll see at eleven.'

Later that evening I heard the phone ring, and a moment later Steph and Dyann were both standing in my room.

'It's Mike, for you,' Steph announced, holding out the phone with the receiver covered. 'Find out how they're reacting, okay?'

I glowered at them like I was a teenager and they were my parents. 'I told you, they won't have heard. They're not even in town.'

Mike was calling from the hotel room, and I could hardly hear him over the music and noise in the background. They'd gone through two cases of beer on the road, he told me, and the gas station attendant had refused to let them use the toilet after Charlie puked in his trash can, so out of desperation they'd all stumbled across the highway to piss into the cornfield. 'There we all are with our dicks hanging out, all in a row!' Mike hollered. 'Longest, fucking best piss of my life! And then this hay truck goes right into the ditch, right beside us!'

'Get off the fucking phone, Chet, it's a hundred bucks a minute!' someone yelled.

'Do you mind?' Mike replied, with the exaggerated dignity of the very drunk. 'I am talking to my wife!'

I hung up. When the phone rang again I lifted the receiver and slammed it back down. 'I told you,' I said again. 'They don't get home until Wednesday. And they're not even going to care about the stupid video. They're going to think it's hilarious. You guys don't understand frat boys at all.'

'Fuck me,' Dyann said, and wheeled around and stomped from my room.

'She knows she should have brought you in on it,' Steph said after a moment.

I opened the book I'd been reading. If this was her idea of an apology, I wasn't accepting it.

'These photos are gorgeous, Karen.' Steph leaned over my desk to peer more closely at one of the enlargements of my tree-planting photos that I'd taped to the wall. A shot of the clearcut, looking down from a hilltop. She stepped back to regard the images as a group. 'Wow. It's sort of disturbing how a scene of so much death and destruction can be so beautiful when you frame it a certain way. Look at how those tractor marks radiate out from that central point. Like a web.'

'It's not beautiful when you're standing in it,' I said. 'It's sweat and black-flies and sore muscles and bad smells.'

'But you had your camera. I mean, you must have seen something.'

'Something, yeah.' Was it beauty I'd seen, and not recognised it as beauty?

Steph shook her head. 'It's amazing. I could never do it. I can never see past what's right in front of me.'

27. PSOGOS

(blame)

All that weekend and all the next week, every moment I wasn't at work or in class, I watched TV. We all did. With Mike away I had time to help out at the Women's Centre, painting placards and bedsheet-banners for the upcoming Our Streets Too vigil and march. The Centre's television set was ceiling-mounted and had no remote control, so while we worked we took turns climbing a stool to flip from one news station to another.

But there wasn't nearly enough buzz about the frat video for Dyann's taste. She kept worrying about what she called 'uptake' and the 'critical window'. Steph had prepared a spreadsheet to track media coverage of the story, but by Wednesday she'd still added less than a dozen lines to it.

Thursday morning Dyann and I met Jen Swinburn locking up her bike beside ours outside the Student Life Building. A misty rain had needled through my jeans and numbed my fingers, but Jen wore a high-tech cycling jacket – longer in the back, edged with reflective tape, cuffed with a placket for her fingers and a hole for her thumb – and the water beaded right off her. There was a nylon sheath over her saddlebag, too, which she balled up and stuffed into its front pocket.

She slipped back her hood and shook out her sleek blonde hair. 'Hey, you guys.'

'I like your lipstick,' I said as I held the door for her.

'It's a lip stain. Like a balm, with just a hint of colour.'

'Kill me,' Dyann said.

'It's organic, if that makes you feel any better,' Jen told her. 'Not animal-tested.'

'Put a gun to my head. Pull the trigger.'

We went up the stairs. I tweaked the griffin's beak on the way past.

'Listen, you guys,' Jen said. 'Sigma Kappa voted not to participate in Our Streets Too this year.'

'What?' Dyann had stopped a few stairs down, her upturned face a search-light in the damp tangle of her hair. I shuffled back down to her level.

'We've got this fund-raiser thing the next night. They just felt it was spreading ourselves too thin.' Jen had paused and turned, but now she started climbing again, and Dyann was forced to follow.

'A fund-raiser for what? Spa Weekend?'

'Alzheimer's. Three of our sisters have grandparents with it, so ...'

'So that takes precedence over women's right to safety and freedom from violence.' Dyann clipped each word in her struggle to keep her voice even.

Jen slipped her keys from her bag and slung it back over her shoulder. 'You should come, Karen. The frats are invited. It's a costume thing – nine-teenth century.'

The Women's Centre door was ajar. Dyann jogged past it and planted herself in front of Jen. 'How come the *Campus Eye* hasn't given more space to the frat party video?'

Jen looked at me, and I shrugged. 'We've given it plenty of coverage,' she said. 'It was Monday's cover story.'

'You should be printing pictures of those frat boys' faces on the front page. You know who they are.'

'We can't do that, Dyann.'

'With those black bars over their eyes, then.'

'We can't print pictures. We can't do anything more than we already have. It'd be libelous.'

'Not if it's the truth! Not if it's rape.'

'We report facts, Dyann. There are no facts in that video.' Jen crossed her arms and put her head to one side. 'Unless you have some facts you'd like to contribute? You keep harping on the need to spread this story. Why don't you go over to the frat house yourself and find out where the tape came from, then? Find out who that girl is, because no one in any of the sororities I've talked to has any clue.'

'Dyann! Oh, thank God. You guys better come see this.' Melanie's round face peeked out of the Women's Centre door.

Chairs were overturned. The trash and recycling bins had been dumped and scattered. Red spray paint striped and speckled the room's walls. Posters were torn down, and some of the placards for next week's Our Streets Too rally were defaced, folded, and cracked off their wooden stalks. I smelled urine.

'Nobody called Security yet, right?' Dyann said. She closed the door carefully behind her.

Melanie said, 'Not yet.'

'Good. Let's do this on our own terms.'

A girl was crumpled forward on the sofa, sobbing, with her hands hiding her face. Another girl sat beside her, rubbing circles round and round between her shoulder blades, saying, 'I know, I know, sweetie, I know.'

'What happened to your friend?' I asked her, thinking of assault, hostage-taking, torture.

'It's just the violation,' she said. 'Of our space, you know?'

'Holy crap,' Jen Swinburn said. She was standing in front of the Wall of Shame. 'Holy, holy crap.'

It was obvious that the bulletin board had been the main target of the vandalism. The rest of the room was incidental, haphazard, an afterthought. Someone had brought pages from a hardcore porn magazine – not torn out, either, but neatly X-Acto-knifed – and tacked them in two long, tidy rows across the board directly under Dyann's hand-lettered SHAME header, so that they covered over many of the boys' photos and the accompanying notes of accusation. The vandal had then attempted to render, with the red paint, a pair of testicles and a penis splashing ejaculate onto the centrefolds. Objectively speaking the image could just as well have been a volcano, or a bunch of balloons bobbing in the rain, but the necessary context was helpfully supplied by a message scrawled in big, block letters across the board's bottom half: *SLUTS DESERVE IT.*

'You'll print a photo of *that* in your paper, right?' Dyann called over to Jen. Still wearing her jacket and backpack, Dyann was bent over the table, writing fast. After a moment she capped her pen and thrust the notepad into Melanie's hands. 'Get Lillian to read this on camera, over by the windows, where the light is better. Do it before she stops crying.'

Then she grabbed Jen by the shoulders, spun her around, and marched her toward the door. 'Go, go, go already! Get your gear and meet me back here in a minute. Karen, go with her, and grab the video camera too.'

Dyann followed us out into the hall and headed the other way.

'Where are you going?' I said.

'Calling the TV station from the main admin office. Maybe then one of those desk drones will finally take it upon herself to tell the Dean of Students what's going on.'

Jen unlocked the door to the *Campus Eye* office, and we gathered our stuff. We had to search for extra batteries for the camcorder.

Jen slammed a drawer hard and wrenched open another one. 'She just doesn't get it, does she? Stuff like this never happens to sorority girls. That's the whole point.'

'What are you talking about?' I said.

'That mess in there? And that video – all that Black Bag bullshit. Dyann hates sororities because she thinks they're antifeminist, but they *protect* women. The whole point of sororities is to protect women.'

'Well. I think for Dyann it's more about the whole system,' I said. 'The fact that women would need protection in the first place –'

'It's like unions.'

'Pardon?'

'If there was a workers' union that refused you membership, wouldn't it make sense to form your own union?' Jen clicked the Dictaphone on and off to make sure it was working. 'You know, you should really think about pledging, Karen, especially if you and Mike are serious. Especially now.'

'Thanks,' I said. I was still trying to catch up to her union analogy. 'Why "especially now", though?'

She locked the door again behind us. 'I'm just saying, if you're involved with a fraternity it's better to have a sorority at your back. Just to represent you, you know?'

'For protection?' I don't need protection, I wanted to tell her. I'm a free agent; I'm neutral. I am Switzerland.

'Just so that people know where to put you. So they know you're not a Dyann Brooks-Morriss.'

*

Looking through the camera's viewfinder, I could tell right away that Lillian was the perfect spokesperson for the Women's Centre on this occasion. The softly curled hair, the hand-knit blue scarf, the enormous, rawbrimming eyes. 'We call on the administration of this university to protect the rights and dignity of its female students,' she read, and her voice wobbled magnificently on the word 'dignity'.

'Hate speech is an act of violence, an assault that contravenes both the laws of this institution and of this country. A short week ago, some of the Women's Centre members dared to turn a camera on the rape culture of fraternities on this campus. We collected visual evidence of the abusive and –'

Lillian broke off, and turned to look at Melanie. 'Wait. Is she saying *we* made that sex tape?' she said.

Melanie shook her head. 'It came in the mail. We had nothing to do with it.'

Lillian's lips moved as she read over Dyann's words. I struggled to hold the camcorder steady. So Dyann was trying to make Operation Black Bag a Women's Centre thing instead of a Dyann Brooks-Morriss thing. She was trying to get some real political weight behind it, to make it a collective action rather than the action of a few individuals.

'No,' Lillian said. 'I'm skipping this part. It sounds pretty good, but we can't just start piggybacking like this.' She faced my lens, cleared her throat, and reorganised her face back into its expression of wounded astonishment:

'This vandalism is just one more instance of the abusive and misogynistic assaults that occur every weekend, at every fraternity party across campus, in the name of male bonding and the so-called right to party.

'This is an assault on all women, and we call on you now to respond to it with outrage and swift, effective action. Show us, *prove* to us' – and here Lillian looked up from Dyann's notebook, directly into the camera – 'that women-hating attitudes will no longer be tolerated on this campus.'

I took photographs of the damage: wide-angle surveys of the disarray, close-ups of the Wall of Shame. I focused in on the scratches by the door-jamb where the lock had been jimmied. Jen interviewed Lillian and Melanie, who'd been first in the door, and then she left to get something down in time for the next day's issue of the *Campus Eye*.

The local TV crew showed up almost three hours later, by which time campus security had cordoned off the room and had stationed officers at either end of the hall to turn away gawkers. I'd skipped two classes and spent the morning hanging out in the *Campus Eye* office with Gita and Steph and Marie-Jeanne, who had been summoned by Dyann and turned up with trays of take-out coffee and bagels for everyone. At Dyann's direction I gave the TV cameraman the video footage I'd taken of Lillian's statement. Dyann handed the reporter several pages from her notebook, too, and he looked them over with what seemed like real interest.

'You have to feed them the story word for word,' she told us afterward. 'I realised it the other night, when the news hardly said a word about the video. They can't talk about it because they don't even know how. They have no idea how to tell a *new* story; left to their own devices they'll just ignore it or revert to clichés – "boys will be boys", or whatever.'

28. SKOTISON

(obscure and confusing speech)

Last Monday's *Eye* was laid out across one of the coffee tables in the GBC lounge. The brother known as Frodo raised his voice to read to the others: 'A multicoloured pile of used condoms rests on the floor beside the weight bench, and each frat brother appears to search through the condom box for his favourite colour before tearing open the package. Is this an agreed-upon identification system? Does each rapist leave his own signature colour condom behind as proof of his participation?'

The gathered brothers fell over each other in their laughter. Someone kicked over his beer and scooped an abandoned T-shirt off the floor to cover the spill.

'Were they flavoured?' someone shouted. 'I bet they were flavoured rubbers, right?'

'I call red. Red is my signature colour.'

'I'm Alec, all right? I'm Alec!' Frodo bellowed. 'Ooh, yummy, lemon-lime!' He sprawled across the others on the couch and pretended to brandish his cock in his fist. 'Want a lollypop, little girl?' He was shoved to the floor, where he curled under the coffee table to avoid the brothers' kicking bare feet.

'Grace is so pissed,' Charlie said. 'That dude is way past the doghouse.' Grace was the one who'd warned me that the brothers liked to share every-thing. I guessed she wasn't thrilled about her boyfriend's starring role in the Black Bag.

Mike had summoned me to the house that afternoon. He'd showered and slept and now he was dying to see me, he said. 'Can't you tell the art fags you're sick, or you have your girl thing, or something?' he wheedled when I said I had to model until six. The crass vocabulary told me he was on the phone in the kitchen and the others were nearby.

Now he grabbed both my hands and pulled me out of my chair. 'Karen, my love. Let's go get reacquainted. I've been saving myself for you since last Friday.'

'Chet, you are such a douchebag!' someone shouted.

Charlie pointed a finger at us. 'Karen, you need to bring some friends over here to help out with Frodo's quota. He needs to hook up, like, eight more times this term.'

'Or what?' I said over my shoulder as Mike dragged me to the stairs. Frodo regarded me with bulging, wet blue eyes from his headlock under Charlie's arm.

'Or his dick falls off!' yelled a brother.

'Or he has to suck all our dicks.'

'Or we turn him ass-up on the gold car and leave him there, and see what happens.'

Look at them, I thought, these lawless, brazen boys. I'd been right, obviously, when I told Dyann and Steph that the video 'scandal' would be nothing for them but a source of hilarity. They were rolling around as usual, soft and silly as puppies but, pausing on the landing to survey them, I felt uneasy. I thought of manslaughtering Ares in the *Iliad* and his human legion of henchmen. At the battle horn wouldn't this whole fraternity pack suddenly snap to attention? Wouldn't they give themselves as one to the bloodfrenzy?

A copy of the most recent house meeting minutes was pinned to the bulletin board in the upstairs hallway. Under 'Service to the Community' someone had penciled in, *Sheri Asselin serviced us.*

'Why do you have to announce to everyone when we're going off to have sex?' I asked Mike as we reached his room. 'Am I that much of a status boost for you around here?'

'It's called making love, what we do,' Mike reminded me. 'And yes, you boost my status.' He shrugged, widened his eyes, and spread his hands to underscore his lack of guile.

'It's disgusting what they're doing. What they're saying about that video.' No one had mentioned today's vandalism at the Women's Centre. I guessed they hadn't heard yet.

He rolled his eyes. 'Tell me about it. They've played the tape a hundred times downstairs. I think they're jerking off to it.'

Charla! The surge of protective outrage made my ears ring. 'Who?' I demanded.

'Moretti and a few others. Don't tell Grace.'

'Where did they even get it?' How dare they, I thought. How dare they!

'Blackie's old roommate works for the dean. He stole it, or copied it or something.'

We'd reached Mike's room. There was a cabbagey smell, which I traced to the laundry from his road trip, still piled in a corner. Mike reached for me, and I stepped back and sat down on his bed.

'Don't you think watching the video is kind of another assault?' I'd meant to say 'another rape', but I backed off the word last-minute. 'Rape' was a red word, a ravenous word. It was double-edged, the word 'rape'. It would automatically make me an accuser and Mike an accused. And it would immediately and forever afterward make it my job to justify myself, to defend myself as the accuser against all manner of arguments. I would somehow have to transform myself into an unimpeachable fortress of sexual righteousness.

'Oh, I don't know,' Mike said. 'Half these guys are gay without knowing it, I swear. If you ask me it's the sight of Comfort's ass that really does it for them.' He stroked my neck, smoothed my hair, and leaned in for a kiss.

I didn't really want Mike to touch me. 'You haven't opened your early Christmas present yet,' I reminded him.

He retrieved the box from his desk and brought it over to the bed.

'Be careful, it's delicate.' I'd brought him a wax sculpture of me, gifted to me by the new mom in Desso's art class. Her name was Deborah. She'd made the sculpture on her own, at home. She shaped it in clay and then cast it in bronze, and she brought it in to show us. I'd been so pleased by its likeness to me – My ribs! My knees! The strong thigh muscles! – and the gracefulness of its posture that I'd asked her if I could photograph it. 'I'll do one better,' she'd promised, and at the next class she'd given me a wax casting of the piece.

Mike opened the box and lifted me out. 'Wow,' he said.

'It's from this woman in the art class. Pretty talented, right?'

'Where am I supposed to put it? It won't last two seconds in this house.'

'You keep your door locked, though,' I said.

'That's your roommate in the video, isn't it?' Mike said. 'The Medusa one. What was her name?' His eyes moved from the statue in his lap to my face, but I kept my eyes on the statue. Of course Mike would know Charla when he saw her again without clothing so shortly after Halloween. Flesh made image – or was it image made flesh?

Mike's hands made a circle around the statue. 'Karen, I want to protect you,' he said, 'but I need to know the truth.'

'Charla,' I whispered.

'You said they were at the S&M party. Did you know? Were you in on it?'

'In on the gang bang, you mean?' I said.

'Call it a gang bang, fine. But it's not a crime if Charla agreed to it.'

'It is if she was drunk, though,' I said. 'Incapacitated, like that girl Sheri was, on the gold car. You saw her. She was way beyond consent. She was incapacitated.'

'Was she?'

'You saw her.'

'Charla, I mean.' Mike's thumbs rubbed at the statue's waxen knees.

Careful, I wanted to say, you can rub dents in it, it's that soft. 'I don't know,' I said. 'I wasn't in on it. I wasn't even there; I was out with you, remember?'

He shrugged, and I crossed his room, opened the window, and inhaled the leafcooled breeze. 'What about that newspaper article?' I said. 'Are the condoms really colour-coded?'

Mike snorted. 'Don't believe everything you see in the media, Karen.'

'Well, don't you think they might start asking questions about the whole fraternity?'

Mike wrapped his arms around me from behind. He murmured at my ear, 'Are you worried about me? You know I have the perfect alibi.'

I turned and looked past him. My statue was back in its box. 'What alibi?'

He laughed. 'Same as yours: I was with you. Besides' – he leaned in and licked at my lips – 'it's just a sex tape. It's just TV. Nobody takes TV seriously.'

'It's newspapers too,' I said.

'Newspapers, neither. Definitely not the campus ones.'

Mike tried to lift my T-shirt, but I clamped my arms across my chest. 'Are you going to tell your brothers who made that tape?' I asked.

'Are you kidding? They'd crucify you for letting a bunch of dykes in here.' He took my wrists in his hands and coaxed my arms back to my sides. 'Plus, I love that we have a secret, you and me. It glues us tighter together.'

After we'd made love and Mike fell asleep, I played the video in my mind. I played Bruce and Charla over in my head: his broad hand cupping her hip, his head resting in the crook of her neck, the lazy arch of his back. I let the lewd, redgolden light fill up my body until my hands tingled and my fingers, flicking and plunging between my legs, grew numb. I heard myself groan and gasped to stifle the sound. I tasted gold; my jaw ached with it. My whole body filled up with Bruce until my flesh grew too heavy with him and was slit open, and all the light poured forth, and I lay gasping, laughing, licking at the empty air.

The women of Raghurst hold forth amongst themselves on the subject of the two posters above the sofa:

       Karen: You know, those images make no sense up there together. Janis Joplin flamed out at – what, twenty-five? She's in no way a role model.

Marie-Jeanne: Joplin *was* a Woman who Ran with Wolves. She howls when she sings!

      Dyann: Janis was a wild woman. You have to remember her time period.

      Karen: Have you read the book? I have it out of the library right now. Dr Estés actually uses Joplin as an example of a creative woman who falls into traps: the trap of leading a double life, and the trap of excess.

      Dyann: She was a martyr to the female spirit. Society killed her for her creativity.

      Steph: Anyway, we all live double lives. We have to, if we want any sort of societal or institutional acceptance.

      Dyann: Not me.

      Karen: It's a pretty great book, actually. Dr Esterhazy would love it. It uses folklore – old wives' tales, fairy tales – to explore archetypes of femininity.

      Steph: Sylvia isn't big on archetypal psychology, actually. It just naturalises gendered power imbalances.

29. ENUMERATIO

(epic catalogue)

The women gathered at Raghurst. They journeyed to us from their dorm rooms and from their shared student-housing apartments and from the rental houses nearby our own and from the high-rise towers downtown and from their parents' homes in the suburbs. Throughout the skylowering early-winter afternoon they came on foot and tramped in heavy shoes up our stairs. They carried their bicycles onto our porch so that they could keep an eye on them through the living room window and thus avoid theft. They carpooled and parked their cars along our street, taking care not to block any of our neighbours' driveways. In our front hall the women shed their coldgoing clothing and relieved themselves of their burdens. Rows and then piles of their footwear covered our floor. There were granny boots and desert boots and secondhand combat boots polished to a fine black shine. There were sturdy Birkenstocks with their stained suede footbeds. There were clogs with hardwood soles and leather stapled all around. There were weblike Tevas meant for climbing waterfalls and gum-soled moccasins lined with shearling.

Rucksacks, they brought, those who journeyed directly from class or study sessions at the libraries: great nylon multipocketed backpacks with reflective tape and hidden adjustable aluminium frames, woven canvas haversacks with detachable shoulder straps, army-surplus parachute bags with superfluous buckles. Carabiner-clipped to the straps there were eco-mugs and bamboo sporks and water bottles with bendy straws advertising the name and address of ski resorts. The women brought with them their daygoing things, the things without which they never left their homes. Yoga mats in sleeves fashioned by their own hands from vintage floral living-room drapes at Women's Centre DIY workshops or in sleeves of recycled sari fabric from the Fair Trade Sisters store downtown. There were dogeared copies of *The Tao of Pooh* and coffee-stained copies of *Manufacturing Consent* and copies of *Gender Trouble* with the covers missing. There were quilted goosedown parkas and quilted flannel slackjackets and Guatemalan patchwork bombers and US Navy-issue peacoats with hand-sewn rainbow flags at the elbows and Peruvian sweaters knit from oatmeal-coloured wool and turd-coloured wool and emblazoned with geometric llamas and with possibly spiritually significant tribal motifs. And all the purses jackets berets backpacks sweaters scarves everywhere on the linoleum floor at Raghurst were bespangled with message buttons big and small bright and dense as meadow flowers: MY BODY MY CHOICE. FARMERS FEED CITIES. DOG IS LOVE. NO MEANS NO. JANE'S ADDICTION.

The women bore with them their great gifts of feasting. From cardboard boxes padded with dish towels they unpacked their Corningwares of broccoli-tofu bake and ginger-yam bake and macaroni-tuna bake. From foil packets they unrolled maple-roasted salmon and sesame-marinated tempeh and beef kofta studded with pine nuts and pomegranate seeds. From Tupperware bowls they unlidded kale-and-beet salad and wild-rice-and-lentil salad and baby greens with raspberry vinaigrette. Spelt bread, they brought, and cornmeal muffins, and samosas and spinach börek, and for dessert there was apple tart and brownies and plumcake and baklava. And all the breads soups salads casseroles desserts everywhere on the countertops and tables at Raghurst were one hundred percent gluten-free and lactose-free and nut-free and shellfish-free as agreed upon beforehand so that all, fearless, might partake.

Michelle Shocked was turned up loud. Incense burned on the windowsill. Many bottles of wine were opened, poured, and drunk. Speeches were made, and toasts proposed, and joints passed round, and dancing broke out in the narrow floor space between the chair and the stereo. Thus the women gathered together at Raghurst from every corner to celebrate and to console one another about the recent gender-based scandals and acts of violence on campus and to fortify themselves for the upcoming Our Streets Too vigil and march.

But we residents of Raghurst were all waiting for our guest of honour. She had promised Steph she would do her best to drop in, but the food was almost gone and Dyann was grumbling. Steph said, 'It's to see us, it's not like she necessarily wants to eat with the mob, I mean if you were Sylvia, would you?'

And then, at last, Dr Esterhazy was sitting at our table, flushed and smiling beneath her fairywhite hair. The temperature outside was dropping fast, she told us. She ate apple tart from a plate hastily washed. She asked if we had cream, said oh no, yes of course, milk would do fine, and then we watched her pour a little milk directly onto the plate with the apple tart and dab each forkful through the milk before bringing it to her lips.

*

Dyann squatted on the arm of the sofa wearing a Bikini Kill T-shirt and a baggy pair of camo pants cinched with what looked like a telephone cord. She was surveying her encampments. She hadn't eaten much all evening, I noticed, had taken only a sip or two of her wine. After the Wall of Shame vandalism, the women were all talking about the frat-party video with new interest, without any prompting from Dyann. She sat and surveyed our ranks and appeared satisfied with what she heard and saw.

'They should be castrated,' one woman said.

'At least expelled. The university has done nothing! They haven't even issued a statement.'

Another woman said, 'The fraternities aren't the exception to the rule, though.'

'Rape is the basic unit of human heterosexuality,' Steph said.

'No, no. Rape has nothing to do with sex.' It was Melanie from the Women's Centre. She looked over at Dr Esterhazy as she spoke, as if we were in class. 'It's about humiliation. About power.'

'Rape has nothing to do with *romance,*' someone corrected her. 'And even that's not true, if you've ever read a Harlequin. It's actually integral to all of our gendered mythology.'

Cross-legged on her chair, Charla held a lighter to her quartz pipe, inhaled, and passed the pipe and lighter to the woman standing next to her. Dyann followed my gaze in her direction and frowned. 'Can we stay straight, please?' she hissed. 'We're marching later.'

'Not if you guys keep on like that,' Charla retorted, her voice plugged with smoke.

'Like what?' Dyann said.

She exhaled. 'Like, *rape is nature's way.*'

'Yeah,' Melanie chimed in. '*Society* teaches men violence against women.'

Dr Esterhazy had been helping clear the dishes, rinsing mugs for tea. We'd all said *don't bother, it's okay, please sit,* but she insisted. She moved softfooted amongst us, pouring more wine, determining who wanted coffee, setting out saucers with irregularly shaped pieces of dark chocolate she'd brought in bar form and broken by hand.

Of course, the entire debate – Charla's pot-smoking too – was staged for Dr Esterhazy's benefit. We were all dying to hear the professor's opinion of the video. But we also wanted to show her what we thought, to show her *that* we thought, that we had intelligent thoughts even outside of the walls of her classroom. And, observing Dr Esterhazy's graceful comings and goings from the room while we talked, I was aware that every eye in the room was following the professor's every movement, and I realised that Dr Esterhazy was aware of this, too, and that she was staging something for us in return. A self-humbling, a service. A foot-washing ritual. 'That one has orange rind,' she stage-murmured, touching a fingernail to the plate beside a shard of chocolate, 'and that's organic ginger.'

And then she floated all the way around the table to my chair and crouched there right next to me. Me! Her slim fingers rested next to my wineglass and her gray-eyed gaze shone up at my face. 'How is your piece on Helen coming along?' she asked.

Loving that she called it a 'piece' rather than an 'essay', I answered, 'Pretty good, except I've got a lot more questions than answers at this point. Oh, wait!

You have to see this book I found. Maybe you already know it. I'll go get it.' I bounded up three stairs at a time to fetch it for her.

I wished I'd had the courage to ask her to come up to my room. I wanted Dr Esterhazy to see where I slept, to see all the books piled on my nightstand and scattered on the floor beside my bed. Maybe she would ask me about the photos on the wall above my desk. Maybe she'd say, 'Yes, Steph told me you'd taken some beautiful shots of logging operations in Canada. These are marvelous, just marvelous.'

Sorry for all the disarray, I'd say, but my professor would be thinking, 'What dedication to art and to the life of the mind. Now *this* is a scholar!'

'… to have women feed *themselves*, and *each other*, before going out into the public realm to be seen and heard,' Steph was saying when I returned, breathless, to the dining room. 'That's what this evening is all about.'

'It bends the narrative,' Dyann said. 'We're mirroring the mythic structures, but twisting them out of shape on purpose.'

Dr Esterhazy had taken my vacated chair. She sipped her coffee and made a face. 'I applaud the effort, you know I do. Anything that brings women together.'

'But you don't think it makes any difference.' Dyann's glare swung my way. 'Go ahead, Karen. Show Sylvia your book, and we can talk about it just like we talk about everything, all the time, without ever lifting a finger to do anything about any of it.'

Dr Esterhazy took the book from me and laughed. 'Oh, Diana! Our class-room Artemis! Women and Myth just isn't the same this year without you.'

'Artemis is the huntress, right?' Charla said. She'd gotten up from her chair and moved to sit beside Dyann on the sofa.

'Yep,' Steph said. 'Shoot first, think later.'

Dr Esterhazy raised a finger. 'No, no, Artemis is Goddess of Virtue, too, don't forget. Chastity, also' – and Dyann grinned at this despite herself – 'defender of the forest, et cetera. But such extremity! The purity of vision itself becomes a kind of violence.'

'Somebody you want on your side, in other words,' Charla said. She touched Dyann between the shoulder blades. Dyann stiffened and leaned away from her, and Charla dropped her hand.

'Well, yes. And you mustn't sneak up on her, or she might turn you into a stag to be torn apart by your own dogs.' Dr Esterhazy smiled, and finally, *finally* she riffled through the pages of my book.

It was a verse translation of the *Iliad* by a British poet. I'd bought it at a used bookstore in Toronto back in high school but had never read it until I started working on my Helen paper.

'It's so amazing,' I said. 'He transliterates the Greek sometimes, so that the images, the metaphors, don't make "sense", like, in common usage. But he creates these amazing visual clashes, this imagery ...' My tongue seized. I sounded immature. Had I just said 'like' in the middle of a sentence? Had I just used upspeak? Had I said 'common usage' like a question not a statement, just now, with my roommates and practically half the female student population watching?

But Dr Esterhazy nodded and smiled at me. 'It's such a treat, isn't it, when the love of language becomes an end in itself? May I borrow this until next class?' she said.

Dyann stood up. She tossed her dreadlocks back from her face. 'Look, Sylvia, you're always telling us that men are violent toward women because they live in terror of the feminine, right?'

Dr Esterhazy gave a quick glance around the table.

'You've taught us that everything we call culture, all of society's so-called progress, aims to subdue the female. Eviscerate it. Humiliate it.'

'Yes,' Dr Esterhazy said. She folded her hands together on the table, waiting for Dyann to come to the point.

But Dyann had already made her point. The CD had ended a few minutes earlier, and in the relative silence Dyann's words had doused the room. The silence deepened as Dyann waited, too, standing straight-spined, feet spread and hands relaxed at her sides, surveying and waiting for the words to soak in or condense into a puddle one of us might try to mop up.

Eviscerate. I knew Dyann hadn't been talking about Mother Earth, or not exclusively, but I was picturing the clear-cut, the pine forests cleaved and combed machine-bare, all that clawed earth.

Finally someone said, 'So, Dyann. Where does that leave us?'

'It leaves us with clear eyes for a change.' Dyann flashed an unexpectedly warm grin around the room. 'You can't tear something down until you see how it's put together.'

'I once was blind, but now I see,' Steph crooned – but softly, in pleasing timbre, and her smile returned Dyann's smile as a gracious tribute to her for winning the argument, and I felt the general mood lift again at once as we shook our heads and chuckled and began to put aside the dirty dishes.

'Come and see what's on the news,' Marie-Jeanne called. She fiddled with the antenna while we gathered around the television to see that the main campus quadrangle was teeming with students, police cars, and media vans. The activity appeared to be centred on McGibbon Hall, the largest of the dorms. A reporter was saying, 'The fraternity videotape has generated tension on campus over the last few weeks, especially between the students living in fraternity houses and several campus women's groups. Recent evidence from the security tapes at the Student Life Building points to some of these male residents as suspects in the recent vandalism of the campus Women's Centre. Tonight this tension erupted into what some sources are calling a full-scale riot. Campus security has called in the local police force to restore order, but most of these students show no signs of going home quietly.'

'This is it. It's happening.' Dyann snapped off the television. 'Let's get our asses over to campus.'

'Aren't we supposed to meet downtown?' someone asked.

'Oh, we'll go downtown,' Dyann assured her, 'only we'll bring a whole lot more people with us than we'd even hoped for.'

Dr Esterhazy murmured that she had to be on her way.

'You're not coming to the vigil?' Steph said. She shot a worried look at Dyann, but Dyann had moved out of earshot.

Steph brought Dr Esterhazy's coat back upstairs from her room, where she'd put it for safekeeping. It was cream-coloured wool with wide sleeves and a built-in scarf that Dr Esterhazy wound around her neck twice. The coat, and the oversized felt hat the professor plucked from her purse and pulled down over her ears, made her gnomelike and otherworldly.

'Are you sure I can't give you a ride somewhere?' Steph said.

Dr Esterhazy stepped into her arms for a hug. 'It will be a wonderful, bracing walk.'

Then she reached out the swinging sleeves and wrapped them around me in turn. Me! I gasped at the silky cheek pressed to mine and the scent of something – gardenia? Was it gardenia? Adoration cartwheeled through my head. 'Okay, thanks. Thank you. Bye,' I babbled.

Back in the living room, Dyann had not seen the professor hug me. Charla had missed it, too, and so had Marie-Jeanne. I stood in the archway, still softstruck, marveling at what my roommates missed.

30. ANACOENOSIS

(demonstrating common interests)

There was a last-minute scramble for winter accessories. I ended up with Charla's wool mittens and a red fleece watch cap Marie-Jeanne had borrowed from Stick. It smelled like a dirty sock.

I dawdled at the door, wanting to walk alone to campus in order to clear my head of the potluck chatter. I heard someone still behind me in the living room, and through the archway I watched as Charla stretched herself out on the sofa. Her foot knocked an empty soup bowl off the side table, and she sat up to retrieve it and add it to the stack of dirty dishes on the carpet.

'You're not coming to campus?' I said.

She shook her head. 'Not with all those cameras. I keep thinking someone is going to figure out it's me in the video, and I don't want to deal with that yet.'

'Does Dyann know you won't be there?'

Charla stretched out again, and the shrug she gave me was sideways, one-armed.

Something in the gesture prompted me to take my boots off and cross the room to her. I lifted her ankles and sat under them so that her feet rested in my lap. 'What's going on?' I said.

Charla stared up at the *WOMEN WHO RUN WITH WOLVES* poster. Finally she said, 'There are aftereffects from the Black Bag for me. I've been trying to shake it, but it keeps sneaking back.'

'What effects?' I said.

'I feel like Susannah.'

My stomach dropped. 'You're pregnant.'

Her gaze jerked to my face. 'Oh, no. God, no.' She gave a short laugh. 'Sorry, that's not what I meant. It's not a good comparison, maybe.'

'Then why Susannah?'

'Shame, I was thinking. I'm fighting off shame for what I did.'

I hadn't thought of Susannah as ashamed. Stubborn, maybe, in her insistence that the baby was her cross to bear. Weak, to allow her parents to yank her out of school. What was the term Steph had for that reaction? *Internalised misogyny*, she'd called it.

Charla sighed, picking at a loose thread in her shirt. 'You know how you're supposed to tell a sexual assault victim it wasn't her fault? You're supposed to keep on repeating it to her, right? "It wasn't your fault. It's not because of who you are, or the way you dressed that night, or the way you conducted yourself."'

I saw her point. No one was saying that to Charla. How could any of us, in good faith, say that to her? 'Why did you do it, Charla?' I asked.

She knew what I was asking. She knew I wasn't asking about self-sacrifice for a feminist cause. Charla rose to a sitting position, pulled her knees up, and rested her chin on them. It was her classroom thinking-and-discussion posture. 'What if I told you I was into it?' she said.

I shook my head. 'No way. I'm sick of you guys all acting like you've found this sexual nirvana or something. Like you just go around getting off all day long, and it makes you so much more enlightened than the rest of the world.'

She just looked at me. Waited.

I closed my eyes. 'Okay. Explain it to me, then.'

'Here we are at college exploring ideas. Seeking to broaden our minds, right? Enrich our intellect. It's not supposed to be just about getting a job afterward. There's some guiding mission here to be curious, to honour our curiosity and follow it and allow it to guide our learning. But it's all about the mind, the brain.'

'Okay.'

'So, I have this parallel project to do the same with my body. With my desires. I want to honour my body's curiosity and let it guide my learning. And I want to be sort of systematic about it, like college is systematic about our brains.'

'A sexual curriculum?'

Charla snorted. 'Well, that's just it. There is no sexual curriculum. All we have is a bunch of rules. Pretty much all of them set by men.'

'So the Black Bag was … what?' I said. 'A tutorial? A test?'

'I already knew I liked being blindfolded. Bound. You know: surprised.' She flushed. 'For me sex is hottest when my fantasy has to change tack a few times, when it has to kind of race to catch up to what my body's experiencing.'

What fantasy? I wanted to ask, but I was suddenly afraid to interrupt. Suddenly I was listening hard.

'I wanted to see how far I could push it, I guess. How far I could submit before it got, I don't know, *un*erotic, I guess. I wanted to chase down my body's boundaries. Find my limit.'

Charla flung out her arms in a self-mocking 'ta-da'. 'Needless to say, I found it.'

'When, though? How far in?' I asked.

She looked at me. 'Well, that's interesting.'

'What?'

'No one has asked me that. No one is interested in that particular information.'

Dyann wasn't interested, she meant. I could only imagine how Dyann felt about Charla's 'limits'. She needed her to be willing, but Dyann must have wanted to believe there'd be nothing sexual about it whatsoever for Charla.

Charla said, 'I guess it was about halfway through. I couldn't come anymore. I got sore and irritated. And then I just sort of shut down.'

'You couldn't come …? You're saying you had an orgasm – more than one – in the Black Bag. During a supposed gang bang.' My scalp tingled. For a second I thought I might tip over.

Charla narrowed her eyes. 'Damn, Karen,' she said. 'Are we even having the same conversation?'

I laughed. I was so dizzy I had to hold on to the edge of the couch. 'I'm … I'm like a newborn baby, listening to you. I don't even get – I don't understand the vocabulary.'

'Haven't you ever tried it?' she asked. 'Bindings? A blindfold, at least?'

181

'Well, I will now,' I said.

I couldn't stop laughing, and Charla finally chuckled, too, watching my delirium. 'Does it feel a tiny bit like freedom, hearing this?' she asked me. 'In your body, I mean? Is that why you're laughing?'

I wiped my eyes. 'Maybe,' I said. 'It feels unhinged. I mean unbound. Uncaged. Like something inside me is running amok.'

She nodded, smiling. 'To me that's freedom, or the first inklings of it. That's what I'm talking about.'

'My God,' I said. 'There are no rules for this, are there?'

Charla arched an eyebrow. 'Funny. That's just what Dyann kept saying all along. And now we can't talk about it at all anymore.

'And Steph's the same. For Steph it's all become this big, heavy, emotional burden. Any conversation about it just seems to pile up on her shoulders and weigh her down. She's worried about me, sure, but the worry isn't really about *me*, because she's not even talking to me about it. She's made me into this object of guilt, or added me to her general catalogue of sorrows, or something.'

Charla plucked a dessert spoon from between the couch cushions and lobbed it across the room onto the dining table, where it clattered into the piled-up plates. 'You know, it's not like we didn't discuss it in advance,' she said. 'We discussed it ad nauseam beforehand – the necessity, the risks, the ethical implications – and now none of us can even bring up the subject.'

I took hold of Charla's toes and wiggled her foot back and forth. 'We just did. You and me.'

'Yeah,' she said.

There are no rules for this. It was exactly the type of aphorism Dyann would invent, I thought. All we ever did at Raghurst, really, was quote Dyann.

*

Dyann and Steph had taken their bikes to campus, and by the time I fought my way through the crowd into the quad, the Women's Centre banners were already unfurled and the placards were waving and Dyann was speaking into her megaphone. Several TV reporters held their microphones out to her.

'Fraternities are finished on this campus!' she declared. 'We're gathered here tonight to say that we're not going to stand by while our campus is overrun with violent crimes against women. We refuse intimidation. We refuse violence. We refuse fear!'

There was scattered cheering, although many of the students, I thought, looked a bit uncertain as to what was going on. They'd come out to be part of the general upheaval, not to participate in a political rally. Dyann pointed at the women's placards, so that the cameras swung to capture the Our Streets Too slogans. 'We're marching tonight to end violence against women. Join us! Tonight we take back our city!'

Steph took one female reporter after another aside and retold the story of the vandalism earlier that week at the Women's Centre. She handed out colour copies of the photos I'd taken of the destroyed Wall of Shame. Over and over again, I heard her say that the attack on women's safe space was a direct act of retaliation for the video of the frat party. 'Their backs are against the wall,' Steph said. 'They know they're being publicly called to task for their behaviour, and they're getting desperate.'

One reporter called to her cameraman, and the two of them followed Steph across the quad into the Student Centre to check out the damage for themselves. The initial newspaper coverage had been less than ideal, despite all our efforts to control the messaging. *Girlfriend Grudge Board Becomes Battleground*, the headline had read. Even Jen Swinburn had been miffed by that: 'I told that reporter my headline. First he steals it, and then he goes and waters it down,' she'd complained. Her *Campus Eye* piece had been head-lined *Wall of Shame Warzone*.

We had cleaned up the garbage and shampooed the carpets at the Women's Centre, but we'd left the red paint on the walls and the centrefolds plastered across the bulletin board. All week we'd worked on new posters for Our Streets Too amid that scrawling red graffiti, and there'd been ongoing arguments about the risks of allowing all that negative energy to taint our efforts and about the unseen effects of the violence inherent even in the colour and the angle of the paint daubs – *They're slash marks*, one woman had insisted; *They're open wounds!* – yet Dyann had been right, I saw now, to insist on leaving the evidence intact. It gave us another shot at getting the story out. Getting the story straight.

When Steph and the TV crew returned to the quad, I stood beside Dyann and watched the reporter beckon the camera directly over to some of the women holding placards and begin to interview them in more detail. A tall black woman in a green ski jacket leaned over the microphone, and Steph waved us a thumbs-up.

Dyann threw an arm around my shoulders. 'Look at her – she's unstoppable. See that? She's even getting women of colour on board.'

There had been no women of colour in attendance at our potluck except for Araniya and Mai from Dr Esterhazy's Women and Myth class. Steph had told me that in the Students of Colour Alliance, one of the groups that shared the room with the Women's Centre, some were leery of adding their voices to the antifrat campaign. Sexual-violence accusations had a history of being used as a racist tool against black men, they said. And if the accusation was against a white man, then a woman of colour suffered a higher chance of being called a false accuser, or of having her own sexual history trotted out to discredit her. It was precarious for them, they said, to demand justice under a system already stacked against them. Others in the group felt that fraternity violence was a white issue, or that their social-justice priorities were elsewhere.

'Steph has been so *blah* lately, have you noticed?' Dyann continued. 'This is exactly what she needed to pull her out of her own head.' She laughed and turned me slowly in a 360-degree circle to take in the throng. '*Bellum omnium in omnes*,' she murmured in my ear.

'What's that mean?'

'War of all against all,' she said, and laughed again. 'The whole fucking place in flames. This is exactly what we need.' O Dyann the burnished general, the vanquisher, splintering the enemy spears!

After the excitement on campus, the Our Streets Too candlelight vigil downtown seemed boring and unnecessarily somber in tone. I could see many women in our group shivering and yawning with the aftereffects of the potluck wine and the long trek downtown. The wind funneled between the office buildings and slapped at us and kicked cold grit into our faces. I needed to pee. The hair on my legs bristled and scraped against my jeans. Candle wax had dripped all over Charla's mittens, and my feet were numb. Finally I snuck off and found a bus and rode home, alone, with bits of frostbitten leaf whirling by and striking the window beside my head.

31. PHRONESIS

(common sense)

We'd taken to having sex right after I arrived at the frat house. We'd find the first opportunity to slip away from the party, as soon as Mike was done mixing the first round of potions and powders. Sex at the outset suited me fine, since it took the edge off Mike's clinginess and still left me the rest of the party to enjoy. We'd only have sex a second time later on if his buzz demanded it of him.

Sex on cocaine was athletic and mean. I hated Mike with a voracious intensity, bruised him and striped his pale hips with my nails. He finished within a minute or two but it felt like hours, hours of sweat-stung skin and cramp-clenched limbs. Sex on E was my favourite – 'sextasy', Mike called it, although he had to combine the drug with speed or it would make him impotent. Sextasy was dissolute, languorous, all about the aesthetics. Little details would fix my focus, like Mike's earlobe or the fuzzy mole above his collarbone, and I loved these details with every fiber of my being. Mike said I talked crazy poetry. He'd be soft and sentimental the next morning, even more than usual, and I wouldn't mind it at all.

In honour of Thanksgiving just around the corner, the brothers had received a massive free take-out delivery from the new Portuguese place downtown, and the whole house, now full of girls from the Grant-Montgomery women's dorm, still reeked of barbecue. I ate a cold drumstick from the foil bag in the fridge while Mike crushed a pill into a drink for us.

'Not that one,' he told a girl who was rinsing a glass from the sink. He reached into a lower cabinet and gave her a plastic disposable beer mug instead. He and I exchanged a companionable shudder of disgust: several parties ago the left-hand kitchen sink had somehow turned into a urinal, and even though the cleaning service had been through several times, the sink's contents had remained suspect ever after. The 'pissoir', we all called it. Same with the right-hand produce drawer in the fridge, and the cooler outside the garage door. This was the sort of insider information I enjoyed about life at GBC, one of the many tidbits I felt set me apart from the other girls. This was the fraternal stuff of which the fraternity was made.

'If this is Purple Jesus,' the girl asked Mike, filling her cup from the giant cooler on the table, 'why's it red?'

Mike looked over her shoulder. 'It's Baby Jesus,' he said, 'with cherry instead of grape.'

She took a sip and made a face. 'Why "Baby"?'

'Christmas is coming.'

'Oh, right.' The girl laughed. She tipped back her head, drained her cup, and refilled it again to the brim.

'Go easy,' Mike warned, but she was already leaving the kitchen. 'This is going to be supremely foul,' he told me. 'You know Antoine? He smuggled a forty-ouncer of *alcool* in from Quebec. Ninety-four percent, and I think they dumped the whole thing in there.' He clucked his tongue. 'People go blind from that stuff all the time.'

'Okay, Dad,' I said. To point out his hypocrisy, I raised my beaker of what-ever he'd just concocted.

'That's chemistry,' he protested, as usual. 'I know exactly what's in my drinks, and it's not *poison.*'

Nirvana played on the main-floor stereo. Soon the girls would be tipsy enough to dance, and they'd demand different music, but for now Kurt Cobain's voice tour-guided Mike's potion into my system, the baritone moan scraping pleasantly at my entrails, the bass-beat buffeting my skull. Some girls I recognised as State students were grouped around a bong in the living room.

To avoid them I veered upstairs, with Mike on my heels. We found a spot on a couch in the second-floor lounge. There was a string of Christmas lights and a tree propped in the corner, already dropping needles on the carpet.

We watched a circle of cross-legged girls play Century Club. In the dorm the target had been one shot of beer every minute, on the minute, for one hundred minutes, but the brothers upped the ante with whatever was in the cooler – Baby Jesus, in this case. Anyone who didn't quit or puke got to wear a Century Club button, a yellow happy face with Xs for eyes. Mike told me they were giving out more buttons now than at the start of the school year. Four to five nights of heavy drinking per week for a whole semester had boosted the girls' tolerance.

The music from downstairs stopped, and then started again at much lower volume. Then a brother poked his head through the lounge door. 'There're cops downstairs,' he announced.

Panic and disorder broke out amongst the drinking-game players, all of whom, like Mike and me, were underage.

'It's okay, it's okay,' said the brother in the doorway. Trey or Trent, I thought his name was. 'Just go pour your drinks over the balcony and you're fine. You don't have to give them your real names.'

'It's because of that sex tape,' I heard one girl say as Mike and I helped pour out cans of beer and cups of Baby Jesus into the dark yard below. 'They're probably going to arrest Bruce and them.' The lines from the *Iliad* popped into my head: *And Rumor walked blazing among them, Zeus's messenger, to hasten them along.* Dyann would be extremely happy to hear about a raid on GBC.

An underage-drinking charge could jeopardise my US student visa. I thought of using the fire escape from the balcony and remembered that it had come detached at some point, years ago, and lay in the yard, a rusty, shin-scraping hazard, under a pile of leaves. If nothing else the cops would find a fire code violation.

'They're asking for Duncan,' Trent told Mike.

'He's already gone home for the holidays,' Mike said. 'They're on a cruise with the girlfriend's parents or something. See if you can find Melon.'

'Melon left yesterday,' Trent said.

'Well, there's nowhere to go,' Mike said. 'Everybody, just relax.'

A gray-haired policeman entered the lounge, followed by another male officer and a young female one. 'Everyone have a seat for a minute, all right?' the older cop said, and we obeyed, Mike and I sliding along the wall and sinking to our haunches. People sat on the furniture and on the floor, whispering, murmuring, clearing their throats, while the three cops moved from person to person asking questions in calm, pleasant voices: 'What's your name?' and, 'Are you a member of this fraternity?' and, 'Are you a student?'

The younger male cop took Trent out into the hall, and a girl began to cry noisily.

'We're not out to get anyone here,' said the gray-haired officer. 'We're just interviewing, just trying to establish who's who.'

'Let's go for a walk, Karen,' Mike said, and pulled me up from the floor by my elbow.

'Sorry, and your name is …?' The female cop turned to us and flipped her notepad to a clean page.

'We're leaving.' Mike's voice broke a little. He squinted at the cop's badge and jerked his head back as if he'd seen a cobra. He squeezed my hand so hard it hurt.

'Could you stay a minute?' the policewoman asked. Gently. Gentling him.

But Mike's potion – whatever drug he'd mixed with the drink we'd downed in the kitchen – had evidently taken him by the throat. 'You have no right!' he shrieked. He tugged me into the hall. The younger cop with Trent put a hand on Mike's chest and said, 'Hold up, buddy,' but Mike wrenched past him and fled, dragging me down the stairs and out the front door at a run into the cold night.

We tore down one street and another, eventually slowing to a jog when it became apparent the police weren't behind us.

Mike's terror flipped into elation, and he let go of my hand and whooped. 'I'm on fire!'

I laughed and speed-walked after him, struggling to catch my breath as he spun and leapt along the leaf-strewn sidewalk. My nerves were jumping under my skin too. My spine itched from my ass right up to the crown of my head.

'I am a burning man!' Mike declared. 'My skin is crackling. Look! I've become a tree. I have bark.'

'You are so fucked up,' I said. Mike would talk and talk when he was tripping, always telling me to 'Look!' and 'Listen!' to everything he was experiencing. It sometimes made it hard to figure out what *I* was experiencing. At the moment, except for the itching, I couldn't tell if I was high at all.

He pinned me to a chain-link fence to kiss me. His eyelashes were huge, waving insect legs against his white skin. I watched the wet surface of his eyeball growing larger as his face approached. Nausea tore through me, and I shoved Mike away and loped ahead of him on the sidewalk.

'I'm a tree! I can't keep up with you, human!' Mike whined from somewhere behind me. A truck rattled by, bouncing on the concrete. I ran faster, looping around the block, leaving him behind. I arrived back at the frat house sweaty but calmer, racked by a terrible thirst and hunger. In the abandoned kitchen I poured a beer down my throat, cracked another can, drank again.

'Hi, Karen? Can I talk to you a minute?' It was the female cop.

I couldn't believe it. I'd forgotten all about the raid. 'How do you know my name?'

She lifted the Baby Jesus cooler from the table onto the floor and motioned me into a chair. 'I'm Officer McRae. Same first name as you – Karen – so I remembered it when I heard your boyfriend say it before.'

'Oh.' She seemed nice, but I knew I should be careful. 'I'm not telling you my last name, though.'

'That's fine, for now,' Officer McRae said. 'I'm just wondering, since you're dating one of the fraternity brothers, whether you might have been here the night of October twenty-eighth, at the S&M party?' She made quotation marks with her fingers around the words 'S&M'.

'No, we were at an awards banquet. I mean, we slept here, but we came home late.'

'But you were here. In the house, that night.' She leaned back in her chair. 'Congratulations. You are the first person I've spoken to who's been honest enough to admit even being here.'

Shitshitshit. Cornered, my brain addled by the chemical thrumming in my spine, I went on the offensive: 'Probably you guys are supposed to have a warrant, and we're supposed to have lawyers and everything, right?'

'There are no charges being laid, so no, Karen. It's just a conversation.'

I crossed my arms and stared at her, determined not to say anything else.

'Look. This isn't only about that videotape going around. Someone got hurt the night of that party. I would like to figure out how it happened.' Officer McRae leaned forward again and propped her elbows right in the sticky pools of Baby Jesus. This detail – that she didn't care about her uniform, or was too intent on her job to notice – suddenly absorbed all of my attention. A female cop. What must it be like, being a female cop? Why would a woman choose policing as a career? Officer McRae had a square jaw and freckled cheeks, reddish hair pulled into a tight ponytail under her hat. She was young, I thought, late twenties, maybe thirty.

She'd asked me something, and I'd missed it entirely.

'I'm sorry, what did you say?' I asked.

'Rohypnol. Have you ever heard of it? Roofies?'

'The date-rape drug?'

'Yeah. Have you ever encountered it, here at the house?'

'No.'

She watched me closely. 'Never overheard the brothers talking about it? Making jokes, maybe?'

'No,' I said. 'Really, no. Why?'

'What about unusual drinks?' She caught my expression and smiled, and said, 'Beyond Hunch Punch and Purple Jesus, I mean. Like special-occasion shooters. Limited-edition stuff that they don't serve to just anyone at the party?'

Holy shit, this woman knew her frat culture. And holy, *holy* shit – my mind waded through Officer McRae's words and finally caught up – she was talking about Mike's concoctions. Implicating Mike, even.

'Like I said, we weren't at the party.'

She changed tack. 'Do you know a girl named Sheri Asselin?'

I shrugged. 'Everyone knows her *now*, right? The golden ticket.'

'But did you know her before?'

'Not to talk to her. She goes to State.' I felt impatient. I was waiting for her to ask me about Charla Klein. My heartbeat sped, waiting for this cop to say Charla Klein's name. In fact I suddenly wanted quite badly to hear her say it. To know that it would finally be taken out of our hands, that the authorities would be taking over from here on in.

But Officer McCrae didn't say Charla's name. Instead, she asked, 'Do you know anyone who might have witnessed what happened to Sheri that night? Do you have any guesses who might have been in the house that night with a camera?'

I'd witnessed what happened to Sheri, or its aftermath, anyhow. Suddenly I remembered some legal thing I'd heard Dyann talking about at Raghurst. There was a law called 'Duty to Rescue'. What if I'd been obligated by law to rescue Sheri Asselin? What if, instead of putting her in a cab, I was supposed to call an ambulance – or police? That was way worse than an underage-drinking charge. 'If there are no charges, why are you investigating?' I said. 'Sheri's not on that sex tape. And the tape – it's just circumstantial evidence, right?'

'Is that what the brothers say?' Disgust coated Officer McRae's voice.

'I'm sorry,' I said, instantly ashamed. It *was* disgusting, the way I was dodging, trying to save my own hide. 'It's just … I'm actually really tired.'

Officer McRae stood up, patted my shoulder, and pressed a card with her name and phone number into my hand. 'Call me if you want to talk, okay?' she said. Her voice was gentle, but I thought I still heard traces of the disgust. And no wonder. I retained just enough self-awareness to know that I hadn't upheld my end of the conversation whatsoever.

I went straight up to bed and dropped into half-sleep. My thoughts were driven snow in the drugscape and drifted far away from Sheri Asselin and my roommates and the Black Bag.

*

Bruce came into the bathroom, yawning, shirtless, scratching his sternum. 'Are you riding your lighthorse?'

I laughed. 'I guess so.' No sleep had found me. Frozen black branches had clacked together ceaselessly outside the window, and Mike had returned shivery and plaintive to curl up beside me and murmur in his sleep.

Bruce wrapped warm arms around me and sighed. 'You know, Karen, I could never keep up with you.'

'What?'

'If you and I … I mean, you run on a totally different track than me, is all.' His arms slipped down mine to fall at his sides. 'I get why it's Chet and not me.'

'Bruce. You don't want' – I made a circling motion with my finger between the two of us – 'something like this. You want girls. Plural. And you can't stand it when girls talk.'

'I like talking to you, though.'

'You like groping me. The words are neither here nor there.' I winced at my prim wording.

'You trying to tell me you don't like being groped?'

'Not … lately.' Not by Mike, lately, I meant.

His eyes narrowed. He rubbed his scalp hard, until his hair stood at crazy angles. 'It's because of that video.'

Of course, the video. Bruce in the video. It flooded back. 'No,' I said.

'Fuck,' he said. His eyes watched mine in the mirror, watched me as I remembered the heavy golden hands sliding over Charla's white flanks. O lavish, lawless Bruce! Those slowmoving honeyed hands. Heat billowed over my skin. My nipples got so hard they hurt. My body was doing the exact opposite of my mind, which was spinning wildly, trying to think of something to say that wouldn't sound like an accusation or a reprimand or a demand for explanations or an effort to make excuses for Bruce.

'Fuck,' he repeated. And he left the bathroom.

I wanted to call after him, but there wasn't a good thing to say.

The bathroom door opened again. But it was Grace, Alec Moretti's girl-friend. 'Oh!' she said. 'I thought … I just saw Bruce …' She looked over her shoulder at the sound of Bruce's bedroom door clicking shut. 'Um. Are you okay?'

There wasn't a good thing to say to Grace, either. I'd assumed that she would have disappeared after seeing Alec in the Black Bag. I'd assumed she would have broken up with him immediately. But here she was in a lacy nightie in the second-floor bathroom of the fraternity house at 3 am, and here I was in boxers and a tank top, and Bruce Comfort had been in here with me moments earlier, and Grace knew this. There was nothing good to say. I nodded, my eyes on the floor, and I stepped around Grace and fled.

32. MONOMACHIA

(single combat)

The whole week before the holidays, the Faculty Club was dead. Most professors had evidently chosen to grade their exams from home. I'd picked up all kinds of extra shifts, partly because I needed the money and partly because I needed an excuse to see Mike less often. It was coming to that. I'd tried telling Mike I didn't want to plan every night of the week in advance, that I wanted to be free to join friends last-minute, sometimes, and he'd said, 'We'll just pencil in our plans, and if you want to change them, that'll be fine.' I'd tried telling him I was the sort of person who needs lots of time to herself, and he'd said, 'I can give you all the time to yourself that you want. We can just hang out together and not talk, and you can be totally alone, in your own head.'

So I booked extra shifts at the near-empty restaurant, and by day two I'd scratched all the chores off the manager's holiday close-down list, and I sat at the bar sneaking sips from the gin bottle and reading my way through most of the next semester's books, including six full Shakespeare plays from my anvil-like edition of the *Complete Plays*. I left the book at the Faculty Club instead of lugging it home with me at night, and I lucked out when Dr Davis happened to come in for martinis with a group of grad students and saw me reading ahead.

I had the house to myself as well as the restaurant: Marie-Jeanne had flown home to Trois-Rivières, and Charla had invited Steph and Dyann to her parents' chalet upstate. They'd suggested I join them after Christmas – there was a bus, and they would pick me up at the depot if I called ahead – but, to compensate for having stayed away all semester, I'd promised my parents I'd be home for all of Christmas break.

On Friday, right before we closed, someone scrawled down a phone message for me from Sheri Asselin. I sought out Hamish, who was cleaning out the auxiliary freezer. 'What did she want?'

He pressed Pause on the Discman in his apron pocket. 'What?'

'Sheri Asselin. What did she say?'

'To call her back. Obviously,' he added, and scowled, and pressed Play.

I dialed the number. She'd remembered hearing I worked there, she said. She wondered if we could meet somewhere and talk. Her voice sounded normal, like anyone's voice. I couldn't match it up with my memory of the torpid girl Mike and I had dressed and put into a taxi at the frat that morning after the S&M party. I couldn't remember her saying much of anything that morning.

I suggested we meet at the Thirsty Camel. I got there early and, without really meaning to, drank fast enough to be halfway through my second pint when she arrived. Sheri was tiny – not just petite, when I stood up to greet her, but small-boned and flat-chested too – and pretty in a wan, sexless way. She had streaked blonde hair with dark roots and lots of dark eyeliner that made her eyes older than the rest of her face.

Sheri ordered herself a beer. She lit a cigarette for each of us, and I thanked her, and then she unfolded a piece of paper from her purse and pushed it across the table to face me.

It was the GBC house meeting minutes, the one with *Sheri Asselin serviced us* written in under Community Service. Since the day I'd seen it pinned in the hallway the brothers had embellished upon this wisecrack, riffed on it, so that there was now a haphazard list, in various boys' handwriting, under the initial joke:

– *She was Asselin for it.*

– *Asselin and you Shall receivalin.*

– Sheri got my wang up her Asselin.

'How'd you get this?' I said. Had she been back to the house?

'One of my friends grabbed it,' she said.

I reread the last line. 'This is disgusting.'

'You think?' she said. Still her tone was neutral, normal.

'I didn't – I mean, I saw this on the wall, but not with all this stuff added to it.'

Sheri nodded in a preoccupied way and took a long pull on her cigarette. I decided not to say anything else until she told me why she'd sought me out.

After a minute, Sheri did talk. She talked fast and looked all around the bar. She didn't look at me even once. 'I got tested after,' she told me. 'I went to the ER, and they did the routine stuff. The thing was, I couldn't remember shit. I hadn't had all that much to drink, but it was, like, a total blackout, even the next day, a total blank. I mean, I was sore, bruised and stuff, so I knew something was up, but ...'

She paused for a drag, and I swallowed the mouthful of beer I'd been holding in my mouth in case I missed anything. That was how fast Sheri talked. She snapped out the words as efficiently as a croupier dealing cards. She had told this story before, I thought. Repeatedly. Recently.

'And then they told me they found traces of Rohypnol in my system,' she said.

'What?'

'Roofies.' She looked at me through a stream of smoke. 'Bad enough, right, if I drank too much and passed out and got hot-boxed for it? But then I find out those assholes *set me up.* Me and that other girl. That poor hooker down in the Bag.'

I blinked. 'She was a hooker?'

'Nobody knows her. She was never at any other parties.'

'Who would have hired her, though?' This was a stupid line of questioning – Shut *up*, shut *up*, Karen, thumped in my ears – but it was the same as when I'd spoken to the police officer at the frat: I wanted to hear that Sheri had figured it out, that she knew it was Charla in the Bag and Dyann, Steph, and Marie-Jeanne behind the lens. I didn't want to tell Sheri. I just wanted it to be known. I wanted it to be something no longer up to me to tell or not tell.

'You'd know better than I would,' Sheri said. 'Don't their girlfriends help plan the parties?'

'No.' Alarm thrummed though me. 'I wasn't even there. Mike had this awards banquet.'

'That's what the cop said, but she said I should still talk to you.'

'Who? Officer McRae?'

'Yeah.'

'Why?'

'She said just talk it through, maybe it would jog my memory of the party. Because you drove me home, and because you're so tight with those guys.'

'I didn't drive you home. I just called you a taxi, remember?' I didn't recall telling the cop that, though. My heart beat hard. Worried about potential charges against me, I'd looked up Duty to Rescue after my conversation with Officer McCrae. There was a state law on the books but nobody ever enforced it, except, rarely, in one of two circumstances: you could be liable under Duty to Rescue if you'd created a hazardous environment, like if a bucket you'd perched on a ladder fell on someone's head and knocked them out, or if the person in peril was an invitee in your home. GBC wasn't my home, though, and Sheri hadn't been my invitee.

I was guiltily aware that this thinking crossed over into victim-blaming. But legally it was sound. In fact, I was fairly sure that any of the frat boys would make the same argument. They'd invited the State girls for the Tribal Warfare party, not the S&M party. It's just that Sheri had become a regular at GBC events since then.

'I *don't* remember, remember?' Sheri stubbed out her cigarette, lifted her hair off her neck, and smoothed it into a ponytail, fastening it with an elastic band from her wrist. She wore tiny crosses in her earlobes.

'Sheri, I swear, I don't know anything about roofies at GBC. I don't think they'd ever go that far, do you?'

She shot me a look I couldn't quite read. 'Some of them would, sure.' Then, 'Not Chet. He seems really sweet.'

Her expression resolved itself for me into a blend of pity and disdain. She pitied my naiveté. Sheri Asselin felt sorry for *me*. I fought an urge to laugh.

'What? He does, he seems sweet.'

'I'm getting more beer. Want one?'

'What is so funny?' Sheri shook her head, pushed herself into the corner of the booth, and stretched out her legs along the vinyl bench. 'Okay, I'll go again. A pint.'

I brought back our drinks, then excused myself and went downstairs to the filthy restroom. I needed the extra minutes to think.

Sheri believed the brothers had drugged her – had drugged Charla, too – in order to make a sex tape. Maybe it was good. Perfect even, maybe. Sheri's accusations would lead to more police raids, more external scrutiny of the mixers, the initiation process, the Black Bag, the gold car – all the parts of GBC culture that needed fixing, in other words. And meanwhile the Raghurst women's videotape would become less central to the whole thing. We'd fall off the radar.

I bought cigarettes from the machine in the basement and gave Sheri one when I sat down. 'I think you're brave to do this,' I told her. 'To strike back. After what you went through. It's brave.'

She leaned in to the flame from my lighter. 'I didn't "go through" anything. I told you: I was completely checked out. I mean, if you're going to get banged, I highly recommend roofies, actually. Except that now we can't press charges, because I can't remember any details.'

'You must remember the beginning of the party, at least. Who gave you the drink?'

'It could have been anyone, really. Sure, there's stuff I remember. They had this swing in the living room. One of those slings, like in sex clubs, you know?'

I hadn't heard this part. No one had been recounting party stories the next day at the frat house. They were all too groggy and hungover. Nor was I at all certain what went on in sex clubs.

'Anyway, there was this kind of show, with a guy and a girl in leather – they must have been professionals, because they disappeared at some point – and then we all sort of danced and fooled around on the swing. And then it fell.' Sheri laughed a little, recalling it. 'It was a pretty good party, actually. There was this chick with a whip, like a dominatrix. And this cocktail waitress with blue and pink shooters. Blue for boys, pink for girls.'

Something nudged me inside, some uneasiness. 'They hired waitresses?'

'Not a real waitress, probably. I thought maybe it was the shooters they spiked, but I only drank a blue one, so.'

I frowned. 'So what?'

'They wouldn't want to drug *themselves*, right? Plus I know lots of girls who drank the pink ones, and they were all fine.'

My tongue was dry. 'What did the waitress look like?'

'Blonde. Pigtails, is all I noticed. I told you, she wasn't really a waitress. The cops talked to the dancers and called around at catering companies, et cetera. It all came up blank.' Sheri swung her crossed legs over the side of the booth and joggled her foot up and down. 'Anyway, probably nothing will happen. McRae told me ninety-nine percent of complaints against fraternities go nowhere. Those guys can, like, line up and piss on your front lawn every morning, and you can't do a thing about it.'

'Getting your lawn pissed on is a little different than getting gang-banged,' I said.

She looked at me. 'Yes. Thank you for pointing that out for me, Karen.'

'I didn't mean … It's just, that *is* how they treat you,' I said. I flicked a finger at the page of house minutes still on the table. 'Like your body is their property to piss on.'

'Thanks for the lecture.' She held up a small hand to stop me from speaking. 'No, I get it. I don't respect myself enough. I'm just one of their skanks, and shit happens.'

'No, that's not –' The beer furred my brain and gummed my words together on my tongue.

'I "fail to grasp the complexity of the situation". That's what the suits and ties at your Student Life Office told me. They weren't even going to put the complaint through, until I went back to McCrae. They weren't going to investigate squat.' She rubbed savagely at a smear of ash on the tabletop. 'I gotta piss,' she said, and stalked off to the stairs.

I rubbed at the ash, too, and used my sleeve to mop up the rings of condensation. It was true: Sheri did fail to grasp the complexity of the situation. But it wasn't her fault. It was mine, for not telling her who'd really been in the Black Bag that night. Who was behind the camera.

When Sheri came back, she didn't sit down. 'McRae said you write about feminist stuff in the school paper. She was all, like, "You should talk to Karen; she may be friendly with the frat but she's got a brain in her head." Meanwhile she totally doesn't get that that's the exact reason *not* to talk to you.'

'Because I'll lecture you.' Where was Officer McCrae getting all this information? It wasn't even accurate. I took pictures for the *Eye* sometimes, that was all.

'Because you think you know better! I can see you thinking it: it's too bad it happened to me, but I put myself into the situation, right? As if they see you as any different than me. As if they see you as anything but red meat.'

33. THAUMASMUS

(marveling at something)

The three pints of beer made my bike ride home wobbly and reckless. I locked up on the porch and was startled by my reflection in the living room window. The house was silent and pitch dark, a rotten food smell emanating from the kitchen.

I'd told Mike I was exhausted from the work week, that I was going out with work people and straight home to bed afterward. He'd wanted to come over, 'just to sleep, and wake up together', but I'd said no and left him sulky on the phone.

It was after eleven, and I rolled into bed as per my alibi, but my bedroom spun unpleasantly and my thoughts kept rearing up, racing forward, and collapsing in a jumbled heap inside my skull. I opened my window for air and heard irritating, repetitive strains of guitar from the boys' house next door. Finally I threw on my plaid shirt and a pair of leggings and went to visit.

The half-pipe was lying in pieces in the living room. Stick crawled down the hallway toward me on all fours. 'Hello,' he greeted me, in a heavy Russian accent, 'I have injury of ankle from catastrophic collapse of skateboard infrastructure.'

'I can't sleep,' I told him.

Stick jabbed his finger ceilingward. 'Aha! This problem, I can help you. Come.' Turning himself gingerly around, he crawled ahead of me into the kitchen. At the dining table I saw a group of boys, including Jake and Wheeler, hunched over a game of Risk. The guitar music came from some-where upstairs.

Stick lifted at least two dozen cans of beer out of a cooler and put them on the floor. 'Pass me big pot from stove,' he instructed.

'Why are you talking like that?' I said, handing him the pot.

He scooped handfuls of ice into the pot. Then he lifted a false bottom on the cooler, revealing a compartment crammed with baggies, pill bottles, and foil packets. 'I am practising new persona for Vampire. Is role-playing game,' he explained. 'We begin game at midnight. Also, perhaps, is influence of ketamine,' he added. He selected and rejected several prescription bottles from his stash before opening one, shaking two tablets onto his palm, and handing them to me.

'How much?' I said.

He shook his head. 'Is gift from pharmacopeia of Vladimir Vronsky. I think perhaps Vronsky will be great physician and healer as well as assassin.'

I got some water and took the pills. Then I sat next to Stick on the lino-leum and helped him stack the cans back in the cooler. 'Do you ever sell Rohypnol?' I asked.

He raised one eyebrow at me. 'Is trick question?'

'Did you sell it to Dyann?'

'Nyet.'

'Marie-Jeanne, then. Or you gave it to her free.'

'Marie-Jeanne is most beloved friend of Vladimir. I do not entertain such question.'

'Holy shit, you did, didn't you?' The kitchen spun, and I rocked up to my haunches. 'They fucking roofied her.'

'Who?'

'Sheri Asselin.'

'Who?' Stick repeated.

'This girl at GBC. She was tested. She was roofied.'

'Keep your voice down.' The Russian accent had evaporated. 'You don't know what you're talking about, Karen, all right?'

I left him there on the floor and stumbled up the stairs. I found the guitar player on Stick's bed, his girlfriend fast asleep next to him. His name was Eugene, he said when I introduced myself. I stretched out on the floor and waited for Stick's prescription to take hold.

When I woke up the next morning, someone had spread a sleeping bag over me. Eugene and his girlfriend had vacated the bed but Stick lay beside me on the floor, shirtless, snoring, his sprained ankle propped on a stack of pillows.

My mouth was dry as cotton from the pills. I went to the washroom and drank a long time from my cupped hands. My head felt light, as if my skull would lift off my neck. I lay back down on the sleeping bag beside Stick, who stirred and groaned as his foot slid off the pillows.

'Who won the game?' I asked.

'It's not that kind of game,' he told me. 'It just goes on forever and ever.'

We fell into companionable silence. I drifted in and out of a fluffy, sunlit sleep.

Then he said, 'Would you consider sex with me?'

'I have a boyfriend,' I told him, half-awake, mumbling the words so automatically that Stick laughed.

'There must be *something* you find attractive about me.' He was teasing now. Back to chumming around.

I looked at him. He was pale, freckly, with wide blue eyes and a snub nose. A wiry rock-climber's body. 'You have a nice head,' I offered. Under his brush cut the skull was shapely, peaked at the back, broad across the brow.

Stick shifted on the carpet and rested his head on my stomach. I stroked his bristly scalp, his delicate ear. He was one of those daredevil boys who, in another part of the country – not a campus town – would ride a dirt bike, do flips and jumps on it, and ride in a big rodeo arena with monster trucks and crushed school buses. 'I could probably have sex with your head,' I said.

'You Esterhazians.' Stick sighed. 'I've never met anyone like you. You're like vestal virgins.'

I laughed. 'What?'

'Priestesses. You know, cloistered.'

'I know what a vestal virgin is,' I said. 'But I have a boyfriend; I told you.'

'A GBC boy.'

'Yeah. Well, sort of. He's atypical.'

Stick raised his head off my stomach and propped it on his elbow. He regarded me a moment, closing first one eye and then the other, alternating. It should have been comical, but it wasn't, somehow. 'I don't know how you can stand the cognitive dissonance,' he said finally.

'What? The boyfriend?'

'The campaign. The scandal.' Stick poked my bicep. 'I saw you in that video, Karen. You looked like you were ready to blow the whistle. Abort the whole mission.'

'I wasn't in the video,' I said.

'What do you mean, you weren't in the video?'

Then it clicked, and I flushed at my stupidity. What my roommates released was just a clip. The camera would have been running in the Black Bag the entire time. 'Do you have the tape? The original?' I said.

He shook his head, and I sat up and shoved hard at his shoulder. Off balance, he flopped flat onto his back. 'Ouch. Watch the foot!'

'Where is it?' It all snapped together in my mind now: my roommates had brought roofies to the frat house that night. They'd drugged some of the brothers' drinks – no, it wasn't the brothers' drinks. They'd brought Jell-O shots with them to the frat house. Sheri Asselin had said there'd been pink and blue shooters, and she'd chosen a blue one. They'd spiked only the blue shooters, for the frat boys.

Stick said, 'I thought you would have watched the tape with them. I thought you knew.'

'Where is it?' I looked under his bed, reached in and yanked out a tangled mass of climbing ropes, an empty suitcase, a pair of ski boots. Dread crawled over the skin of my belly, my ribs, and my breasts, leaving my armpits damp. How dare they, I thought. How dare they. 'I swear to God, I will tear this place apart!'

'They left it with Charla. They gave it to Charla,' he said.

I slumped onto his bed. I felt like crying.

'Hey.' Stick came up to his knees to look me in the eyes. 'Nobody's going to put you on TV or anything.'

'That's not it,' I said. Blue for boys, pink for girls. I was sick to death of being left out, left behind, left in the dark. How dare they, I thought – but they did dare, my roommates. They were daring and fearless and shameless, and they'd left me entirely in the dark.

After a moment he said, 'You know they deserved it, right? Boyfriend or no boyfriend, you must know those fraternities are a blight on the earth. Even if some girl was caught in the crossfire by accident, it was still worth it.'

'That girl's name was Sheri. And for your information, she got gang-banged that night. Raped.' Saying the word was like punching Stick in the face. I was shocked at how good it felt.

But Stick didn't react as if I'd punched him. He simply nodded. 'This is the whole point. Those assholes all deserve to be gelded like steers.'

Steers had been Dyann's analogy too. No, elk. She'd compared the brothers to rutting elk.

'Let's keep our heads on straight here,' Stick said. 'I mean, imagine a place where taking drugs and passing out means you'll get gang-banged. That place shouldn't even exist.'

34. ENARGEIA

(vividness)

The videotape sat in plain view in the pencil drawer of Charla's desk. It took me almost an hour of further searching, though, to locate the video camera in its Styrofoam-packed box on a shelf at the top of Steph's closet. I also found, under Steph's mattress, a photo of her stretched out beside Dyann in a hammock, her head on Dyann's breast. In Dyann's room I found a tea canister full of marijuana buds, a gay pornography video entitled *Cocksure*, a flexible stick with a leather tassel, and a threadbare stuffed lamb with yarn Xs for eyes. Marie-Jeanne's bedside table yielded a bulk supply of birth control pills past their expiration date and a bundle of letters in French, addressed to her, postmarked Trois-Rivières, Quebec, and dated 1990. By the time I got back around to Charla's bedroom with the camera, I was too tired to snoop any further. I hooked up the camcorder to the television, lay down in Charla's bower, and smoked some of Dyann's pot, intending to watch the videotape from beginning to end.

But Raghurst's doorbell rang, and when I answered it, it was Mike. I'd promised to phone him first thing that morning so that we could go Christmas shopping, and by now it was nearly two in the afternoon. He was irritated beyond measure to find me still in pajamas, bloodshot, and oblivious to the fact that he'd called 'at least twenty times, probably thirty' since eight o'clock.

Mike sat down on the sofa and reached into his book bag. 'I brought these for you. You left them in my room.'

I knew right away what they were. They were photographs. I'd kept them tucked in my *Iliad*, and they must have fallen out when I was at GBC. Or Mike had paged through my book and found them.

He laid the photos on the steamer trunk and sat back, arms crossed.

I picked them up. 'Thanks.'

'You're in love with Bruce,' Mike said.

'What?'

'Don't smile like that. Don't mock me, on top of everything else.'

I concentrated all my willpower on the muscles of my face. I sat in the chair opposite him with the photos on my lap, not looking at them. There were six images, if indeed Mike had found them all. They were extreme close-ups, most of them blurry and overexposed. The drugstore where I'd had them developed at nineteen cents a print hadn't even charged me for four of the six – just included them in the envelope with black stickers to indicate that the mistake was mine, not theirs. I'd peeled off the stickers and kept them, planning to work with the images further in the darkroom sometime.

'Grace saw you,' he said. 'She told me she saw the two of you, you and Bruce. And I was like, "Oh, that's ridiculous. Karen and Bruce? That doesn't even make sense." And then I saw *those*.'

I refused to follow his glance to the photos in my lap. Only the last two images – the in-focus ones – could have upset Mike like this. One was the nape of Bruce's neck: a burnished swell of vertebrae, the flat gold plain above it with its shimmer of hair, and, away in the distance, the lurid blur of earlobe.

When it became clear I wasn't going to defend myself, Mike cleared his throat and leaned forward, forearms on his knees. 'Listen to me. Bruce is evil, all right? It's not just that he's an idiot, and that he's had his whole life handed to him on a silver platter and will never have to lift a finger, his whole life, to get what he wants. It's that he treats women like shit. He's using you, like he used Charla on that video, like he used that girl Susannah. Like he uses everyone. How can you not see that?' He glanced at the photos again with disgust.

I looked down. The small pile of prints lay on my lap like a lolling tongue. The top image depicted the soft gully between Bruce's hipbone and his pelvis, where a vein floated just beneath the golden skin. Quickly, I flipped the whole stack facedown to protect Bruce from the profanity of Mike's eyes.

'He was drugged,' I said.

'What?'

'On the video. I think Bruce was doped up with Rohypnol. Roofies. Remember how wasted everyone was? All the puking, the blackouts? All the brothers, that night – they were all drugged.'

'By whom?'

'My roommates. It was part of the whole plan, I think, so none of the brothers would remember being taped.'

Mike stood up. 'Is this supposed to make me feel better? You defending Bruce?'

'I don't know,' I said.

'I never knew you were this shallow. Falling for that.' He jerked his chin at the photos in my lap.

'Falling for what?'

'An image. His image.'

＊

I finally viewed the entire videotape in the unfinished area of my parents' basement, back home in Canada. I'd stashed the tape in my backpack on the assumption I'd be at Raghurst again before Charla and the others got back from their chalet trip. My parents' video camera proved compatible, so I set it up with an old computer monitor and watched with headphones, late one night after Christmas, my feet aching with cold on the concrete floor, my index finger poised to hit the Stop button if my brother Keith happened by.

My mother was happy to have me home but unhappy about how long I slept and how little I talked. And she was especially displeased with how often Mike called and how long our conversations were. She said it felt like I wasn't really home at all – like I was there in body but not in spirit. She eavesdropped by the door of my bedroom and didn't try to hide the fact of her having eavesdropped when I came out.

'Let me make you an appointment with Dr Howe,' she begged. Dr Howe was the therapist my father had been seeing for the last couple of years for his anxiety. 'You just seem so tense and worried about this boy, and he seems so obsessive about you. You don't seem yourself.'

The news about the roofies had made Mike feel better after all. 'The only two things I care about are GBC and you,' he'd said on the phone. 'Knowing the video was a setup makes me feel better about those guys on the tape: they weren't really themselves. And knowing Bruce was part of that setup makes me feel better about you, Karen. You were right, right? It's not *Bruce* you want – he's just a pretty face, a model for your art, or your feminist campaign, or whatever. You're using him, not the other way around.'

'Using him? That's a good thing?' I'd said.

'Compared to you falling for him, sure.'

'I'm in a *relationship*,' I told my mom. 'This is how it works, right? Relationships require work, and communication.'

It was eerie to hear Mike's words coming out of my mouth – he'd said exactly this on the phone earlier that day – but they got my mother off my back. She bought me a last-minute Christmas present: a self-help book called *The Dance of Intimacy*. When I unwrapped it, I felt like throwing it at her. She was welcoming me to some kind of club I didn't want to join. I do drugs, I wanted to tell her. Mike and I fuck like animals. I live with *queers*!

What I saw on the videotape, when I finally did watch it, was fifty-five minutes of redlight jostle and shuffle and heave all blurring together into a monotony of flesh. The brothers stumbled and swayed around the room. They laughed like morons at one another and at Charla. They mumbled obscenities. They held on and humped or thrust in a perfunctory fashion, and many didn't appear to come at all but just pulled the rubber off after a few minutes, or went limp and let the rubber slide off by itself. It was the most boring show I'd ever watched.

The only interesting moments of the tape were those featuring the Raghurst girls. Marie-Jeanne in the earliest segment, in the backseat of what must have been Steph's car. Steph's voice close to the microphone, saying, 'Test. Test.' And then: 'Where does a person even buy false eyelashes nowadays?'

Marie-Jeanne wore a black leotard and vinyl suspenders. Her hair was slicked into two tight pigtails, and her face was caked in enough sparkly makeup to make her utterly unrecognisable.

'No seconds for anyone.' Dyann's voice came from just outside the frame. 'If someone grabs one, you're going to have to grab it back, or jostle him and spill it somehow.'

Marie-Jeanne's eye-roll was exaggerated by her mascara, and she said something sarcastic in French that was cut off when the camera stopped rolling.

There were moments when no brothers were in the Black Bag. Dyann couldn't risk being seen, of course, but once or twice she couldn't seem to help herself. Once she emerged into the frame, touched Charla's bare shoulders, and whispered something at her ear.

'You're a coward, you know that?' Charla barked at her. 'Get the hell back in the closet. And make sure the tape is still rolling!'

Later on, between frat boys' visits, Dyann's voice came close to the microphone: 'Charla, please say the safeword. Please, let's get out of here now.'

And later still, Dyann saying, still off-camera, 'Fuck, Charla. Fuck.' The words choking into a sob.

Then I was in the frame too, looking overdressed in Mike's T-shirt and boxers. My hands fluttered, and my eyes goggled with the effort to take everything in at once under the red light. And then Dyann charged across the room to body-check me into the closed door, trying to angle her whole body into my sight lines, to hustle me out of the room. 'Find Steph,' she said. 'Tell her we're done here.'

What I saw in the video wasn't erotic, or even pornographic in any proper sense of the word. Nothing about it stirred anything in me beyond the queasy fascination a tabloid or multivehicle accident might have done. And yet afterward, in my old bedroom on my old twin mattress with my head on the pillow that was firmer than the one at Raghurst and smelled of all my high school yearnings, I pictured Charla's naked body awash in red light. I reverted to my own version of the video, the one I'd played over and over in my mind after seeing the initial scandal-clip. And I added to my version, innovated upon it: Charla lay in her bower now, and Bruce was there with her, and Charla clawed at his flesh and called him a coward while they fucked.

And lying there picturing this with both hands between my legs I came again and again, furious and convulsive and each time accruing what felt like clarity, taking on what felt like light, until I was suspended somewhere high above myself, looking down from above upon the foreshortened red figures below, looking down upon the embowered girl whose soul spilt out around her in a shimmering pool.

35. TOPOTHESIA

(description of an imaginary place)

The morning after viewing the tape in my parents' basement I bought a one-way bus ticket to the ski town near Charla's family chalet. I left a message at the chalet with my arrival time, but I almost hoped my roommates wouldn't get it in time. I had a vision of myself striding for hours through a snowstorm and then flinging open the log-cabin door with the blizzard howling at my back, so that the fireplace would explode embers over the hearth and they'd all have to leap up and beat out the sparks with their slippers.

Disruption, that was what I was after. I wanted to disrupt their cozy retreat – their *cloister*, as Stick had referred to it – and haul them one by one into the broad light of accusation and accountability. I was only sorry Marie-Jeanne wouldn't be there to answer for her part.

Steph's orange Corolla was waiting for me at the Sunrise Inn bus terminal. The snow had blinded the highway an hour back, but here it was clear, and I walked to the car under a flat white sky.

'Howdy, stranger.' Charla climbed out of the driver's seat to unlock the trunk for my bag. 'I never asked you. Do you ski?'

'Not really. How's the snow been?' Charla had come alone. The backseat was full of boxed groceries. I moved her copy of *The Voyage Out* from the passenger seat to the back before getting in.

'I only went one day. Dyann doesn't ski, either, and Steph hasn't gotten out of bed all week.'

'Is she sick?'

Charla shrugged. 'Maybe she'll confide in you.' She pulled off one of her gloves to light a smoke, opened her window a crack, and replaced the glove. Her cheekbones stood out when she inhaled. A strand blew into her face and came close to the glowing tip of her cigarette. Her lips were chapped.

I thought of telling her about my meeting with Sheri Asselin, but my guts knotted as I searched for the right opening. It wasn't Charla I wanted to accuse anyway. Charla was a nervous driver – hands at ten and two even holding the cigarette, neck craned toward the windshield, humming to herself to stay calm – and yet she'd come in person to pick me up as promised. She'd never been bent on secrecy and exclusivity to the same degree as the others. And if she'd helped engineer the fraternity setup, she'd paid for it, hadn't she, with her own body? Charla had put her money where her mouth was, so to speak.

We shared the twenty-minute drive in silence. The snow-covered hills grayed and blackened and swallowed their stands of pines as night came on.

The car slowed and then turned into the trees – a narrow driveway I hadn't noticed among the shadows. Charla parked at a turnaround ringed by snowbanks.

'It's so dark,' I observed, struggling up the shoveled path with my backpack and a box of groceries.

'The solstice is just past,' Charla said. 'These are the longest nights of the year.'

Charla had suggested I see Steph right away, so after dropping my bag in the tiled hallway and putting the groceries on the kitchen counter, I waved a quick hello to Dyann and followed Charla down the hall to the third bedroom door. The room was dark and stuffy. The bedside lamp had a shade made from Popsicle sticks. I turned the switch, and slatted light struck the pile of quilts on the bed. The pile stirred and groaned.

I touched Steph's shoulder, and she turned onto her back. Her face was doughy, the eyes sunken and shadowed.

'Are you wearing all your clothes under there?' I said.

'I can't get warm,' she told me.

'What's the matter?'

Tears filled her eyes. 'I'm just so tired. I shouldn't have come. Those guys don't want me up here like this.' Her words were slowed down, thick and effortful, like she was trying to speak under water.

'Of course they want you. Why wouldn't they?'

Her hands came out from the quilts, and I folded them between my own. Her fingers were those of a younger girl than Steph. 'I'm not equal to this,' she said.

I thought she meant she felt like a third wheel. 'Well, I'm here – it'll even things out.'

She shook her head. 'I mean, I'm unequal to the task. I keep telling them: go on without me, I'm not up to it anymore, I want out. And Dyann keeps treating me like a defector, like I'm AWOL and it's up to her to haul my ass in.'

I let go of Steph's hands to pull at a bit of orange yarn sticking out of the quilt. What an ugly piece of handiwork. Some grandmother imagined she was making an heirloom. Or maybe this particular quilt was never intended to be art but merely a way of stitching things together to keep warm. I wanted to get my camera from my bag, to capture this weird double patchwork of rags and lamplight.

Steph was still shaking her head, squinting and blinking at the window. Tears came again, more of those silent, slippery ones with no other symptoms of weeping. 'It's not fair of Dyann to ask me to hold on to this,' she whispered. 'We think these problems are just on our campus. But they're everywhere; there are no battle lines to draw. It's too big. It's bigger than us now – bigger than any of us.'

I did not want to hear Steph's confession. I had not come to serve as their confessor. I wanted to accuse, not absolve. My righteous anger was as heavy in my guts as a heap of stones.

But Steph wasn't confessing exactly, at least not right now. She said, 'I keep having this daydream that I have tuberculosis. My lungs are bogged down with blood. Whenever I speak my words are plain, pure drops of blood here on the sheet, or a red spray that makes a pattern on the floor.' She turned onto her side with her mouth at the edge of the mattress; I could tell she was seeing the pattern at this very moment.

Red drops on white: I thought of pricked fingers, of Snow White's mother, of the spindle and the sleeping castle. Enchantment. 'You wish the whole world would stop,' I guessed.

'Yes!' Steph grabbed my hand again. She even smiled. 'Yes, that's it exactly.'

'She's really depressed,' I reported when Charla and Dyann looked up from putting the groceries away in the cupboards.

Charla shrugged, just as she had in the car. Her eyes were on Dyann, who hoisted the recycling wastebasket to her hip and began clanking empty wine bottles into it from the cluttered countertop.

'What should we do?' I said.

'There's nothing we *can* do,' said Dyann. 'We've been over it and over it, trust me.'

'Over what? The fact that Steph has a conscience?' My anger was piled up inside me like a stone cairn.

Dyann lowered the bin to the linoleum and shoved it toward the back door with her foot. She sighed. 'Karen, you don't even know what you're talking about, all right? It's not *conscience* bothering Steph. She's just sulking because she's thought of a way to suck up to Sylvia, and I won't let her do it.'

'I don't know if it's only about sucking up,' Charla said.

'Do you really think Sylvia's going to show up on a white horse and say, "I'm yours. I'm at your service. Let's all sit down and figure out our best course of action given the present circumstances?" Come on.'

'Steph wants to tell Dr Esterhazy?' I said. Maybe all of this would take care of itself. I wouldn't have to confront anybody about anything. I wouldn't have to do a thing. I could just climb up into the stone tower of my anger and sit there, high above them all, watching it unfold.

'Steph wants to *fuck* Esterhazy,' Dyann said. 'Steph wants to *marry* Esterhazy. Telling her? Confiding in her? It's just a pathetic attempt at seduction.'

Charla was laughing now. 'We all want to marry Esterhazy. I want to marry her. You want to marry her, right, Karen?' I made a lovesick face and nodded, joining her joke. 'Dyann, don't deny it, you would marry her in a heartbeat, if only she would propose to you.'

'I'm going out to chop more wood,' Dyann said.

I offered to help with dinner, and Charla showed me the ingredients she'd bought for pizza. She sat on the dishwasher reading Woolf to me while

I sliced the veggies, flattened the dough and spread it with pesto, shredded the cheese.

'We've been going to bed super-early up here,' she explained when, at nine o'clock, Dyann tossed the couch cushions to the floor and pulled open the sofa bed. Charla disappeared into her parents' bedroom, alone.

I waited until Dyann and I were both finished in the washroom and she'd just turned out the living room light. Then I whispered, 'Did you really dump Charla the day after the Bag?'

'What?' Dyann sat up straight in the bed. She was wearing men's long underwear and a toque pulled over her dreadlocks. In the dark she looked small.

'You stopped touching her because of the Black Bag. You've pulled away from her completely, like she's got a taint or something. How do you think that makes her feel?'

'I think … it's none of your goddamn business, Karen.'

'Of course it isn't. None of this is any of my business, is it?' Her pause was enough, though. I wanted no confessions, especially not from Dyann, tonight; I'd just wanted to shock her for a moment, just enough to appease my anger. I mumbled a stiff good night and retreated to my room.

The quiet at the chalet oppressed me. It wasn't the cloying, carpeted quiet of my parents' house after my parents went to bed – the acquiescent silence that kept me tossing restless in my old bedroom and then left me asleep long into the mornings while my brothers played Nintendo and ate Cheerios. Here at the chalet the silence dropped straight down on me from a great height. Here it pinned me down like the silence of gravity itself. Here was mid-winter quiet, the forest's mouth stuffed with snow.

I am unequal to this too, I thought. I lay in my bunk and felt sullied in body and soul, my heart frayed with doubts. This feeling – my corruption, my unworthiness – drained me. My limbs seemed to sink through the mattress to the floorboards beneath. The anger rotted in its cairn and I flowed away from it in all directions. I ebbed away and was asleep in moments.

36. KATABASIS

(descent)

For two days and two more nights we did nothing, said almost nothing to one another. Meeting Sheri, viewing the videotape – it was there, at the back of my mind, but all the urgency and resolution that had gathered in me was muffled, at a standstill. Mike too – our capital-R Relationship that needed so much analysis and attention – seemed far away and inconsequential. After all, Mike didn't even know where I was. The torpor made me hungry, but no one else seemed interested in the kitchen, so I cooked and brought food to the others on trays. I took Steph's car and consulted a local map and fetched more groceries. I mixed drinks and brewed tea. Charla got a nosebleed from the dry air, so I soaked bath towels and hung them over the backs of chairs in front of the baseboards to humidify the space.

I found a videotape library in the cabinet and, though Charla and Dyann scoffed at the titles I read out, Steph actually seemed mildly interested, so we watched *Terms of Endearment, Tootsie, Dead Poets Society*. The silence padded from room to room on great white paws. At night it turned tight circles, flattening us underfoot, then flopped its shaggy body down to sleep.

On the third afternoon – it was our last full day at the chalet – Charla roused us all to go for a hike. The Scenic Caves were only a ten-minute drive away, and we absolutely needed to see them before we left. 'We really need this,' she insisted, 'all of us. You'll see what I mean when we're standing there.'

Surprisingly, it was Steph who agreed first. 'Maybe I can throw myself over a cliff,' she suggested – but we could hear that it was a joke, that she was back to some degree of her usual dry, self-deprecating humor. She and Dyann sorted through their clothing to find suitable gear for me to borrow, Charla consulted the map, and I put together a makeshift trail mix with left-over granola, mixed nuts, and M&M's.

'It's never been logged,' Charla read from the little pamphlet she had pulled from the wooden welcome box at the trailhead. 'They couldn't risk bringing horses this close to the chasm. Some of these pines are three hundred years old. Karen, I bet it'll remind you of tree-planting country.'

Ninety minutes we hiked in, and eventually the conversation petered out and the silence crept into our ears. It wasn't at all like the tree-planting cutovers with their splayed-open trenches crisscrossed by slash piles. An alien light filtered down across our path as we walked, a weaker light than summer's but somehow more intensely green. Crevices would sneak up on us, invisible ahead until the path veered and disappeared downhill. The deciduous trees scrambled naked and scrawny among the pines, desperate for the sun.

I lifted my camera from its case around my neck and took a few pictures. The twisting trunks reminded me of Ovid's Daphne, who, Dr Esterhazy told us, turned herself into a tree to save herself from Apollo's amorous advances. Those were the words Dr Esterhazy used: 'amorous advances'. In class I'd imagined Dyann's hand shooting up and her voice saying, 'Can we please say "rape"? May we please have permission to call it what it is?' Later I'd read that Daphne had emulated the goddess Diana, preferring woodland sports, hunting, and perpetual virginity to sex. Perhaps life as a tree wasn't such a terrible outcome for Daphne.

O, but let us not forget the amorality of the earth! Look at these stone-dark faces whiskered with ferns. See how the hoarfrosted leaves disguise the waiting jaws beneath. We humans who walk groundling and gaze at the middle distances, we are but gossamerboned and velvetskinned. We walk the thinnest crust over our own crypts.

My feet and ankles grew chilled. I'd drunk all the water from my bottle. The strap of my daypack chafed my collarbone. It may not have been a clear-cut but it felt like tree-planting, this numbing, animal movement across the terrain. I loved the way it scraped out the inside of my brain until I was just a body, merely a creature. Ninety minutes we hiked, and the silence leapt down our throats.

'Karen, what the hell!' Dyann had repeated my name several times already, apparently. 'We need your vote.'

'On what?'

'Holy space cadet. Where have you been for the last twenty minutes? We're lost.'

The blue painted dots marking the trail were mostly too faded or snow-caked to read. Steph thought we should have taken the other path at the fork, thirty minutes back. Charla was certain the trail would still loop around. 'If we're actually still on the trail,' she added.

Dyann was for retracing our steps: 'At least then we know it's an hour and a half to the car.'

'I don't want to climb back up all those gullies we slid down,' Charla said.

As usual, though, Dyann's will was strongest. We turned around and plodded back the way we'd come, and soon we were picking our way single file, up along the rockfall trail between the cliff faces. It was slow, treacherous going.

O, but look how the black rock weeps even below freezing! Look how the cold green light strikes bronze through Dyann's tangled mane! She tosses her head like a warhorse and thrusts her hips into the climb. We who follow her steady tread throw our hearts at her feet again and again. We lay out our hearts like acolytes, looking for her blessing. But she grows impatient with the caves' wet whispering. Sure-footed, prancing, she hears the far-off echoing war cry, sees the signal fires high on the summit.

I was second in line, watching every step Dyann took so I could place my feet where she had. 'Just answer me one question,' I said to her. 'If you were so certain about filming that video, why did you need the Rohypnol?'

Dyann heaved herself atop the boulder she was scaling, straightened, and turned to look down at me. I felt the others pull up short on the trail behind us. We were all panting from the steep climb, and my heart kicked double against my ribs.

'I don't understand the question,' she said.

'Sure you do. MJ the cocktail waitress? Blue for boys, pink for girls? You wanted to make sure none of the brothers remembered what happened in the Black Bag.'

Dyann glared down on me from her great height, a raptor in her eyrie. 'You always refer to it as "what happened",' she said. 'Why can't you say, "what they did"? Or call it "rape". Call it what it was, for God's sake!'

There it was, that red word. Swung like an axe. But Dyann wasn't going to bully me out of having this conversation, not now I'd finally begun it. This time I was ready to swing the axe too.

'If a girl is too incapacitated to say yes or no, it's rape,' I said. 'So let's follow the logic, then. Charla wasn't incapacitated at all' – I threw an apologetic glance back at Charla – 'but the frat brothers *were* incapacitated, thanks to you.' Dyann huffed and rolled her eyes, and I raised my hand to stop her from interrupting me. 'Many of them are totally incoherent on the tape. Some of them can barely stand up.'

It was gratifying to watch the fact close its fist on Dyann: 'You found the tape. You watched all the footage?'

'It's not nearly as close to rape as you'd like it to be, is it?' I said.

Dyann turned her back and commenced her climb again, moving faster than before. 'That is such bullshit, Karen!' she growled. 'That's exactly the kind of sexist, legalistic jargon you hear every time a man sticks his cock where it's not wanted!'

'Mike and I found this girl the morning after the party.' I had to scramble to catch up with her; she was already ten or twelve feet above me on the trail. 'Her name is Sheri Asselin. She was passed out in one of the bedrooms upstairs, and she'd been raped for real. Gang-raped.' I was out of breath, light-headed, but I rushed to say the rest before Dyann could cut me off: 'She'd also been roofied. By you. You guys drugged her along with all the frat boys.'

Dyann half-turned; she shifted her boot on a rock and reached for the tree root above her. And then, somehow, she lost her footing. Her fingers grabbed at the empty air. She fell.

Dyann's body slammed down into mine, her elbow striking hard into the top of my skull, and then we were both falling, tumbling straight past the others – there was a shriek from Charla – grabbing in all directions at nothing and bashing into each other with knees hips shoulders and striking one sharp rock after another on our way down. I felt my camera fly out from my neck – I hadn't yet tucked it back into its case after the last photo – and smash against a solid surface, then break from its strap altogether.

Dyann and I plummeted, rolled, were jounced from side to side and plummeted again. There wasn't time to do anything but grunt at the pain. We hit the bottom of the gully, where the path widened and was carpeted with pine needles, and we had picked up so much speed that we slid down the slope, me headfirst, Dyann sideways, for another twenty or thirty feet before landing in a stand of poplar saplings.

For long moments the trees tilted and spun, and the sky flickered above me. Then things settled, and I coughed out a mouthful of snow.

'You're bleeding,' Dyann said. 'Your nose.'

I craned to see her. '*You're* bleeding.' Blood bubbled on her lips, and she spat blood into the snow. There were sharp parallel scratches across her cheekbone, and one of her eyelids was puffing up.

I worked to untangle myself from the greenery, testing each muscle, feeling for deeper pain beneath the surfacethrob of my bruises.

Dyann got to her hands and knees and shuffled closer to me. 'You must be hurt if I'm not,' she said. 'Ribs? Collarbone?'

I raised my hands over my head to show her no, I was fine. She'd slurred, though. 'Concussion,' I suggested.

She took off her one remaining glove and felt her scalp. 'I don't think so.'

'Internal bleeding. That blood in your mouth.'

'Bit my tongue.' Dyann stuck out her tongue at me, showing me the punctures. She grinned. 'It's not even possible. A fall like that?'

I smiled back. 'We should be dead.'

'You kneed me in the tit so bad.'

'You brained me with your elbow.' We lay there, nose to nose, grinning like morons at each other, chuckling at our luck, at having fallen and not been killed or maimed.

We heard our names shouted, and we remembered the others and sat up to see Steph and Charla emerge from the cleft.

They were both white-lipped, crying, and they wept even harder with relief to find us unhurt. They helped us clean up with mittfuls of snow. They fed us water and trail mix and slices of apple that Steph had brought. Charla handed me a shattered lens and the camera housing with the film compartment door and advance lever both missing and the hot shoe bent flat on one side. It was all she could find, she said.

I pried out the reel of ruined film and tried to cram its tangled spirals into my coat pocket. 'You know, you guys are responsible for Sheri Asselin,' I said. It was words before it was a thought. We weren't even on the subject anymore; we'd been discussing an alternate route up the gully and whether we had enough time left before nightfall.

The three of them looked around at each other. 'Look, Karen,' Dyann began, 'if this girl was drugged, it was a mistake.'

'Her name is Sheri. And you say she "was drugged", passive verb, like it just magically happened. But *you* did it. Oh, no, I know it was an accident,' I said over her protest. 'Blue for boys, pink for girls; I know. But Sheri is collateral damage in all of this. She wasn't even there, is how she describes it. She can't remember anything, so she can't even properly press charges against the frat. She tried to register a complaint, but they laughed her off.'

'You talked to her?' Steph said.

I nodded, and let that sink in.

'It's more heat on the frats, though.' Dyann said. 'Even the possibility of charges. That's good news.'

They were missing the point. I said, 'It's a miracle no one at GBC died that night.'

Charla said, 'We didn't use that high a dose.'

'Still. You know how much booze those guys drink.'

'Well, we tested it with booze,' Steph said.

'On whom?'

'On ourselves. On Dyann and Charla. Remember that night at the T-Cam?'

I looked from Charla to Dyann. 'You took *roofies* that night?'

'Not that they remember it,' Steph said, smiling at the recollection. 'Or the next day, for that matter.'

'Wow. Good times,' I said.

Steph looked at my face and stopped smiling. 'We couldn't have let you in on it, Karen. It was early in the school year; we barely knew you. Imagine if we'd told you, "We'd like to set up a gang rape to bring down Gamma Beta Chi. Charla's volunteered for the job." You would have thought we were insane.'

'You *are* insane. All of you. And Sheri Asselin is paying for it.'

Dyann wrapped her arms around her knees. 'You want to talk about responsibility, Karen? What about your responsibility? This Sheri Asselin is a poor, friendless girl being thrown under the bus by a bunch of feminists for political reasons. So what are you going to do about it?'

There was a silence, and then Charla burst out laughing. 'Holy God, Dyann, you do think fast! You heard about Sheri five minutes ago? Ten? And you've already figured out your next move.'

Dyann frowned. 'What?'

'Or was this your plan all along?'

'What are you talking about?'

'You want Karen to report us. You don't want it to be Steph, or MJ, or me who comes forward, because if one of us has a change of heart it'll look like we made a mistake.'

'We *did* make a mistake,' Steph said.

'But Karen only just found out,' Charla said, 'so Dyann wants her for the role of turncoat. The betrayer.'

'That's ridiculous,' Dyann said.

'That way you can stay true to your principles. A hundred percent pure. No guilt, no second thoughts.' Charla laughed again, and shook her head. 'Karen gets to be the Judas, and that way you get to be the Christ.'

'No. No, you guys, I'm not –' I broke off. I couldn't be the betrayer. To betray someone – to rat them out, or even to accuse them – you had to be sure. You had to be one hundred percent confident that you were in the right and they were in the wrong.

Look at us backed into corners, I thought. Look how we lash our tails and stare. We are all become like Dyann now: rovers and raveners circling the arena. Bareclawed. Lionmaned. Justice in our eyes. I couldn't do it. I didn't have that kind of certainty.

I stood up, wincing at the stiffening in my quadriceps. 'They have this rating system at the frat,' I told my roommates. Steph and Charla, I noticed, had unconsciously adopted Dyann's posture, hunkered forward with their forearms looped around their knees. 'They put coloured stickers on the girls' clothes when they arrive at the party. White for virgin, green for cold fish, red for red meat, black for skank, pink for little sisters –' I could see they didn't recognise the term. 'The girls who've been "trained" in the Black Bag, or who've blown every brother in the house, or danced topless or some other kind of initiation.'

'I guess I'd get pink, then,' Charla said, half-smiling.

'Little Sister!' Steph fist-bumped her.

'What sticker did they give you?' Dyann asked me. She looked a little ill.

'Blue.' And just like that, whatever satisfaction I'd felt from schooling my roommates in the vagaries of frat culture dropped away. I felt my face go red. I dropped to my haunches, back into their circle. 'It's like "blueblood" or something,' I explained. 'I'm sort of off limits, since I'm a girlfriend. Sorority sisters sometimes get blue, too, or if an actual family member of one of the frat boys is visiting. That kind of thing.'

'So what are you telling us?' Dyann said. 'I mean you're preaching to the choir here if you're saying that this sticker system objectifies women.'

'I'm saying that I think you're right about fraternity culture being a massive problem for women. Girls are invited into the frat house for one reason only: to cement the bonds among the brothers. Even me. We're a means to an end.'

Dyann shook her head. 'No. That's still too soft-focus. It isn't only that we're a means to an end. Those brotherly bonds *depend* on our debasement. The homosocial contract hasn't changed since the Trojan War, Karen. It operates the same way in the military, with sports teams – anywhere men get together in any organised fashion.'

'Don't lecture her,' Charla said. 'She's agreeing with you.'

'And you guys just fell off a cliff,' Steph reminded us.

Dyann said, 'Okay, okay,' rolled to her hands and knees, and stood up. She groaned and rubbed her right knee, where there was a rip in the fabric of her pants. But she couldn't resist a final declamation: 'It's not that rape is a *risk* of frat culture. Rape is a basic *necessity* for frat culture.'

'Are the right people suffering for your actions?' I said.

'Yes,' Steph said. 'That's exactly our dilemma.'

'No,' Dyann said. 'Suffering is a question of individuals, and this is about the wider, systemic oppression.'

'Are the right people suffering?' I asked her.

'That's not the question,' Dyann insisted.

'It's not *your* question. But it's *a* question,' I said, 'and it's an important one.'

Silence. We picked our way back up the gully slowly, in silence. I couldn't ignore the pain and fatigue in my body, so I concentrated on it fully, feeling it roll around my limbs with each step until I was again a dumb creature and my mind was still.

On our way back to the chalet we pulled in at a mom-and-pop restaurant in town. The waitress described the dinner special in such laudatory terms – 'slow-braised pork roast, really incredibly tender, our famous smashed pota- toes with sage gravy' – that we all ordered it.

'I think the fraternities are in real trouble,' Dyann said. 'The inquiry into the video is one thing. But if there's an actual rape victim pressing charges against them –'

'Sheri isn't pressing charges,' I corrected her. 'I told you: she can't remember enough of what happened. And of course no one's stepping forward as a witness. The police have nothing to work with.'

'Still,' Dyann said. 'It's more concrete than the video. The Dean's Office can ignore the video, to an extent – they have been ignoring it – but they can't ignore a real, live person with a complaint.'

'This is Bisto mix,' Charla complained about the gravy. 'You can taste the cornstarch. They just added dried sage.'

'Shut up. I love it here,' Steph said.

I liked the restaurant too. The place was perfect after the frigid hike. It was replete with homey fortifications, and I loved them all: the dusty-rose balloon valences on the steamy windows, the plastic gingham-printed table-cloths, the grammatically shaky menu descriptions, the collection of porce-lain horses on the mantel.

After our meal we browsed the sale items in the adjacent gift shop: hemp-based soaps, crocheted dishcloths, imported Thai jewellery. There were rings with Egyptian cartouches, all manner of Celtic knots, but none like the one I was looking for, nothing shield-shaped.

That night in the chalet the quiet purred at my ear. In the morning, after I stripped the bed, I opened the window to listen, astonished by birdsong.

Book III

EPODE

(after-song)

37. MARTYRIA

(testimony from experience)

Compared to the other two panelists' presentations, 'Domestic Dreams' is as pitiful as I'd feared. The panel host has explained Annabeth's family emergency, explained that I'm pinch-hitting at the last minute, but still. There are about fifty people in the audience, and the room is staggered so I can see every single expectant face. The other presenters' talks are written out in full, peppered with clever phrasing and laughter-generating anecdotes. They use quotations from experts to prove their points. I am scheduled last, and when my turn comes my dismay has almost canceled out my nervousness.

'I'm just a photographer,' I begin, 'so my perspective on blogging, on storytelling, might not be very helpful.' I flick through my slideshow of Annabeth's farmhouse photos: the reclaimed-wood floors, the mismatched chairs painstakingly collected from antique stores and painted butter-yellow. 'As you can see, she's a big fan of the lens flare,' I say. '"Can we sunny it up a bit?" "Can we wash in just a little more light?"' Without meaning to, I've started imitating Annabeth's broad, competent tone, the slightly British cadence of her sentences.

'"Wash in" isn't a photography term, but I'm sure you all know what it means. It's what everyone wants in this business, isn't it? Natural light but not natural. When we started I just used whatever was handy to bounce the light onto the thing I was shooting.' I pause on an image of a pie cooling on the windowsill. 'See the penumbra, the shadow, under the sill? With the window behind it, the contrast would be too high without something to reflect the light into it. I would use whatever was around – a magazine, a white plate. Now I use strobes to hit everything with that clean, cool, sunny light.' I don't mention that Annabeth has recently started taking more and more of her own photos for the blog. Her husband bought her a Canon Mark II for Christmas last year, but she says her new phone does nearly as good a job, with the filters.

I flip through more pictures. The henhouse. The oak tree with its vintage-saddle swing. The beeswax candles on the mantel. 'Don't get me wrong,' I say. 'There's always some satisfaction in making a beautiful photograph. It's just … I don't know. The aesthetic of interiors has become so rigid. *Urban Idyll* is successful because it makes an ordinary home look like a magazine. A regular family looks like celebrities. I'm not shooting the bickering or the jammy counters or the temper tantrums.'

As if on cue, the shaky wail of a baby rises from somewhere in the room. Everyone laughs. Hands are going up here and there. People have questions.

I try to head them off. 'As I said, I'm not complaining,' I say. 'When I first started working, I'd send my portfolio – all these beautiful art prints I'd prepared in school – and then I'd be hired to take twelve hundred shots of a doorknob or something. This is artistic paradise compared to that, which is probably why it doesn't pay.'

More laughter. More hands. 'We'll take questions at the end,' the panel host reminds the audience. But I am already finished; I've reached the end of the slideshow. 'That's the end, actually,' I tell her. 'Thank you.'

The hands have gone down now, though. There's silence in the room except for the baby's fussing and the *shh-shh*ing of its mother trying to soothe it.

'What is that?' a woman calls out, not waiting for the host to acknowledge her hand. I turn around in my chair and see that the image on-screen has reverted to a tableau on a smoky-black background: a decanter of wine, a cleaved pomegranate with scattered ruby kernels. In the bottom right quadrant a dead moth lies on the flange of the serving tray.

I fumble with the mouse, trying to reopen my farmhouse slide-show. 'That's nothing; sorry. I was trying to figure out some technical thing,' I say. 'Just fooling around.'

'But you've done more of those shots, haven't you?' the woman says. 'I've seen them on Fotomarkt: I've just realised you're the same Karen Huls. Am I right? All those dark, moody still lifes?'

My online album is visible to the public but no one views it. No one knows about it. The sudden revelation that someone has viewed it, that someone does know about it, makes me light-headed. 'Yes, but,' I say, 'those are just technical exercises, they're just –'

'There is certainly nothing domestic about *those* pieces.' Now the woman stands, hands on her broad hips. She has black-framed glasses and a stylish gray bob with heavy bangs. 'Those shots aren't about beauty at all, are they,' she says, 'not in any aesthetic sense. They reference beauty, of course, but the effect is shock, disruption. One wants to look away, but one cannot.'

The other panelists are shuffling papers, shifting in their chairs. The host says, 'I think we'd better use the remaining time for questions on our topic …?'

'We'll talk later,' the stout woman says, and sits down, and other hands go up again.

The baby begins to cry in earnest, a fastgasping newborn holler. The mother rises from an aisle seat halfway back and turns to mount the stairs. A collective cooing erupts at the sight, over her shoulder, of the tiny tomato-coloured face with its fluff of dark hair. Most of the people in this crowd are women of mothering age, I realise. Children are an integral part of the Domestic Dream, even if they're notoriously hard to photograph.

Obviously embarrassed by the attention, the mother squares her hips to the climb and quickens her pace, her heavy black boots thumping the treads. A long, single braid leaps against her back.

38. TAPINOSIS

(debasing language)

Something was wrong with my statue. My head – its head – lolled too far forward, the chin fused to the chest. One shoulder had sunk into a nub. My breasts – its breasts – were gone, hollowed into craters, and stalactites of wax poked from the thighs where they'd dripped.

'I'm really sorry,' Bruce said. He'd brought the statue to me at the Faculty Club. Hamish had told me somebody was waiting for me outside, and there was Bruce Comfort. He pulled the statue, wrapped in a T-shirt, out of his duffel bag and handed it to me.

'Did Mike do this?' I asked. This naked slump. This droop. I couldn't look at Bruce.

'I don't think so,' he said. 'He was probably too embarrassed to tell you about it, though, so he tossed it out.'

A line came to me, something Steph had quoted, once, from one of her theorists: 'Love is giving what you haven't got to someone who doesn't want it anyway.' Was I angry about the statue? Was I sad? All I could feel was Bruce.

'But I thought, you know, you'd care, so. I'm sorry,' he said again.

'I do care.' I looked at Bruce then, and I could have wept with the relief after weeks of not looking at Bruce. Even with the snow out here on the patio, with snow outlining each needle of each tree in Faculty Hollow, it seemed to me that Bruce Comfort wore too many clothes: a varsity hoodie, track pants, Nikes. His body hid itself loose and lavish under his clothes.

He cleared his throat and scuffed at the snow with his toe. 'Some of the guys are saying it's you on that sex tape, in the Black Bag.'

'Who is saying that?'

'Moretti, mostly. A few others. Mike keeps saying you were out with him that night.'

I turned the waxen lump round and round between my hands. 'What about you?'

'What?'

'Is that why you came? To ask me if it's me on the tape?'

He reached out and slid his palm along my jaw. Broad daylight. O, but look how his eyes are a summersky blue made sunnier by the snow! How was it that a person could be this beautiful and I'd never even stood outside in daylight with him before this very moment? It was an injustice to both of us, to beauty everywhere.

'I know it's not you,' he said. 'I've seen you up close often enough.' His half-grin was aimed at my breasts, which were smaller than Charla's by several cup sizes.

I flicked his shoulder in mock-offense. 'I miss you,' I said, before I could remember not to say it.

He closed his eyes. 'The thing is, it doesn't matter.'

'What?'

'Which girl is on that tape. I've fucked girls, all right? Like, lots.' His fingers tangled in my hair and made a fist of it. 'They can say whatever they want about me, and it may as well be true.'

I frowned. 'You didn't even know what you were doing. You don't even remember, remember?' His furred voice on the video, his big sleepy body stumbling around. I slid my right hand under his hoodie up to his chest, the ball of my thumb over his nipple, my fingertips curling into his armpit.

His eyes sprang open, met mine, widened. His heart thumped under my hand. It was an intimate touch. It was more than I'd ever touched him in private, in the bathroom at GBC.

'It wasn't your fault,' I said, 'that night. Do you remember drinking shooters? There were these blue –'

'Why don't you leave her alone!' a voice called.

Bruce hurled himself back from me. I squawked when, trying to shake his hand free, he accidentally yanked my hair. A group of students had stopped on the sidewalk. One of them leaned over the wrought-iron fence. Her wool scarf dangled almost to the patio stones. 'That's him, for sure,' she said.

'Asshole!' shouted one of the boys.

'Trying to add harassment to sexual assault now?' said the girl.

'Um. I'm fine,' I called to them.

'You don't have to talk to him,' said a girl in a long overcoat. 'I can call Security if you want.'

'Come on.' I pinched Bruce's sleeve to get him to follow me inside, but he twisted from my grasp and loped away, down the length of the building.

'That's right, run, you cowardly, piece-of-shit frat boy!' the first girl yelled after him, and the others laughed.

Bruce disappeared around the corner. His footprints were smeared where he'd slipped in the snow and caught himself.

*

It kept happening. Girls I barely knew would come up to me after class and say, 'We support you, Karen,' and, 'Just know you're not alone in this.'

'It's not me,' I would say. 'I don't know what you're talking about.'

But I did know. The tape was being copied and watched more widely. And with it the rumour was spreading; they thought I was on the video.

A nearby college ran a whole newspaper series on 'The Future of the Fraternity' and interviewed a Women's Studies professor who'd written a book on hazing and initiation rituals. The video got renewed play at the local news stations and was even picked up on the West Coast, after a high school hockey team was accused of drugging cheerleaders at a party.

Mike told me that four of the brothers had quit GBC and moved their stuff out of the house over the holidays. 'It wasn't their choice, of course,' he said. 'It was their parents, worried their little darlings might suffer some kind of taint.'

Even so, Mike kept saying he wasn't planning on telling the frat about the roofies. 'I'd choose you over GBC, of course,' he said, 'but I'd rather not have to choose.' He was treating it like a juicy conspiracy between us. 'I love sharing a secret with you,' he'd say. Whenever the mistaken-identity situation came up he'd say he was enjoying the fame by association. 'My girlfriend, the porn star,' he'd joke.

Someone hung up posters of Bruce around campus. He was in a swimming pool, floating with a blowup doll, his cheek pressed between her breasts. It was an old photo – it might have been high school, even, Bruce looked that young. Big block lettering across the bottom of the poster said FRAT PARTIES, and under that, the letters of PARTIES had been rearranged into RAPEIST. The posters showed up everywhere, all over campus. No one but me seemed to notice the misspelling.

People I didn't recognise would say, 'Stay strong, Karen!' and give me a thumbs-up. 'You've been objectified, but you are not a sex object.'

'It's a mistake,' I'd say. 'It wasn't me.'

Sheri Asselin called me at the Faculty Club a few days after Bruce's visit. Officer McCrae had suggested she ask me to file a complaint against the frat, she said. After I went through my 'It wasn't me' refrain, she said, 'What if it *was* you, though? What if you were roofied, too, and you can't remember anything?'

'You want me to lie,' I said.

'I want you to do the right thing. I know Chet's your boyfriend and everything, but you shouldn't protect those guys. The silence is part of the problem.'

'I'm not protecting anybody,' I told Sheri. 'I'm just not going to lie.'

After I hung up I felt sick. I wasn't going to lie but I was lying, of course, by not telling anyone the truth. And I wasn't protecting the fraternity per se, but I was protecting my roommates and, on the other hand, I wanted to protect Bruce. I'd started to tell Bruce the truth on the patio of the Faculty Club, but now that I hadn't seen him for a few days it felt like too radical an act to seek him out specifically for confession purposes. I decided to wait until the next time I saw him in the bathroom at GBC.

But things were heating up for Bruce too. He was getting the brunt of it. I saw him with a few of the GBC brothers in the parking lot behind the

Athletic Centre. There was a little mob of students – lots of girls, but boys, too – following them and shouting insults as the brothers hurried to Bruce's car. 'Hey, hey, ho, ho, Bruce Comfort has got to go!' the students chanted. Not 'GBC has got to go', but 'Bruce Comfort'. The mob blocked Bruce's car and pounded on the hood.

Stick came over to tell us he'd heard a rumour that a couple of major engineering and design firms were backing out of their annual fraternity meet-and-greets. 'It's working, in other words,' he crowed. 'Business turning its back on the Greeks? That's massive. That's a disaster for the school's public image. As soon as the provost gets wind of it, GBC is done. Never mind an inquiry or disciplinary hearings; they'll carve them out of here like gangrene.'

*

I considered asking Deborah if she'd make me another wax casting of my statue, but I was too embarrassed to tell her I'd let a bunch of frat boys melt the first one. Even the adult-ed students in Desso's Advanced Charcoal class had heard about the videotape and the ongoing controversy about gang bangs at the fraternities.

'Girls go to those all-male places, they know what to expect,' said Robert, a part-time ER nurse. 'They drink until they can't stand up, they gotta know what's coming, pardon my honesty.'

'That's only one step away from saying girls shouldn't wear tight jeans,' said Chantelle, grandmother of a teenage girl, a two-time Highland dancing champion. 'Or they shouldn't go out after dark if they expect to be safe from assault.'

'Well, there's something to that. No, I'm serious,' Robert said when the other students jeered. 'It's just facts. It's statistical.'

I posed on the plinth and half-listened, unable to feel angered or even interested. My legs were twisted to one side under me, and I was braced on one arm, head bowed. I drifted and daydreamed, imagining the plinth was made of glass instead of plywood. What would they see from below? All my hidden and tucked parts would show there: the unshaven folds, the smears. As a precaution I always wore a tampon, string tucked, when I modeled, but now I imagined myself glued to the glass floor by my own juices, flowing, spreading, pasted down. And I saw myself growing a carapace, smooth-sanded like a mollusk. A reverse Venus on my glass-bottomed boat. A bearded merman with his trident coming to strike the glass, to pry the shell, to pierce the soft flesh and suck me loose.

'We don't wear our masks at dinner,' my mother chided, and she pointed me at the stairs. A waterfall cascaded the treads, and I told her, 'Look, Mom!' and she looked and said, 'It's him. Poseidon.'

I had fallen asleep with my forehead resting on my knee. There was spittle on my leg where I'd drooled. 'Sorry,' I said to the artists, and I took a moment to stretch my spine. I'd gotten good at this, sleeping in place. I'd sway, then catch myself, wake myself sometimes with a moan.

My shadow was sharp on Desso's studio floor. I saw sand rippling, chasing itself away from my toes. My bent elbow looked like a clipped wing. The crown of my head was hot under the lights.

'She looks ashamed,' one of the artists complained about the pose. 'I don't want to depict her like that.'

'Picture her hiding from a lover,' Desso suggested. 'She's not ashamed – she's being coy. She's flirting.'

Picture an arrow stuck in my breast, I thought. Picture me curled around a wound. Picture my skull cleaved by heat, the feathers melting from my back. Picture me falling from the sun, down into the sea.

*

A week after the interrupted conversation with Bruce on the patio, I was walking to meet Dyann and Marie-Jeanne at the T-Cam when something heavy hit me between the shoulder blades. The blow startled me into a stumble, and I scraped my palms on the sidewalk and ripped both knees of my jeans.

A girl's voice yelled, 'Slut!' A hand stuck out the passenger window of a passing car to give me the finger. It was a metallic-blue car with white racing stripes. It was Alec Moretti's car. The Ginomobile. It was Grace's voice.

I looked around to see what had hit me. It was a full, unopened can of beer.

The women of Raghurst hold forth amongst themselves on the subject of the biological basis for gender:

Steph: Look. If we agree that there's no such thing as male and female, then how do we explain all the crimes committed by men against women?

Charla: *All* men? *All* women? Who are you even talking about?

Dyann: Well, she's right. Statistically, women have a very good chance of being harmed by a man, and it doesn't bear out the other way around.

Charla: I'm sorry, no. I refuse, as a woman, to be equated with 'victim'. I just refuse.

Steph: Then you are in total denial about what it means to be a woman in our society!

Dyann: But Steph, you're saying that it's our sexed bodies deciding where we stand in society. That everything about our cultural circumstances follows from our biology. But that's exactly the story patriarchy has told itself to make sure things seem natural. To make sure they stay the way they are.

Charla: To explain itself to itself.

Steph: It's not 'just a story', it's *the* story we need to tell! If you stop noticing that women's bodies are different, if you stop paying attention to the fact that it was sex determining where women stood in patriarchal arrangements throughout all of history ... Well, then you wipe out the long record of female oppression, just like that, and that gets us nowhere.

Charla: Fuck history.

Steph: What? You don't believe in history now?

Charla: I refuse to be yoked to it, is all.

Dyann: Sex was never grounded in human nature. It's a mythical construct.

Steph: Go tell a woman she was raped by a construct. Go tell her the power used against her was a myth.

39. CATAPLEXIS

(threatening or prophesying payback)

Mike and I had to mix up a second batch of Lemon Demon only two hours into the GBC Rush Hopefuls party. The numbers were down this semester because of all the controversy, but the house was still packed with freshman boys hoping to be considered for frat membership. Bruce wasn't even there, and I couldn't ask anyone where he was because Mike would overhear me asking.

They looked so young to me, the Hopefuls! They wore polo shirts and blazers and were nervous despite all the booze they were ingesting: the brothers could pull any one of them aside at any point in the evening for a scored interview, in which the Hopeful would have to demonstrate Gamma Beta Chi's Key Virtues of intelligence, wit, wisdom, and loyalty.

'They make them smoke a bowl and read a bunch of dirty song lyrics, is all,' Pits had told me. 'But don't tell them that.'

'Don't tell *anyone* that.' Mike scowled at Pits. 'They need to take us seriously or we won't get quality pledges.'

Pits grinned and elbowed me. 'He's pulling up the ladder, see that? They let Chet into the tree house, and now he doesn't want anyone else to have it so easy.'

'It wasn't easy,' Mike said.

We crashed early that night. Mike had been doing a lot of drugs since the holidays, even more than the usual stuff he shared with me at the frat. He couldn't sleep, he told me, if I wasn't in his bed. Yet every time I slept over he passed out before me, and he slept so deeply that I couldn't wake him up even when I shook him and shouted.

When I'd asked Mike where my statue had gone, he'd told me he left it at his parents' house after Christmas for safekeeping. I couldn't call him out on the lie without telling him it was Bruce who'd fished the statue out of the trash and brought it to me.

I woke up, sober and jittery, at 3 am. As usual the frat house was infernally hot. I climbed over Mike and found my underwear and his T-shirt on the floor. I went down the hall to the lounge. Christmas lights were still strung from the light fixture to the mantel of the boarded-up fireplace, and I plugged them in instead of turning on the overhead light. They threw a tinselly glow over the furniture. I selected the least-stained couch and lay looking at the multicolour constellation reflected in the balcony doors.

The melted sculpture, and Mike's lying about it, nagged at me. I knew of course that defacement was one of the fraternity's most beloved pastimes. There wasn't a poster in the house not marred by graffiti. Every plastic cup had a hole burnt in it, for bongs or for funnels or for fun. I'd seen the haircuts and the permanent-marker doodling when one of them passed out. Even their sports trophies wore liquid-paper mustaches and condom hats.

The statue was no different, but it felt different. The whole place felt different. I listened to the waning party sounds downstairs, the last, drunken Hopefuls careening around hollering insults at each other. They sounded foreign, like I was a foreigner in the house, or an intruder.

It's not fatal when it's a shallow dive. Was that the sum of my philosophy? Was that why I hadn't come straight home from Charla's chalet after confronting my roommates and telephoned Officer McCrae – I still had her card in my backpack, after all – and told the police who had really drugged Sheri Asselin? Was that why I didn't say anything even when Sheri had me on the phone? Maybe all I wanted, all along, was to dabble, to dip toes only, to skim for dross instead of plunging deep. I wanted to wade the shallows and watch while others drowned.

I swear it didn't feel that way at the time. My whole body shivered and thrummed with the risk of it, the thrill. The whole world shimmered around me, all its surfaces moist and springlike, pressing back at my lightest touch. I squinted, and shivered, and yes, I dove in, again and again I dove and splashed; I gasped at the enveloping, sparkling pressure against my skin. It wasn't only Dyann who swung and struck the world at its roots. It wasn't only Charla who chased desire, Marie-Jeanne who strode boldly, Steph who suffered and sorrowed. I felt everything, I swear it. I felt it all.

I lay there listening, and I heard footsteps. I sat up and turned to see Alec Moretti in the door. Narrow shoulders, boxer shorts, black hair all over his body. He flicked on the light. Scowled.

'Enemy lines'. The words pressed themselves into my mind. 'C'mon in, soldier,' I drawled. 'Put your feet up.'

'You're inviting me into my own lounge?' Alec was hammered, or maybe high on something. He swayed a little as he stood before me.

'Ha ha,' I said, but he wasn't grinning. The bulge in the front of his boxers was soft, but he thrust it forward like a gun. Well, hardly a gun. A grenade, maybe. A beanbag. The cliché of penis as weapon was silly and also, somehow, true. How was it a man could look aggressive in his underwear? It was never the case with breasts.

'Waiting for Bruce?' Alec asked.

'I wasn't – no, I wasn't waiting for Bruce.' It was so hot. I pulled Mike's T-shirt down over my knees.

'What I wonder: how come Chet hasn't thrown you out on your ass yet?'

'I wasn't waiting for Bruce,' I repeated.

'You know we might get revoked.'

'What?'

'GBC National might revoke our charter. Not to mention getting disaffiliated from the college.' He stepped closer. 'I'm not Bruce. I'm not Chet. You can't bullshit me.'

I stood up. 'I don't know what you're talking about.'

Alec leaned his head to one side. He looked less drunk now; he was waking up. His breath came at me hot and sour, and he said, 'You set us up, you slutty little piece of shit.'

'Come on, Alec, you know I had nothing to do with any of that.'

'You're a Women's Studies major.'

'No I'm not.'

But Alec wasn't listening. 'You live with a bunch of dykes,' he said. 'You go to all those fucking rallies and marches. You think Grace doesn't tell me all this shit? You think Chet doesn't tell me all about your dyke roommates coming in here with their pills and their cameras and stirring up this massive shitstorm on campus?'

'No. Alec, listen. I'm not –'

'Maybe it doesn't matter to Bruce. Maybe his parents have the money for good lawyers.' Alec stopped talking and looked out the window, arms crossed. Sparse black hairs curled here and there from the skin on his biceps, like escapees from the thatch of his armpits.

I slid my foot sideways on the rug, between Alec and the couch, toward the door. 'I'm going back to bed,' I said.

He shook his head. 'You are fucked, you know that?'

I eased farther sideways, and he grabbed my arm, fingers digging. 'Hey. Ouch,' I said. 'Take it easy.'

'You are one seriously fucked up bitch.'

'Stop it!'

Alec jabbed both his thumbs straight into my mouth, right to the back of my throat, and clamped his fingers into the hollows behind my jaw. I gagged and tried to bite down but couldn't. His hands kept shoving until my knees caught the edge of the couch and I fell back onto it. He pressed my head down into the pillow until the cushions muffled my hearing.

My hair covered my eyes. I breathed quick little breaths whenever I could get them in. I slapped at him and scratched, but he brought his chest down and pinned my arms. I felt his knee wedge down hard between my thighs, pinching the skin against the sofa frame until I screeched into his hands.

My fingers found his chest hair, and I yanked as hard as I could. He yelled, rearing back so his thumbs came out of my mouth, and he slapped my face.

Something happened to me then. Something – the shock of the slap, maybe, or the sheer force of Alec's fury – made me suddenly stop fighting altogether. He pulled me off the sofa, out of the lounge, down the hall, up the stairs. My vision blurred with tears. He had me by the hair but I was following him too; my legs were walking along underneath me, and I didn't kick or punch or scratch or scream or do anything to escape.

Alec dragged me into the room with the bunk beds and the gymnastics vault that they called the gold car. I thought he was going to bend me over the vault – my mind raced with the possible ways I might buck or bite from that position; at least he wouldn't be looking at me! – but instead he shoved me to my knees, pressed my head against the side of the wooden box, and, before I could figure out what was going on, lifted the top and slammed it back down so that most of my hair was trapped in the seam. I couldn't move my head at all.

Alec snapped a latch on the other side of the vault. He took Mike's T-shirt in both fists, ripped it apart, and yanked the shreds off my shoulders. 'This is more like it,' he said, and laughed. 'Chet should see this.'

'Very funny,' I said. My teeth chattered. I bit down to stop them. Chet, I thought, Chet Morton. Chet had told Alec about Dyann, about the roofies – or he had said enough, anyway, that Alec had figured it out.

'Welcome to the gold car, Karen. See?' He thrust his groin into my face. 'You're the perfect height. I just have to lean in.'

'Come on, the joke's over, Alec.'

He slapped me again, and again, and again. 'Shut up. Shut up. Shut up.'

Alec pulled his penis out of his underwear and stuffed it into my mouth. He held me tight around the throat. My head knocked hard against the vault as he plunged. I gagged and tried to focus on breathing but I wasn't breathing, really. I closed my eyes and opened them but I couldn't see either way for the tears.

Alec was only half-hard, though, his flesh spongy in my throat. Panting, he pulled out. 'Bruce should see this,' he said, 'and everyone else.' He tucked himself back into his shorts and bared his teeth. 'Hey, check it out, Karen.' He pointed to the back of the bedroom door.

A Magic Marker hung from a nail, and beside it, written on the door, was a list of girls' names.

'Golden tickets, see?' Alec crowed. He uncapped the marker and scrawled *Karen Huls* at the bottom of the list. 'Everyone has to see this. Everyone should come and get some of this,' he said. Then he left the room, closing the door behind him.

Alec would come back with the rest of them. They would all see me like this; they would all hurt me like Alec had, or worse. My mind jumped suddenly to Charla in the Black Bag. I struggled to remember what she'd told me she'd been feeling when she was hung up in those handcuffs. She was into it, she'd said. She was chasing down the limits of her body's pleasure. For a brief moment I turned my attention to my body, wondering if I could somehow maybe turn this around. My teeth wouldn't stop clacking together. My nipples stung where Alec had pinched and yanked them, my knees were bruising against the hardwood floor, and my neck ached from trying to keep my head still in order to stop my trapped hair from pulling.

It would only be a minute or two and they would all be here. I looked at the list and found Sheri Asselin a few names up from mine. A bizarre feeling of smugness came over me. At the T-Cam, that time, Sheri had accused me of patronising her. Look at me now, I thought. I couldn't say I knew better than her now.

If my body couldn't find Charla-like pleasure, maybe it could achieve numbness, dullness – that resigned, creaturely feeling I'd mastered on the tree-planting block and had accessed that time in the gorge with my room-mates. But I was distracted when a car horn sounded somewhere outside the bedroom window, far away. The frat house was quiet. *Hey, Karen,* a mild voice inside me spoke up. *Maybe they're not coming.* I wasn't sure what had me more afraid: the possibility of the others coming in or of Alec, alone, coming back. The shivering had turned into a series of muscle spasms. I couldn't feel my legs and feet, and my head hung despite the pulling at my scalp.

'Help,' I said. My voice, barely audible, tore at my throat. I hated the feebleness of the voice.

They're not coming, Karen, really, the voice said. It was such a weird contrast, to hear my own voice weak and panicky from my mouth and then to hear this other, inner voice speaking with immense detachment and calm.

'Help,' I called, louder. It sounded horrible – croaky, full of snot – but I did it again. 'Help me.'

The door flew open. 'Holy fuck. Oh, holy fuck.'

It was Bruce. His nose was bleeding. He circled the vault and snapped the latch on the box. He lifted the lid, allowing my head to fall free, and I collapsed forward onto all fours. Bruce tried to lift me up, tried to cover me with the rags of Mike's T-shirt, and then he gave up and sank to the floor and wrapped his arms around me and gathered me into his lap.

'Oh fuck, Karen, fuck. I thought he had you in the Bag. I went down there and it – there was no one there, so I thought he was lying about the whole thing. Holy, holy fuck. That twisted son of a bitch.'

I tasted blood. I wasn't crying but there was that sound, that horrible wet sound I was making. 'Where were you?' said the sound. 'Where were you where were you?'

'You're good,' he said. 'You're good now, it's all good.' The words were supposed to comfort me, but Bruce had to raise his voice so that we could hear it over mine.

40. PARAMYTHIA

(consolation)

I dreamt I was getting my hair cut by a barber. It was a real barbershop with a striped pole outside and an old man in a faded smock doing the cutting. He used a serrated kitchen knife and worked with a sawing motion, like carving a roast. Half my hair came out by the roots. I woke on a gasp, my scalp crawling and my eyes clambering frantically over the darkness of my bedroom as the nightmare tumbled back down the chasm of my sleep.

I stumbled to the bathroom and turned on the light. My eyes in the mirror reminded me of something. I was half-asleep, still adrift in the bad dream, and my eyes had that look: Bruce's look, from the video. That dumb-animal look, dull and instinct-driven, the look on a dog's face kicking up grass ten feet from where it has defecated or humping a much smaller dog so that its hips are pumping air. Bruce Comfort on Rohypnol, trying to fuck Charla, missing his mark. Barking up the wrong tree.

It was not at all the same look on Alec Moretti's face when he stared me down in the lounge, when he slapped my face. Alec had been furious, exulting in the violence. What did it matter, though? What difference did it make, the look on an assailant's face?

I got the scissors from my desk drawer and went back to the bathroom. I unrolled toilet paper and laid strips of it across the sink for easier cleanup. The scissors were dull, and I had to take up one small section of hair at a time. I started the haircut in the back, working from my nape. My arms were bloodless and sore halfway through the job, and my back ached from leaning over the sink. When I was finished I stood in the shower and let the hot water run over my bare neck and shoulders. Then I spread a towel on my pillow and lay there not sleeping, dreaming nothing.

*

'Why do women metamorphose so much more frequently than men, in the myths?' Dr Esterhazy asked us. 'In the last months we've read what – ten or twelve examples? Kallisto becomes a bear, Io a heifer, Daphne a tree. Women get snakes for hair, dogs sprouting from their waists, bestial hindquarters' – she got to her feet, swished her hips and fluttered her arms behind her like tailfeathers, so that we all laughed. 'But why is it always women who are transformed, or who catalyse the transformation in men?'

'Well, women are considered like property, right?' said Alyssa Coxwell from the far end of the table. 'They're more like objects, in stories, than subjects. So stuff happens *to* them?'

'Yes, of course, as feminists we know how narrative traditions in general tend to map out in gendered ways – the male agent moving through the female landscape, et cetera, et cetera.' But Dr Esterhazy was dissatisfied with Alyssa's answer. Her nodding head scanned the seminar room for a better guess.

There was a chart on the blackboard with two columns illustrating antiquity's fundamental duality between wet/cold on the one side and dry/hot on the other. The male body was seen as being dominated and motivated by its warm, airy spirit, while the female body was cool and wet. Reason, a quality gendered male, was a dry phenomenon; emotion was wet. The trouble with wet was its tendency to leak, to flow, and to liquefy dry things. In the Greek epic, 'wet fear' could swamp a soldier's strategy in battle; anxiety could 'fall in drops', soaking into stupor an otherwise thoughtful man.

As always during her classes I found myself covertly looking to Dr Esterhazy for the embodiment of the feminine qualities she recounted. Today, though, in the 9 am winter light from the windows, the professor looked anything but moist. The fluff of her hair was less luminous than usual; it looked like she'd walked a dusty road or slept on a beach somewhere. Her skin appeared paper-crumpled and then ironed flat again.

At the start of class she'd told us that she'd planned to hand back our first-term essays today but that her TA hadn't dropped them off in time. That meant Steph. I wondered what was wrong. I hadn't crossed paths with Steph at Raghurst at all the last couple of days.

'It boils down to a question of boundaries,' Dr Esterhazy said. 'Women's bodies are believed to be less boundaried, less circumscribed within an autonomous and coherent selfhood, than men's bodies. If you're governed by a liquid element, then your body is necessarily porous and mutable. It flows from one form to another without resistance. And conversely, women in these stories become agents of boundary violation. They adapt to the boundaries of others and adopt their forms.'

Porous, (un)circumscribed, mutable, flowing, I wrote in my notes. I liked to list Dr Esterhazy's adjectives. The way she spoke enchanted me. All those elegant cadences, delivered as seamlessly as if she'd just written a book and was reciting it to us verbatim. She wove delicate nets of syntax and studded them with synonyms and I hung them, sparkling, in my head.

'The plot always resolves the same way in Greek epic,' Dr Esterhazy said. 'And like everything else, the plot resolution is sharply gendered. For the male heroes: *kleos aphthiton,* imperishable glory via death on the battlefield. For the women, who are apportioned out to the victors: sexual slavery.'

There was silence in the room.

'Now, this might be all well and good in mythology.' Then the professor waited, cocking her head to one side and looking from one to another of us. This meant she wanted someone to follow the line of her thought and draw it to its conclusion.

I wanted so badly to be the one that I raised my hand before I knew what to say, and my heart knocked into my chest when she pointed at me. My mind raced. 'Our myths don't only reflect the way we live,' I said. 'They shape it, too.'

She raised her eyebrows, waiting for more.

'If we buy into the idea that women are' – I gulped and glanced down at my notes – '"uncontained", then we'll go right ahead and set up ways to contain them. Create rules and regulations for how women have to behave in public.'

Dr Esterhazy nodded at last, and my relief made me almost dizzy.

'It's even worse than that.' Charla's voice came from one of the chairs not pulled up to the seminar table, one near the door, where she must have slipped in late. Everyone turned around.

'I'm sorry – what was that?' Dr Esterhazy wasn't fond of people speaking without raising their hand first.

Charla didn't apologise, though. She was in her usual pretzel position: knee raised, arm hugging her shin, swanlike neck arched. 'Without bound-aries, women's bodies are polluting, sure, but they're also pollute-able,' she said. 'We already read that, pretty much, in Hesiod; he goes on and on about how women are more "subject to defilement", or whatever, than men.'

I glanced back at the professor and wondered if she could see Charla's underwear. My roommate's vintage peasant skirt spilled to the floor on either side of her bare knee. From my angle the scuffed toe of her combat boot just blocked the space between her splayed legs.

I'd walked to Raghurst from the frat house yesterday at five thirty in the morning. I'd fallen straight into bed and stayed there, except for giving myself that haircut, all day and night. This morning I'd woken hungry but hadn't wanted to run into my breakfasting roommates, so I'd tiptoed downstairs and out the front door, eaten a bagel at the cafeteria, and spent the hour before class in the library.

Charla continued, 'So society sets up these rules and regulations to so-called protect women, but at the same time, everyone kind of expects a woman to be violated at any moment. If she gets raped, or killed, or beaten or whatever, then okay, a rule has been broken, but it's seen as kind of natural for that to happen because she's … permeable.'

'Hm,' said Dr Esterhazy. 'Yes, that's a very interesting point.'

Permeable, I added to my list. *Subject to defilement*; *Hesiod*. I couldn't remember reading that in the pages we'd been assigned.

Maybe it was in a different Hesiod text, one from Dr Esterhazy's 'Suggested Supplementary Readings'.

I glanced over at Charla again. She didn't look permeable to me. She looked the opposite of that. Impenetrable. Shielded. Her body itself was her shield. That polished-marble face of hers, irreproachable as the *Mona Lisa*. 'Go ahead,' she seemed to say, 'Go on and impale yourself upon me, I can take it.' Dyann had once said that the myths had nothing whatsoever to say about women, that we had to build our own mythology. If anyone could build her own mythology, I thought, it was Charla.

Charla frowned at me, pointed to her head, and mouthed, 'Are you okay?'

Was it just the haircut, I wondered, or were the bruises on my throat visible from all the way across the room?

41. ACCUMULATIO

(forceful repetition of main points)

When Charla and I got home from class at eleven, Dyann called to say that Steph had tried to kill herself. Her voice was calm on the phone. 'I'm at the hospital, but they won't let me see her yet,' she told me. 'Apparently she's sleeping it off.'

'Sleeping what off?' I said.

'Pills. She filled a prescription twice, or something. Planned it all out in advance.'

Dyann said this like she was reporting the weather. 'Are you okay?' I said.

'Sure. Of course.'

'Okay. What do you want us to bring?'

'Oh, no, there's no point in all of us sitting here waiting. I'll call again in an hour when I see how she's doing. And she can only have one visitor at a time, so let's take turns with the bedside vigil.'

'Oh, fuck, Steph. Fuck, fuck, fuck,' Charla said when I told her, and she started to cry.

'We knew she's been really depressed,' I said. I wanted to hug Charla but for some reason I just stood there.

'She has been, hasn't she? She's been a sponge for all of it: all the stress, the guilt, the second-guessing.' Charla crossed her arms over her breasts, hunching her shoulders and gripping her collarbones with her fingertips. It was a signature Charla-posture I'd seen before once or twice, a little-girl gesture of preoccupation and self-soothing.

'I can't deal with this,' she said. 'First you, and now her, in the same day? We're imploding here.'

'Me? I'm fine,' I said.

'You got beat up, or worse. And if someone else didn't do that to your hair, then it pretty much falls into the category of self-harm.' She gave a shuddering sigh, dropped her hands to her sides, and straightened her spine. 'Go next door and get something for us, will you? And come meet me in the bower.'

I told Stick what was going on. He crushed four pills and scraped the powder into an envelope. 'That's for you *and* Charla, okay? Don't take it all yourself, or you'll be in the hospital right next to Steph.'

'I'm not suicidal,' I snapped at him. 'I just cut my hair weird.'

'All right, all right,' he said.

Charla's bower was the best place in the world. My body sank into the down comforter, and I moaned with the ease of it, the rightness.

Charla used one fingertip, light as a thread, to trace the bruises on my neck and jaw. 'Tell me what happened to you,' she coaxed. 'Did Mike Morton do this?'

I smiled at her. I felt alert and unafraid in the serenity of the bower.

She placed her hand, open-palmed, in the centre of my chest. I wished there were a secret panel somewhere on my body that she could press so that feeling would pour out of me. Or in.

Upstairs the phone rang. Both of us knew we should answer it. It might be Dyann with an update about Steph.

I moved to sit up, but Charla's hand pressed me back. She brought her lips to my ear. 'You need to say who hurt you. Otherwise your head gets messed up. Trust me.'

I did it to myself, I wanted to say. My stupidity and arrogance, to think that I was somehow exempt, neutral, immune. That I was Switzerland. But I knew this would be the wrong answer, so I stayed quiet.

'You need to sort it out: what were you responsible for, and what was him hurting you? They're two different things, even if they were part of the same thing.'

The phone rang again. I pushed Charla gently aside and got out of the bower. 'The thing is,' I said, 'I think Dyann's right, after all. It's a war. *Bellum omnium in omnes.*'

What a great parting line, I thought; I know how to tread my measures on the grim floor of the war god. Stick's powder had made me clever and light on my feet. I took the basement stairs two at a time.

It was Mike calling, saying that we needed to talk. I told him I had to go to the hospital to visit Steph. He wanted to come with me, and I said no thanks, and then he got such an edge in his voice that I agreed to let him drive me to the hospital, at least.

Charla had followed me upstairs with a pair of scissors. She sat me down in the kitchen and snipped at my hair to even it out. 'You know, that video we made was never intended to start a war,' she said. 'Dyann said it was supposed to open the frat to public scrutiny. It wasn't supposed to start some personal, us-versus-them vendetta thing.'

'I was talking about the war between men and women in general,' I said.

'Oh Jesus,' Charla said. 'Don't start with that.'

'Because everything Dyann says is bullshit now?'

'No. Because … because I think we're as free as we want to be. The problem is fear. We're afraid of ourselves.' Charla scooped up the bits of my hair from the floor and put them in the compost. 'Those guys, those terrified little boys all huddled together in that house. And now Steph. Freedom is a terrifying thing to contemplate.'

I wanted to ask Charla more about freedom. I knew she meant sexual freedom, specifically – or sex as a microcosm of the wider freedom she was contemplating. Being a woman in a woman's body without conceding to the rules laid out for her by others. But how were we supposed to achieve freedom without fighting the war first? Dyann would say it was impossible.

I watched her fill the kettle, scoop a teaspoon of dried mint leaves into her tea egg, and run the tap water hot to warm the teapot. These rituals of comfort, of care. I watched her tip her head back and forth on her long, white neck, press her fingers into the base of her skull. I watched her feel for a loose strand of her hair, wind it into the knot with the rest, and tuck it under the elastic. These rituals.

No one in his right mind gives up power peaceably, Dyann would say. No one is ever going to hand over our freedom to us, just like that. Yet here was Charla, uninterested in war, calmly exploring her own idea of freedom. How much more I wanted to ask her! How much more I still needed to learn from her! She said crazy things, Charla, rulebreaking things. She set my brain on fire.

But Mike was on his way over, and I wanted to be dressed and ready for him, waiting outside, when he pulled up. I dug through my dresser for the one turtleneck sweater I owned, and I wrapped a fluffy scarf around my neck too, for good measure. I stuffed what was left of my hair into a beret.

Mike showed up in Bruce's car. I wondered if Bruce had said anything to him. Bruce had retrieved my clothes for me from Mike's room after the gold car. Mike hadn't stirred, he'd told me. Bruce had wanted to drive me to Raghurst but I'd insisted on walking home.

'I think you should move into the house with me,' Mike said as soon as we were underway.

This was unexpected. 'The fraternity house?'

'Into my room, yeah. You don't have to give up your lease or anything. Just move some clothes and books and stuff in. It's not that long until the end of the term, and then we can switch to a bigger room.'

I couldn't think of anything to say. There were no girls living at Gamma Beta Chi. The brothers would never let me move in even if I wanted to, even if Mike begged them.

The winding commuter corridor was already congested at three o'clock. We passed baby furniture stores, travel agencies, ladies' clothing boutiques, and home décor shops with names like Nest, Hutch, Trove, Cache.

'I feel like you disappear whenever you're not with me,' Mike said. 'It's like I say goodbye to you, and the second you're out of my sight you drop off the face of the earth.'

This couldn't possibly be a normal conversation for a boyfriend to have with his girlfriend, not for college sophomores. Maybe it was Stick's pills making it seem so utterly boring and absurd. 'The brothers hate me,' I said.

'They do not.'

'They hate all women. Especially girlfriends – we compromise your loyalty. You're supposed to be such a brilliant guy, Chet! How can you be too stupid to see it?'

'Don't call me that.'

'It *is* stupid, though.' A fleet of spandexed women jogged by, tacking around fire hydrants and sandwich boards. Moving targets, I thought, like antelope. Safety in numbers. Maybe it was even worse for women out here in the real world than it was on campus.

'Chet, I mean,' he said.

I hadn't realised I'd said 'Chet'. A throbbing started up behind my ear. 'Why can't I call you what they call you?' I said.

'I want to be "Mike" with you, not "Chet". Come on, Karen. You know it's a different thing.'

St Michael's Hospital was located beside a private school campus and across the street from a golf course. A queue of cars snaked back from the hospital's gates. 'You were incapacitated,' Mike said.

I looked at him. 'What?'

'You were so drunk, that first night. I asked you if you were drunk, and you said yes. And I still went ahead and fucked you.'

'I thought you didn't like calling it that.'

'In your opinion, Karen, am I a rapist?' he said.

'No.'

'You bring naked statues of yourself to the frat house. You model naked in front of everyone who wants to see.'

'I ... model for art students, Mike.' The throbbing in my head was worse. My brain bounced around my skull. 'That statue is art. Or it was art, before you took a lighter to it.'

Mike flushed. The car crawled forward and lurched to a stop. 'You and Bruce, behind my back. And now your name up on that door.'

'What?'

'Your golden ticket? It's all over the frat, Karen. Did you think I wouldn't hear?'

I realised that I had been waiting for this. I said, 'You think it was my fault.'

'Well, what am I supposed to think if you're all over the house doing whatever the hell you feel like with whomever the hell you feel like?'

I had known Mike would say this. I had the impulse to take off my scarf so he could see the bruises on my neck; I wanted to show him my brutal haircut. These would serve as proof that I was in physical and emotional pain.

But the fact that he'd need to see proof – that my bruises were my only hope of escaping the 'slut' category and reclaiming the 'girlfriend' category, as far as Mike was concerned … 'This is the rapeability conversation all over again,' I said.

'No it isn't.'

I had known this would happen. 'If I get drunk I become rapeable. If I take off my clothes I become rapeable. If I leave your room at night when you're passed out I become rapeable.'

'So you *do* think I'm a rapist.'

I opened my door and swung my feet to the pavement.

'Karen, it's still too far to walk,' he said.

I clicked the door shut and started to walk away from the car.

Mike jumped out and said over the hood, 'Call me when you know how Steph is doing.'

I looked back at him. 'I'm not going to call you, Mike. And don't call me, either. This is it. We're done.'

'Karen!' he yelled. 'Karen!'

42. AXIA

(first principles)

Mike was right, of course: the walk took forever, in a knifing wind across enough tarmac for an airport. I passed loading docks, ambulance bays, a cancer wing, and something called 'Community Development and Relations' before I found a door I was allowed to enter. By the time I'd located the correct elevator to the third floor and hallwayed back along much of the distance I'd covered outside, I was forty minutes later than I'd told Dyann I would be. An orderly led me around a nurses' bay to the back corner, past a window overlooking the hospital gates.

Steph lay flat on her back under a pink blanket. Her closed eyelids were gray under the fluorescents. Her feet, crossed at the ankles, stuck out the bottom of the blanket. I couldn't remember ever noticing Steph's bare feet before – they were small and pink, soft-looking, with little round toenails like seashells. A little girl's feet. Her freckled arms were extended at her sides, wrists at the edges of the bed; there was an IV plugged into one forearm and some sort of monitor band on the other, a heart rate clip on her index finger. She was Saint Stephanie on her martyr's cross, broken and exalted. If I lifted the blanket there would be cherubs snuggled round her waist.

Dyann, by contrast, was a profane black scowl hunching in a chair beside the heart monitor. 'She's not asleep,' she said. 'These people are such assholes. They told her she could have brain damage, so now she's convinced she'll flunk out of school. You know: *I'm going to kill myself, but I also want to graduate.*'

Steph opened her eyes and blinked at me. Tears leaked out of her eyes. I perched on the bed at her hip, but she winced, so I stood up again.

'No, it's okay.' She was hoarse.

I sat down again and took her hand. 'God, you're freezing. Do you want me to get another blanket?'

'I can't feel anything,' she said.

'They pumped her stomach, but she's still high as fuck.' Dyann stood up. 'Look, I have to go. MJ should be here in an hour or so. You'll have to tell an orderly if you need to leave before that. It's a suicide watch.' She made quotation marks around the words 'suicide watch', as if the whole thing might be a hoax. 'Hang in there, Steph.' She gave Steph a quick pat on the knee, scooped up her coat, and turned to go.

I followed her around the corner. 'Are you sure you're okay?'

'Why do you keep asking me that?'

'Because you were the first one here. It must have been frightening.'

She arched one eyebrow to inform me that 'frightening' wasn't the right word to use in the context of Dyann Brooks-Morriss.

'Stressful, at least,' I conceded.

Dyann shook her head and gazed out over the parking lots. 'Turns out it's all about Sylvia. She told Steph she won't be her thesis supervisor anymore.'

'What? Why not?'

She shrugged. 'Steph told her everything. About Charla, the video, the roofies, everything.'

'And Esterhazy dropped her?' That would kill Steph, I thought. Then I thought, Oh – it nearly did.

'I don't get why she didn't come to me,' Dyann said.

'It's not your fault,' I said.

'Actually, it is,' she said.

'No it's not, Dyann.'

Dyann turned her head and pointed her gaze at me. 'It's the most dramatic gesture a woman can make, isn't it? Killing herself. She's never more interesting or eloquent than when she offs herself. Look at us, Karen: we're right in the middle of a freaking masterpiece of literature! Steph kills herself, and the world swoons with the poetry of it all.'

'It's not *literary*, Dyann. It's personal. Steph's a person.'

Dyann gave a growl of sheer exasperation. 'God, it's like trying to explain gravity! You just don't *get* it, Karen; you never have. It's like you missed the very first class and never caught up.'

'What?'

'The. Personal.' She was overenunciating, as if to a lip-reader. 'Is. Political.'

'Okay.' I felt my face redden. Oh, Dyann, I thought, don't bother with the bait, the harpoon, the catchnet. I'm here, aren't I? I'm yours.

'Everything follows from that. Everything.'

'Okay, Dyann. I got it, all right?'

'I'm sorry to have put you in this position. All of you,' Steph said when I pulled the chair up to her bed.

'It's no problem,' I said. It didn't feel like quite the right thing to say, though. I tried to think of something less small-talky. 'Did you leave a note somewhere?' But this was too direct. 'Sorry,' I said. 'Oh, Steph. I'm so sorry.'

Steph's tears came fast, with no sniffles or gasps or any change at all in her breathing. They just slid straight down her cheeks, into her ears and onto the pillow. 'I'd never write a note,' she said. 'I'm not *that* self-centred. No,' – she shook her head and dropped to a whisper – 'no note.'

'Charla sends her best wishes. We figured we should take turns visiting.'

'I can't face Charla!' Steph grasped my hand and squeezed. 'Did Dyann tell you what I did? I told Sylvia it was Charla at the frat house that night. I never meant to do this to her, on top of everything. To expose her. Please tell her I'm so, so sorry.'

'She won't blame you, Steph,' I said. 'And you can tell her yourself, as soon as you're home.'

'No. They're admitting me to the ninth floor. The psychiatric ward. I'm not safe, you see.'

'Safe from what?' I thought of the fraternity. Of Alec Moretti.

'Self-harm.'

'Oh.'

Steph wanted a reaction from me, I realised. She kept shooting me little sidelong glances through her eyelashes. She wanted me to say that I hadn't known how bad things had gotten, that I'd never guessed how much she was suffering. Maybe this was what Dyann had meant about being in the middle of a masterpiece, or what had irritated her into that train of thought. Maybe Dyann was right that suicide wasn't private or personal; it was public. It was a demand of some kind, a declaration.

'I need a huge favour, Karen. Sylvia's – Dr Esterhazy's – essays are there, in my backpack.' Steph had stopped crying. She seemed more alert now; maybe the drugs she'd taken were wearing off. She pointed at her bag on the floor. 'I meant to deliver them, and I couldn't do it. I just couldn't face her again.'

'Shall I drop them off?' I said.

'Her home number is in the folder. Maybe ... Could you talk to her for me, Karen?'

'What do you want me to say?'

'She likes you. Maybe you can undo the damage I've done.'

'But what would I say, Steph?' There was nothing I could say. There was nothing more *to* say, I thought, now that Steph had said, had done, it all.

43. DEUS EX MACHINA

(divine rescue)

'I feared something was amiss,' Dr Esterhazy said when I told her the news over a pay phone in the hospital lobby. Her phone voice had a slight British accent, a shortening of the vowels, an emphasis on the 't' and 's'. 'Stephanie called me earlier today. I thought she was drunk, and that was rather uncharacteristic, not to mention rather early in the day.' A titter crawled under her words. Was Dr Esterhazy nervous? Guilt-ridden? 'She kept telling me she was sorry. I called her home number but didn't get an answer. Oh, I *am* glad to hear she'll be all right.'

'They're going to keep her longer, though,' I said, and I told her I had the essays for her.

'Oh, excellent, yes, I'll need them at once. Do you have a pen? I'll give you the address.'

I had assumed, since I'd just seen Dr Esterhazy in class that morning, that I would be bringing them to her campus office. It was a long bus ride to the professor's suburban neighbourhood. I slept, dry-mouthed from the waning effects of Stick's pills, all the way to the end of one bus route, then another. I walked the nautilus of sidewalks under a heavy sky.

A garbage truck chewed noisily at a box-spring mattress, and a group of toddlers had gathered on the sidewalk to spectate. They clung to their nannies' hands and hopped around in tense exuberance. I looked at the kids' fat bellies and red cheeks. One of the girls sported a column of green snot under each nostril. Everyone at my school was the same age. Weeks spent exclusively on campus made these kids as exotic as zoo animals to me, though I knew my environment was the unnatural one, like a military base or a convent.

One sixty-two Cliffmount Drive was a backsplit like its neighbours but fronted with fieldstone and teak. A path meandered its way to the front doors. To one side a lamppost illuminated an island of pea gravel surrounded by burlap-shrouded shrubbery.

The doorbell produced the lingering sound of a Buddhist gong. A boy came to the door – acne, headphones, game controller, big toe poking from his sweat sock – and when I asked for Dr Esterhazy he bellowed 'Sylvia!' over his shoulder and shuffled off, up the stairs.

She wore tweed slacks and a gray cashmere wrap. 'That was Zach, my stepson.' She draped my coat over the newel post. 'Meghan is downstairs somewhere. They're only here alternate weekends,' she added as if custody, not adolescence, was responsible for the bad manners.

Dr Esterhazy led me down the hall and paused in front of a doorway. 'Everyone, this is my student Karen; Karen, this is everyone.' Five gray-haired men and women seated on leather couches looked up, nodded, and waved or called hello. A two-storey stone chimney housed a gas fire; on either side of the fireplace a window soared up from rolling lawns into ink-drawn clouds.

'I'll just be a few minutes,' said Dr Esterhazy. 'Don't decide anything without me.'

'We're going to Tuscany for the winter press,' she explained to me as we descended a couple of carpeted steps and passed a dining room behind French doors. 'Patrick's a birder, so he wants to squeeze in a side trip to Marseille, but I don't think we can fit it all in, even if Stephanie is well enough to teach my Tuesday class. Which she may not be.'

We'd reached the kitchen, and she took the stack of essays from my hands and set it on the marble-topped peninsula next to a tray of hors d'oeuvres.

She offered me some mulled wine and ladled out a mug from a steaming pot on the massive black stove. There were eight burners. *Wolf*, the stove read, in chrome cursive above a long row of knobs. I perched on a stool in a fog of soured spices and tried hard to memorise everything I saw. There was a Persian rug over the hardwood, right there in the kitchen where everything would spill on it, and another, larger one underneath a café table with four more stools. Three hammered-copper pendant lamps cast bright circles on the countertop.

Dr Esterhazy's hair was crushed to one side of her head as if she'd napped on it. That and the sight of her slim feet in velvet ballet slippers made me yearn for her touch, for at least a look of fondness from her. I wished that she would kiss my cheek as I'd seen her kiss Steph's that first day in the Faculty Club. What was the winter press in Tuscany? Olives? Or some kind of skiing? Did they have mountains there? I heard a bird call somewhere in the house.

She was peering expectantly into my face. I realised that her last comment about Steph had, in fact, been a question, and that Steph must still be the TA for Dr Esterhazy's course even if the professor wasn't her PhD supervisor anymore. 'Um, yeah, Steph's pretty sick,' I said. 'I guess she might be in the hospital a while.'

Dr Esterhazy gestured toward the hors d'oeuvres on the tray. 'Spanakopita?' she said, and I took one. 'Self-harm is a difficult truth to face, isn't it? A "soul truth", the Greeks called it. They say Sappho took her own life; did you know that?'

'Well, with everything that's been going on,' I began.

One of the men came into the kitchen. He picked up the tray of spanako-pita and tilted the little pies into a basket lined with paper towels. 'What do you think?' he said, nodding at the half-eaten one in my hand. 'I tried them with goat cheese instead of feta.'

'It's delicious,' I said, and I put the rest of it into my mouth.

'Geoffrey's insisting on Pensione Bianca Collina again,' he told Dr Esterhazy.

She sighed. 'Did you remind him how cold it was? I doubt they've instal-led central heating since last year.'

'He says we'll bring blankets.' He put his free hand on Dr Esterhazy's neck and ruffled the hair behind her ear with his fingers. So this was him, the husband. Patrick Esterhazy. Or no – probably Sylvia had a different surname than Patrick. She would have kept her maiden name. Wouldn't she? He had a full beard, Patrick. Shaggy blond hair threaded with gray. Khakis, plaid flannel shirt, bandanna tucked into his collar like a cravat.

Wine, I remembered. Tuscany was wine. The winter press must be about grapes. And Patrick, Patrick was a birder. He birded.

Dr Esterhazy rolled her eyes and leaned back a little into Patrick's palm. The smile on her lips was the same smile as his: a secret smile, or shared anyhow, some shared knowledge about the pensione or Geoffrey and his luggage or the folly of their friends in general.

Patrick scooped a stack of side plates and balanced the basket on top of them, reached a bottle from a cupboard, snagged a half-dozen liqueur glasses by their stems, and made us a maître-d's bow before exiting the kitchen. His khaki trousers, I noticed, had various-sized pockets on the outer thighs, and a loop for a flashlight or pickaxe.

'I'd like to send along a card for Stephanie, if you can spare another minute or two,' Dr Esterhazy said. 'Shall we complete the tour? There's a lovely view of the garden, if it's not already too dark outside.' Carrying my wine, I followed her back past the dining room and down a different set of carpeted stairs. Another set of French doors opened onto a sort of patio enclosed with curving glass and filled with tropical plants.

A cockatiel in a cage chattered at our approach. 'This is Dido,' said Dr Esterhazy. She opened the cage and coaxed the bird onto her finger. When she drew it from the cage it hopped to her shoulder, pecked at her earlobe, and buried its head in her hair where Patrick's fingers had been. 'Dido is Mummy's good girl, isn't she? There's a pretty girl.' Dr Esterhazy reached up to scratch the bird's head.

Outside, isolated flakes of snow fell from the rapidly dimming sky. I moved to the window to examine the garden she'd mentioned. Five beds edged with trimmed boxwoods formed a perfect circle, like slices of a pie. The wedges were divided by gravel paths, and a cedar gazebo sat at the centre. Under the gazebo roof hung a sign that said THESMOPHORION. 'What does it mean?' I asked Dr Esterhazy.

'Ah, yes. The Thesmophoria was a women-only festival in Athens,' she said. 'It was a three-day retreat: fasting and feasting, the *teletai* initiation rites and the celebration of the goddess Kalligeneia. That's my tenure garden out there. I always said, "Once I have tenure I'll have time for gardening."'

'Do you?' I said. 'Have time?'

She smiled. 'Not really. Nor do I write very often in my thesmophorion: it's too windy here on the bluffs. But it's nice to look at from the sunroom.' She moved the bird to the top of its cage. It squatted and shat, through the bars, into its food dish. 'Oh, silly Dido, that's yucky,' said Dr Esterhazy, and she reached in with her finger and scooped the green blob out, onto the cage floor.

Dr Esterhazy crossed the sunroom to an antique rolltop desk, from which she drew a box of note cards and a pen. She lifted a plant off the chair – 'Jasmine,' she said. 'You're seeing it in all its glory today!' And it was true: even the slight swaying of the hoop wound with white flowers filled the room with a sweet perfume.

Dr Esterhazy sat down to write Steph a get-well message. 'Charla is having a hard time too,' I said as she wrote. 'Charla Klein? You know, from Women and Myth?' I added when she looked puzzled. 'We all are, actually. It's all this stuff with the fraternity.'

Dr Esterhazy held up a hand, veined, ringed with silver. 'Oh, don't let's talk about that. I really do find it best practice not to get involved in student politics.'

I took a breath. 'Um, well, it's more college politics. And it's not only about students; it's more about sexism in society, in general.'

Dr Esterhazy licked the envelope flap and pressed it closed. She blew a little air through pursed lips. 'Nonsense. It's about whose parents have the money to send their darlings off to an Ivy League institution. Class is so much more of a barrier to equality than gender, you know. And race! Did you know that the ancient Greeks didn't divide people by race at all? Their measure was language: if one spoke Greek one was Greek, and if not one was a barbarian.'

I tried again. 'Steph was … I mean, we're all just trying to get the school to recognise that the fraternities sort of excuse' – I groped for Dyann's wording – 'that they *institutionalise* violence against women.'

Dr Esterhazy, legs crossed, back straight, rested her forearm on the chair back. Her other arm was draped on the desktop, dangling Steph's card from the edge with two fingers. I suddenly thought she might let it slip from her fingers into the trash can below. 'If you want to get involved, you should run for student president,' she told me. 'Leadership can really strengthen a CV.'

She extended her fingers and inclined her head for me to take the note. I came forward and took it. With Dr Esterhazy gazing up at me, my arms seemed to hang at awkward angles from my shoulders. My turtleneck sweater cowered, threadbare and ill-fitting, next to her cashmere. 'I don't have a CV,' I said.

'Are you crying?' she asked.

'No,' I said, but I was. The word had come out a sob. I turned away from her and moved to the window, where the thesmophorion swam before my eyes.

She was beside me at once. 'Oh, Karen.'

'You have such a beautiful house,' I gasped.

'I know it.' Dr Esterhazy paused. 'We … we don't always find ourselves where we thought we'd be, in this life.' A hand alighted on my shoulder. 'Karen, I am so sorry. I should never have said all that just now.'

'It's okay,' I managed. 'I'm fine.'

'No. It is typical of me, to retreat into my books like that when faced with a discomforting situation.' She turned away and came back with a box of tissues. I took one and blew my nose, and she jiggled the box to indicate I should take another. 'But you do understand, don't you, that I can't become involved in this?'

'Why not, though?'

'Committing a crime is always only an act of self-sabotage. It is kneeling down and putting their gun into your mouth.'

I cringed, picturing it – a gun in the mouth of this beautiful, gentle woman! – and glanced at Dr Esterhazy, but she gazed straight ahead, out the window.

'Poor Dyann.' She sighed. 'Our Diana! She was never going to be satisfied until she made herself a pariah.'

The women of Raghurst hold forth amongst themselves on the subject of moral and sexual corruption:

Marie-Jeanne: Absolute power corrupts absolutely. That is the problem with fraternities: there are no walls to hold the boys in.

Steph: Absolute power is a door into dreaming.

Marie-Jeanne: Ugh, *mon dieu*. Freud again.

Steph: Yes. It's related to polymorphous perversity. Or infant sadism, anyhow. Picture a little boy pulling the legs off dragonflies. What's going to stop him? His parents, friends, an overall cultural context with standards of humane behaviour – he's only going to stop when he internalises the limits.

Marie-Jeanne: Wait, I know how this works. Now we picture the boy all grown up to be the king of the whole world. Like Caligula. The Emperor.

Steph: Exactly. No ministers or counselors to cross him. No laws that apply to him. No taboos.

Karen: Worse, even: picture an army of supporters egging him on to more and more outrageous cruelties.

Steph: Yes. Good. Instead of constraining him, his social circle pushes him past every internal boundary.

Karen: All those monstrous perversions that most people only have bad dreams about, or maybe fantasise about. Those things would become the everyday menu of the Emperor.

Steph: And it would get boring really fast. And so he would need more, and more.

44. ACCISMUS

(coyness, affectation)

I am on the phone with Jane Moscovitch, the woman who interrupted my 'Domestic Dreams' presentation to ask about my still-life photographs. She left a message at the hotel room with her number, saying she couldn't stay for the rest of the conference but wanted to talk. I looked her up and discovered that Jane Moscovitch owns art galleries in Brooklyn, Berlin, and The Hague.

It is halfway through the closing banquet of the conference. I'd planned to call Jane back tomorrow, but I excused myself between courses, during an onstage Q&A with a celebrity interior designer whose name I was too distracted to remember. I'm now sitting on my bed with a pillow in my lap and the receiver pressed hard to my ear.

'I've spent all evening with your Fotomarkt folio,' Jane is saying. 'Honestly, I haven't seen work this exciting in a long while, Karen.'

'Thanks,' I say. 'Thank you.'

'The Dutch masters are the obvious intertext, of course. A seventeenth-century still life was designed to show off the painter's technical skill, and you're clearly doing the same thing with photography. But you know, they were always *memento mori* too, right from the start of the tradition. Reminders of death. Are there any prints out there? Large format?'

'Not yet,' I say.

Thanks. Not yet. Have I been speaking monosyllabically for our entire conversation? Have I offered a single intelligent statement about my images? *Could* I offer such a statement, if she asks me? I am so accustomed to working on them in secret, in silence, that I have no vocabulary ready. It is surreal to hear Jane talking about them. It's like hearing her describe a dream I've had.

'They're brutal, really,' she says. 'This melon splayed open like this ... They're really hard on the committed viewer, you know, the person who lingers past a first glance.' She is clicking through the folio. 'The chicken – oh my God!'

I picture the dimpled gray skin where the three feather stumps protrude. Heat rises to my face. It's like I've had a recurring dream of being naked in front of the class and suddenly, this time, someone is in the dream with me. It's like it isn't a dream at all but waking up.

'Destruction,' she says.

'Pardon?'

'Destruction. Violation. It's not just a *memento mori*, a reminder; it's a ... I don't know, what do you call an image of destruction and decay? Of beauty *in* decay, like this? The longer I look, the more obvious it becomes, and the more sullied I feel, looking. It's like being dragged to the Underworld.'

'How ...' I take a breath. 'How did you see that?'

Jane laughs. 'I didn't see it, Karen. You saw it. I'm seeing what you saw.'

*

O alas, Dr Esterhazy! Our Thetis, our Athene, our Regina Coeli, our Britomartis. Maybe I had imagined that Sylvia Esterhazy was a spinster. Chaste and pure, wed only to her own intellect. Or I'd assumed her a lesbian, at least, cloistered with other anarcha-feminists in a desert compound somewhere. I couldn't decide why this home life of hers – my discovery of her home life – was so disappointing. If it represented a compromise, what was the nature of the compromise? A dilution, it felt like. A leakage. The deep, still well leaked out into rivulets and brooks that burbled haphazardly, this way and that, without purpose.

Don't let's talk about it. My professor's nineteenth-century diction needled at me more than anything else.

Dyann had known it all along, I realised. I'd always wondered about her antipathy for Dr Esterhazy – or ambivalence, anyhow – and assumed she was jealous of Steph's relationship with the professor. But Dyann had seen what Steph didn't, what Charla and I had overlooked. She saw what the rest of us missed. O farseeing Dyann, swinging her axe, cutting the world down to its roots.

*

It was seven thirty by the time I got home from Dr Esterhazy's house in the suburbs. Marie-Jeanne's eyes widened when she saw me. 'You cut your hair.'

I glanced at my reflection in the hallway mirror. The beret had begun to itch on the bus home and I'd stuffed it into my bag. 'It's awful, I know.'

Loud voices – Dyann's, then Charla's – came through the floor.

'That newspaper girl is here,' Marie-Jeanne said. 'You know, from the *Campus Eye?*'

'Jen Swinburn?'

'She told us you were assaulted at the fraternity. She was worried about you.'

I started toward the basement stairs, and Marie-Jeanne followed me and stroked her palm over my head, trying to smooth down the shaggy bits. She said, 'Karen, *je suis vraiment désolée.*'

The voices went silent as I came down the stairs to Charla's bedroom.

'What did they do to you?' Dyann asked before I even had a chance to close the door behind me. She was very pale. She clutched an orange silk pillow from Charla's bower.

Charla sat cross-legged in the nest of quilts. She'd been crying. She patted the bed beside her. 'Karen, c'mon over here.'

Jen Swinburn had been perched against Charla's desk with her backpack at her feet and her parka still bundled in her arms. She stood up when I came in, put the parka down, and held out her arms for a hug.

I shook my head, stepped back, and held up both hands to fend her off. 'I'm fine,' I told everyone.

Charla freed herself of the bower, crossed over to me, and unwound the scarf from my neck. She lifted the sweater over my head until I stood before them in just my tank top. I cupped a hand to either side of my jaw to hide the bruises, but Charla nudged my hands away and turned me this way and that to show the others.

'Oh, Karen,' Jen said. 'Oh, Jesus Christ, Karen. I mean, we heard about this big fight at GBC over you: about how Alec went after you, and now Bruce and everyone else is taking sides. But this is disgusting. You should go to the police.'

'Why didn't you tell us?' Dyann said. 'Why did you hide that' – she waved the pillow at my head – 'when I saw you at the hospital? I mean, how the hell am I supposed to – how do you expect me to try to make things right when I don't even know what's wrong?'

Was Dyann imagining herself some kind of avenging angel now? 'Make things right?' I said. 'What things?'

Charla spoke at the same time as me, and louder: 'That's just it, Dyann: you know exactly what's wrong.'

Dyann rolled her eyes. 'Oh, so things are black-and-white for Charla Klein all of a sudden. The woman for whom all of life is shades of gray.'

Charla rounded on her. 'You've known what's wrong right from the start. We've all known it. Karen asked you straight out, remember? *Are the right people suffering?*'

I picked up my scarf from the floor and put it back on. 'I'm fine,' I said again. 'It was just one guy.'

'You're obviously not fine,' Jen told me. 'Stop saying that.'

I knew I wasn't fine. I knew I was glassy-eyed, clumsy, slurring even, and I knew they could all see this and hear it. Stick's pills from this morning after class had worn off somewhere between the hospital and Dr Esterhazy's house. It had been altogether too long a day.

Charla caught her breath on a sudden sob. 'Goddamn it, Dyann!' She jabbed the tip of her index finger into Dyann's sternum, so hard that Dyann dropped the pillow. 'How much suffering will actually be enough for you?' She grabbed the doorknob, flung open the door, and ran upstairs.

The remaining three of us stared at one another. After a moment Jen put her parka down beside her, bent over to unzip her backpack, and pulled out a notebook and pen.

Dyann rubbed at her chest with the palm of her hand. 'It's going to be me, and only me,' she said to Jen. 'I'm the only name you name.'

'But it *is* her, right?' Jen tilted her head toward the open bedroom door. 'Charla's the woman in the video.' She waited a beat. 'And you're the one who recorded that video, aren't you, Dyann?'

Dyann straightened. Her hands fell loose at her sides. 'Mine is the only name you mention,' she said. 'I mean it. Otherwise I'll deny everything. I'll say you made it all up.'

'Dyann,' I said, 'wait. Don't do this.' I'd wanted the truth to come out, but that was before. Bruce was Bruce, but the rest of them? The rest of them – even Mike – deserved everything we could possibly do to them. Maybe Bruce did too.

'Well, I'm here now,' Jen said. 'It seems like the right time for talking, Karen.'

Dyann looked into my face. 'Charla's right. *You* were right. It isn't the right people suffering. It's none of the right people.'

'But I didn't mean …' I faltered. O Dyann, our breastplated general! Dyann the bright-eyed, the keen, the unwavering, swinging your double-sided axe.

'Go upstairs and see if you can calm Charla down, will you?' Dyann gave my shoulder a soft shove toward the door. 'This won't take very long; it's a pretty short story, really.' And she gave me her gentlest smile.

O Dyann, I thought. But I left her down there with Jen Swinburn and her notebook.

45. DECORUM

(proper fit between subject and style)

Jen's story came out in the *Eye* three days before the V-Day celebration we were supposed to host at Raghurst. There was talk of relocating the party, but none of the other Women's Centre members who lived close to campus had enough space for that many women. We thought Steph's being in the hospital was a legitimate enough excuse all on its own to cancel the party, but on Marie-Jeanne and Charla's next visit Steph begged them to go ahead with it. She told them it was important that our individual failings didn't undermine the more significant groundswell happening on campus.

V-Day was Valentine's Day changed by the Women's Centre to Vagina Day. The idea was to subvert the commercially driven, heteronormative mandate by making the holiday into a celebration of women's bodies and women's relationships with one another.

The boys next door had somehow convinced Marie-Jeanne to invite them too. Marie-Jeanne waited to break it to Dyann until Dyann got home from the library a couple of hours before the start time.

'We're not having any men,' Dyann insisted, fists to hips in front of the patio doors. 'The women expect us to offer them sanctuary after everything that's happened. This is supposed to be about women being *in* their bodies, not parading their bodies in front of men.'

'I told them that,' Marie-Jeanne said. 'They have promised to behave.' The tension grew when Charla, whose job it was to script an indoor version of the circle we'd performed for the Meditrinalia back in October, called to say she had a last-minute thing to attend and would be late to the party.

'It's a date, with a man.' Dyann banged the dishes in the sink. 'And she won't come out and say it because she knows it's a fucking pathetic thing to do at Imbolc.'

In the old calendar, Imbolc marked the start of spring, midway between the Winter Solstice and the Equinox. In Ireland it was the Feast of St Brigid.

'I am so sick of all her so-called sex-positive feminism bullshit,' Dyann said.

I crossed my arms and leaned against the kitchen doorway. 'Surely sex can be positive, though,' I said, knowing it was a goad.

She knew it was a goad, too, and grinned and lobbed the dish towel so it hit me in the chest. But she still couldn't resist a retort, though she put on a self-parodying bulldyke voice: 'Not when it's with a man. Not when it's probes and orifices.'

'Listen, I'll take care of Imbolc,' I said. I had a library book on Wiccan spirituality up in my room. 'You guys get the booze and stuff for the party, and I'll make us a ritual.

'Not a full circle,' I warned Dyann, who'd followed me into the hall to start instructing me, 'just something ad-libbed, over dinner, before everyone arrives. All right?'

'Okay.' Dyann said. She stood a moment looking at me, and then turned back to the kitchen. 'Fine. Good.'

In fact we were already more than a week late for Imbolc because of Steph, and also because of Dyann's confession. The morning after Jen Swinburn's visit to Raghurst, Dyann had decided to come clean on all fronts. She'd made an appointment with the Dean of Student Life and told him the whole story. He had suspended her on the spot. There would be a disciplinary hearing, he told her, and she would almost certainly be expelled for violation of the Student Code of Non-Academic Conduct.

Next Dyann got Officer McCrae's number from me and was picked up in a cruiser and taken to the police station to make a statement. We wondered whether she would be arrested and held, jailed even, but she was home again an hour later. There likely would be charges, she told us, but McCrae said it could take ages. 'She was pissed,' Dyann said grimly. 'She delivered a massive lecture about Sheri Asselin, and how I'd squandered the community's will to act on years of complaints against frat houses.'

Jen Swinburn had been angry, too, when she'd come upstairs from Charla's room after talking to Dyann. 'She's delusional,' she'd fumed. 'She wants to come off as some kind of feminist folk hero. Like she's Gloria Steinem infiltrating the Playboy Mansion or something.'

'Well, I can sort of see the comparison,' Charla had said, trying to be loyal. 'Speaking truth to power? Like Antigone, maybe?'

'Steinem didn't drug people's drinks,' Jen said. 'She didn't break the law.'

For our Imbolc dinner I made a vegetable soup using sweet potatoes, onions, a turnip – whatever I could find in the fridge. I raided Charla's spice shelf and added anise and cloves for spiritual clarity. I walked over to the strip mall and bought a fresh loaf of grainy bread. Everything else I needed – the dish of salt, the mirror, the black candles – was still stashed in the bathroom cupboard from the last time.

It felt good to be doing something specific. I'd been skipping class the last four or five days, avoiding campus altogether and walking to the T-Cam as soon as it opened at 11 am. The first time I brought a book and sat alone in Raghurst's usual booth. But after a couple of hours, when I went up to the bar for my third pint, Stan pointed out that I hadn't looked down at the page once but had been staring into space. 'You know the place is empty, right?' he said. 'I keep looking over to see who it is you're watching. It's like there's a hologram on the pool table or something.'

'Sorry,' I said. 'I haven't been sleeping well.' In fact I hadn't been able to sleep at all since the gold car. Night was a waste. A void.

'So's I'm not creeped out, why don't you just come sit up here at the bar,' Stan suggested. And after that I didn't bother with the pretense of schoolwork. I just waited on the sidewalk outside the T-Cam until it opened for the day, and then I sat on a bar stool and drank and talked to Stan.

At six o'clock there was a knock, and I opened the door to see Wheeler, Stick, Jake, and Josh on our porch. 'Get Dyann,' Stick said. 'We want her to admit us personally.'

I tried to keep a straight face when I fetched Dyann, but she said, 'Oh, great. What now? What did they do this time?'

'We come as you asked us,' Stick announced with great formality. They were in drag, all four of them: miniskirts, frilly tops, makeup, junk-store jewellery. Stick wore stiletto boots and had a pair of sequined fairy wings strapped to his bare shoulders.

There was a moment of silence. Look how Wheeler shifts from left foot to right, how Josh drags a finger under his lower lip in case his lipstick has bled. They look like banished prophets waiting to be struck blind.

'And we come bearing gifts,' added Stick. He opened his palm and held out his trump card: a beribboned plastic baggie containing generous portions of grass, pills, and foil-wrapped hash brownies.

'Hm,' said Dyann. She looked at me and bit her lip. 'What do you think?'

'Me?' I was so surprised that Dyann wanted my opinion that I suddenly found myself thinking hard about Imbolc, about whether the presence of cross-dressing skateboarders would jeopardise the integrity of the ritual. O, but look how they shift from foot to foot, how they hold forth their open hands! They are chastened prophets begging admittance at the city gates. 'As long as they're women they're safe, I think,' I said.

Dyann sighed. 'Okay,' she told them, 'but your lives are in your own hands.'

I served the brownies around first, as soon as the music was turned off and they'd all brought their drinks to the table.

'Drink the cedar water next,' I told them. I'd filled glasses with one of Charla's infusions.

'I hate cedar water,' Stick whined, but they all drank it down, fast, to get on to their wine. We became surprisingly easy around the table together, chatting about nothing and nibbling on olives and dried fruits I'd dug out of the pantry for appetizers.

Dyann squirmed as I lit the candles. I had written out the invocation on a separate piece of paper in tidier handwriting than my usual, because I knew she'd need to participate to feel comfortable. I handed it to her now and switched off the dining room light.

She leaned forward to read it in the candles' glow. 'Here is light, in this winter's darkness. Here is life in this winter's deadness. These women gather'

– Jake tittered, and Wheeler shushed him – 'to share the bounty offered by thrift and cunning, by wisdom and togetherness.'

'Solidarity,' I interrupted. That was the word I'd searched for an hour ago and not found. 'Togetherness' was too touchy-feely.

'Wisdom and solidarity,' said Dyann. Again that alien feeling came over me, that Dyann was deferring to me, that she was following my script.

'Now we eat the soup,' I said, and ladled it out into the bowls.

The phone rang. Marie-Jeanne picked it up in the kitchen and told me it was Mike calling.

'Tell him no,' I said. 'No matter what, it's no.' I hadn't spoken to Mike since the ride to the hospital. Had that really been only a week ago? Between the daytime drinking and the nighttime sleeplessness, I'd completely lost track.

Marie-Jeanne came back to the table. 'He said to tell you he met someone. He wants to make sure there are no hard feelings.'

'Good ol' Chet Morton,' I sighed.

'Wasn't that a character in the Hardy Boys?' Josh said.

I laughed and felt anger knuckling, sharp and surprising, under my rib cage. The hash was already nosing its way into my bloodstream. It was time to break the bread. I held the loaf aloft and squinted at the notes beside my plate: 'We tear this bread, and share it amongst us, in memory of other bodies broken and lost.' There was the Catholic Communion, of course, but my book had explained that the breaking of bread went back much further than the Corpus Christi, back to Dionysus and Osiris and to endless indigenous variants about flayed and dismembered gods.

I'd decided to stick with the Greek idea: 'Bread is life: the fruit of last summer's harvest and the promise of springtime resurrection. Broken and shared, it also means *sparagmos*, the rending and scattering, the destroying in order to seed the new.'

I tried to rip the loaf of bread in half, but it was tougher than I thought, too fat for me to get a solid grip. I swung it over to Marie-Jeanne beside me, and we each took one end.

'*Sparagmos!*' Marie-Jeanne pronounced, in the manner of a toast. She dug her fingernails in, sheared off the loaf's heel, and bit into it. In the moment between biting and chewing there was a flicker of Marie-Jeanne's anorexic ghost peering from its bonecage.

We passed the bread around, each tearing off our own piece and saying, 'Sparagmos.' Dyann succumbed to a fit of uncharacteristic giggling when Wheeler's bread landed in his half-finished soup.

'Dude, I think you still have to eat it,' Stick told him, and Wheeler fished out the bread and took a careful, conscientious bite. They were taking it seriously, the ritual. They all were.

The hash spread itself into a gritty layer under my skin, like sandpaper. I became nervous about the next portion of the ritual. 'We take our shirts off now,' I instructed. 'We need bare skin.'

I'd imagined bras, but Dyann wasn't wearing one. Her nipples were dark brown, with large areolas.

'Nice,' Jake said, and the others shushed him. Josh wore a lacy pink bandeau under his blouse. Stick had only his wings, and the others stayed in their bikini tops to maintain appearances.

'You can choose the back or the chest,' I explained. 'We face each other, recite the words, and slap three times. Open hands.' I splayed my fingers to demonstrate. My thoughts were racing forward, though, whipped up and spurred on by the drug. Jostling and vying through the narrow passages, they ran together, neck and neck.

Dyann's laughter bubbled through her words. 'Wait, we're *slapping* each other now?'

The boys caught the laughter up and swallowed it; it came back to their vivid lips doubled, tripled, quadrupled. 'Why are we slapping each other, Karen?'

My thoughts came all at once, leaping on one another's backs. 'Kittens are taught with blows – oh, you guys, don't you wish we were all lions? You're struck: you can be struck by insight, struck by a thought. Did you know that at the onset of her first period a Jewish girl used to be slapped by her mother?'

We sat shirtless, laughing. Marie-Jeanne poured more wine, and Stick lit a joint and passed it around the table. I missed Charla and Steph. I was embarrassed by my loose words and the loosening of whatever logic had held the ceremony together. It was silly, what I'd planned. It was as dumb as the frat boys' drunken pileups. Dumber, because it took itself too seriously.

But after a few minutes Dyann sobered. 'Give me what you wrote,' she said. 'Let's see.' She spent some moments deciphering my penmanship, then said, 'No, this is good, actually. This fits with Imbolc's theme of purification, and – what else is it?' Again, she looked at me, looked *to* me, for the information, and this time I felt a flash of irritation, anger almost, at her subservience. 'Purification, initiation, dedication, right?' she said.

I didn't know which of my thoughts might break through the gate next, so I just nodded.

Dyann stood up and circled to my chair. She read out what I'd written: 'Here we enact the punishing gestures of initiation. Here we purge evil and open ourselves to insight.

'Stand up,' she ordered, and when I did she slapped me, hard, in the face.

Without thinking, I slapped her back with equal force.

'Oh, *mon dieu*,' Marie-Jeanne said.

Stick turned to Wheeler and, with both hands, slapped his friend's shoulders once, twice. Then he dealt a loud blow across his cheek.

'Ow! Fuck, man!' And Wheeler slapped him back.

There were still a few other items on my Imbolc agenda, but they fell away in the general hilarity of the slapping. After we cleared the dishes, Stick doled out MDMA pills, Josh served as DJ, and we all danced. At one point some of us paraded next door to try out the climbing wall the boys had built in their living room in place of the half-pipe. I remember straddling someone's shoulders, reaching for one of the top holds – and when we returned, Raghurst was humid, clamorous, packed with bodies. The guests were all girls, just like we'd planned.

Because I'd been avoiding campus, I hadn't been constantly reminded of my newfound fame. But now I was being congratulated again for standing my ground against the fraternity. I was hugged. I was told it was courage like mine that would win the war on rape. News of Dyann's role in things was spreading, but not fast enough to shake this crowd from its belief that I was still the victim and Bruce Comfort was still the perpetrator. Dyann may have muddied the waters but she hadn't stemmed the tide.

The only party guest more popular than me was Ms Dentata, our Viking-helmeted mannequin. She was lifted by the women and passed around and danced with and kissed. It wasn't only the party's V-Day theme; it was St Brigid's Day, too – someone had said you were supposed to make a sacred doll and parade it from house to house in the village. You were supposed to bring it food and invite it into your bed for luck.

Marie-Jeanne told me that Charla had returned, so I went downstairs to see her. She was in her bower smoking a joint. She wore her red geisha dress. Her bare legs shone marble-white.

'Nice shirt,' she said.

I looked down. I was still topless; I'd forgotten my shirt at the dining table and had failed to notice my nakedness all evening. More and more of the women upstairs were getting naked, in fact. Our Imbolc hijinks had set the tone for the evening, for the newcomers as they trickled in. The neighbour boys in their frilly outfits were starting to look grossly overdressed.

Charla beckoned me under the canopy, and I flopped down next to her. The bass thumped down through the ceiling, causing the fabric to quiver overhead. I remembered the tree-planting camp next to a nickel mine where the machines ran through the night, a subsonic pulse that kept extinguishing the pilot light on our propane showers. My tent had trembled. The whole week of that contract, every night, I'd dreamt of quicksand: of sinking and of being swallowed.

'How was your date?' I asked.

Charla laughed. 'Is that what Dyann told you guys? That I was on a date? Oh, poor Dyann!'

'She was mad you missed Imbolc.'

'Well, I had an appointment. I was looking at a condo.'

I blinked at her. *I was looking at a condo.* I'd never heard anyone my age say that sentence before. I wasn't even sure I knew what a condo was. Shag carpeting came to mind.

'My brother wants to invest,' she explained, 'and I want to get the hell out of this house. So it's win–win.'

I rolled over and clutched both her arms. 'Don't go,' I planned to say. I was going to say, 'Charla, I'd miss you.'

But instead what came out was, 'Charla, I miss Bruce Comfort.' And at the words my heart wriggled like a pup from my arms and bounded from the bed.

'The frat boy?' she said. 'For real?'

'I really like him,' I whispered. My heart yapped interruptively, turning circles on her rug.

She moved onto her side to face me and curled her knees up, against my ribs. There was a little line between her eyebrows.

'I liked him from the start. I like him more and more.' *Yapyapyap*. Surely Charla could feel my heartbeat through her kneecaps. I waited for her to pull them away.

She blinked. She didn't pull away. She said, 'It feels like freedom, doesn't it, in your body. It's terrifying, freedom. If you want it you have to go way out there on a limb, all alone.'

'I'm not alone; I'm in the bower, with you.'

'Yes, you are.' She reached out and stroked my hair away from my cheek.

A few minutes or maybe more passed in the warm racket of our companionship and shared understanding. Desires as dense as melons swelled in my chest and sent their furred vines down between my legs. I arose from the bower laden with desires, hobbled with them.

'Did you know that Helen of Troy married Achilles in the afterlife?' I asked her.

'I thought it was Paris she was hot for,' Charla said. 'That's what started the whole war.'

'Maybe he wasn't divine enough, in the long run. Apparently Poseidon made them their own island and everything.'

'So, are you going to call him?'

'Who?'

'Bruce Comfort,' she said.

'To come here? That would be pearls before swine.' That wasn't the right expression, though. It was hard to think with the swollengold thought *Bruce, Bruce, Bruce* suffusing my body. I tried again: 'Dogs, I mean. It would be like throwing him to the dogs.'

Charla was laughing at me. 'You're not obliged to stay at this party, you know, Karen. You are allowed to leave this house.'

'It's late, though.'

'Yes. And you might need some clothing.'

46. EPIDEICTIC

(ceremonial oratory)

I confirm on the Department of Women's Studies website that Steph's memorial service is scheduled for nine thirty in the morning. When I arrive at nine twenty the many-windowed, carpeted room is empty except for rows of chairs facing a podium and screen. I fret about getting the location wrong – try unsuccessfully to log on to the campus Wi-Fi, walk one way and then the other down the hall, searching in vain for an admin office – before two young women show up with a stack of photocopied programs on blue paper and a grocery bag full of potted tulips. I help distribute the tulips beside the podium and along the refreshment table. There's a big round tray of pastries, a stack of Styrofoam cups, and a bowl of creamers nestled in ice, though no coffee yet.

I take a seat. By now a steady trickle of people are entering the room, talking in subdued tones, shaking hands. Women's Studies must be just upstairs, because eight or ten women whom I assume to be Steph's colleagues arrive together, without jackets, several of them gripping mugs of coffee from their offices. A short, florid woman with burgundy stripes in her black hair strides to the podium, taps at the microphone, and asks one of the young women to help power up the projector.

I contemplate slipping out for a coffee before things start, if they are starting late anyhow. I decide against it, in part because I stick out in this crowd enough without a Starbucks cup. I haven't been on a college campus since I graduated. I chose a navy twinset and a charcoal skirt – thinking funeral wear, thinking whatever was still clean – and then I added heels and a chignon. The profs, of course, wear either jeans and T-shirts or ankle-length rayon skirts and oversized sweaters. Not a single person in the room other than me is wearing makeup. The academic uniform has not changed since my days as an undergraduate. Karen Huls, lifestyle photographer, is what my outfit says to this crowd. Lightweight. Sellout.

The flyer says the service will open with a blessing from the interfaith chaplain, followed by welcome messages from the Dean of Arts and the Chair of Women's Studies. An image of Steph appears on-screen: grainy, out of focus, obviously cropped from a party shot of some kind. She gazes off-camera, half-smiling, her small hand wrapped around a champagne flute. She has aged some since I knew her, of course. Hair still cut short but temples touched now with gray. Lines run from the outside edges of her nostrils to the outside corners of her mouth, and there is a softness to the flesh under her chin.

Looking at her I feel a door inside me come off its latch and swing ajar. Beyond the door is sadness, and the sadness does have some of Steph in it, I think. I only knew her for a year. Less. O Steph, shining among women, our pale saint lying prone. Steph is protected from herself again – protected permanently, now, in death. The funeral and cremation have already taken place, the flyer informs me, back in Rochester where her father and her brother and their families live. The McNamaras have established a bursary in Steph's name for students with mental health challenges. The family is collecting donations, and the Faculty of Arts will be matching the funds.

My sadness has Greg in it too – the memory of Greg reading aloud to me from the newspaper over breakfast, of our sunrise walks by the lake, of our plans to build a cabin in the woods where I could take pictures and he could hike, maybe take up the guitar. The sadness of having been mistaken, of second-guessing one's memories, of revising them.

But looking through this inner door I also consider the prospect of mourning for myself. Sitting in that brightly lit public room with Steph's face looming before me, I mourn for something of myself that I have lost along with Steph – lost not recently, with her death, but back while we were still roommates at Raghurst.

A shell has grown over me. It's a toughness built of routine and of the gradual closing down of my contact with others. After I left Raghurst, I exiled myself from other women. Whenever I met a woman like my roommates, who seemed to care about women in general and our place in the world, I veered sharply in the opposite direction. Whenever I met any woman with whom I thought I could become friends I avoided her. This exoskeleton of mine has grown thick and rough, and it's becoming less and less possible to make contact. That phone call last night, the conversation with Jane Moscovitch the gallery owner – the effort to connect felt like boring through stone. I've grown so accustomed to sucking on my little pearls in private that I've stopped noticing how I am locked away, how I am living inside a shell.

47. SAPHENEIA

(clarity)

And what of myth? What of destiny's rising tide that swells and crests and sweeps us to its titanheights before dashing us upon the reef? Maybe I believed the storm had already broken. Maybe I thought we'd been sufficiently tossed and battered and were now lying, grateful for our very lives, on the shore. As if myth might engulf the lives of mortals and then simply recede. As if myth might relent!

I took the cordless phone up to my bedroom and called the frat house. A girl answered, promised to get Bruce for me, and hung up.

I called again, and she answered again. 'Leave it off the hook,' I reminded her, but I knew she was probably too drunk to stay on task. It was the telephone on the GBC kitchen wall, right next to the screen door. I could hear the rusty spring shrieking as people went in and out. I listened to the party noises there, and here at Raghurst – on the phone were baritone laughter and the jackhammer bass of a dance track; downstairs were the shouts of dancing women and Tori Amos on the stereo.

After a minute a male voice came on the line. 'What's aaaap?' it drawled.
'It's an emergency,' I tried. 'Can you get Bruce Comfort? This is his sister.'

There were a few more minutes of background party noises, and then someone hung up the phone again.

I was very patient. It had begun to feel like a game. Like a quest. I lay down on my bed and dialed again, went through the emergency routine again. This time it was only a short wait; he must have been close to the kitchen.

'Hey,' Bruce's voice said.

'Hooray!' I said.

'Who is this?'

'It's Karen Huls. Can you please come and take me away?'

'From where?'

'My house. You remember. You picked Mike up here, at Halloween.'

'Are you okay?' he said.

'Pretty high,' I confessed.

Bruce laughed. 'I don't think I should fetch you to the frat house, Karen.'

'No, no,' I agreed. 'And I don't think we can stay here at my house, either. We'll have to go someplace new.'

'Hell, why not,' Bruce said. 'I'm on my way.'

I went downstairs to find my shirt, but Raghurst's living and dining rooms were too crowded with nude women dancing, and there were too many other shirts and skirts and pants and bras and panties strewn over the floor and draped over the chairs and piled on the dining table. As I wound through the throng, women hugged me. Women kissed me on the mouth. Women slapped me on the back. Women cheered and whistled. Women called out my name.

Someone must have tried to let in some air, because the patio door had gotten jammed again. It stood six inches open to the winter night, listing off its track and running with condensation. Dyann was sitting out there on the deck railing, all alone, looking off across the yard. For a second I thought I'd mistaken her for someone else, but they were her dreadlocks, her broad shoulders and bare breasts, her high-bridged nose in profile. It was her expression that threw me. I'd never seen that expression before, and I squeezed out through the gap to get a closer look at her face.

She turned, and I shivered with the strangeness as much as the cold. Her lips were parted a little, her eyes wide, her gaze soft. It wasn't so much something new on her face as something missing. Some surety, some conviction, had been torn away.

Lost. That was it: Dyann Brooks-Morriss looked lost. 'What's wrong?' I said.

'They just ... They threw me out.'

'Who?'

'Them.' Dyann jerked her head at the house. 'That lynch mob in there.'

That lynch mob loves me, I thought. 'They can't throw you out of your own house, Dyann.'

'Not the house. The Women's Centre. Melanie just told me they're booting me out of the Women's Centre. They're releasing a statement "officially condemning my actions", she said.'

'Well, you're going to be expelled anyways, right? So you can't really keep your Women's Centre membership.'

Dyann was silent. No snappy comeback, no sharp retort.

I wrapped my arms across my chest. The deck was encrusted with ice, and we were both in bare feet. 'Come on, let's go back inside.'

'You go ahead,' she said. 'I can't fit through there. I tried to close the door behind me and it got stuck.'

'So we'll go around front. Come on. You can't stay out here.'

Dyann bit her lip. 'They're like a pack of wild animals.'

'Well, Dyann, that's exactly what you wanted.'

She looked at me. 'I wanted to organise. I wanted to act.'

'You wanted chaos,' I said. '*Bellum omnium in omnes*, remember?'

There was shouting from inside. I heard my name. I heard Bruce Comfort's voice.

'Oh, shit,' I said. Blurry bare limbs flashed through the fogged-up doors. I moved to the opening to see, Dyann's cold flesh pressing in behind me.

Bruce was coming through the house toward me, toward the jammed doors. He was trying to elbow his way through the women, but some of the women were shrieking at him, crowding and jostling and shoving him. Bruce looked scared.

'What is he doing here?' someone hollered.

'Rapist!' someone screamed.

'Get out, you pig!' someone shrieked.

It happened so fast. The women pushed in on Bruce and some reached out and clawed at his hoodie and his belt and his hair. He tried to back away but they pressed in around him as one naked writhing mass of limbs and hands clutching and tearing and shoving each other and shoving Bruce until he stumbled, or flung himself, or was thrown, violently forward.

'Watch out!' somebody cried. There was screaming.

I flinched back from the gap just as Bruce's body struck the patio door and exploded out, onto the deck, in a shower of flying glass. He slammed into Dyann and me with such force that all three of us telegraphed straight across the ice, shot under the deck railing, and landed in the snowdrift five feet below.

Amid the tangle of us in the deck's shadow, I thought at first my arm had been severed. I'd hit my head, and a solid weight crushed my thigh and my stomach, but the sharpest pain was just below my elbow. My chest flooded with hot liquid from what I thought must be the stump of my severed arm.

If all this blood is your blood you'll be dead soon. If not not. The logic was simple as a shrug. It was the same quiet, detached voice that had come to me when I was pinned to the gold car, but now it had burrowed itself even deeper inside my brain. It had walled itself off. It had no interest whatsoever in the screaming careening limbstruggle taking place in the snow.

I lifted my other hand and felt hair. I heard a thick bubbling sound, a spraying. I felt a hot spray across my belly. It was Bruce, lying on top of me.

'Fuck,' said Dyann, up on her elbow beside us, 'Oh. Oh, fuck.'

Bruce rolled a little and slid partway off me, into the snow. The top of his head wedged itself into my armpit. I wriggled to escape, scraping my bare back along the snow, but we were on an incline and I couldn't get any traction.

'Karen. Oh, Karen, look,' Dyann said.

Bruce's face was pierced all over with glass. Pieces of glass glittered in his cheek, his forehead. A shard protruded from his eye. But worse than that was his throat: a jagged fragment as long as my hand was lodged sideways in Bruce's neck. The wound bubbled. Red blood burbled and fountained as he coughed.

I reached over him, thinking to stanch the flow somehow, but my fingers nudged the glass and it tipped sideways from the wound, onto my ribs. The blood came faster, pumping now in a rhythm, spraying and gurgling when Bruce breathed.

My fingers slipped and scrabbled at his throat. 'Dyann,' I said, 'help me with this. I can't move my arm.'

The waterlogged breaths stopped, but Dyann lifted her hand and placed it over mine, pressing flat. The blood welled up between our fingers. I felt the pulse weaken, and then it stopped altogether. Dyann's head came down heavy on my shoulder.

The others came, screaming, from all sides. They looked down from the railing, circled around behind us, crowded in on both sides. Someone dropped a blanket down on us. Sirens wailed, and the paramedics ordered everyone away. They shone flashlights. They pulled Bruce clear of me, farther out into the yard, and did some CPR on his body there in the snow while everyone watched. Wherever the flashlights struck, Bruce's flesh was liquid, inert, the red blood dulling as it cooled.

I kept twisting and reaching around to see, frustrated when my limbs wouldn't cooperate, and they kept telling me to lie still while they felt through all the blood for injuries. 'I'm good, I feel good,' I assured them. 'I can't feel a thing, except my arm hurts.'

'It's the snow numbing you,' they told me. 'You have some serious lacerations in your legs and back.'

Finally they lifted me onto one stretcher and Dyann onto another, and carried us out of the backyard to separate ambulances. She was concussed, they told me. And because I wouldn't stop asking, they told me that Bruce Comfort was dead.

48. ANAGNORISIS

(recognition)

A woman leans across the empty seats between us. 'You're Karen, right? Karen Huls?' She has curly dark hair and glasses, and I struggle to place her. 'Janine Jeffries. I knew Steph back at grad school. You were her roommate, weren't you?'

'Yes,' I say. Janine does look familiar, once I mentally remove twenty or thirty pounds and pull her hair back into a braid. She worked at the Women's Centre. Ate with us at Raghurst, danced with us. Marched with us.

'Do you remember Seema?' Janine sits back so that I can see the woman next to her: brown skin, high cheekbones, thick bangs.

'Did you come together?' I say.

'No, we just met at the door,' Seema replies. 'It's been at least ... five years, right, Janine?' Janine pats Seema's knee.

'Seema was Steph's partner for, what, six years?'

'Seven.' Seema sighs. 'We broke up in 2005.'

The three of us look up at the picture of Steph still projected at the front of the room. I remember then how I know Seema: 'You were in the same program as Marie-Jeanne Ouellette, weren't you?'

Seema smiles and nods. 'MJ and I dated for a few months in 1997, senior year. That's how I first met Steph. Then we moved out here after graduation, and MJ went the other way, out to the Wild West somewhere.'

'The oil fields, wasn't it?' I say. 'Last I heard, she got a job consulting for some oil company in Alaska.'

'Oh, that was ages ago. It was Alberta after that,' Seema says.

We sit quietly a few minutes, the three of us, once we realise none of us has any up-to-date information. The sadness of obsolete knowledge, I think. The sadness of having lost track.

'I wonder who else might show up,' I say, thinking of Dyann but not wanting to say her name. 'Any of our old profs? I'd love to see Dr Esterhazy again.'

'You didn't hear.' Janine glances at Seema.

'What?'

'Sylvia Esterhazy died of breast cancer just over a year ago.' Seema shakes her head, gazing up at the screen as she speaks. 'It was really fast. Steph hadn't seen her in years, but they were supposed to present a paper together at some conference, and apparently when the date got close she called Steph from the hospital. And then she died before the conference. Steph never actually got to see her in person.'

'That's terrible,' I say.

'Yeah. Steph tracked me down and told me about it a couple of months after it happened.' Seema turns to look at Janine and me, and her eyes are shiny with tears. 'You know, I could already hear it in her voice then.'

Janine says, 'Hear what?'

'The sorrow. I mean, Steph struggled with depression when we were together too. But this was worse. You know, way beyond being sad because someone died. More like sad because you're still alive.'

*

I was scrubbed clean, bandaged, bound, plastered, put to bed. O blessings upon these tiled white rooms with their subdivided pools of curtainquiet! Blessings upon all the murmuring nurses who pierce the skin who anoint the skin who bind the skin! Thus are our flows stanched, our ravings soothed. Thus are our toxicities siphoned off and neutralised, our bodies put to restorative rest. Thus are we saved always and again from ourselves.

They kept me in the hospital the next day on an IV drip because I was so dehydrated. I woke sometime mid-morning and spent five full minutes engaged in the silent, paralysing work of figuring out where I was. Then I lifted the sheet to inspect my injuries. My arm lay on the mattress beside me in a cast. It hurt to move it – it hurt even when I tried to roll it slightly back and forth. My shoulder, chest, and upper arm were dark with bruises. There were big patches of gauze taped all over my body: on my upper arm, here and there on my back, across my thigh, over my hipbone, and behind my left knee. Where I didn't hurt, I itched. I dug a crust of dried blood from my navel, and another from behind my ear. The hair at my nape was stiff and left rusty flakes on the pillow.

A nurse slipped inside my curtain, checked my blood pressure, and made a note on my chart. Then she said, 'You have a visitor. A policewoman.'

Panic dove down my throat and cannonballed into my stomach. 'No!' I croaked. I swung my legs over the side of the bed, but Officer McCrae had already filled the gap in the curtain with her shining brass buttons and her smooth, reddish-gold hair.

I lay back down and drew the sheet up to my chin. Muscles spasmed throughout my body, and the nurse *tsk*ed and dabbed at my forearm where I'd yanked on the IV port.

'How do you feel?' Officer McCrae asked once we were alone.

I closed my eyes. My skin crawled, and nausea rose in my guts. I said, 'Please, can I have some water? Can you call the nurse back?'

Officer McCrae ducked out through the curtain and came back a moment later with a cupful of water. My hand shook so badly trying to take it from her hand that I nearly spilled it on the bed. She had to help steady the paper cup to my mouth.

'You're in rough shape,' she said. 'Are your parents coming for you?'

'Am I under arrest?' I asked.

Officer McCrae frowned. She set her hat on the blanket and sat down on the bed. 'Why would I arrest you, Karen?' she asked.

'Because it was my fault.'

'We've talked to a lot of the party guests,' she said. 'We have a pretty good picture of what happened.'

'But it was me who called him,' I said. 'I asked him to come over.'

'You weren't even inside the house when the accident happened.'

My head spun. I couldn't stand to have her weight on my bed. I couldn't bear the gentle pity in her voice. I said, 'You say it "happened" like nothing caused it. But I caused it.'

She sighed. 'This is a really common response to trauma, to blame yourself. Are they sending someone to talk to you? A social worker?'

I didn't say anything. I wasn't accusing myself falsely due to trauma. I had lied to Officer McCrae when she asked me whether I knew how Sheri had been drugged. That night she interviewed me at the frat house – had I known about the roofies back then? Had I known about the video? I couldn't remember. But I'd lied and lied, and now Bruce was dead.

As if she'd followed my thoughts, Officer McCrae said, 'Did you know that blaming and denying blame follow exactly the same pattern? It doesn't matter whether someone's trying to blame someone or protect someone. People always look to themselves first. Then those closest to them: family, loved ones, roommates, et cetera. And only then do they look beyond that, to other people, to the bigger picture.'

She got back to her feet. She picked up her hat and tucked it under her arm. 'Except, of course, when it comes to rape,' she said. 'No one will believe himself or his loved ones capable of rape. When it comes to rape it's always the victim who gets blamed first.'

I lunged over and threw up onto the tiled floor. My weight on my cast hurt, and I collapsed flat against the mattress. I choked on a bit of vomit and coughed and coughed, my bruised ribs pounding pain.

Officer McCrae went away after that, and I fell asleep again. When I woke up the IV was gone. I drank lots of water and ate the sandwich sitting on the tray.

Charla came in with a bag of clothes she'd collected from my bedroom. Even with her help, it took me forever to get dressed. Charla had to fasten my bra for me and help me pull my tank top over my head. She'd brought my plaid shirt, too, my Kerouac one. I put it on even though I had to leave it draped over the shoulder of my broken arm. Charla did up a couple of the buttons for me to stop it from slipping off.

'You'll have to cut a sleeve off some stuff,' she said. 'I couldn't find anything in your closet that would work with a cast.'

'Maybe they have a special store,' I said.

'A store for the one-armed?' she said.

'For amputees, maybe.' Laughter knuckled at my diaphragm, a ghostly return of the long stretches of hash-driven giggling the night before.

Charla put her arms around my waist and held her cheek to mine. 'Dyann and Marie-Jeanne are up in the psych ward getting Steph up to speed,' she said. 'They wanted to come see you, but I said I would ask you first.'

'Wasn't Dyann hurt?'

'Not much. She just whacked her head. She was still sitting in the waiting room last night when MJ and I arrived.'

The thought of my roommates gathered around my hospital bed made me queasy again. Instead, Charla helped me sneak past the nurses' station to the elevators, so we could go up to Steph's room.

Marie-Jeanne snoozed beside Steph in the bed, their fingers interlaced. Dyann was reading by the window.

There was an empty chair beside Steph's bed, but I didn't sit down. 'Are we going to be in trouble because of all the drugs at the party?' I said.

Charla snuggled in on Steph's other side. 'Stick had the sense to leave when the police arrived, so he's okay. I think you guys ingested everything there was to ingest, because they didn't seem to find a stash anywhere.'

'Maybe liability, though,' Dyann said. 'We were the hosts of the party.'

Steph shook her head. 'If anyone is liable it's the landlord.'

'What if he evicts us?' Marie-Jeanne said.

Another firm shake of Steph's head. 'That patio door was never up to code. We'd have every right of appeal if he tried to evict, but he knows it would mean his ass if he drew attention to the whole thing like that.'

Steph was holding court, here in the psych wing. Steph the captive suffering saint, the martyr lying abed as though behind shatterproof glass. There were special plastic bubbles screwed over the electrical outlets. Nothing in the room long enough for hanging oneself.

'We're kind of not talking about the main thing here,' Charla said. She reached for my good hand and pulled me down until I was sitting on the bed with the others. 'The main thing is that someone died.'

They all looked at me.

'No,' I said, shaking Charla off. 'Don't.'

'It's okay, Karen,' Dyann said. 'You can say whatever's there.'

'Whatever's in your head,' said Steph.

'Whatever's in your body,' Charla corrected.

'Why?' I said. 'What would be the point?'

Dyann stood up and dropped her book on the chair. She came around Steph's bed and looked down into my face. 'The point is that you're a part of this, Karen. You're central to it, actually. So you can't pretend to be watching from the periphery.'

'Dyann, come on. It's not the time,' Steph said.

'No, it's okay. She's right,' I said. 'It's my fault he's dead.'

'No,' Charla said.

'You know that's not what I meant,' Dyann said.

I stood up and pulled away from them. I was remembering Steph's tuberculosis fantasy: all those pretty coughed-up drops of blood on the snow. My own throat by contrast was a flamethrower. When I spoke, things shriveled and crisped.

'I have to go back downstairs to get discharged,' I told them. I couldn't remember having given anyone my parents' number, but the nurse had informed me they were driving down from Toronto and would be here by five o'clock.

I waved goodbye to my roommates from the hospital room doorway. 'Dyann is right,' I repeated, because the others were glaring at her. 'Look at her.' Warburnished Dyann, insatiate of battle. Speaker of unbearable truths. 'Have you ever noticed? Dyann is always right in the end.' I knew the smile twisting my mouth must have looked ghastly, demented. My words landed black and burnt, leaving my mouth full of ashes.

O Dyann the dreadful. Dyann blinking her keen eyes, flaring her nostrils, sniffing out truth. Dyann redglistening with blood, sniffing at the wet, red blood.

49. PATHOS

(appeal to emotions)

My parents took me home with them that same night, all the way back to Toronto. 'I need you home with us, at least a week or two,' my mom insisted. I didn't want them to see Raghurst, so they waited in their car in the driveway while I went in to pack a bag. The patio door had been taped over with cardboard, but the house was otherwise still in disarray from our party.

I looked out my bedroom window at the wan crimson patchwork in the snow. Look how the ground ran with his blood, I thought, look how the earth groaned with his blood. I turned for my camera but it wasn't on my desk, and I remembered it had been smashed in the gorge weeks and weeks ago. Then I stood at the window again and felt sick at how beautiful the backyard appeared to me with its marks of death. Someone had died – my brain shied from his name – and I wanted to photograph the bloodpattern. I sickened myself. I made myself so sick that I rushed into the bathroom and vomited into the toilet.

My mom didn't cry in the car, but her voice was tight with tears. Her lips clenched tight against her tears when she spoke. 'Drugs. Ecstasy pills, no less! Oh, Karen, there could be lasting repercussions. Memory loss. Flashbacks, even years later.'

'Did you black out?' my dad kept wanting to know. He'd cornered a doctor in my hospital room and demanded to know whether they were certain they'd checked everything, tested everything. 'You need to collect all the evidence right now, even if she's insisting nothing happened,' my dad had said, and the doctor had upset him further by saying no, that's not how it worked, they didn't do that unless the patient requested it.

Once I'd been home with them for a couple of days, though, my parents calmed down. My mom drove me to her hairdresser for what she called a 'pixie cut', and then to the mall for knee-length skirts and three-quarter sleeve tops to hide what would always be ugly scars, despite the doctors' competent suturing. 'A fresh start,' she kept calling it. 'Now that you've got that boyfriend business behind you, you can focus your energies on taking care of yourself.'

My parents went back to work. There were arguments over dinner about my brother Keith using the car on a weeknight and about him cutting class. I went to bed early and lay there in my old basement bedroom listening to *Law & Order* on the television upstairs and wondering why my parents always turned up the volume so loud.

Nostalgia zipped itself around me like a sleeping bag. I was nostalgic for washing the dishes after dinner and for bickering with Keith over whose turn it was to dry them. For playing Mastermind and Probe around the dining table, for doing jigsaw puzzles. For rewinding *Purple Rain* over and over on my ghetto blaster. I was nostalgic for smoking cigarettes down by the creek, for sleepovers, for lying to my parents, for pit parties and for being driven to school the next day by my girlfriends' hungover or still-drunk older brothers. For frosh week and freshman year, for my shopaholic roommate Rachel Smythe. For tree-planting. I was nostalgic for everything, everything, before the present.

I'd been in Toronto four days when Charla telephoned my mother. I would have listened in on the call, but Dad took the extension into the study. The three of them talked for a long time, and afterward my parents decided that it was important for me to attend Bruce Comfort's funeral. Dad would drive me to Bruce's hometown, they decided, and accompany me to the service. Then he would bring me back to Raghurst, back to school. A fresh start.

On the way to the funeral, we listened to an unabridged audiobook of *Les Misérables*. Dad stopped the tape for the border crossing, and when we were back on the highway, before he pressed Play again, he said, 'Do you want to talk, Karen? I can leave it off so we can talk, if you want.'

'I'm okay,' I said. 'Really.'

Four hours later we found a coffee shop and used the washroom, then drove around Bruce's town for forty minutes so as not to be too early for the service. We passed a construction crew guiding a telephone pole into place with a crane. We passed an elementary school playground with children running around and screaming. That it was a weekday, a workday, surprised me. That people could be so innocent, so oblivious. That they could have no idea.

The church was an old one in a residential neighbourhood, and even though we were early for the funeral we had to park four blocks away. A frigid wind was blowing dry snowflakes over the roofs. My dad had lent me his parka in Toronto, and now he draped it around my shoulders and zipped it up for me over the sling. The cold shriveled my lungs and made my eyes sting with tears.

The coffin at the front of the sanctuary was surrounded by flowers and flanked by an easel displaying an enormous picture of Bruce. Closed casket: I hadn't thought about what that meant when Dad had mentioned it earlier, what that implied. I remembered the glass protruding from the eye socket and cheek. I remembered the burbling red throat. For a moment, daring myself, I imagined marching up the aisle and lifting the lid and looking down at – what? Would Bruce's face be sunken in, graying, gaping? Or tacked together like Frankenstein's monster?

Bruce's family sat in the front pew. Mr and Mrs Comfort were not how I would have imagined the CFO of Comfort Insurance Services and his wife. Mrs Comfort had dyed hair in that shade Charla called 'menopause red'. Her gray roots made a thick line down her part. Mr Comfort was bald, with ruddy cheeks, sloping shoulders, and a thick neck.

Bruce's sister Sandra played a classical piece on the flute. Her friend, accompanying her on piano, blinked tears and sniffled and made mistakes the whole way through, but Sandra kept her back straight and her eyes steady on the score.

I hadn't read the order of service and was surprised when Duncan Larson took the podium. Duncan wore an expensive dark suit and hair gel. I turned in my seat and saw a whole pew crammed full of GBC brothers, shoulder to shoulder in charcoal, black, or navy suits with muted striped ties. Before I turned back to the front of the church I recognised Tim Burns, Charlie, Chris, and Pits.

Look at them all sobershowered, each whose duty it is to carry the bones back to a man's children. All their bronze helmets held in their laps. Look how they are ennobled by loss, valourvaunted by grief. O warmaking Dyann, thou stark of courage, where are you now when I need you?

Duncan unfolded a piece of paper from his suit pocket, introduced himself, and began his eulogy, reading too fast and stumbling every few words: 'Bruce Comfort, known affectionately as "Jangles" in our house, was one of the best men the fraternity has ever known. His athletic abilities put the rest of us to shame but he never lorded it over us – he was always happy to toss a ball around just for fun with any of us. Loyalty was his number one quality.'

They will carry the hero's bones back to his family, but first they must gather stones from the roadways and pile them high. Four by four they must shoulder the timbers onto the pyre. The women's keening death song will echo across the sunbaked sky, carrying his name to Olympus.

But how could the epic hero die? I wondered suddenly. It made no sense; he couldn't die. And he certainly couldn't be called 'Jangles', I thought. I'd never heard that nickname used at the frat house; it must not have stuck past the day Bruce pledged GBC. This was a fiction I was listening to. A fable, a bedtime story. Duncan's clichés rolled on and on, like a postgame interview with a linebacker. Mr Comfort emitted loud, rumbling sobs throughout the speech.

My dad and I followed the shuffle of guests up to the front of the church after the service. The Comforts stood in a line beside the coffin to receive condolences. One of Bruce's older brothers held his wife's hand, and the other, taller brother held a toddler on his hip.

'You weren't there when it happened, were you?' the taller one asked me. It was the sling. People looked at my sling and imagined right away that I must be integral to the tragedy.

Bruce's brother's looks were halfway between Bruce's and Bruce's father's: handsome but bloated, with thinning hair and saggy jowls. Looking at him – looking at Bruce's future, the future Bruce did not have – made the air go out of the room. 'No, I wasn't there,' I lied. 'I'm sorry for your loss.'

My dad was talking to an old woman – Bruce's grandmother, maybe, her frame so small and stooped that Dad had to hunch over to hear her – and I squeezed in behind them, next to the tiered rack of flickering candles in their ruby jars. Duncan was hugging Mrs Comfort, shaking Mr Comfort's hand. Behind him came the whole line of boldsorrowing brothers, all dressed the same. And Mike Morton was in the line too, looking puffy and pale in his yellow dress shirt.

He had spotted me. When he was finished with his condolences, he came through the crowd and took my good hand and held it. 'Hey,' he said.

'Hi, Mike,' I said. The skin of his neck was flushed, with deeper red lines where his collar had pinched. Poor Mike, I thought, and I realised it was the first time in weeks – months, maybe, even – that I'd felt anything but rage toward Mike Morton.

'This is Alexandra,' he said. He turned to a girl behind him, slipped his arm around her waist, and drew her closer. 'Alexandra, this is my ex, Karen.'

'Oh, Karen, it's so good to meet you finally,' Alexandra said. She was tall, with a handsome, freckled face and strawberry-blonde hair halfway down her back. 'How's your arm? Are you okay?'

'Alexandra's in pre-med,' Mike told me. 'She won the freshman bio award. Remember, at the banquet?' There was pride in his voice.

'Are you two dating?' I said.

'Not *dating* dating,' Alexandra said.

'We're going to see where things go,' Mike said.

Alexandra's cheeks had reddened. 'It's just – a couple of parties, so far. You know.'

Mike kissed Alexandra's temple and smoothed her hair behind her ear. 'This girl is brilliant. *Brilliant.* Karen, you should remember the name Alexandra Cavell. She's going to be a famous pediatrician someday.'

'Okay,' I said.

Mike said, 'We're having a wake at the house tonight. I think you should come.'

Fright charged me. Not that house. Not that third-floor room, that list on the door. I laughed to hide my fright. 'I don't know if that's a good idea,' I said.

'You know he would have wanted you there.' Mike looked over his shoulder at the coffin as though Bruce might be listening.

I saw with relief that my father was moving down the aisle toward the exit.
'It's closure, Karen, you know?' Alexandra said. 'You should come.'
'I'll have to see,' I told them.

50. APOTHEOSIS

(deification)

Sheri Asselin was dancing. She lashed her body back and forth like she was wearing a rubber suit rather than skin. She crashed into a lamp and tore a poster off the wall. She lurched over to where I was sitting on the buffet cabinet and hugged me hard. 'Karen. Fuck, Karen, can you believe it? That poor, poor guy. Fuck.' She was wasted. One of her tears ran down my sternum behind the sling.

'What are you doing here, Sheri?'

'Eric called me. He said I should be here, and I thought he was right. Don't you think? I mean, don't you think this kind of trumps everything else?'

Bruce Comfort's wake was just another frat party. The beer keg and the plastic cups. The giant cooler of PPD, aka Pink Panty Dropper, for the girls. Groups of already-drunk boys and girls playing Quarters and FUBAR and Century Club and Flip, Sip or Strip. Bon Jovi and Nirvana and CCR and Green Day on the stereo. Blackie and Tim Burns bickering over who got to DJ. Frodo taking off his shirt to prove how many spoons he could stick into his armpits without dropping any. Except for the dress code – the brothers were still in their suits, the girls wore dresses and pumps – it was just the same as always.

It was just the same, but it was completely different of course. Mike and Alexandra were mixing drinks in the kitchen. I was nobody's girlfriend. I was worse than nobody: my name was on the door in the room with the gold car. I was even worse than that: I was Dyann Brooks-Morriss's roommate.

Across the room Eric Vine raised his beer bottle to us. He and Pits were laughing. Alec Moretti held a camcorder and was filming Sheri and me in each other's arms – Sheri Asselin and Karen Huls, the pair of skanks, the golden-ticket girls, the dirty little sistersluts.

'Neither of us should be in this house, Sheri,' I said. Fear spiked my voice. 'Coming back here to party like this, after everything that's happened. It's stupid.'

'It wasn't even these guys' fault,' Sheri said. 'They didn't do anything.'

'Come on, you don't really believe that.'

She clutched at my shoulders for balance. 'It was that bitch roommate of yours, that feminazi. McCrae says she could end up with jail time.'

'You're going to press charges?' I asked her.

Sheri leaned in farther, overbalanced, and collapsed against me, her elbow digging hard into my lap. 'Accessory to rape,' she said. 'S'perfect, right? Bitch is all, like, "Frat boys are rapists," and now who's the rapist, bitch?'

Over her shoulder I saw Duncan Larson come in and hook a hand over Alec's shoulder and take the camera away from him. He pressed Alec against the doorframe and crowded in on him so that their backs were to me. I heard Alec's voice raised and saw Duncan lean in.

'What's going on?' Mike said. He and Alexandra had brought me a drink.

Sheri pushed off me and snatched one of the cups from Mike's hand. 'Thanks, Chet, baby,' she slurred.

'Hey, that was for Karen,' Alexandra said, but Sheri was already halfway across the room.

'It's okay, I don't want it,' I told them. 'It was stupid of me to show up here.'

Mike followed my gaze to Duncan and Alec. He gripped my elbow. 'They're just working it out, Karen. Just give them time.'

'For God's sake, Mike, he died at *my house*,' I hissed.

'I still have your copy of the *Iliad* in my room,' he said. 'We'll give you a lift home, at least.'

We went upstairs, Mike and Alexandra and me, past the open door of Bruce's bedroom, where I stopped and stared. It was wrecked, deserted. The stripped bed listed like a beached ship, flanked by shoals of bookshelves fallen off their pins, an empty CD tower, and a curled-up poster. The floor was a spindrift of cassettes, empty bottles, mismatched socks, a pair of pink varsity sweatpants.

'We told the cleaners to take everything, but they were probably worried his parents would sue or something, so they just left it,' Mike said.

I went in and plucked a paperback book from the flotsam at my feet. *Zen and the Art of Motorcycle Maintenance.* 'Oh, hey, that's mine,' said Mike.

'Bruce read it?'

'Bruce hated it. He thought it was going to be about motorcycles.'

I closed my eyes. The warm animal scent of Bruce was gone from the room, flooded out by strong cleaning products and the house's everyday aura of stale beer. I felt a shifting of sands inside my body, a receding tide, an ebb. Grief drying salty on my tongue.

'It's just so confusing, from a moral standpoint,' Alexandra said.

I looked at her.

'Mike told me everything that happened.' She took Mike's hand, lacing her fingers through his. 'The poor guy didn't deserve to die.'

I stared at their interlocked hands. 'The gods are monsters beyond the comprehension of man,' I said.

Mike kissed Alexandra's temple. 'But that doesn't mean Bruce was right, either. Moretti sure as hell wasn't right. Those guys just give the frat a bad name.'

'Karen,' Alexandra said, 'your roommate, Dyann – I mean, do you think she was right, to do what she did?'

I shuffled my feet through the trash on Bruce's floor. I stood, eyes closed, in the centre of the wreckage. Oh, just look at the farce of the three of us, Mike and the old girlfriend and the new girlfriend circling these ruins. How dare we? Look how we flap and caw and pick over the bones, justice strewn at our feet.

'Is she okay?' I heard Alexandra ask.

Mike touched my shoulder so I would open my eyes. 'Karen, we're trying to have an honest conversation here. Some kind of closure.'

'I know,' I said. 'I'm sorry. I'm sorry.'

From downstairs a male voice cried, 'To Bruce! To fucking Bruce!'

'Bruce! Bruce! Bruce!' And the chant was taken up outside in the hallway and up the stairs and across the second and third floors and outside on all the terraces and balconies, until the entire house resounded with the lusty basso grunt of Bruce Comfort's name reverenced and repeated and reabsorbed into the purebeating heart of the brotherhood.

51. ELEGEÍA

(lament for the dead)

The Dean of Arts speaks, and then the Chair of Women's Studies, and then someone named Dr Susan Green, a Djuna Barnes scholar and co-editor with Steph of a recent collection on something called 'spatial affect' in modernist women's literature. Apparently Steph has become – had become – quite an expert in 'affect theory', because each eulogist praises her 'groundbreaking' work in this field except for her brother, Lawrence McNamara, the only nonacademic to take the podium.

I confront my growing disappointment. These are not the right people, I tell myself. These people didn't know Steph like we did. But really what is bothering me is that Dyann isn't here; she didn't come after all. She isn't coming. I slip out of my chair without bothering to say goodbye to Janine and Seema – they have each other, after all, to chat with over coffee afterward. I ease the door closed behind me so that it doesn't make a sound.

There is a woman nursing a baby on a bench here in the hallway. Her worn chambray shirt is unbuttoned in the front, one shoulder exposed along with a wide white bra strap. I take in the thick braid slung over her other shoulder, the baby's red ear moving up and down as it swallows. Something is familiar.

'You came to my presentation,' I say, 'at the Lifestyle Photography Conference – right?'

The woman looks up at me. A gyrfalcon looks up at me.

'Dyann!'

Dyann lifts her eyebrows. 'Well, I *tried* to come to your presentation. I only caught bits.' She mock-glares at the baby and then gives it a soft pat on the back to compensate. 'How was the thing?' she says, tilting her head toward the door.

'Steph wasn't there,' I say. I frown and blink. I can hear that what I've said is illogical, but my brain refuses to fix it. My mouth refuses. Seeing Dyann out here on this bench after all these years. It throws a breaker in my mind.

Dyann just looks at me. 'Karen. It's really good to see you,' she says.

I sit down next to her on the bench. She is wearing a nursing bra that appears to be sewn of two layers: one that flips down, for access, and another featuring a circular cutaway to expose the nipple. Most of Dyann's breast is spilling from the cutaway, or she has pulled it through: she squeezes and rolls it with one hand while the other holds the baby's head steady. Her flesh is filigreed with silvery stretch marks.

I think of the nursing-wear shop down the street from my apartment building in Toronto. In the window are elegantly draped blouses with panels and pleats disguising vertical access slits. The old Dyann wouldn't, of course, have gone looking for such a store. She'd have been scornful of its very existence.

Dyann is a midwife now. I heard this somewhere, a few years after graduation. After she was kicked out of the university she worked in a women's bookstore, and then as a receptionist at a midwives' collective, and then she went back to school for a midwifery diploma. It makes sense to me, in a purely theoretical way, that a midwife would eventually want her own baby. 'How old is he-slash-she?' I ask her.

'Almost nine weeks. And he's a he. His name is Bruno.' She looks sidelong at me and gives an exaggerated sigh. 'I guess my male-bashing days are officially over, right?'

'You never male-bashed.'

'Ha.'

'You called it like you saw it, Dyann. I always admired that,' I say.

She shrugs. 'Then I suppose I'm going to have to start seeing it differently.'

*

'You've got to let yourself heal, Karen,' my mother had told me when she sent me off to Bruce's funeral with my dad. 'Don't just bury yourself back into your schoolwork. Leave time for healing too.'

Many people said things along those same lines over the next couple of weeks at school. 'It takes time,' said the counsellor they made me see at the Student Health Centre. 'Give it time,' said Dr Esterhazy, whom Steph had filled in on my situation, once the professor was back from her holiday and Steph was home from the hospital. Dr Esterhazy granted me what she called a 'blanket extension' on the rest of the assignments for the term. 'Take all the time you need,' she insisted.

There was no time for healing, though. Or maybe it was that there was no space for it at Raghurst. Dyann had picked up some kind of virus at the hospital, some kind of superbug, and she sprawled on the sofa, coughing and wheezing, for what seemed like weeks. Steph was released from the psych ward and immediately took up the sickroom vigil. Every time I came in the front door, there were the two of them hunkered down in our living room with blankets and books and teacups and cough syrups and tissues.

I slept little, and when I did my dreams poured and ran in every direction. I dreamt of caves and gullies, of groping blindly through underground paths. I dreamt of mountain passes, of goats hobbled at the roadside, every swerve a kill. My dreams rushed back and pooled around my ankles. I kept drowning myself awake.

I went to the movies with Charla or Marie-Jeanne, or alone. I hung out next door with Stick more and more, enough that his roommates told Marie-Jeanne we were dating and Marie-Jeanne warned me not to break his heart. She was right to be suspicious: I was dating Stick's pharmacy, mostly. He wouldn't give me more than one dose of anything at a time – to keep it safe, he insisted, since I was mixing so many different sorts of drugs, but also because he wanted me, plain and simple. O sad Simon Alastair Pinkney, Jr, with the eager arms.

Meanwhile I wrote essays. I got all my assignments done early, working late in the *Campus Eye* office or on Stick's desktop while he snored in the bed nearby. I typed with my left hand plus the two semi-motile fingers on my right. Nights passed in the tunnelglow of the screen with my eyes stinging and a thumping ache in my skull. Except for exams and some reading, I finished my term by the end of March.

But I couldn't bring myself to attend Women and Myth. I knew my participation grade would suffer, but I'd received an A+ on my reading responses and midterm from first semester. So long as I eventually turned in my Helen of Troy paper, I was pretty sure I could still pass the course. The problem was developing a defendable argument. After almost six months of Women and Myth, all I had on Helen were questions. Is Helen a naïve girl oblivious to her own uncanny beauty? Is Helen culpable for the destruction of nations if we can find logical reasons for her behaviour? I had lists and lists of questions in my notes. Is Helen inherently indescribable? Would depicting Helen's beauty diminish it? Every scholarly article I read about Helen generated more questions for me. And these questions seemed to me utterly unanswerable.

Dyann's virus morphed into an eye infection. Her student health card had been suspended along with her student status, pending a decision from the Disciplinary Board, and she refused to ask her parents for help with medical bills. Steph brought her over-the-counter eye drops, but they didn't work. Charla made a tincture of eyebright and witch hazel, but Dyann said it felt like hot needles. After a week both her eyes had swelled shut and crusted over.

I barely talked to her. I never went into the living room. Whenever my chemical fog thinned enough that I had to notice Dyann lying there on the sofa with an herb-soaked dishrag over her eyes – or worse, sitting up and squinting at me through the shiny, reddened flesh of her lids – I felt a grim, queasy kind of satisfaction. She'd wanted to organise, to act, she'd said. She'd wanted to be active rather than reactive to male violence, to strike rather than wait to be stricken.

Well, she was certainly stricken now. Maybe she'll die, I caught myself thinking.

The crying waited two weeks after Bruce's funeral and wake. Then it began to stalk me everywhere. It ambushed me in class: loud, choking sobs that sent me scrambling for my things and scuttling out of the room in embarrassment. The crying struck at the T-Cam so that I heaved and gasped, doubled over at the curb, while Charla patted my back and eventually went inside and told the others she was taking me home. The crying sprang from the mirror and throttled me whenever I forgot not to look at myself. Once it had me, the crying hung on for fifteen minutes or more, pummelling my belly and clawing at my throat until I was faint, shaky, wrung dry. There were no words in the crying – no thoughts, even – just a gulf opening beneath my feet and a great howling painstorm all around me.

The only place safe from the crying was pills, so I spent more and more time swallowing them. I swallowed pills to be alert, to get my work done, then to calm me down afterward. Pills to sleep and pills to wake up. There was one pill – a small, mint-green tablet taken in threes whose name I never learnt from Stick – that had a way of expanding my skin and padding it over so that I felt that I was cocooned deep inside it and that everything touching me was actually touching only the outermost layer of something ultimately impenetrable.

Is Helen even meant to be understood as a flesh-and-blood woman? Is Helen a mere apparition of male desire? Is Helen a commodity to be traded amongst men in the warrior economy? Is Helen, herself born of rape, an emblem of female victimhood?

Pills are their own kind of exile, though. I spent week after week looking in on things from outside. I chewed food that tasted like it was in someone else's mouth. It seemed to me that everywhere I went, I'd seen it all before. It seemed I'd made a big mistake believing that my life was a story never previously told. Every telling is just a retelling, I realised. So this is what myth is, I thought, all this donning of outsized masks and flowing robes and declaiming in foursquare flowery epithets. This is the trouble with myth. Each of us scoops out our own rotten core and spits it out onstage. We stand around the heap of smoking corpses and declare it fate.

*

Lamenting has been my slow death, Helen says in the *Iliad*. I know what she meant. O Bruce. I know full well you were never real. I know I fashioned you out of the depths of my longing, an idol to worship in the darkness of my own savage heart. I erected you and excepted you from every rule and made you lawless, blameless, soulless, footless, until it was inevitable you should tumble.

Still I keep hauling the stones for you, Bruce. I keep heaping the stones, and laying on the timbers, and piling the brush, and striking the match. But you won't go quietly to your pyre. You won't stay put. O goldbright boy who lives in my blood, you've coursed your way through me for fifteen years. My heart is dammed with you.

52. ARETE

(excellence of character)

'You're so pulled together.' Dyann figure-eights her fingers in the air between us, and I roll my eyes. 'No, I don't mean the fashion, or whatever,' she says. 'I mean you've aged, but in a good way.'

We've moved to the Harbour Room, a student-run café two buildings over from where Steph's memorial is being held.

'Thanks. You've pulled together, too.' It's true: it's as if all Dyann's skin has pulled in toward her bones a bit. Or been sucked. Squint lines radiate from the corners of her eyes. A single silver hair, more wiry than the rest, arcs away from her head and waves in the air as she looks down at the baby on her shoulder. Even as we sit here, though, the Dyann in front of me is overwriting my memories of her from the past. That whole year we lived together I never got a photograph of Dyann. She was right at the centre of Raghurst, she was the organising centre of every activity on campus that year, yet somehow she evaded my camera entirely.

'I'm not who I used to be, that's for sure,' Dyann says.

'What do you mean?'

'Do you remember how Steph used to talk about border violations all the time? That identity is made up of these imaginary boundaries?'

'Yeah.' We all used to talk like that – it was Dr Esterhazy's influence. I wonder if Dyann knows that Dr Esterhazy is dead.

'Well, my borders are breached. I guess I thought when I grew older I'd feel less vulnerable, you know? But now, thanks to him' – she lifts the shoulder on which Bruno is sleeping – 'my boundaries are just … dissolved. Just like that. I feel unmanned.'

We both laugh at her word choice, and Dyann groans. 'Oh, God, I can't believe I just said that.'

'Well, maybe it's appropriate. No man could give life to that' – I nod at the baby in her arms – 'nurture something with his own *body* like that.' Dyann's filigreed body.

Tears well up in Dyann's eyes. 'I've midwived for seven years, so I've seen it every day. But I had no idea it would be this hard.'

Dyann's tears are something I have never seen before. I think carefully about my wording. 'Does Bruno have another parent?'

'He was supposed to.' Dyann knuckles the tears away and sniffs hard. 'She wanted to be a mother more than anything, but she couldn't get pregnant, so then *I* got pregnant, and then she decided she didn't want to parent someone else's kid.'

'Ugh. Just like that?'

'Well. She said she'd "be there" for me, all that obligatory penance crap. I left before he was born, which in retrospect was stupid of me. I should have taken whatever help I could get.'

'Oh, Dyann.'

She gives her head a sharp little shake. I recognise the gesture and can picture her dreadlocks flying. I remember what comes next, too: the raptor-glance of those keen dark eyes, the head cocked slightly to one side. Dyann changing the subject, Dyann shifting focus.

How I've missed you, I want to tell her. I thought I'd feel less vulnerable too. But instead I'm just lonely. How I've missed you!

'You've kept your course, though,' she says. 'Stayed true to your creative work, et cetera.'

I laugh. 'I'm an interiors photographer, Dyann.'

Dyann smiles, shakes her head. 'I mean the still lifes. I looked up that album of yours on Fotomarkt. They're amazing. They kept me awake last night, actually, even after Bruno finally passed out.'

'Why?' I'm not fishing for compliments. It is honest bafflement.

'Curiosity, I guess. It was like seeing what you see. How you see the world. You were never really one for saying what was going on inside your head.'

Again, that sensation of nakedness, of being seen when I thought I was hidden. 'That woman from the conference wants to represent me,' I tell Dyann. 'She's putting together an exhibit about beauty and the female gaze or something.' On the phone Jane Moscovitch had said the show would be called 'Objects of Desire'. She'd asked, 'As women artists, how do we participate in the traditions without replicating their power structures?'

The waitress brings our food: onion soup for Dyann, a tuna wrap for me. Dyann pierces the melted cheese with her spoon and broth spills over onto the table. She sighs. 'I keep forgetting to order foods that I can eat with one hand.'

I rotate our dishes so Dyann has the wrap instead. 'Do you ever hear from Charla?' I ask. I almost don't want to know. Charla attended a homeopathy college in Oregon after graduation, I remember having heard somewhere, but she and I lost touch as soon as I moved back to Toronto. After all this time Charla inhabits my imagination more as light source than person. She is a white planet, all cool sparkle. I thought of the photograph I'd saved of Charla – the one of her blazing up her little stone pipe – and wondered if I still had it tucked away somewhere.

Dyann shakes her head no.

And yes, I find I am relieved. 'I was so in love with her,' I confess. 'I wanted to be her knight in shining armor, but I didn't know how.'

'Me neither,' Dyann says. 'And I was too young to realise, back then, that being a knight only makes sense in a kingdom where someone higher up is in charge. You know, someone actually interested in justice.'

'Charla was kind of our Helen,' I say to Dyann. 'She was our *casus belli*, the cause of war. That year, everything that happened with the fraternity? Charla was our Helen of Troy.'

Dyann chokes on her food. She is laughing, choking, waving away my help, bouncing the baby in her arms with her vigorous coughing. 'Oh my God,' she gasps, when she has recovered enough to speak. 'It was *you*, Karen, not Charla. You were our Helen of Troy.'

53. CONFIRMATIO

(proof)

Gamma Beta Chi received an official reprimand from the Office of Student Life for 'maintaining a reckless environment' and 'failing to provide for the safety, well-being, and/or privacy of its guests'. That was the extent of any disciplinary action. The fact that Dyann had confessed to drugging them exonerated the brothers from any willful wrongdoing. All fraternities on campus, the dean's report stated, were 'strongly exhorted to uphold the positive values the Greek tradition represents within the university and the wider community'. There was speculation that GBC National's legal counsel would turn around and sue Dyann for damages, but nothing ever materialised.

I ran into Frodo one day early in April. The first real summerpromising days – brash sunshine, newflying green on every tree – had brought on a campus bacchanal of class-cutting and weed-smoking and general loafing around on the lawns. The university was once again nothing but a playground with a city grown up around it. Frodo jogged up to me shirtless and barefoot from an Ultimate Frisbee game, his gray sweatpants covered with grass stains. His brush cut showed his scalp reddening in the sun.

'Hey, Karen!' he panted. He reeked of beer.

'Oh, hi, Fro – ' I caught myself. 'I'm sorry, I don't even know your real name.'

'It's Fred,' he said.

'Hi, Fred.' I looked for other brothers on the lawn but spotted only Pits among the players.

'Yeah, so, I pretty much failed everything so I'm on probation,' Frodo said, as if we were already fifteen or twenty minutes into a conversation.

'Oh. I'm sorry.'

'So technically I can't be in a frat next year. But GBC is letting me stay for the summer anyhow.'

'Oh. That's good.' I took a couple of steps away from him, to indicate I was continuing on my way. Frodo really was a moron, with those weepy-looking, pale eyes and that high-pitched laugh. I couldn't believe I'd ever found him cute or charming. Outside the frat house he was like a snail with no shell.

He walked along beside me, slapping his bare feet on the sidewalk. 'You know Moretti got booted, right?'

I stopped. 'Alec? He's not graduating?'

'From the frat, I mean. We booted him out. Chet put in a complaint about him – basically ratted out a brother, but whatever; I don't blame him.' Frodo talked fast, like he knew he didn't have much time with me, like he was afraid someone else would run up beside him and stop him before he had a chance to tell me.

'Alec really had it in for Chet, man. After Bruce died Alec went sort of apeshit. Painted this giant pussy – pardon my French – but like, this massive fucking monster vagina all over Chet's wall, with the word WHIPPED, you know? Oh, man, it's good you never saw it. You would of fuh-reaked.'

I hadn't seen Mike's room the night of the wake. I'd left the wake right after Sheri's wild dancing, right after Mike had shown me the wreck of Bruce's room. Mike had left me with his new girlfriend, Alexandra the future world-famous pediatrician, while he fetched my *Iliad* for me, and then there had been a strained round of well-wishing and hugs amongst the three of us after I declined their offer of a lift home, and then I'd fled the fraternity house for the last time.

'Anyhow. I just thought you should know that we voted him out.'

'Okay. Thanks, Fro – Fred.'

'Bruce was really a good guy, you know. Even with everything.'

'Yeah, he was. Thanks, Fred,' I said again.

He clapped me on the shoulder, hitched up his waistband, and jogged back across the grass. Fred was a good guy, too, I thought. It was just Frodo that was the moron.

Marie-Jeanne decided to accept a bid from Theta Phi for her senior year. 'They approached me. They are becoming friendlier to lesbians,' she explained.

Every part of her statement unseated me. Marie-Jeanne was so quiet about her sexuality – so serious about school, so busy with the squash team and the role-playing games with the boys next door – that I tended to think of her as asexual.

'You should consider joining too,' she went on. 'I think they would be interested in you, after everything that happened this year.'

'After everything that happened, the last thing I'm about to do is go Greek,' I said.

'It is like refusing a promotion at your job because you disapprove of capitalism,' Marie-Jeanne said.

'A sorority isn't a job, MJ.'

'It leads to a job. After we graduate, you and I will need a way to get a green card, or it will be straight back to the Great White North.'

'I can't be a sorority sister,' I told Marie-Jeanne.

She shrugged. 'Suit your own taste.'

It wasn't only my distaste for Greek life, though. It was my unworthiness. How could I pretend to pledge fealty to anyone after so much lying, so much betrayal? Exile – that was the appropriate outcome for me. Exile to the Great White North.

Is Helen bound by fate to instigate earthbreaking violence? Is Helen the 'shameless bitch' she names herself in Book I of the *Iliad*? Is Helen dishonourable, fickle, narcissistic, toxic? Does Helen deserve everything she gets, namely 3,000 years of being maligned and/or lauded as an agent of extermination?

Dr Esterhazy took ages to grade my essay, and in the end she gave me a C. There were no margin comments, just a short note at the bottom of the last page penned in her fountain-pen ink.

Reading the note, I could picture the professor bent over her rolltop desk in her jasmine-scented sunroom with Dido chattering on her shoulder. My essay did not conform satisfactorily to the assignment rubric, she wrote. It didn't assert a specific thesis regarding Helen, or develop a convincing argument supported by evidence from the primary source(s). My inquiry remained too loose and wide-ranging to be effective; after all, to say that Helen is defined by her passivity is to state the obvious. However, given my exemplary work last semester and the 'special challenges' I'd recently faced, she had decided to grant me a final grade of B in Women and Myth. She sincerely hoped I'd consider registering for her senior seminar, Sapphic Poetry, next year.

I told myself that I hadn't really written the Helen essay for Dr Esterhazy anyway. I wished I hadn't turned in anything at all, or that instead of the essay I had written her an eloquent letter about how she'd failed us when we needed her most. I wished it were Dr Esterhazy's course title on my transcript that made me queasy, and not the B. But the truth was that the mediocre grade stung. I even considered asking Dr Esterhazy if I could redo the assignment and pull up my grade, but I thought Steph would find out and feel it as some kind of betrayal.

Steph had been forced to finish out her TA contract for Dr Esterhazy even though the professor had dropped her as a grad student. Steph was ostensibly out of danger, out of the hospital, but she still cried all the time. Every time she had to talk to Dr Esterhazy she cried for hours. She seldom left Raghurst. She'd paid for a cable package and now spent all day watching television. She'd gotten addicted to soaps in the psych ward, she told us. Dyann couldn't stand the TV being on all the time, and as soon as she was well enough to express her irritation, there was constant bickering at Raghurst.

Dyann had been officially expelled from school, and then officially charged with accessory to rape. In the end it was Gerry, Dyann's stepfather, who came to her aid. At some point in Dyann's illness someone, Marie-Jeanne maybe, had put in a call to Dyann's parents, and Gerry took time off work to fly out for a visit, during which he dragged Dyann to an ophthalmologist, paid her medical bills, accompanied her to her disciplinary hearings on campus, and hired a lawyer to deal with the criminal charges. No one was being prosecuted for Sheri Asselin's rape – Sheri had dropped the charges, apparently, when she realised how many questions she'd have to answer about all the other times she'd partied at GBC, especially the times after the assault – and they could hardly prosecute Dyann for being an accessory to a crime that had never happened, whether she'd confessed or not. It didn't take long for Gerry to 'clear it all up', as he put it. I wondered if he intentionally left it vague whether he was referring to the eye infection, the rape charge, or both.

'What really gets me is the hypocrisy,' Steph complained. 'She natters away at me about being a drone and a traitor because I still want to finish my degree. She goes on and on about my loyalty to the capital-S System, and meanwhile she's letting Gerry pay tens of thousands of dollars into the legal system so she can have a life after all this.'

It seemed to me there was a more specific hypocrisy haunting us at Raghurst. Sheri Asselin hadn't received any kind of justice at all. She was an imperfect victim, sure. But wasn't the imperfect victim exactly the victim we should champion most? We had victimised her once by setting her up to be assaulted, and then the taint of guilt had stood between us and our supposed sisterhood.

As usual in these debates Dyann wanted to focus on the systemic rather than the individual. She had started to lecture all of us about the corruption of the higher education system in America. College in general served the interests of the elite, she said, the white patriarchal hegemony, but the Ivy League was worst of all. 'Did you know they don't even pay taxes?' she told us more than once. Marie-Jeanne had tried to point out that our school was the second-biggest employer in the state and offered better pay equity and benefits than any other. 'What other employer is allowed to treat crime as an in-house problem?' Dyann had retorted. 'What other employer actively covers up for criminals?'

Surprisingly, it was Charla who agreed with Dyann on this one. 'Maybe misogyny is everywhere,' she said. 'Corporations, sports franchises, politics, churches. Maybe the campus isn't the only place rape happens. But an educational institution is supposed to be where social change starts. You hear that all the time, right? A liberal education is supposed to create freethinking and culturally informed citizens, blah blah blah. It's the hypocrisy that makes it so disgusting.'

Whatever my own thoughts, I stayed mostly quiet during these conversations. I was so tired of talk. All people ever did at school was talk. Everyone loved to accuse everyone else of hypocrisy, of saying one thing and doing another. Well, wasn't I the biggest hypocrite of them all? I'd been determined to ally myself with both Raghurst and the frat house. I thought I could stay neutral, live in both camps and travel unhindered between. I thought this meant freedom. I thought it meant live and let live. Instead it meant murder.

'You know, you got that Audre Lorde quote all wrong,' I told Steph.

'What do you mean?'

'About the master's tools dismantling the master's house? Using a sex tape to beat the gang bangers at their own game? I looked it up. What Lorde actually said was that the master's tools will *never* dismantle the master's house.'

'But some of us really do want to change the system,' Steph said. 'You need access to the institution in order to transform it, right? You can't just turn your back on it like Dyann. You can't just walk out.'

54. PROLEPSIS

(*futurity*)

Dyann leans way forward, over the baby in her arms, to take another bite of the tuna wrap. She's been eating quickly, talking and chewing at the same time like she's afraid someone will snatch away her plate. O burnished Dyann, I find myself thinking. How you would wing your way unreluctant into battle!

'What you said before, about your boundaries being dissolved by mother-hood. The breach,' I begin.

She looks at me warily, swallows her food. 'Please don't say it'll make me a better person.'

'God, no. But how do you want this to turn out? I mean, what did you want when you decided to have a baby? What were you after?'

She is silent. I hope the question didn't sound presumptuous or bitchy. Suddenly I recall, with a sour flutter of panic, how Dyann used to feign boredom and walk away from conversations that made her uncomfortable. O Dyann, how you would splinter the spears and batter the bright shields! Stay, oh stay with me.

'Did you want to be untouchable? Invincible?' I persist. 'I mean, that's how it used to be, I think. You were after immortality.'

'I wanted to feel real.' She says it very quietly. Then she rolls her eyes and laughs. 'Now, thanks to the sleep deprivation, nothing feels real!'

'Well, this is real, right?' I wave my hand back and forth between Dyann and me, to indicate the two of us, here, together. 'That's what you told me once.'

'When?'

'When we were doing the circle in the woods that time, for that Roman festival. Meditrinalia, remember? I said I wanted something real, and you said, "Women in the woods – this is real."'

Dyann looks past me, out the window. Her free hand rests at the base of her throat.

'You were happy that night.'

'I was *arrogant*,' she says. 'I had no idea what life was really like.'

'You were right, though. It was real,' I say. I take off my cardigan, reach out my arms, and wiggle my fingers for Bruno. 'I don't know anything about babies,' I warn, but Dyann passes him over to me anyhow. He rests, damp and dense, against my shoulder. I cup the warm velvet skull. 'You know, this is your whole problem right here,' I joke. 'You're not supposed to hog these things. You're supposed to share them around.'

Dyann grins. 'Sure, sure. You want him now. Just wait till he shits and starts shrieking.' She lifts her hands straight up to stretch out her shoulders, rolls her head side to side. A grunt of pleasure escapes her.

Then she says, 'Didn't you write an essay on Helen of Troy for Esterhazy that year?'

My face heats. 'How do you know that?'

'Steph showed us, probably. I mean, we were horrible. We had zero respect for privacy or property.'

'Esterhazy didn't like that essay, if I recall,' I tell her. 'Too many questions, not enough answers.'

'That woman could be such a cunt,' Dyann says, and gives a little bark of shocked laughter at the word.

It makes me laugh, too, the blasphemy. The baby is jostled on my shoulder. I breathe deep to calm myself. Then I say, 'Did you hear about her?'

'What?'

'She died.'

'Dr Esterhazy died?'

'I just heard today.'

Dyann reaches across the table and touches the three-inch scar on my tricep. I flinch. Her fingertip hovers there, just above my skin, like a question.

I keep my eyes on my shoulder, on Bruno, swallowing the tears that are filling my throat.

'I do not know if I'm ready to be real,' she says.

'Me neither,' I say, and I look up to see Dyann's eyes shining with tears again. My own tears blur my vision, but I don't look away and neither does she.

Dyann touches my scar again, very softly. She traces its length twice. Then she moves to the fold of flesh at Bruno's nape, strokes her way down the tiny arm. Although the baby is still fast asleep, his miniature fingers close and squeeze around his mother's finger.

*

O sing of the American student body, glorious and young. We are the future! *Look, the future,* outsiders think when they wander onto the campus. Everyone on a university campus is equally young. We are all the same social class, give or take a country club membership. We all wear the same clothes and listen to the same music – or anyhow we buy our clothes and music from adjacent stores, or stores across the street from one another downtown. We are all giddy and hyperventilating in the superoxygenated atmosphere of attention and information and privilege and power.

We all thought we were different but we weren't. We all thought we were resisting something but we weren't. We all thought that life would be like this forever but it wouldn't. We were going to spend the rest of our lives trying and failing to re-create this feeling of urgency, of specialness, of being smack at the epicentre of everything important and real happening in the world. For the rest of our lives we would yearn for this feeling of exigency and belonging and fullness and passion. From here on in, it would be nostalgia.

I sat at my desk at Raghurst and stared at my tree-planting photos on the wall. Steph had commented, months ago, on the beauty I'd captured in the scene of destruction. Not captured. Created. By framing the shot a certain way I'd created beauty out of the violence of the logging cutover. Gazing at the images now, though, it seemed to me that the destruction *was* the scene's beauty. The presence of death guaranteed something in the image, or fixed it, or made it available to the viewer. Something Dr Esterhazy had said in class came back to me: 'Beauty resists capture, like desire.' She'd been talking about Helen in the *Iliad* again, but it was true of photography too, I thought. The camera was always trying to capture beauty and always falling short, always failing. But when you took a picture of something wrecked, something violated, something dying, maybe you got a little closer to your goal.

I'd lost the negatives to these images. I'd left them in the darkroom by accident, and they'd been tossed out by whoever had used the room after me. I could just destroy these prints, I thought, and they wouldn't exist anymore. All that work. The idea pleased me, that I could erase the whole scene, all evidence of it, all traces of it, so easily. I peeled the pictures off the wall and found a lighter in my desk drawer and held it to the top image. The small flame curled and blackened the corner but then died in a gasp of smoke.

I took the photos and the lighter downstairs and went out to Raghurst's backyard. The new grass was damp and spongy underfoot, and I looked around for something to elevate the images while they burnt. On the boys' side, by the cedar hedge, was a set of wicker patio furniture so old and busted up that one of the chair seats lifted right off. When I laid the seat on the grass and set the pictures on top, though, it still didn't feel like enough. I went to our front porch and unwound the cedar garland Marie-Jeanne had bought for Christmas. It was rust-brown now and left a trail of needles as I dragged it to the back and dumped it onto the wicker seat. I jumped on the chairs to crack them apart, dragged them to the pile, and crisscrossed the arms, legs, and sections of the backs.

This time the fire got going on my first try. The photos disappeared as the crackling cedar sent a plume of sparks swirling up, higher than my head. Already overwarm from breaking up the chairs, I peeled off my wool shirt and knotted it round my waist. The night air pursed its lips against my bare shoulders and nosed at me through the thin cotton of my tank top. My cast had come off only days earlier, and my right forearm looked pale and shiny as a grub.

I found the boys' disassembled skateboarding ramp next to their back door, and I carried the sections one by one over to my fire. The wax or shellac they'd applied to the plywood ignited at once. The flames jostled and shoved at each other to climb skyward. When I couldn't lift anything else high enough to add to the pile, I sat on my haunches to watch it burn.

Steph came out on the deck in her pajamas and bathrobe. 'I only saw the flames reflected in the TV screen when I turned it off,' she said. 'Can you imagine? The whole world burning, and nobody notices because *Friends* isn't over yet.'

Next came Marie-Jeanne and Dyann. 'Charla! You have to see this,' Dyann called back into the house, and soon all three of them were crouched alongside Steph and me. Charla had brought out a bottle of wine. Each finger of her right hand was hooked through the handle of a coffee mug, and Marie-Jeanne unhooked them one at a time and handed them out as Charla poured.

'We need lawn chairs,' Steph said.

'I burnt them,' I told her.

'What's the occasion?' Charla asked.

'All this stuff lying around,' I said. 'It was just such a waste.'

'Is that Wheeler's skateboard ramp?' Marie-Jeanne said.

I'd found my theme, though. 'This whole year. This whole year was a waste.'

'You know, that's what people always say about college,' Steph told us. 'In alumni surveys people always say they wish they hadn't wasted so much time partying.'

'Is that how you all feel?' I said. We'd decided to give up Raghurst's lease in May. Charla and her brother would take possession of their condo May first, and Steph was moving into graduate housing to be closer to the library. Marie-Jeanne would have the sorority, and Dyann kept saying only that she'd play it by ear.

Marie-Jeanne gave my shoulder a soft pat. 'I wanted to set a fire too,' she said.

'Me too,' Steph said.

'But you have to tend it,' Dyann said. 'As soon as you stop throwing fuel on it, it just goes out.'

I took a gulp of my wine and threw the rest into the flames.

'Hey, that is a good merlot,' Marie-Jeanne protested. But Charla lifted her mug high, sipped, and then flung the glistening liquid against the pyre.

'You guys,' Steph said.

'It's in the *Iliad*, remember?' Charla said. 'Hektor's funeral?'

'The *Iliad*'s a poor excuse for dumping good booze,' Dyann said.

We were silent a moment. Charla's love at my shoulder was silken, a moon-lit moth.

'Maybe our fire went under the ground,' Marie-Jeanne suggested. 'Like in the forest, when lightning strikes.'

Our crew had planted a burn site last summer. No undergrowth or slash piles impeded our movement, and it was easy to follow our lines of seedlings against the black earth. But the earth was so dry that our ATV's tailpipe kept picking up bits of dead moss and igniting them. Thirty minutes after a tree delivery I'd be stomping out smoky little fires all along the road. And two weeks after we finished the contract we got word that the whole site had burnt again: 45,000 red pine seedlings up in smoke.

The new tree-planting season still didn't start for another three weeks. I wanted to be up there in the bush so badly I could hardly stand it. I wanted to be a creature without a mind, trudging through the frost-hardened mud, chafing and sweating under the weight of the seedlings, not caring if all the labour was for nothing. I wanted to pack a bag and head north tonight.

'Maybe it's more like we were sending up a flare,' Charla said. 'You know, so someone would see it in the distance.'

'Enough with the fire metaphors now,' Dyann said.

'It's like the Olympic flame.' Steph sniggered.

Dyann shoved Steph over, but they were both laughing now. Laughing, Dyann stood up and poured out her wine in a thin stream over the flames. She yelped when the heat caught her forearm, cursed, laughed again.

And the laughter of farseeing Dyann, of highhearted Dyann, gave the rest of us reason to laugh too. And O, let us not forget the deathlessness on these five faces! Look how these bright leaping lights are fed by the darkness pressing in. They are creatures shoulder to shoulder even with their separate minds aflame. Look: five women circle here on the prospering earth, their faces rapt to the fire and their backs resolute to the night.

ACKNOWLEDGEMENTS

I am grateful to Monica Pacheco, first and most enduring champion of this story. To Amy Hundley for her incisive and generous editorial guidance, to Susan Renouf for offering the book an ideal Canadian home, and to the stellar production teams at Grove Atlantic and ECW. To Sarah Davis-Goff and Lisa Coen at Tramp, for helming the project so skilfully across the pond. To those who read earlier drafts and gave helpful feedback: Suzanne Alyssa Andrew, Kathryn Kuitenbrouwer, Neil Vander Kooy, and Martha Webb. To my Artscape Youngplace posse, especially Jill Margo and Sarah Selecky, for daily motivation and companionship, and to the folks at Spark Box Studio and Small Pond Arts for providing quiet, beautiful places to write. To Kristin Sjaarda for her photography expertise. To the Dogbeard Circle – Dennis Denisoff, Morgan Holmes, and Kevin McGuirk – for sharp eyes on the opening scenes and for general inspiration and tomfoolery. To Johann Lotter and Heidi Reimer for assiduous error-catching in the final stages. Thank you, thank you, thank you!